Enid Blyton

THE FAMOUS FIVE

COLLECTION 4

FIVE ON A HIKE TOGETHER

FIVE HAVE A WONDERFUL TIME

FIVE GO DOWN TO THE SEA

Illustrated by
Eileen A. Soper

**Hodder
Children's
Books**

KU-183-249

HODDER CHILDREN'S BOOKS

Five on a Hike Together first published by Hodder and Stoughton in 1951
Five Have a Wonderful Time first published by Hodder and Stoughton in 1952
Five Go Down to the Sea first published by Hodder and Stoughton in 1953

Enid Blyton ® Famous Five ® Text copyright © Hodder and Stoughton Ltd

This edition published 2017

1 3 5 7 9 10 8 6 4 2

Enid Blyton ® The Famous Five ®
Enid Blyton's signature is a Registered Trademark of Hodder and Stoughton Limited
Text copyright © Hodder and Stoughton Limited
Illustrations copyright © Hodder & Stoughton Ltd

All of the author's moral rights are hereby asserted.

*All characters and events in this publication, other than those clearly
in the public domain, are fictitious and any resemblance to real persons,
living or dead, is purely coincidental.*

All rights reserved.
No part of this publication may be reproduced, stored in a retrieval system,
or transmitted, in any form or by any means, without the prior permission in
writing of the publisher, nor be otherwise circulated in any form of binding
or cover other than that in which it is published and without a similar condition
including this condition being imposed on the subsequent purchaser.

A CIP catalogue record for this book is available from the British Library.

ISBN 978 1 444 93516 5

Typeset in Times by Avon DataSet Ltd, Bidford-on-Avon, Warwickshire

Printed and bound in Great Britain by Clays Ltd, St Ives plc

The paper and board used in this book are made from wood
from responsible sources

Hodder Children's Books
An imprint of Hachette Children's Group
Part of Hodder and Stoughton
Carmelite House, 50 Victoria Embankment
London EC4Y 0DZ

An Hachette UK Company
www.hachette.co.uk
www.hachettechildrens.co.uk

Five on a
Hike Together

CONTENTS

CHAPTER ONE

A letter from Julian

'ANNE!' SHOUTED George, running after her cousin as she went along to her classroom. 'Anne! I've just been down to the letterboard and there's a letter from your brother Julian. I've brought it for you.'

Anne stopped. 'Oh thanks,' she said. 'What *can* Julian want? He only wrote a few days ago – it's most extraordinary for him to write again so soon. It must be something important.'

'Well, open it and see,' said George. 'Hurry up – I've got a maths class to go to.'

Anne ripped open the envelope. She pulled out a sheet of notepaper and read it quickly. She looked up at George, her eyes shining.

'George! Julian and Dick have got a few days off at our half-term weekend! Somebody's won a wonderful scholarship or something, and the boys have got two days tacked on to a weekend to celebrate! They want us to join them in a hike, and all go off together.'

'What a glorious idea!' said George. 'Good old Julian. I bet he thought of that. Let's read the letter, Anne.'

But before she could read it a mistress came along. 'Georgina! You should be in class – and you too, Anne.'

1

George scowled. She hated to be called by her full name. She went off without a word. Anne tucked the letter into her pocket and rushed off joyfully. Half-term with her brothers, Julian and Dick – and with George and Timmy the dog. Could anything be better?

She and George talked about it again after morning school. 'We get from Friday morning till Tuesday,' said George. 'The boys are getting the same. What luck! They don't usually have a half-term in the winter term.'

'They can't go home because the painters are in our house,' said Anne. 'That's why I was going home with you, of course. But I'm sure your mother won't mind if we go off with the boys. Your father never likes us in the middle of the term.'

'No, he doesn't,' said George. 'He's always deep in the middle of some wonderful idea, and he hates to be disturbed. It will suit everyone if we go off on a hike.'

'Julian says he will telephone to us tonight and arrange everything,' said Anne. 'I hope it will be a nice fine weekend. It will still be October, so there's a chance of a bit of warm sunshine.'

'The woods will be beautiful,' said George. 'And won't Timmy enjoy himself. Let's go and tell him the news.'

The boarding-school that the two girls were at was one that allowed the children to bring their own pets to school. There were kennels down in the yard for various

dogs, and Timmy lived there during term-time. The two girls went to get him.

He heard their footsteps at once and began to bark excitedly. He scraped at the gate of the kennel yard, wishing for the thousandth time that he could find out how to open it.

He flung himself on the two girls, licking and pawing and barking.

'Silly dog. Mad dog!' said George, and thumped his back affectionately. 'Listen, Tim – we're going off for the weekend with Julian and Dick! What do you think of that? We're going on a hike, so you'll love it. All through the woods and up the hills and goodness knows where!'

Timmy seemed to understand every word. He cocked up his ears, put his head on one side and listened intently while George was speaking.

'Woof,' he said, at the end, as if he approved thoroughly. Then off he went with the girls for his walk, his plumy tail wagging happily. He didn't like term-time nearly as much as the holidays – but he was quite prepared to put up with kennel life so long as he could be near his beloved George.

Julian rang up that night as he had promised. He had got everything planned already. Anne listened, thrilled.

'It sounds super,' she said. 'Yes – we can meet where you say, and we'll be there as near as we can on time. Anyway, we can wait about if you others aren't there. Yes – we'll bring the things you say. Oh, Julian, won't it be fun?'

'What's he say?' asked George impatiently when at last Anne put the receiver down. 'You might have let me have a word with Julian. I wanted to tell him all about Timmy.'

'He doesn't want to waste an expensive telephone call listening to you raving about Timmy,' said Anne. 'He asked how he was and I said "fine", and that's all he wanted to know about Tim. He's made all the arrangements. I'll tell you what they are.'

The girls went off to a corner of their common-room and sat down. Timmy was there too. He was allowed in at certain times, and so were three other dogs belonging

4

to the girls. Each dog behaved well – he knew that if he didn't he would be taken back to the kennels at once!

'Julian says that he and Dick can get off immediately after breakfast,' said Anne. 'So can we, so that's all right. He says we've got to take very little with us – just night things, toothbrush, hairbrush and flannel and a rolled-up mac. And any biscuits or chocolate we can buy. Have you any money left?'

'A bit,' said George. 'Not much. Enough to buy a few bars of chocolate, I think. Anyway, you've got all the biscuits your mother sent last week. We can take some of those.'

'Yes. And the barley sugar one of my aunts sent,' said Anne. 'But Julian says we're not to take much because this is to be a proper hike, and we'll get tired if we have to carry a heavy load. Oh, he said put in two pairs of extra socks.'

'Right,' said George, and she patted Timmy who was lying close beside her. 'There's going to be a long walky-walk, Tim. Won't you love that!'

Timmy grunted comfortably. He wondered if there would be any rabbits on the walk. A walk wasn't really exciting unless there were rabbits all over the place. Timmy thought it was a pity that rabbits were allowed to live down holes. They always disappeared most unfairly just when he had nearly caught one!

Anne and George went to see their house-mistress to tell

her that they were not going to Kirrin Cottage after all, but were going walking.

'My brother says he has written to you,' said Anne. 'So you'll know all about it tomorrow, Miss Peters. And George's mother will be writing too. We can go, can't we?'

'Oh, yes – it will be a lovely half-term for you!' said Miss Peters. 'Especially if this sunny weather lasts. Where are you going?'

'Over the moors,' said Anne. 'In the very loneliest, most deserted parts that Julian can find! We might see deer and wild ponies and perhaps even a few badgers. We shall walk and walk.'

'But where will you sleep if the parts you are going to are so very lonely?' asked Miss Peters.

'Oh Julian is arranging all that,' said George. 'He's been looking up little inns and farmhouses on the map, and we shall make for those at night. It will be too cold to sleep out of doors.'

'It certainly will!' said Miss Peters. 'Well, don't get into trouble, that's all. I know what you five are when you get together. I imagine Timmy is going with you too?'

'Of *course*!' said George. 'I wouldn't go if he didn't go! I couldn't leave him here alone.'

The two girls got their things ready as Friday came near. The biscuits were taken out of the tin and put into paper bags. The barley sugar was put into a bag too, and the bars of chocolate.

Both girls had rucksacks with straps for their shoulders. They packed and repacked them several times. One by one more and more things were added. Anne felt she must take a book to read. George said they must each take a torch with a new battery.

'And what about biscuits for Timmy?' she said. 'I simply must take something for him. He'd like a bone too – a big one that he can chew and chew and that I can put back into the bag for another time.'

'Well, let me carry all the biscuits and chocolate then if you're going to put a smelly old bone into your bag,' said Anne. 'I don't see why you want to take *anything* for Timmy – he can always have something to eat when we do – wherever we have a meal.'

George decided not to take the bone. She had fetched one from his kennel, and it certainly was big and heavy, and equally certainly it was smelly. She took it back to the kennel again, Timmy following her rather puzzled. Why keep carrying his bone here and there? He didn't approve at all.

It seemed a long time till Friday, but at last it came. Both girls woke up very early indeed. George was out in the kennels before breakfast, brushing and combing Timmy to make him look spruce and tidy for Julian and Dick. He knew it was the day they were to set off and he was as excited as the two girls.

'We'd better eat a good breakfast,' said Anne. 'We might have to wait some time before our next meal. Let's

slip off immediately after breakfast. It's lovely to feel free
of school and bells and time-tables – but I shan't feel
really free till I'm outside the school grounds!'

They ate an enormous breakfast though really they were
too excited to want much. Then they got their rucksacks,
ready-packed the night before, said goodbye to Miss Peters,
and went to fetch Timmy.

He was waiting impatiently for them, and barked madly
when they came near. In a trice he was out of his kennel-
yard and capering round them, almost tripping them up.

A LETTER FROM JULIAN

'Good-bye, Anne and George!' yelled one of their friends. 'Have a good time on your hike – and it's no good coming back on Tuesday and telling us you've had one of your usual hair-raising adventures, because we just shan't believe it!'

'Woof,' said Timmy. 'Woof, woof!' Which meant that *he* was going to have adventures with hundreds of rabbits, anyway!

CHAPTER TWO

Setting off

JULIAN AND Dick were also on their way, very pleased to have such an unexpectedly long weekend.

'I never liked Willis or Johnson much,' said Dick, as they walked out of the school grounds. 'Awful swotters they were – never had any time for games or fun. But I take my hat off to them today! Because of their swotting they've won medals and scholarships and goodness knows what – and we've got a weekend off in celebration! Good old Willis and Johnson!'

'Hear hear,' said Dick. 'But I bet they'll sit in a corner with their books all the weekend – they won't know if it's a brilliant day like this, or pouring with rain like yesterday! Poor mutts!'

'They'd hate to go off on a hike,' said Julian. 'It would be utter misery to them. Do you remember how awful Johnson was at rugger? He never knew which goal he was playing against – always ran the wrong way!'

'Yes. But he must have got terrific brains,' said Dick. 'Why are we talking about Willis and Johnson? I can think of plenty of more interesting things. Anne and George, for instance – and old Tim. I hope they'll manage to get off in time all right.'

SETTING OFF

Julian had carefully looked up a large-scale map of the moors that lay between the two schools that he and the girls went to. They were vast stretches of lonely heathery land, dotted with farms here and there, with a few small cottages, and some inns.

'We'll keep right off the main roads, and the second-and third-grades,' he said. 'We'll take the little lanes and paths. I wonder what Timmy will say if we see deer. He'll wonder what in the world they are!'

'He'll only be interested in rabbits,' said Dick. 'I hope he's not as fat as he was last hols. I think we must have given him too many ice-creams and too much chocolate!'

'Well, he won't get that in term-time!' said Julian. 'The girls don't get as much pocket money as we do. Buck up – there's the bus!'

They ran for the little country bus that rumbled along the country lanes, taking people to market, or to the tiny villages that lay here and there tucked away in the moor. It stopped most obligingly for them, and they leapt in.

'Ha! Running away from school?' said the conductor. 'Have to report you, you know!'

'Very funny,' said Julian, bored at this joke, which the conductor produced regularly every time a boy got on board with a rucksack over his shoulders.

They had to get out at the next village and cut across country to get to another bus route. They managed to catch a bus there easily and settled down comfortably in their seats. It was half an hour's run from there to where they had planned to meet the girls.

'Here you are, young sirs,' called the conductor, as the bus ran into a village. It had a wide green on which geese cackled, and a small pond for ducks. 'You wanted Pippin Village, didn't you? We don't go any farther – we just turn round and go back.'

'Thanks,' said the boys and got out. 'Now – are the girls here or not?' said Julian. 'They have to walk from a tiny railway station about two miles away.'

They were not there. Julian and Dick went to have a drink of orangeade at the village store. They had hardly finished when they saw the two girls looking in at the door.

'Julian! Dick! We guessed you'd be eating or drinking!' said Anne, and she rushed at her brothers. 'We came as quickly as we could. The engine broke down – it was such a funny little train! All the passengers got out and advised the engine-driver what to do!'

'Hallo!' said Julian, and gave Anne a hug. He was very fond of his young sister. 'Hallo, George! My, you've grown fat, haven't you?'

'I have not,' said George, indignantly. 'And Timmy isn't fat either, so don't tell him he is.'

'Julian's pulling your leg as usual,' said Dick, giving George a friendly slap on the back. 'All the same, you've grown a bit – you'll soon be as tall as I am. Hallo, Timmy! Good dog, fine dog! Tongue as wet as usual? Yes, it is! I never knew a dog with a wetter tongue than yours!'

Timmy went nearly mad with joy at being with all four of his friends. He leapt round them, barking, wagging his long tail and sending a pile of tins crashing to the floor in his delight.

'Now, now!' said the shop-woman, emerging from a dark little room at the back. 'Take that dog out. He's gone mad!'

'Don't you girls want a drink of ginger-beer or something?' asked Julian, getting hold of Timmy's collar. 'You'd better, because we don't want to have to carry heavy bottles of drinkables with us.'

'Where are we going to set off to?' asked George. 'Yes, I'd like ginger-beer please. Get down, Timmy. Anyone would think you'd been away from Julian and Dick for at least ten years!'

'It probably does seem like ten years to him,' said Anne. 'I say – are those sandwiches?'

She pointed to a ledge at the back of the counter. There was a little pile of sandwiches there, looking most appetising.

'Yes, they're sandwiches, Miss,' said the shop-woman, opening two bottles of ginger-beer. 'I've made them for my son who works over at Blackbush Farm – he'll be in for them soon.'

'I suppose you couldn't make *us* some, could you?' asked Julian. 'We wouldn't need to bother about trying to get to some village at lunch time then. They look jolly good.'

'Yes. I can make you all you want,' said the shop-woman, putting two glasses down in front of the girls. 'What do you want – cheese, egg, ham or pork?'

'Well – we'd like some of all of those,' said Julian. 'The bread looks so nice too.'

'I make it myself,' said the woman, pleased. 'All right – I'll go and make you some. You tell me if anyone comes into the shop while I'm gone.'

She disappeared. 'That's good,' said Julian. 'If she makes plenty of those we can avoid villages all day and have a really good day of exploration – treading where no foot has trod before and all that!'

'How many can you manage each?' asked the woman, suddenly reappearing. 'My son, he has six – that's twelve rounds of bread.'

'Well – could you manage eight sandwiches for each of us?' said Julian. The woman looked astonished. 'It's to last us all day,' he explained, and she nodded and disappeared again.

'That's a nice little sum for her,' said Anne. 'Eight sandwiches each, making sixteen rounds of bread – for four people!'

'Well, let's hope she's got a bread-cutting machine!' said Dick. 'Or we'll be here for keeps! Hallo – who's this?'

A tall man appeared at the entrance of the shop, a bicycle in his hand. 'Ma!' he called.

The children guessed who he was at once – the son who worked over at Blackbush Farm. He had come for his sandwiches!

14

'Your mother is hard at work cutting sixty-four rounds of bread,' said Dick. 'Shall I get her for you?'

'No. I'm in a hurry,' said the man and he set his bicycle by the door, came in, reached over the counter for his sandwiches and then went back to his bicycle.

'Tell my mother I've been in,' he said. 'And you might tell her I'll be late home today – got to take some stuff to the prison.'

He was off at once, sailing away down the road on his bicycle. The old woman suddenly came in, a knife in one hand, a loaf in the other.

'Did I hear Jim?' she said. 'Oh yes – he's got his sandwiches. You should have told me he was in!'

'He said he was in a hurry,' explained Julian. 'And he said we were to tell you he'd be late today because he had to take some stuff to the prison.'

'I've got another son there,' said the woman. The four looked at her. Did she mean he was a prisoner? And what prison?

She guessed their thoughts and smiled. 'Oh, my Tom isn't a prisoner!' she said. 'He's a warder – a fine fellow. Not a nice job there though – I'm always afraid of those men in prison – a fierce lot, a bad lot!'

'Yes – I've heard there is a big prison on this moor,' said Julian. 'It's marked on our map too. We're not going near it, of course.'

'No. Don't you take the girls near there,' said the woman, disappearing again. 'If I don't get on with your

16

sandwiches you'll not have them before tomorrow morning.'

Only one customer came in while the children were waiting – a solemn old man smoking a clay pipe. He looked round the shop, couldn't see the woman, took a packet of blancmange powder, which he slipped into his pocket, and put the money down on the counter.

'Tell 'er when 'er comes,' he mumbled with his pipe still in his mouth, and out he shuffled. Timmy growled. The old man smelt very unwashed and Timmy didn't like him.

At last the sandwiches were finished and the old woman appeared again. She had packed them up neatly in four parcels of grease-proof paper, and had pencilled on each what they were. Julian read what she had written and winked at the others.

'My word – we're in for a grand time!' he said. 'Cheese, Pork, Ham and Egg – and what's this?'

'Oh, that's four slices of my home-made fruit cake,' said the old woman. 'I'm not charging you for that. It's just so that you can taste it!'

'It looks like half the cake!' said Julian, touched. 'But we shall pay for it, with many thanks. How much is all that?'

She told him. Julian put down the money and added five pence for the cake. 'There you are, and many thanks,' he said. 'And that money there was left by an old fellow with a clay pipe who took a packet of blancmange powder.'

'That would be Old Gupps,' said the woman. 'Well, I hope you'll enjoy your tour. Come back here if you want any more sandwiches cut! If you eat all those today you won't do badly!'

'Woof,' said Timmy, hoping that he too would share a few. The woman produced a bone for him, and he took it up in his mouth.

'Thanks!' Julian said. 'Come on – now we'll really start!'

CHAPTER THREE

Across the countryside

THEY SET off at last, Timmy running in front. School already seemed far behind them. The October sun shone down warmly, and the trees in the village glowed yellow and red and golden, dressed in their autumn colourings. A few leaves floated down in the breeze, but not until there was a real frost would many come whirling down.

'It's a heavenly day,' said George. 'I wish I hadn't got my blazer on. I'm cooked already.'

'Well, take it off and carry it over your shoulder,' said Julian. 'I'm going to do the same. Our jerseys are quite warm enough today!'

They took off their thick blazers and carried them. Each of them had a rucksack, a mac rolled up tightly and tied to it, and now a blazer to carry. But none of them noticed the weight at the outset of their day.

'I'm glad you girls took my advice and wore your thickest shoes,' said Julian, looking with approval at their brogues. 'Some of our walking may be wet. Have you got changes of socks?'

'Yes. We brought everything you told us to,' said Anne. 'Your rucksack looks a bit fuller than ours, Ju!'

'Well, I've got maps and things in it,' said Julian. 'It's

a strange place, this moor – miles and miles and miles of it! Strange names on it too – Blind Valley – Rabbit Hill – Lost Lake – Coney Copse!'

'Rabbit Hill! Timmy would love that,' said George, and Timmy pricked up his ears. Rabbits? Ah, that was the kind of place he liked!

'Well, actually we're going towards Rabbit Hill now,' said Julian. 'And after that there's Coney Copse, and as coney is a country word for rabbit, Timmy ought to enjoy himself!'

'Woof,' said Timmy joyfully and bounded ahead. He felt very happy. His four friends were with him, their rucksacks were full of delicious-smelling sandwiches, and a long, long walk lay ahead, teeming, he hoped with rabbits!

It was lovely walking along in the sun. They soon left the little village behind and took a winding lane. The hedges on either side became so high that the four couldn't see over the tops at all.

'What a sunken lane!' said Dick. 'I feel as if I'm walking in a tunnel! And how narrow! I wouldn't like to drive a car along this lane. If I met another car I might have to back for miles!'

'We shan't meet anyone much,' said Julian. 'It's only in the summer that cars come along these lanes – people on holiday, touring round the countryside. Look – we take that path now – it leads to Rabbit Hill, according to the map!'

20

They climbed over a stile in the high hedge and walked over a field towards a curious little hill. Timmy suddenly went mad with excitement. He could smell rabbits – and he could see them too!

'You don't often see so many rabbits out in the day-time,' said George, surprised. 'Big ones and little ones too – what a scampering.'

They came to the hill and sat down quietly to watch the rabbits. But it was quite impossible to make Timmy do the same. The sight and smell of so many made him quite wild. He pulled away from George's hand and went bounding madly up the hill, scattering rabbits by the dozen.

'Timmy!' yelled George, but for once Timmy paid no attention. He rushed here and rushed there, getting very angry as first one rabbit and then another neatly popped down a hole.

'It's no use calling him,' said Dick. 'He won't catch one, anyway – see how nippy they are. It's my belief they're having a game with our Timmy!'

It did look rather like it. As soon as Timmy had chased two or three rabbits down one hole, a few more would pop up from another behind him. The children laughed. It was as good as a pantomime.

'Where do you mean to have lunch?' asked Anne. 'If we stay here much longer I shall really have to have something to eat – and it's not nearly time yet. I wish I didn't always feel so hungry in the open air.'

'Well, come on then,' said Julian. 'We've got some way to go before we get to our lunch-place. I've made a pretty good time-table of our tour – we're going to go all round the moors and finish at the place we started at! I've really marked it all out pretty well.'

'Do we sleep at farmhouses or something at night?' asked George. 'I should like that. Will they mind having us, do you think? Or do we go to inns?'

'Farmhouses for two nights and inns for the other nights,' said Julian. 'I've marked them all.'

They went up Rabbit Hill and down the other side. There were just as many rabbits there. Timmy chased them till he panted like an engine going uphill! His tongue hung out, dripping wet.

'You've had enough, Tim,' said George. 'Be sensible now.'

But Timmy couldn't be sensible with so many rabbits about. So they left him to chase and dart and race at top speed and went on down the hill. Timmy came rushing after them when they got to the bottom.

'*Now* perhaps you'll stop tearing about like a mad thing and walk with us,' scolded George. But she spoke too soon, for soon they were in a small wood which Julian informed them was Coney Copse.

'And as I told you, coney means rabbit, so you can't expect Timmy to stop being mad just yet,' said Julian.

They very nearly lost Timmy in Coney Copse. A rabbit disappeared down a very big hole, and Timmy was

22

actually able to get down a little way. Then he got stuck. He scrabbled violently with his feet but it was no good. He was well and truly stuck.

The others soon discovered he wasn't with them and went back, calling. Quite by chance they came on the hole he was in and heard the sound of panting and scraping. A shower of sand flew out of the hole.

'There he is! The idiot, he's down a hole,' said George in alarm. 'Timmy! TIMMY! Come on out!'

There was nothing that Timmy would have liked better, but he couldn't come out, however much he tried. A root of a tree had got wedged into his back, and he couldn't seem to push himself out again, past the annoying root.

It took the four children twenty minutes to get Timmy out. Anne had to lie down and wriggle in a little way to reach him. She was the only one small enough to get into the hole.

She caught hold of Timmy's back legs and pulled hard. Somehow the root slid off his back and he came backwards. He whined loudly.

'Oh, Anne, you're hurting him, you're hurting him!' shouted George. 'Let him go!'

'I can't!' yelled back Anne. 'He'll only go down deeper, if I leave go his legs. Can you pull me out? If so Timmy will come too – he'll have to because I've got his legs!'

Poor Anne was pulled out by her legs, and poor Timmy came too, pulled by his. He whined and went to George.

23

'He's hurt himself somewhere,' said George anxiously. 'I know he has. He wouldn't whine like that if he wasn't hurt.'

She ran her fingers over him, pressing here and there. She examined each leg and each paw. She looked at his head. Still he whined. Where could he have hurt himself?

'Leave him,' said Julian, at last. 'I can't see that he's hurt anywhere – except in his feelings! He probably didn't like Anne hauling him out by his hind legs. Most undignified!'

George wasn't satisfied. Although she could find nothing wrong, she couldn't help being sure that Timmy had hurt himself somewhere. Ought he to see a vet?

'Don't be silly, George,' said Julian. 'Vets don't grow on trees in moorland country like this! Let's go on walking. You'll see Timmy will follow quite all right, and soon forget to whine. I tell you, he's hurt his doggy feelings, that's all. His vanity is wounded!'

They left Coney Copse and went on, George rather silent. Timmy trotted beside her, also rather quiet. Still, there really didn't seem anything the matter with him, except that he gave sudden little whines now and again.

'Now here's where I thought we might have our lunch,' said Julian, at last. 'Fallaway Hill! It's a good name for it too – it falls away steeply, and we've got a marvellous view.'

So they had. They had come to the top of a steep hill, not guessing that it fell away on the other side. They could

25

sit on the top and see the sun shining on miles and miles of lonely heather-grown moor. They might see shy deer in the distance – or little wild ponies.

'This is heavenly,' said Anne, sitting down on a great tuft of heather. 'It's as warm as summer too! I do hope it's like this all over the weekend. We shall all be burnt brown!'

'It will also be heavenly having some of those sandwiches,' said Dick, choosing a lump of heather too. 'What comfortable seats are provided for us! I've a good mind to take a tuft of this heather back to school with me to put on the very hard chair that goes with my desk!'

Julian put the four packets of sandwiches down in the heather. Anne undid them. They looked wonderful!

'Super!' said Anne. 'What do you want first?'

'Well, speaking for myself I'm going to have one of each, put them all on top of one another, and have a huge bite of cheese, ham, pork and egg at once,' said Dick. Anne laughed.

'Even *your* mouth isn't big enough for that,' she said. But somehow Dick managed, though it was difficult.

'Disgusting behaviour,' he said, when he had managed the first mouthful. 'I think on the whole that one at a time is more economical. Hie, Timmy – have a bit?'

Timmy obliged. He was very quiet, and George was still anxious about him. Still, his appetite seemed remarkably good, so nobody but George wondered any more if he had hurt himself. He lay beside George, occasionally

26

putting a great paw on her knee if he wanted another bit of sandwich.

'Timmy does jolly well,' said Dick, with his mouth full. 'He gets bits from us all. I bet he eats more than any of us. I say – did anyone ever taste such smashing sandwiches? Have you tried the pork? It must have come from a super pig!'

It was lovely sitting there in the sun, looking over miles of countryside, eating hungrily. They all felt very happy. Except George. *Was* there anything wrong with Timmy? It would spoil the whole weekend if so!

CHAPTER FOUR

George is worried

THEY LAZED for some time in the sun after they had finished their meal. There were three sandwiches each left, and half a piece each of the fruit cake. No one had been able to manage a whole piece, much as they would have liked to.

Timmy seemed to think he could finish all the cake that was left, but Julian said no. 'It's such a gorgeous cake it would be really wasted on Timmy,' he said. 'You've had enough, Tim. Greedy dog!'

'Woof,' said Timmy, wagging his tail, and eyeing the cake watchfully. He sighed when he saw it being packed up. He had only had a bit of George's half-slice – what a cake!

'I'll pack three sandwiches and a half-slice of the cake into each of four bags,' said Julian. 'Anyone can eat his or hers whenever they like. I expect we shall have a good meal at the farmhouse I've chosen for tonight, so you can eat when you like before then.'

'I don't feel as if I could eat anything till tomorrow morning,' said Anne, putting her bag of food into her rucksack. 'But it's odd how hungry you keep on getting, even if you feel you can't possibly be for hours and hours.'

'Well, Timmy can wolf anything you don't want,' said Julian. 'Nothing wasted when Tim's about. Now, are we all ready? We're going through a little village soon, where we'll stop for a drink. I could do with a ginger-beer. And then on we go to our farmhouse. We ought to try and arrive about five, because it gets dark so soon.'

'What's the farmhouse called?' asked Anne.

'Blue Pond Farm,' said Julian. 'Nice name, isn't it? I hope it's still got a blue pond.'

'Suppose they haven't room for us?' said Anne.

'Oh, they can always put a couple of girls somewhere,' said Julian. 'Dick and I can sleep in a barn if necessary. We're not particular!'

'*I'd* like to sleep in a barn too,' said Anne. 'I'd love to. Let's not ask for a bedroom, let's all sleep in a barn – on straw or hay or something.'

'No,' said Julian. 'You girls will have to be in the house. It gets cold at night, and we've brought no rugs. We boys will be all right with our macs over us. I'm not letting you two girls do that.'

'It's *stupid* being a girl!' said George, for about the millionth time in her life. 'Always having to be careful when boys can do as they like! I'm going to sleep in a barn, anyway. I don't care what you say, Ju!'

'Oh yes you do,' said Julian. 'You know quite well that if ever you go against the orders of the chief – that's me, my girl, in case you didn't know it – you won't come out with us again. You may look like a boy and behave like a

29

boy, but you're a girl all the same. And like it or not, girls have got to be taken care of.'

'I should have thought that boys hated having to take care of girls,' said George, sulkily. 'Especially girls like me who don't like it.'

'Well, decent boys like looking after their girl cousins or their sisters,' said Julian. 'And oddly enough decent girls like it. But I won't count you as a girl, George, decent or otherwise. I'll merely count you as a boy who's got to have an eye on him – my eye, see? So take that look off your face, and don't make yourself any more difficult than you already are.'

George couldn't help laughing, and the sulky look went at once. She gave Julian a punch. 'All right. You win. You're so jolly domineering these days I feel quite afraid of you!'

'You're not afraid of anyone,' said Dick. 'You're the bravest girl I ever knew! Aha! That's made old George blush like a girl! Let me warm my hands, George!'

And Dick held his hands up in front of George's scarlet face, pretending to warm them at her fiery blush. She didn't know whether to be pleased or angry. She pushed his hands away and got up, looking more like a boy than ever with her short tousled hair and her well-freckled face!

The others got up and stretched. Then they settled their rucksacks on their backs again, with their macs fastened to them, threw their blazers over their shoulders and set off down Fallaway Hill.

Timmy followed, but he didn't bound about as usual. He went slowly and carefully. George looked round for him, and frowned.

'What *is* the matter with Timmy?' she said. 'Look at him! Not a jump or a scamper in him!'

They all stopped and watched him. He came towards them and they saw that he was limping slightly with his left hind leg. George dropped down beside him and felt the leg carefully.

'I think he must have twisted it – sprained it or something, when he was down that rabbit-hole,' she said. She patted

31

him gently on the back and he winced.

'What's the matter, Tim?' said George, and she parted the hair on his back, examining the white skin underneath to see why he had winced when she had patted him.

'He's got an awful bruise here,' she said at last, and the others bent to see. 'Something must have hurt his back down in that hole. And Anne must have hurt one of his legs when she held on to them and dragged him out. I *told* you not to hold on to his legs, Anne.'

'Well, how were we to get him out if I didn't?' demanded Anne, feeling cross but rather guilty. 'Did you want him to stick there for days and days?'

'I don't think there's much damage done,' said Julian, feeling the hind leg. 'I honestly think he's only just twisted it a bit, George. He'll be all right after tonight, I'm sure.'

'But I must be *certain*,' said George. 'Did you say we come to a village soon, Ju?'

'Yes – Beacons Village,' said Julian. 'We can ask if there's a vet anywhere in the district if you like. He'll look at Timmy's leg and tell you if there's anything much wrong. But I don't think there is.'

'We'll go on to the village then,' said George. 'Oh dear – the only time I *ever* wish Timmy was a *little* dog is when he's hurt – because he's so very very heavy to carry.'

'Well, don't think of carrying him yet,' said Dick. 'He can walk on three legs even if he can't on four! He's not as bad as all that, are you, Timmy?'

'Woof,' said Timmy, mournfully. He was rather enjoying all the fuss. George patted his head. 'Come on,' she said, 'we'll soon get that leg put right. Come on, Tim.'

They all went on, looking round to see how Timmy was getting on. He followed slowly, and then began to limp more badly. Finally he lifted his left hind leg up from the ground and ran on three legs only.

'Poor boy,' said George. 'Poor Timmy! I do hope his leg will be all right tomorrow. I can't possibly go on with the hike if it isn't.'

It was rather a gloomy company that came to Beacons Village. Julian made his way to a little inn that stood in the middle, called Three Shepherds.

A woman was shaking a duster out of a window. Julian called up to her.

'I say! Is there a vet anywhere in this district? I want someone to have a look at our dog's leg.'

'No. No vet here,' answered the woman. 'Not one nearer than Marlins over six miles away.'

George's heart sank. Timmy would never be able to walk six miles.

'Is there a bus?' she called.

'No. Not to Marlins,' said the woman. 'No bus goes there, missy. But if you want your dog's leg seen to, you go up to Spiggy House, up along there. Mr Gaston lives there with his horses, and he knows about dogs too. You take the dog there. He'll know what to do.'

'Oh *thank* you,' said George, gratefully. 'Is it very far?'

'About half a mile,' said the woman. 'See that hill? You go up there, take the turning to the right and you'll see a big house. That's Spiggy House. You can't mistake it because of the stables built all round it. Ask for Mr Gaston. He's nice, he is. Maybe you'll have to wait a little if he's out with his horses though – he may not be in till it's almost dark.'

The four put their heads together. 'We'd better go up to this Mr Gaston's, I think,' said Julian. 'But I think you and Anne, Dick, should go on to the farmhouse I planned to stay in for the night, and make arrangements for us. We don't want to leave it till the last minute. I'll go with George and Timmy, of course.'

'Right,' said Dick. 'I'll take Anne now. It will be dark pretty soon. Got your torch, Julian?'

'Yes,' said Julian. 'And I'm pretty good at finding my way, as you know. I shall come back to this village after we've been to Mr Gaston's, and then make straight for the farmhouse. It's about a mile and a half away.'

'Thanks awfully for saying you'll come with me, Julian,' said George. 'Let's go now, shall we? Well, Dick and Anne – see you later!'

Julian set off with George and Timmy up the hill to Spiggy House. Timmy went on three legs, and still seemed very sorry for himself. Anne and Dick watched him, feeling sorry for him too.

'I hope he's all right tomorrow,' said Dick. 'It will spoil our weekend if he's not, no doubt about that!'

GEORGE IS WORRIED

They turned away and walked through the little village of Beacons. 'Now for Blue Pond Farmhouse,' said Dick. 'Julian didn't give me very clear directions. I think I'll ask someone exactly where it is.'

But they met nobody except a man driving a little cart. Dick hailed him and he pulled up his horse.

'Are we on the right road for Blue Pond Farmhouse?' shouted Dick.

'Ar,' answered the man, nodding his head.

'Is it straight on – or do we take any paths or little lanes?' asked Dick.

'Ar,' said the man, nodding again.

'What does he mean – "ar"?' said Dick. He raised his voice again.

'Is it this way?' And he pointed.

'Ar,' said the man again. He raised his whip and pointed up the road where the two were going, and then across to the west.

'Oh, I see – we turn to the right up there?' called Dick.

'Ar,' said the man, nodding, and drove on so suddenly that the horse almost stepped on Dick's foot.

'Well – if we find the farmhouse after all those "ars" we'll be clever,' said Dick. 'Come on!'

CHAPTER FIVE

Anne and Dick

IT BEGAN to get dark very suddenly. The sun had gone, and a big black cloud slid smoothly over the sky. 'It's going to rain,' said Dick. 'Blow! I thought it was going to be a lovely evening.'

'We'd better hurry,' said Anne. 'I hate sheltering under a hedge in the pouring rain, with drips down my neck, and puddles round my feet!'

They hurried. They went up the road that led out of the village and then came to a turning on the right. This must be the one the man had meant. They stopped and looked down it. It seemed to be like one of the sunken lanes they had walked down in the morning, and it looked rather dark and tunnel-like now, in the twilight.

'I hope it's right,' said Dick. 'We'll ask the very first person we meet.'

'If we *do* meet anyone!' said Anne, feeling that they never would in this curious deep lane. They went up it. It would round and about and then went downhill into a very muddy bit indeed. Anne found herself sloshing about in thick mud.

'A stream or something must run across the lane here,' she said. 'Ugh! The water's got into my shoes! I'm sure we don't go this way, Dick. The water's quite deep farther on, I'm certain. I was up to my ankles just now.'

Dick looked about in the deepening twilight. He made out something above him in the high hedge that grew on the steep bank each side.

'Look – is that a stile?' he said. 'Where's my torch? At the bottom of my rucksack, of course! Can you get it out, Anne, to save me taking the thing off?'

Anne found the torch and gave it to Dick. He switched it on, and immediately the shadows round them grew blacker, and the lane seemed more tunnel-like than ever. Dick flashed the torch upwards to what he had thought was a stile.

'Yes – it is a stile,' he said. 'I expect that leads up to the farmhouse – a short cut, probably. I've no doubt this lane is the one used by the farm-carts, and probably goes right round to the farm – but if this is a short cut we might as well take it. It must lead somewhere, anyway!'

They scrambled up the bank to the stile. Dick helped Anne over, and they found themselves in a wide field. In front of them was a narrow path, running between crops of some sort.

'Yes – this is obviously a short cut,' said Dick, pleased. 'I expect we'll see the lights of the farmhouse in a minute.'

'Or fall into the blue pond first,' said Anne, rather dismally. It was just beginning to rain and she was

38

wondering if it was worth while to untie her mac from her shoulder and put it on. Or was the farmhouse really nearby? Julian had said it wasn't very far.

They walked across the field and came to another stile. The rain was coming down fast now. Anne decided to put on her mac. She stood under a thick bush and Dick helped her on with it. She had a small sou'wester in the pocket and put that on too. Dick put his on and they set off again.

The second stile led into another endless field, and the path then came at last to a big field-gate. They climbed over it and found themselves on what looked like a heathery moor – wild and uncultivated land! No farmhouse was to be seen – though, indeed, they could not have seen anything of one unless they had been very close to it, because the night was on them, dark and rainy.

'If only we could see lights somewhere – shining out of a window,' said Dick. He shone his torch on to the moor in front of them. 'I don't quite know what to do. There doesn't seem to be a path here – and I just hate the idea of going all the way back across those wet fields, and into that dark little lane.'

'Oh no – don't let's,' said Anne, with a shiver. 'I really didn't like that lane. There *must* be a path somewhere! It's silly for a gate to open on to moorland!'

And then, as they stood there, with the rain dripping on them and not much else to be heard, another noise came to their ears.

It was so unexpected and so very startling that both of them clutched the other in a start of alarm. It was certainly a strange noise to hear in that deserted bit of country.

Bells! Wild, clanging bells sounding without a stop, jangling out over the dark countryside in peal after peal. Anne held on tightly to Dick.

'What is it? Where are those bells? What are they ringing for?' whispered Anne.

Dick had no idea. He was as startled as Anne to hear this extraordinary noise. It sounded some distance away, but every now and again the wind blew hard and then the noise of the jangling swept round them, close to them it seemed.

'I wish they'd stop. Oh, I wish they'd stop!' said Anne, her heart beating fast. 'I don't like them. They frighten me. They're not church bells.'

'No. They're certainly not church bells,' said Dick. 'They're a warning of some kind. I'm sure – but what for? Fire? We'd see fire if there was one anywhere near us. War? No – bells and beacons were used to warn people of war long long ago. Not now.'

'That village was called Beacons,' said Anne, suddenly remembering. 'Do you suppose it has that name because long ago there was a nearby hill where people lighted a beacon, to send a warning to other towns telling them that the enemy was coming? Did they ring bells too? Are we hearing long-ago bells, Dick? They don't sound like bells I've ever heard in my life before.'

40

'Good gracious! They're certainly not long-ago bells!' said Dick, speaking cheerfully, though he was really just as puzzled and alarmed as Anne. 'Those bells are being rung now, at this very minute!'

Quite suddenly the bells stopped and an enormous silence took the place of the wild ringing. The two children stood and listened for a minute or two and then heaved a sigh of relief.

'They've stopped at last,' said Anne. 'I hated them! *Why* did they ring out on this dark dark night? Oh do let's find Blue Pond Farmhouse as soon as ever we can, Dick. I don't like being lost in the dark like this, with bells ringing madly for nothing at all!'

'Come on,' said Dick. 'Keep close to the hedge. As long as we follow that we must come to somewhere. We won't wander out on to the moorland.'

He took Anne's arm and the two of them kept close to the hedge. They came to another path at last and followed it. That led to a lane, but not a sunken one this time – and then, oh wonderful sight – not far off they saw a light shining!

'That must be Blue Pond Farmhouse!' said Dick, thankfully. 'Come on, Anne – not much farther now!'

They came to a low stone wall and followed it till they came to a broken-down gate. It opened with a squeak, and Anne stepped through – right into an enormous puddle!

'Blow!' she said. 'Now I'm wetter than ever! For a

41

moment I thought I must have stepped into the blue pond!'

But it was only a puddle. They went round it and followed a muddy path to a little door set in a white stone wall. Dick thought it must be the back door. Nearby was a window, and in it shone the light they had seen so thankfully.

An old woman sat near the light, her head bent over some sewing. The children could see her quite clearly as they stood by the door.

Dick looked for a bell or knocker but there was none. He knocked with his bare knuckles. Nobody answered. The door remained shut. They looked at the old woman by the lamp, and saw that she was still sewing.

'Perhaps she's deaf,' said Dick and he knocked again, much more loudly. Still the old woman sewed on placidly. She must indeed be deaf!

'We'll never get in at this rate!' said Dick, impatiently. He tried the handle of the door – it opened at once!

'We'll just have to walk in and announce ourselves,' said Dick, and he stepped on to the worn mat inside the door. He was in a narrow little passage that led to a stone stairway, steep and narrow at the farther end.

On his right was a door, a little ajar. It opened into the room where the old woman was sitting. The two children could see a streak of light coming through the crack.

Dick pushed the door open and walked boldly in,

followed by Anne. Still the old woman didn't look up. She pushed her needle in and out of her sewing and seemed to hear and see nothing else whatsoever.

Dick had to walk right up to her before she knew he was in the room. Then she leapt up in such a fright that her chair fell over with a bang.

'I'm sorry,' said Dick, upset at frightening the old lady. 'We knocked but you didn't hear!'

She stared at them, her hand over her heart. 'You give me such a fright,' she said. 'Where did you come from this dark night?'

Dick picked up her chair, and she sat down in it, panting a little.

'We've been looking for this place,' said Dick. 'Blue Pond Farmhouse, isn't it? We wondered if we could stay the night here – and two others of us as well.'

The old woman pointed to her ears and shook her head. 'Deaf as a post,' she said. 'No good talking to me, my dear. You've lost your way, I suppose?'

Dick nodded.

'Well, you can't stay here,' said the old woman. 'My son won't have no one here at all. You'd best be gone before he comes. He have a nasty temper, he have.'

Dick shook his head. Then he pointed out to the dark rainy night, then pointed to Anne's wet shoes and clothes. The old woman knew what he meant.

'You've lost your way, you're wet and tired, and you don't want me to turn you out,' she said. 'But there's my son, you see. He don't like strangers here.'

Dick pointed to Anne, and then to a sofa in a corner of the room. Then he pointed to himself, and then outside. Again the old woman understood at once.

'You want me to give your sister shelter, but you'll go out into the night?' she said. Dick nodded. He thought he could easily find some shed or barn for himself. But Anne really must be indoors.

'My son mustn't see either of you,' said the old woman, and she pulled Anne to what the girl thought was a cupboard. But when the door opened, she saw a very small, steep wooden staircase leading upwards into the roof.

'You go up there,' said the old woman to Anne. 'And don't you come down till I call you in the morning. I'll get into trouble if my son knows you're here.'

'Go up, Anne,' said Dick, rather troubled. 'I don't know what you'll find there. If it's too bad, come down. See if there's a window or something you can call out from, and then I'll know if you're all right.'

'Yes,' said Anne, in rather a trembling voice, and she went up the steep, dirty wooden stairs. They led straight into a little loft. There was a mattress there, fairly clean, and a chair. A rug was folded up on the chair and a jug of water stood on a shelf. Otherwise the room was bare.

A tiny window opened out on one side. Anne went to it and called out. 'Dick! Are you there? Dick!'

'Yes, I'm here,' said Dick. 'What's it like, Anne? Is it all right? Listen, I'll find somewhere nearby to shelter in – and you can always call me if you want me!'

CHAPTER SIX

In the middle of the night

'IT'S NOT bad,' said Anne. 'There's a fairly clean mattress and a rug. I'll be all right. But what about if the others come, Dick? Will you look out for them? I almost think George will have to sleep in a barn with you and Julian if she comes. That old woman won't let anyone else in, I'm sure!'

'I'll look out for them and arrange something,' said Dick. 'You eat the rest of your sandwiches and your cake, and see if you can dry your wet feet and make yourself really comfortable. There's a shed or something out here. I shall be quite all right. Yell for me if you want me.'

Anne went back into the room. She felt wet and tired, hungry and thirsty. She ate all her food, and had a drink from the jug. Then she felt sleepy and lay down on the mattress, throwing the rug over her. She meant to listen for the others to come, but she was too tired. She fell fast asleep!

Dick was prowling about down below. He was careful because he didn't want to run into the old woman's son. He didn't like the sound of him somehow! He came to a small barn with piles of straw in one corner. He flashed his torch cautiously round.

'This will do for me,' he thought. 'I can be quite comfortable here in that straw. Poor Anne! I wish old George was with her. I'd better wait about and watch for the other two, or I'll fall asleep and miss them, once I bed down in that straw! It's only about six o'clock too – but we've had a long day. I wonder how Timmy is. I wish he was here!'

Dick thought that probably George and Julian would come in through the same gate as he and Anne had used. He found a broken-down shed near the gate and sat down on a box there, waiting for them to come.

He ate his sandwiches while he waited. They were very comforting! He ate every one and then the cake. He yawned. He felt very sleepy indeed, and his feet were wet and tired.

No one arrived at all – not even the old woman's son. She could still be seen sewing under the lamp. But after about two hours, when it was almost eight o'clock, and Dick was beginning to be very worried about George and Julian, the old woman got up and put away her workbasket.

She disappeared out of Dick's sight, and didn't come back. But the light was still there, shining out of the window. Left for her son, probably, thought Dick.

He tiptoed to the window. The rain had stopped now and the night was much clearer. The stars were out and a moon was coming up. Dick's spirits rose.

He peered in at the lighted room. Then he saw the old

woman lying on a broken-down sofa in a corner. A blanket was pulled right up to her chin and she seemed to be asleep. Dick went back to his shed, but now he felt there was no use in watching for George and Julian. They must have lost their way completely! Or else Mr Gaston, or whatever his name was, must have had to do something to Timmy's leg, and Julian had decided to stay at the inn in Beacons Village for the night.

He yawned again. 'I'm too sleepy to watch any more,' he decided. 'I shall fall off this box with sleep if I don't go and lie down in that straw. Anyway I think I'd hear if the others came.'

Using his torch cautiously, he made his way to the barn. He shut the door behind him and bolted it roughly from the inside by running a stick through two hasps. He didn't know why he did that – perhaps because he was still thinking of the old woman's bad-tempered son!

He flung himself down on the straw, and immediately fell asleep. Outside the sky became clearer and clearer. The moon came up, not fully, but large enough to give some light. It shone down on the desolate little stone house and ill-kept outbuildings.

Dick slept soundly. He lay in the soft straw and dreamt of Timmy and George and Blue Ponds and bells. Especially bells.

He awoke suddenly, and lay for a moment wondering where he was. What was this prickly stuff round him? Then he remembered – of course, it was straw and he was in a barn! He was about to cuddle down again when he heard a noise.

It was only a small noise – a scratching on the wooden walls of the barn perhaps. Dick sat up. Were there rats there? He hoped not!

He listened. The scratching seemed to come from *outside* the barn, not inside. Then it stopped. After an interval it began again. Then there came a gentle tapping at the broken window just above Dick's head.

He felt very startled. Rats scratched and scrabbled about – but they didn't tap on windows. Who was tapping so very cautiously on the little window? He held his breath and listened, straining his ears.

And then he heard a voice – a hoarse whisper.

'Dick! Dick!'

Dick was amazed. Could it be Julian? If so, how in the world did he know that he, Dick, was in the barn? He sat listening, stiff with surprise.

The tapping came again, and then the voice, a little louder. 'Dick! I know you're there. I saw you go in. Come here to the window – quiet, now!'

Dick didn't know the voice. It wasn't Julian's, and it certainly wasn't either George's or Anne's. Then how did the owner know *his* name and that he was there? It was astounding. Dick didn't know what to do!

'Buck up!' said the voice. 'I've got to go in half a tick. I've got that message for you.'

Dick decided to go nearer to the window. He was quite

certain that he didn't want whoever it was outside to come into the barn. He cautiously knelt up in the straw and spoke just underneath the window.

'I'm here,' he said, trying to make his voice deep and grown-up.

'You've been long enough coming,' grumbled the one outside, and then Dick saw him through the window – just a face, dim and wild-eyed, with a round bullet-like head. He crouched back, thankful that the face couldn't see him in the darkness of the barn.

'Here's the message from Nailer,' said the voice. 'Two-Trees. Gloomy Water. Saucy Jane. And he says Maggie knows. He sent you this. Maggie's got one too.'

A bit of paper fluttered in at the broken pane. Dick picked it up in a daze. What *was* all this? Was he dreaming?

The voice came again, insistent and urgent. 'You heard all that, Dick? Two-Trees. Gloomy Water. Saucy Jane. And Maggie knows too. Now I'm going.'

There came the sound of someone cautiously creeping round the barn – and then there was silence. Dick sat amazed and bewildered. Who was this wild-eyed fellow, who called him by his name in the middle of the night and gave him extraordinary messages that meant nothing at all to a sleepy boy? But Dick was wide awake now. He stood up and looked out of the window. There was nothing and no one to be seen except the lonely house and the sky.

Dick sat down again and thought. He put his torch on cautiously and looked at the piece of paper he had picked up. It was a dirty half sheet, with pencil marks on it that meant nothing to Dick at all. Words were printed here and there, but they were all nonsense to him. He simply couldn't make head or tail of his visitor, his message or the bit of paper!

'I'm sure I must be dreaming,' thought Dick, and put the paper into his pocket. He lay back in his straw, cuddling in deep, because he had got cold by the window. He lay and thought for a while, puzzling over the curious happenings, and then he felt his eyes closing.

But before he was quite asleep, he heard cautious footsteps again! Was that fellow back once more? This time someone tried the door – but the wooden stick was in the hasps. Whoever it was outside shook the door and the stick fell out at once. The man shook the door again as if thinking it had stuck, and then opened it. He came inside and shut the door behind him.

Dick caught a quick glimpse of him. No – this wasn't the same man as before. This was a man with a head of thick hair, Dick hoped and prayed that he wouldn't come over to the straw.

He didn't. He sat down on a sack and waited. He talked to himself after a while, but Dick could only make out a word or two.

'What's happened?' he heard. 'How much longer do I wait?' Then there was a mumble and Dick could not catch a word.

'Wait, wait – that's all I do,' muttered the man, and he stood up and stretched himself. Then he went to the door and looked out. He came back and sat down on the sack again.

He sat still and quiet then, and Dick found his eyes closing once more. Was this part of a dream too? He didn't have time to think it out because he was suddenly in a real dream, walking along ringing bells and seeing trees in twos everywhere round him!

He slept heavily all night long. When morning came he awoke suddenly and sat up. He was alone in the barn. Where had the second visitor gone? Or *could* it all have been a dream?

CHAPTER SEVEN

In the morning

DICK STOOD up and stretched himself. He felt dirty and untidy. Also he was very hungry. He wondered if the old woman would let him buy some bread and cheese and a glass of milk.

'Anne must be hungry too,' he thought. 'I wonder if she's all right.' He went cautiously outside and looked up at the tiny window of the loft where Anne had spent the night. Her anxious face was already there, watching for Dick!

'Are you all right, Anne?' called Dick, in a low tone. She pushed open the tiny window and smiled at him.

'Yes. But I daren't go down because that son is downstairs. I can hear him shouting at the deaf old woman every now and again. He sounds very bad-tempered.'

'I'll wait for him to go out to his work then, before I go and see the old woman,' said Dick. 'I must pay her something for letting you sleep up in that loft – and perhaps I can persuade her to let us have something to eat.'

'I wish you could,' said Anne. 'I've eaten all the chocolate I had in my bag. Shall I wait till I hear you call me?'

Dick nodded and disappeared into the barn in a hurry. He had heard footsteps!

A man came into sight – a broad, short, hunched-up man, with a shock of untidy hair. He was the man that Dick had seen in the barn the night before. He was muttering to himself and looked very bad-tempered indeed. Dick decided to keep out of his way. He crouched down in the barn.

But the man did not go in there. He walked past, still muttering. Dick listened for his footsteps to die away. He heard the opening of a gate somewhere, then it crashed behind the man.

'I'd better take my chance now,' thought Dick, and he went quickly out of the barn and up to the little white house. It looked very tumble-down and neglected in the daylight, and had a more forlorn air.

Dick knew that it was no good knocking, because the old woman wouldn't hear him. So he walked right into the house and found the woman washing up a few dishes in a cracked old sink. She stared at him in dismay.

'I'd forgotten about you! And the girl too! Is she still up there? Get her down quickly before my son comes back! And then go, both of you!'

'Can you sell us some bread and cheese?' shouted Dick. But the old woman really was stone deaf, and all she did was to push Dick away towards the door, jabbing at him with the wet cloth in her hand. Dick slipped aside and pointed to some bread on a table.

'No, no – I tell you, you're to go,' said the old woman, obviously terrified in case her son should come back. 'Get the girl, quickly!'

But before Dick could do anything, there were footsteps outside and in came the hunched-up fellow with the shock of hair! He was back already, holding some eggs he had been to find.

He walked into the kitchen and stared at Dick. 'Clear out!' he said, angrily. 'What do you want here?'

Dick thought he had better not say he had slept the night in the barn. There were strange goings-on here, and the man might be very savage if he knew Dick had slept the night nearby.

'I wanted to know if your mother could sell us some bread,' he said, and could have bitten his tongue out. He had said 'us'! Now the man would guess there was someone with him.

'Us? Who's "us"?' said the man, looking round. 'You fetch him and I'll tell you both what I do to boys who come stealing my eggs!'

'I'll go and fetch him,' said Dick, seizing the chance to get away. He ran to the door. The man made a clumsy dart at him and almost caught him. But Dick was out and away, running down the path. He hid behind a shed, his heart thumping. He had to wait for Anne. Somehow he had to go back and get her.

The man stood at the door, shouting angrily after Dick. But he didn't chase him. He went back into the house and

after a while came out again with a pail of steaming food. Dick guessed he was going to feed the chickens wherever they were.

He had to take this chance of fetching Anne. He waited till he heard the crash of the distant gate again and then he rushed to the house. Anne's face was at the window, scared. She had heard all that the man had said to Dick, and then to his mother about allowing boys to come to the house.

'Anne! Come down at once. He's gone,' shouted Dick. 'Hurry!'

Anne's face disappeared from the window. She ran to the door, tumbled quickly down the stairs, and ran through the kitchen. The old woman flapped a cloth at her, screaming at her.

Dick ran into the kitchen and put a pound coin on the table. Then he caught Anne's arm and both children tore out of the house and down the path. They came to the hedge they had followed the night before.

Anne was quite scared. 'That awful man!' she said. 'Oh Dick – what a horrible place. Honestly I think Julian must be mad to choose a place like that to sleep in for the night – horrible little house! And it didn't look a bit like a farm. There were no cows or pigs that I could see and not even a farm-dog!'

'You know, Anne, I don't think it could possibly have been Blue Pond Farmhouse,' said Dick, as they walked beside the hedge, looking for the gate that they had come through the night before. 'We made a mistake. It was an ordinary cottage. If we hadn't lost our way we'd have come to the proper Blue Pond Farmhouse I'm sure.'

'Whatever will George and Julian be thinking?' said Anne. 'They'll be dreadfully worried, won't they, wondering what has become of us? Do you suppose they're at the real Blue Pond Farmhouse?'

'We'll have to find out,' said Dick. 'Do I look very messy and untidy, Anne? I feel awful.'

'Yes. Haven't you a comb?' said Anne. 'Your hair's all up on end. And your face is very dirty. Look, there's a little stream over there. Let's get our flannels out and wash our hands and faces with them.'

They did a little washing in the cold water of the stream, and Dick combed back his hair.

'You look a lot better,' said Anne. 'Oh dear – I wish we could have some breakfast. I'm really starving! I didn't sleep awfully well, did you, Dick? My mattress was so hard, and I was rather scared, up in that funny little room all alone.'

Before Dick could answer, a boy came whistling through the gate. He looked astonished to see Dick and Anne.

'Hallo!' he said. 'You hiking?'

'Yes,' said Dick. 'Can you tell me if that place up there is Blue Pond Farmhouse?'

He pointed back to the old woman's house. The boy laughed.

'That's no farmhouse. That's Mrs Taggart's place, and a dirty old place it is. Don't you go there, or her son will drive you off. Dirty Dick we call him – he's a terror! Blue Pond Farmhouse is down along there, see? Past the Three Shepherds Inn and away up to the left.'

'Thanks,' said Dick, feeling very angry indeed with the man who had said 'ar' and sent them all wrong the day before. The boy waved, and set off across a moorland path.

'We certainly went the wrong way last night,' said Dick, as they walked over the fields they had crossed in the dark the night before. 'Poor Anne! Dragging you all that way in the dark and the rain to a horrible place that wasn't Blue Pond Farmhouse after all. I can't think what Julian is going to say to me.'

'Well, it was my fault too,' said Anne. 'Dick, let's go down to the Three Shepherds and telephone Blue Pond Farmhouse from there, shall we? If it's on the phone, that is. I don't somehow feel as if I want to walk for miles and perhaps not find Blue Pond Farmhouse again.'

'Good idea,' said Dick. 'The Three Shepherds was where that woman was shaking a duster out of the window, wasn't it? She told Julian the way to Spiggy House. I wonder how old Timmy is. I hope he's better. I say – this hike isn't as good as we hoped it would be, is it?'

'Well, there's still time for it to be all right!' said Anne, much more cheerfully than she felt. She so badly wanted her breakfast that she felt quite bad-tempered!

'We'll telephone to Julian from the Three Shepherds to say what happened to us,' said Dick, as they came to the lane where they had floundered in the mud the night before. He helped Anne over the stile and they jumped down to the narrow road. 'And what's more, we'll have breakfast at the Three Shepherds – and I bet we eat more than ever the Three Shepherds did, whoever they were!'

Anne felt more cheerful at once. She had thought they would have to walk all the way to find Blue Pond Farmhouse before they had breakfast!

'See – a stream does flow right across the road here,' she said. 'No wonder I got my feet wet yesterday! Come on – the thought of breakfast makes my legs want to run!'

They at last arrived in Beacons Village, and made their way to the inn. On the sign three shepherds were painted, looking rather gloomy.

'They look like I feel,' said Anne, 'but I shall soon feel different. Oh Dick – think of porridge – and bacon and eggs – and toast and marmalade!'

'We must telephone first,' said Dick, firmly – and then he suddenly stopped, just as he was going into the inn. Someone was calling him.

'DICK! DICK! ANNE! Look, there they are! Hey, Dick, DICK!'

It was Julian's voice! Dick swung round in delight. He saw Julian, George and Timmy racing along the village street, shouting and waving. Timmy was first to reach them of course – and there was no sign of limping either!

He leapt on them, barking madly, and licked every bare part of them he could reach.

'Oh, Ju! I'm so glad to see you!' said Anne, in rather a trembling voice. 'We lost our way last night. George, is Timmy all right?'

'Quite. Absolutely,' said George. 'You see . . .'

'Have you had breakfast? interrupted Julian. 'We haven't. We were so worried about you we were just going to see the police. But now we can all have breakfast together and tell our news!'

CHAPTER EIGHT

All together again

IT WAS wonderful to be all together again. Julian took hold
of Anne's arm and squeezed it. 'All right, Anne?' he said,
rather worried at her pale face.

Anne nodded. She felt better at once, now she had
Julian, George and Timmy, as well as Dick. 'I'm only just
terribly hungry,' she said.

'I'll ask for breakfast straight away,' said Julian. 'All
news later!'

The woman who had leant out of the window shaking a
duster the evening before, came up to them. 'I expect it's
a bit late for you,' said Julian. 'But we haven't had any
breakfast. What have you got?'

'Porridge and cream,' said the woman. 'And our own
cured bacon and our own eggs. Our own honey and the bread
I bake myself. Will that do? And coffee with cream?'

'I could hug you,' said Julian, beaming at her. The others
felt the same. They went into a small, cosy dining-room
and sat down to wait. Soon a smell of frying bacon and hot
strong coffee would come into the room – what joy!

'Your news first,' said Dick, patting Timmy. 'Did you
get to Spiggy House? Was Mr Gaston there?'

'No, he wasn't,' said Julian. 'He was out somewhere.

He had a very nice wife who made us wait for him, and said he wouldn't mind in the least looking at Timmy when he came back. So we waited and waited.'

'We waited till half past seven!' said George, 'and we felt rather awkward because we thought it might be getting near their meal-time. And then at last Mr Gaston came.'

'He was awfully kind,' said Julian. 'He looked at Timmy's leg, and then he did something, I don't know what – put it back into place, I suppose – and Timmy gave a yell and George flung herself on him, and Mr Gaston roared with laughter at George . . .'

'Well, he was very *rough* with Timmy's leg,' said George. 'But he knew what he was doing, of course, and now Timmy is perfectly all right, except for that bruise on his back, and even that is getting better. He can run as well as ever.'

'I'm glad,' said Anne. 'I kept thinking of poor old Tim all last night.' She patted him, and he licked her lavishly and wetly.

'What did you do then?' asked Dick.

'Well, Mrs Gaston insisted on us staying to supper,' said Julian. 'She simply wouldn't take no for an answer, and I must say that by that time we were jolly hungry. So we stayed – and we had a jolly good meal too. So did Timmy! You should have seen his tummy afterwards – as round as a barrel. Good thing it's gone down today or I was thinking of changing his name to Tummy.' They all laughed, George especially.

'Idiot,' she said. 'Well, we didn't leave till about nine o'clock. We didn't worry about you because we felt sure you would be safely at Blue Pond Farmhouse and would guess we'd had to wait about with Timmy. And when we got there and found you hadn't arrived – well, we *were* in a state!'

'And then we thought you must have found somewhere else for the night,' said Julian, 'but we thought if we heard nothing we'd go down to the police first thing this morning and report your disappearance!'

'So down we came – without any breakfast either!' said

66

George. 'That shows how worried we were! Blue Pond Farmhouse was nice. They gave us a bed each in two tiny little rooms, and Timmy slept with me, of course.'

A wonderful smell came creeping into the little dining-room, followed by the inn-woman carrying a large tray. On it was a steaming tureen of porridge, a bowl of golden syrup, a jug of very thick cream, and a dish of bacon and eggs, all piled high on crisp brown toast. Little mushrooms were on the same dish.

'It's like magic!' and Anne, staring. 'Just the very things I longed for!'

'Toast, marmalade and butter to come, and the coffee and hot milk,' said the woman, busily setting everything out. 'And if you want any more bacon and eggs, just ring the bell.'

'Too good to be true!' said Dick, looking at the table. 'For goodness' sake, help yourselves quickly, girls, or I shall forget my manners and grab.'

It was a wonderful breakfast – extra wonderful because they were all so ravenously hungry. There wasn't a word said as they spooned up their porridge and cream, sweetened with golden syrup. Timmy had a dishful too – he loved porridge, though he didn't like the syrup – it made his whiskers sticky!

'I feel better,' said Anne, looking at the porridge dish. 'The thing is – shall I have some more porridge and risk not enjoying my bacon and eggs so much – or shall I go straight on with bacon and eggs?'

'A difficult question,' said Dick. 'And one that I am faced with too. On the whole I think I'll go on with bacon and eggs – we can always have more of those if we want to – and those little mushrooms really do make my mouth water! Aren't we greedy? But how can anyone help that when they're so hungry?'

'You haven't told us a single word of what happened to *you* last night,' said Julian, serving out the bacon and eggs with a generous hand. 'Now that you've got something inside you, perhaps you feel able to tell us exactly why you ignored my instructions and didn't arrive where you were supposed to last night.'

'You sound like our headmaster at school!' said Dick. 'The plain fact is – we got lost! And when we did finally arrive somewhere, we thought it was Blue Pond Farmhouse, and we stayed the night there.'

'I see,' said Julian. 'But didn't the people there tell you it wasn't the right place? Just so that you could have let us know? You must have known that we would worry about you.'

'Well, the old woman there was stone-deaf,' explained Anne, attacking her bacon and eggs vigorously. 'She didn't understand a word we said, and as we thought it *was* Blue Pond Farmhouse, we stayed there – though it was a horrible place. And *we* were worried because *you* didn't arrive!'

'A chapter of accidents,' said Julian. 'All's well that ends well, however.'

'Don't sound so pompous!' said Dick. 'Actually we had a pretty poor time, Ju. Poor Anne had to sleep in a little loft, and I slept in straw in a barn – not that I minded that – but – well, peculiar things happened in the night. At least – I *think* they did. I'm not really sure it wasn't all a dream.'

'What peculiar things?' asked Julian at once.

'Well – I think perhaps I'll tell you when we're on our way again,' said Dick. 'Now I think about it in full daylight I feel that either it was all a silly dream – or – well, as I said – something very peculiar.'

'You never told me, Dick!' said Anne, in surprise.

'Well, to tell you the truth I forgot about it because other things happened,' said Dick. 'Having to get away from that man, for instance – and wondering about Julian and George – and feeling so hungry.'

'You don't sound as if you had a good night at all,' said George. 'It must have been awful, too, trying to find your way in the dark. It poured with rain, didn't it?'

'Yes,' said Anne, 'but oh – the thing that frightened me more than anything was the bells! Did you hear them Julian? They suddenly clanged out, and they made me terribly scared. I couldn't think what they were! Whatever were they ringing out for? They were so loud.'

'Didn't you know what they were ringing for?' said Julian. 'They were bells rung from the prison that nice old woman told us about – they were rung to tell everyone in the countryside that a prisoner had escaped! Lock your doors. Guard your folk.'

69

Anne stared at Julian in silence. So that was why the bells had made such a clamour and clangour. She shivered.

'I'm glad I didn't know that,' she said. 'I would have slept in the straw with Dick if I'd known there was an escaped prisoner. Have they caught him?'

'I don't know,' said Julian. 'We'll ask the inn-woman when she comes.'

They asked her, and she shook her head. 'No. He's not caught yet. But he will be. All the roads from the moor are guarded and everyone is on the watch. He was a robber who broke into houses and attacked anyone who tried to prevent him. A dangerous fellow.'

'Julian – is it all right to go hiking on the moors if there's an escaped prisoner about?' said Anne. 'I shan't feel very comfortable.'

'We've got Timmy,' said Julian. 'He would be strong enough to protect us from three prisoners if necessary! You needn't worry.'

'Woof,' agreed Timmy, at once, and thumped his tail on the floor.

At last everyone had finished breakfast. Even starving Anne couldn't manage the last bit of toast. She sighed happily. 'I feel myself again,' she announced. 'I can't say I feel very much like walking – but I know it would be good for me after that enormous meal.'

'Good or not, we're going on our way,' said Julian, getting up. 'I'll buy some sandwiches first.'

The inn-woman was delighted with their hearty praises.

She gave them some packets of sandwiches and waved good-bye. 'You come again whenever you can,' she said. 'I'll always have something nice for you.'

The four went down the street and took a lane at the bottom. It wound about for a short way and then came into a valley. A stream ran down the middle of the valley. The children could hear it gurgling from where they stood.

'Lovely!' said Anne. 'Are we going along by the stream? I'd like to.'

Julian looked at his map. 'Yes – we could,' he said. 'I've marked the path to follow, and the stream joins it some way on. So if you like we could go along by it, though it will be very rough walking.'

They made their way to the stream. 'Now, Dick,' said Julian, when they had left the path. 'What about telling us all those peculiar things that happened in the night? There's nobody about to hear – not a soul in sight. Let's hear everything. We'll soon tell you whether it was a dream or not.'

'Right,' said Dick. 'Well, here's the tale. It does sound pretty peculiar. Listen . . .'

CHAPTER NINE

Dick surprises the others

DICK BEGAN his tale – but it was really very difficult to hear it because they couldn't walk four abreast, as there was no path to follow.

In the end Julian stopped and pointed to a thick clump of heather. 'Let's go and sit there and hear Dick's story properly. I keep missing bits. No one can hear us if we sit here.'

They sat down and Dick started again. He told about the old woman who was afraid her son would be angry if she let them stay the night. He told about his bed in the straw.

'And now here comes the bit I think must have been a dream,' he said. 'I woke up to hear a scratching noise on the wooden walls of the barn . . .'

'Rats or mice?' said George, and Timmy leapt up at once, of course. He was sure she had said the words to him!

'I thought that too,' said Dick. 'But then I heard a gentle tap-tap-tapping on the window.'

'How horrid,' said Anne. 'I shouldn't have liked that at all.'

'Neither did I,' said Dick. 'But the *next* thing I heard was my name being called! "Dick! Dick!" Just like that.'

'It *must* have been a dream then,' said Anne. 'There was no one there who knew your name.'

Dick went on. 'Well, then the voice said – "Dick! I know you're there. I saw you go in!" And it told me to go to the window.'

'Go on,' said Julian. He was puzzled. No one in the world but Anne could have known that Dick was in the barn – and it certainly wasn't Anne out there in the night!

'Well, I went to the window,' said Dick, 'and I saw, rather dimly, of course, a wild-eyed looking fellow. He couldn't see me in the darkness of the barn. I just mumbled, "I'm here," hoping he would think I was whoever he wanted.'

'What did he say next?' said George.

'He said something that sounded stuff and nonsense,' said Dick. 'He said it twice. It was "Two-Trees. Gloomy Water. Saucy Jane." And he said "Maggie knows." Just like that!'

There was silence. Then George laughed. 'Two-Trees! Gloomy Water! Saucy Jane – and Maggie knows about it! Well, it *must* have been a dream, Dick! You know it must. What do you think, Julian?'

'Well – it does sound a bit nonsensical to have someone come in the middle of the night and call Dick by name and give him a strange message that doesn't mean a thing to him!' said Julian. 'It sounds more dreamlike than real. I'd say it was a dream too.'

Dick began to think they were right – and then a sudden thought struck him. He sat up straight. 'Wait a bit!' he said. 'I've remembered something! The man slipped a bit of paper through the broken pane of the window, and I picked it up!'

'Ah – that's different,' said Julian. 'Now – if you can't find that paper, it's all a dream and you dreamt the paper too – but if you *can* find it, well the whole thing is true. Very peculiar indeed – but true.'

Dick searched quickly in his pockets. He felt paper in one of them, and drew it out. It was a dirty, crumpled piece, with a few words on it and a few lines. He held it out to the others in silence, his eyes shining.

'Is this the paper?' asked Julian. 'My word – so you didn't dream it after all, then!'

He took the paper. Four heads bent over it to examine it. No, five – because Timmy wanted to see what they were all so interested in. He thrust his hairy head between Julian's and Dick's.

'I can't make any sense of this paper,' said Julian. 'It's a plan of some kind, I think – but what of, or where, it's impossible to know.'

'The fellow said that Maggie had one of these bits of paper too,' said Dick, remembering.

'Who in the wide world *is* Maggie?' said George, 'and why should Maggie know?'

'Any more to tell?' asked Julian, intensely interested now.

'Well – the son of the deaf old woman came into the barn later on,' said Dick. 'And he sat and waited and waited, and muttered and muttered – and then when I woke up he wasn't there. So I thought I must have dreamt him too. He didn't see me, of course.'

Julian pursed up his lips and frowned. Then Anne spoke excitedly.

'Dick! Ju! I think I know why the second man came into the barn. It was the *second* man that the wild-eyed man wanted to give the message to, and the bit of paper – not to Dick. He didn't want *Dick*. But he had seen him creep into the barn, and I suppose he thought Dick was the man he really wanted and that he was in the barn waiting for him!'

'That's all very well – but how did he know my name?' asked Dick.

'He didn't know it! He didn't know it was you at all!' said Anne, excitedly. 'The other man's name must have been Dick too! Don't you *see*? They must have planned to meet there, the wild-eyed man and the old woman's son – and the first man saw Dick go in, so he waited a bit and then went and tapped on the window! And when he called "Dick! Dick!" of course Dick thought it was he that he wanted, and he took the message and everything! And then the other man, the real Dick came along – and was too late to meet the first one. *Our* Dick had met him and got the message!'

Anne was quite breathless after this long speech. She sat and stared at the others eagerly. Didn't they think she was right?

They did, of course. Julian clapped her on the back. 'Well worked out, Anne! Of course that's what happened.'

DICK SURPRISES THE OTHERS

Dick suddenly remembered the boy they had met on the way down from the old woman's cottage to Beacons Village – the whistling boy. What had he said about the old woman and her son?

'Anne – what did that whistling boy say? Wait a bit – he said that was Mrs Taggart's place – and he said we'd better not go there or her son would drive us off. And he said – yes, I remember now – he said "Dirty Dick we call him – he's a terror!" Dirty *Dick*! His name *must* be Dick then! Why didn't I think of it before?'

'That proves that Anne is right,' said Julian, pleased. Anne looked pleased too. It wasn't often that she thought of something clever before the others did!

They all sat thinking. 'Would this have anything to do with the escaped prisoner?' said George at last.

'It might,' said Julian. 'He might have been the prisoner himself, that fellow who came with the message. Did he say who the message was from?'

'Yes,' said Dick, trying to remember. 'He said it was from Nailer. I think that was the name – but it was all given in whispers, you know.'

'A message from Nailer,' said Julian. 'Well – perhaps Nailer is in prison – a friend of the man who escaped. And maybe when he knew this fellow was going to make a dash for it, he gave him a message for someone – the man at that old cottage, son of the old woman. They may have had a prearranged plan.'

'How do you mean?' asked Dick, looking puzzled.

77

'Well – the old woman's son, Dirty Dick, may have known that when the bells rang out, this fellow was making a run for it – and would come to bring him a message. He was to wait in the barn at night if the bells rang, just in case it was Nailer's friend who had escaped.'

'Yes, I see,' said Dick. 'I think you're right. Yes, I'm sure you are. My word, I'm glad I didn't know that fellow at the window was an escaped convict!'

'And *you've* got the message from Nailer!' said Anne. 'What a peculiar thing! Just because we lost our way and went to the wrong place, you get a message from a prisoner given you by one who's escaped! It's a pity we don't know what the message means – or the paper either.'

'Had we better tell the police?' said George. 'I mean – it may be important. It might help them to catch that man.'

'Yes,' said Julian. 'I think we *should* tell the police. Let's have a look at our map. Where's the next village?'

He looked at the map for a minute. 'I think really we might as well go on with what I had planned,' he said. 'I planned we should reach this village here – Reebles, look – in time for lunch, in case we hadn't got sandwiches. We'd have gone there for drinks anyway. So I vote we just carry on with our ramble, and call in at Reebles police station – if there is one – and tell them our bit of news.'

They all got up. Timmy was glad. He didn't approve of this long sit-down so soon after breakfast. He bounded ahead in delight.

'His leg's *quite* all right,' said Anne, pleased. 'Well I

78

hope it teaches him not to go down rabbit holes again!'

It didn't, of course. He had his head down half a dozen within the next half-hour, but fortunately he could get no farther, and he was able to pull himself out quite easily.

The four saw little wild ponies that day. They came trotting over a hillock together, small and brown, with long manes and tails, looking very busy indeed. The children stopped in delight. The ponies saw them, tossed their pretty heads, turned one way all together and galloped off like the wind.

Timmy wanted to go after them, but George held his collar tightly. No one must chase those dear little wild ponies!

'Lovely!' said Anne. 'Lovely to meet them as suddenly as that. I hope we meet some more.'

The morning was as warm and sunny as the day before. Once again the four of them had to take off their blazers, and Timmy's tongue hung out, wet and dripping. The heather and wiry grass was soft underfoot. They followed the stream closely, liking its brown colour and its soft gurgling voice.

They bathed their hot feet in it as they ate one of their sandwiches at half past eleven. 'This is bliss!' said George, lying back on a tuft of heather with her feet lapped by the water. 'The stream is tickling my feet, and the sun is warming my face – lovely! Oh, get away, Timmy, you idiot! Breathing down my neck like that, and making my face so wet!'

The stream at last joined the path that led to the village of Reebles. They walked along it, beginning to think of dinner. It would be fun to have it in a little inn or perhaps a farmhouse, and keep their sandwiches for tea-time.

'But first we must find the police station,' said Julian. 'We'll get our tale told, and then we'll be ready for our meal!'

CHAPTER TEN

An angry policeman and a fine lunch

THERE *was* a police station at Reebles, a small one with a house for the policeman attached. As the one policeman had four villages under his control he felt himself to be rather an important fellow.

He was in his house having his dinner when the children walked up to the police station. They found nobody there, and walked out again. The policeman had seen them from his window and he came out, wiping his mouth. He wasn't very pleased at having to come out in the middle of a nice meal of sausage and onions.

'What do you want?' he said, suspiciously. He didn't like children of any sort. Nasty little things, he thought them – always full of mischief and cheek. He didn't know which were worse, the small ones or the big ones!

Julian spoke to him politely. 'We've come to report something rather strange, which we thought perhaps the police ought to know. It might help them to catch the prisoner who escaped last night.'

'Ha!' said the policeman scornfully. 'You've seen him too, I suppose? You wouldn't believe how many people have seen him. 'Cording to them he's been in every part of the moor at one and the same time. Clever fellow he must be to split himself up like that.'

'Well, one of us saw him last night,' said Julian politely. 'At least, we think it must have been him. He gave a message to my brother here.'

'Ho, he did, did he?' said the policeman, eyeing Dick in a most disbelieving manner. 'So he runs about giving messages to school-boys, does he? And what message did he give you, may I ask?'

The message sounded extremely silly when Dick repeated it to the police. 'Two-Trees. Gloomy Water. Saucy Jane. And Maggie knows.'

'Really?' said the policeman, in a sarcastic voice. 'Maggie knows as well, does she? Well, you tell Maggie to come along here and tell me too. I'd like to meet Maggie – specially if she's a friend of yours.'

'She's not,' said Dick feeling annoyed. 'That was in the message. I don't know who Maggie is! How should I? We thought perhaps the police could unravel the meaning. We couldn't. The fellow gave me this bit of paper too.'

He handed the piece of dirty paper to the policeman, who looked at it with a crooked smile. 'So he gave you this too, did he?' he said. 'Now wasn't that kind of him? And what do you suppose all this is, scribbled on the paper?'

'We don't know,' said Dick. 'But we thought our report might help the police to catch the prisoner, that's all.'

'The prisoner's caught,' said the policeman, with a smirk on his face. 'You know so much – but you didn't know that! Yes, he's caught – four hours ago – and he's safe back in prison now. And let me tell you youngsters this – I'm not taken in by any silly school-boy spoofing, see?'

'It's not spoofing,' said Julian, in a very grown-up manner. 'You should learn to see the difference between the truth and a joke.'

That didn't please the policeman at all. He turned on Julian at once, his face reddening.

'Now, you run away!' he said. 'I'm not having any cheek from you! Do you want me to take your names and addresses and report you?'

'If you like,' said Julian, in disgust. 'Have you got a notebook there? I'll give you all our names, and I myself will make a report to the police in our district when I get back.'

The policeman stared at him. He couldn't help being impressed by Julian's manner, and he calmed down a little.

'You go away, all of you,' he said, his voice not nearly so fierce. 'I shan't report you this time. But don't you go spreading silly stories like that or you'll get into trouble. Serious trouble too.'

'I don't think so,' said Julian. 'Anyway, seeing that you are not going to do anything about our story, may we have back our bit of paper, please?'

The policeman frowned. He made as if he would tear the paper up, but Dick snatched at it. He was too late. The aggravating policeman had torn it into four pieces and thrown it into the road!

AN ANGRY POLICEMAN AND A FINE LUNCH

'Don't you have laws against scattering litter in your village?' asked Dick, severely, and carefully picked up the four pieces of paper. The policeman glared at Dick as he put the bits into his pocket. Then he made a peculiar snorting noise, turned on his heel and marched back to his sausages and onions.

'And I hope his dinner's gone cold!' said George. 'Horrid fellow! Why should he think we're telling a lot of untruths?'

'It is rather an odd story of ours,' said Julian. 'After all – we found it a bit difficult to believe when Dick first told it. I don't blame the policeman for disbelieving it – I blame him for his manner. It's a good thing most of our police aren't the same. Nobody would ever report anything.'

'He told us one bit of good news, anyway,' said Anne. 'That escaped prisoner is back in prison again! I'm so relieved to know that.'

'I am too,' said Dick. 'I didn't like the look of him at all. Well, Ju – what do we do now? Forget the whole business? Do *you* think there's anything in that message to follow up? And if so – can we do anything?'

'I don't know,' said Julian. 'We must think a bit. Let's go and see if we can scrounge a meal in some farmhouse somewhere. There seem to be plenty around.'

They asked a little girl if there was a farmhouse anywhere near that would give them dinner. She nodded and pointed.

'See that farmhouse up on the hill there? That's my

gran's place. She'll give you dinner, I expect. She used to give dinner in the summer to trippers, and I expect she would give you some too, if you ask her, though it's late in the season.'

'Thanks,' said Julian, and they all went up the lane that curved round the hillside. Dogs barked loudly as they came near and Timmy's hackles went up at once. He growled.

'Friends, Timmy, friends,' said George. 'Dinner here, Timmy. Dinner, perhaps a nice bone for you. Bone!'

Timmy understood. The fur down his neck lay flat again and he stopped growling. He wagged his tail at the two dogs near the farm-gate who sniffed his doggy smell suspiciously even when he was some distance away.

A man hailed them. 'What do you kids want? Mind those dogs!'

'We wondered if we could get a meal here!' called back Julian. 'A little girl down in the village said we might.'

'I'll ask my mother,' said the man, and he yelled in an enormous voice to the farmhouse nearby. 'Ma! MA! Four kids out here want to know if you can give them a meal.'

A very fat old lady appeared, with twinkling eyes and red cheeks like an apple. She took one glance at the four by the gate, and nodded her head. 'Yes. They look decent children. Tell them to come along in. Better hold their dog's collar though.'

The four walked to the farmhouse, George holding Timmy firmly. The other two dogs came up, but as

AN ANGRY POLICEMAN AND A FINE LUNCH

Timmy was hoping for a bone, he was determined to be friendly, and not a single growl came from him, even when the two dogs growled suspiciously. He wagged his tail, and let his tongue hang out.

The other dogs soon wagged theirs, and then it was safe to let Timmy go. He bounded over to them and there was a mad game of 'chase-me-roll-me-over' as George called it.

'Come your ways in,' said the plump old lady. 'Now you'll have to take what we've got. I'm busy today and haven't had time for cooking. You can have a bit of homemade meat-pie, or a slice or two of ham and tongue, or hard-boiled eggs and salad. Bless you, you look as pleased as Punch! I'll put the lot on the table for you and you can help yourselves! Will that do? There's no vegetables though. You'll have to make do with pickled cabbage and my own pickled onions and beetroot in vinegar.'

'It sounds too marvellous for words,' said Julian. 'We shan't want any sweet after that!'

'There's no pudding today,' said the old lady. 'But I'll open a bottle or two of our own raspberries and you can have them with cream if you like. And there's the cream cheese I made yesterday too.'

'Don't tell us any more!' begged Dick. 'It makes me feel too hungry. Why is it that people on farms always have the most delicious food? I mean, surely people in towns can bottle raspberries and pickle onions and make cream cheese?'

'Well, either they can't or they don't,' said George. 'My

mother does all those things – and even when she lived in a town she did. Anyway, *I'm* going to when I'm grown-up. It must be so wonderful to offer home-made things by the score when people come to a meal!'

It was extraordinary to think that any children could possibly eat the meal the four did, after having had such a huge breakfast. Timmy ate an enormous dinner too, and then lay down with a sigh. How he wished he could live at that farmhouse! How lucky those other two dogs were!

A small girl came in shyly as they ate. 'I'm Meg,' she said. 'I live with my gran. What are your names?'

They told her. Then Julian had an idea. 'We're walking over your moor,' he said. 'We've been to lots of nice places. But there's one we haven't been to yet. Do you know it? It's called Two-Trees.'

The little girl shook her head. 'Gran would know,' she said. 'Gran! Where's Two-Trees?'

The old lady looked in at the door. 'What's that? Two-Trees? Oh, that was a lovely place once, but it's all in ruins now. It was built beside a strange dark lake, in the middle of the moors. Let's see now – what was it called?'

'Gloomy Water?' said Dick.

'Yes! That's right. Gloomy Water,' said the old lady. 'Are you thinking of going by there? You be careful then, there's marshland around there, just when you least expect it! Now – would you like anything more?'

'No thank you,' said Julian, regretfully, and paid the

very modest bill. 'It's the nicest lunch we've ever had. Now we must be off.'

'Off to Two-Trees and Gloomy Water, I hope!' George whispered to Dick. 'That would be really exciting.'

CHAPTER ELEVEN

Julian's idea

ONCE OUTSIDE the farmhouse Julian looked round at the others. 'We'll find out how far Two-Trees is and see if we've got time to pay it visit,' he said. 'If we have, we'll go along there and snoop round. If we haven't we'll go tomorrow.'

'How can we find out how far it is?' said Dick eagerly. 'Will it be on your map?'

'It may be marked there if the lake is big enough,' said Julian. They walked down the hill, and took a path that led once more over the moors. As soon as they were out of sight and hearing of anyone Julian stopped and took out his big map. He unfolded it and the four of them crouched over it as he spread it out on the heather.

'That nice old lady said it was in the middle of the moors,' said Julian. 'Also we know there's a lake or at any rate a big pool of some kind.'

His finger traced its way here and there on the map. Then George gave a cry and dabbed her finger down.

'There, look! It's not really in the middle. See – Gloomy Water! That must be it. Is Two-Trees marked as well?'

'No,' said Julian. 'But perhaps it wouldn't be if it's in ruins. Ruins aren't marked on maps unless they are important in some way. This can't be important. Well – that's certainly Gloomy Water marked there. What do you say? Shall we have a shot at going there this afternoon? I wonder exactly how far it is.'

'We could ask at the post-office,' said George. 'Probably once upon a time the postman had to take letters there. They might know. They could tell us the way to go.'

They went back to the village and found the post-office. It was part of the village store. The old man who kept it looked over the top of his glasses at the children.

'Gloomy Water! Now what be you wanting that for? A real miserable place it is, and it used to be so fine.'

'What happened to it?' asked Dick.

'It was burnt,' said the old man. 'The owner was away, and only a couple of servants were there. It flared up one night, no one knows how or why – and was burnt almost to a shell. Couldn't get a fire-engine out there, you see. There was only a cart-track to the place.'

'And wasn't it ever built up again?' asked Julian. The old man shook his head.

'No. It wasn't worth it. The owner just let it fall to rack and ruin. The jackdaws and the owls nest there now, and the wild animals snuggle in the ruins. It's a queer place. I once went out to see it, hearing tales of lights being seen there. But there was nothing to see but the shell of the place, and the dark blue water. Ah, Gloomy Water's a good name for that lake!'

'Could you tell us the way? And how long would it take us to get there?' asked Julian.

'What for do you want to go and gaze at a poor old ruin?' said the old man. 'Or do you want to bathe in the lake? Well, don't you do so – it's freezing cold!'

'We just thought we'd go and see Gloomy Water,' said Julian. 'Such a strange name. Which is the way, did you say?'

'I didn't say,' said the old fellow. 'But I will if you're so set on it. Where's your map? Is that one in your hand?'

Julian spread it out. The old fellow took a pen from his waistcoat pocket and began to trace a path over the moor. He put crosses here and there.

'See them crosses? They mark marshland. Don't go treading there, or you'll be up to your knees in muddy water! You follow these paths I've inked in for you and you'll be all right. Keep your eyes open for deer – there's plenty about those parts, and pretty things they are too.'

'Thank you very much,' said Julian, folding up the map. 'How long would it take us to get there from here?'

'Matter of two hours or more,' said the old man. 'Don't you try to go this afternoon. You'll find yourselves in darkness coming back, and with them dangerous marshy bits you're in danger all the time!'

'Right,' said Julian. 'Thanks very much. Er – we're thinking of doing a bit of camping, as the weather is so beautiful. I suppose you couldn't hire us a ground-sheet or two and a few rugs?'

The other three stared at him in astonishment. Camping

out? Where? Why? What was Julian thinking of all of a sudden?

Julian winked at them. The old man was ferreting about in a cupboard. He pulled out two large rubber ground-sheets and four old rugs. 'Thought I had them somewhere!' he said. 'Well, better you camping out in October than me! Be careful you don't catch your deaths of cold!'

'Oh thanks – just what we want,' said Julian, pleased. 'Roll them up, you others. I'll settle up for them.'

Dick, Anne and George folded up the groundsheets and the rugs in astonishment. Surely – surely Julian wasn't thinking of camping out by Gloomy Water? He must think the message that Dick had been given was very important!

'Julian!' said Dick, as soon as they got outside. 'What's up? What's all this for?'

Julian looked a little sheepish. 'Well – something suddenly came over me in the store,' he said. 'I suddenly felt we ought to go to Gloomy Water and snoop round. I felt excited somehow. And as we've got so little time this weekend I thought if we took things and camped out in the ruin we might make more of our few days.'

'What an idea!' said George. 'Not go on with our hiking, do you mean?'

'Well,' said Julian. 'If we find nothing, we *can* go on with our hike, of course. But if there's anything interesting, it's up to us to unearth it. I'm quite sure there's something up at Two-Trees.'

'We might meet Maggie there!' said Anne, with a giggle.

'We might!' said Julian. 'I feel quite free to go and investigate on our own seeing that we've made our report to the police, and it's been turned down with scorn. *Somebody* ought to follow up that message – besides Maggie!'

'Dear Maggie,' said Dick. 'I wonder who in the wide world she is!'

'Somebody worth watching if she's the friend of convicts,' said Julian, more soberly. 'Look, this is what I thought we'd do – buy some extra food, and go along to Gloomy Water this afternoon, arriving there before dark. We'll find a good place to shelter in – there must be some good spot in the old ruin – and get heather or bracken for beds. Then tomorrow we can be up bright and early to have a look round.'

'It sounds smashing,' said Dick, pleased. 'Sort of thing we like. What do you say, Tim?'

'Woof,' said Tim, solemnly, bumping his tail to and fro across Dick's legs.

'And if we find there's absolutely nothing of interest, well, we can come back here with the things we've borrowed, and go on with our hike,' said Julian. 'But we'll have to sleep the night there because it will be dark by the time we've had a look round.'

They bought some loaves of bread, some butter and potted meat, and a big fruit cake. Also some more chocolate and some biscuits. Julian bought a bottle of orangeade as well.

'There's sure to be a well,' he said. 'Or a spring of some sort. We can dilute the orangeade and drink it when we're thirsty. Now I think we're ready. Come on!'

They couldn't go as fast as usual because they were carrying so many things. Timmy was the only one that ran as fast as ever – but then Timmy carried nothing but himself!

It was a really lovely walk over the moorlands. They climbed fairly high and had wonderful views all over the autumn countryside. They saw wild ponies again, in the distance this time, and a little herd of dappled deer, which sped away immediately.

Julian was very careful to take the right paths – the ones traced so carefully on the map by the old man in the post-office. 'I expect he knew the way well because he was once a postman and had to take letters to Two-Trees!' said Dick, bending over the map. 'We're getting on, Ju – halfway there!'

The sun began to sink low. The children hurried as much as they could because once the sun had gone darkness would soon come. Fortunately the sky was very clear, so twilight would be later than it had been the night before.

'It looks as if the moorland near here gives way soon to a little bit of wooded country, according to the map,' said Julian. 'We'll look out for clumps of trees.'

After another little stretch of moorland Julian pointed to the right. 'Look!' he said. 'Trees! Quite a lot – a proper little wood.'

'And isn't that water over there?' said Anne. They stood still and gazed hard. Was it Gloomy Water? It might be. It looked such a dark blue. They hurried on eagerly. It didn't look very far now. Timmy ran ahead, his long tail waving in the air.

They went down a little winding path and joined a cart-track that was very much overgrown – so overgrown that it hardly looked like a track. 'This must lead to Two-Trees,' said Julian. 'I wish the sun wasn't going down so quickly. We'll hardly have any time to look round!'

They entered a wood. The track wound through it. The trees must have been cleared at some time to make a road through the wood. And then, quite suddenly, they came on what had once been the lovely house of Two-Trees.

It was a desolate ruin, blackened and scorched with fire. The windows had no glass, the roof had gone, except for a few rafters here and there. Two birds flew up with a loud cry as the children went near.

'Two Maggies!' said Anne, with a laugh. They were black and white magpies, their long tails stretched out behind them. 'I wonder if they know the message too.'

The house stood on the edge of the lake. Gloomy Water was indeed a good name for it. It lay there, smooth and dark, a curious deep blue. No little waves lapped the edge. It was as still as if it were frozen.

'I don't like it,' said Anne. 'I don't like this place at all! I wish we hadn't come!'

CHAPTER TWELVE

A hiding-place at Two-Trees

NOBODY PARTICULARLY liked the place. They all stared round
and Julian pointed silently to something. At each end of
the house was the great burnt trunk of a big tree.

'Those must be the two trees that gave the place its
name,' said Julian. 'How horrid they look now, so stiff and
black. Two-Trees and Gloomy Water – all so lonely and
desolate now.'

The sun disappeared and a little chill came on the air.
Julian suddenly became very busy. 'Come on – we must
see if there's anywhere to shelter at all in this old ruin!'

They went to the silent house. The upper floors were all
burnt out. The ground floor was pretty bad too, but Julian
thought it might be possible to find a sheltered corner.

'This might do,' he said, coming out of a blackened
room and beckoning the others to him. 'There is even a
mouldy carpet still on the floor! And there's a big table.
We could sleep under it if it rained – which I don't think
it will do!'

'What a horrid room!' said Anne, looking round. 'I
don't like its smell, either. I don't want to sleep here.'

'Well, find somewhere else then, but be quick about it,'
said Julian. 'It will soon be dark. I'm going to collect

heather and bracken straight away, before it's too dark. Coming, Dick and George?'

The three of them went off and came back with vast armfuls of heather and brown bracken. Anne met them, looking excited.

'I've found somewhere. Somewhere much better than this horrid room. Come and look.'

She took them to what once had been the kitchen. A door lay flat on the floor at the end of the room, and a stone stairway led downwards.

'That leads down to the cellars,' said Anne. 'I came in here and saw that door. It was locked and I couldn't open it. Well, I tugged and tugged and the whole door came off its rusty old hinges and tumbled down almost on top of me! And I saw there were cellars down there!'

She stared at Julian beseechingly. 'They'll be dry. They won't be burnt and black like everywhere else. We'll be well-sheltered. Can't we sleep down there? I don't like the feel of these horrid burnt rooms.'

'It's an idea,' said Julian. He switched on his torch and let the beam light up the cellar below. It seemed spacious and smelt all right.

He went down the steps, Timmy just in front. He called up in surprise.

'There's a proper room down here, as well as cellars all round. Maybe it was a kind of sitting-room for the staff. It's wired for electricity too – they must have had their own electricity generator. Yes – we'll certainly come down here.'

A HIDING-PLACE AT TWO-TREES

It was a strange little room. Moth-eaten carpets were on the floor, and the furnishings were moth-eaten too and covered with dust. Spiders had been at work and George slashed fiercely at the long cobwebs that hung down and startled her by touching her face.

'There are still candles in the candlesticks on this shelf!' said Dick, surprised. 'We can light them and have a bit of brightness when it's dark. This isn't bad at all. I must say I agree with Anne. There's something hateful about those burnt-out rooms.'

They piled heather and bracken into the cellar room on the floor. The furniture was so old and moth-eaten that it gave beneath their weight, and was useless for sitting on. The table was all right though. They soon set out their food on it after George had wiped it free of dust. She caused them all to have fits of choking because she was so vigorous in her dusting! They were driven up into the kitchen till the dust had settled.

It was dark outside now. The moon was not yet up. The wind rustled the dry leaves left on the trees around, but there was no lap-lap of water. The lake was as still as glass.

There was a cupboard in the cellar room. Julian opened it to see what was there. 'More candles – good!' he said, bringing out a bundle. 'And plates and cups. Did anyone see a well outside? If so we could dilute some orangeade and have a drink with our supper.'

No one had noticed a well – but Anne suddenly

101

remembered something peculiar she had seen in a corner of the kitchen, near the sink.

'I believe I saw a pump up there!' she said. 'Go and see, Ju. If so, it might still work.'

He went up the cellar steps with a candle. Yes – Anne was right. That *was* an old pump over there in the corner. It probably pumped water into a tank and came out of the kitchen taps.

He turned on a big tap which was over the large sink. Then he took the handle of the pump and worked it vigorously up and down. Splash! Splash! Water came flooding through the big tap and splashed into the sink! That was good.

Julian pumped and pumped, feeling that he had better get rid of any water running into the tank for the first time for years. The tank might be dirty or rusty – he must wash it round with a good deal of pumped water first.

The water seemed to be clean and clear, and was certainly as cold as ice! Julian held a cup from the cellar cupboard under the tap, and then tasted the water. It was delicious.

'Good for you, Anne!' he called, going down the cellar steps with a cupful of water. 'Dick, you find some more cups – or a jug or something in that cupboard, and we'll wash them out and fill them with water for our orangeade.'

The cellar room looked very cheerful as Julian came down the steps. George and Anne had lit six more candles, and stuck them about here and there. The light they gave was very pleasant, and they also warmed the room a little.

'Well, I suppose as usual, everyone wants a meal?' said Julian. 'Good thing we bought that bread and potted meat and stuff. I can't say I'm as hungry as I was at breakfast, but I'm getting that way.'

The four squatted round on their beds of heather and bracken. They had put down their ground-sheets first in case the floor was damp, though it didn't seem to be. Over bread and butter and potted meat they discussed their plans. They would sleep there for the night and then have all the next day to examine Two-Trees and the lake.

'What exactly are we looking for?' asked Anne. 'Do you suppose there's some secret here, Julian?'

'Yes,' said Julian. 'And I think I know what it is!'

'What?' asked George and Anne, surprised. Dick thought he knew. Julian explained.

'Well, we know that a prisoner called Nailer sent an important message by his escaped friend to two people – one he wanted to send to Dirty Dick – but he didn't get it – and the other to Maggie, whoever she is. Now what secret does he want to tell them?'

'I think I can guess,' said Dick. 'But go on.'

'Now suppose that Nailer has done some big robberies,' said Julian. 'I don't know what. Jewellery robberies probably, because they are the commonest with big criminals. All right – he does a big robbery – he hides

103

the stuff till he hopes the hue and cry will be over – but he's caught and put into prison for a number of years. But he doesn't tell where the stuff is hidden! He daren't even write a letter to tell his friends outside the prison where it is. All his letters are read before they leave the prison. So what is he to do?'

'Wait till someone escapes and then give him a message,' said Dick. 'And that's just what happened, isn't it, Julian? That round-headed man I saw was the escaped prisoner, and he was sent to tell Dirty Dick and Maggie where the stolen goods were hidden – so that they could get them before anyone else did!'

'Yes. I'm sure that's it,' said Julian. 'His friend, the escaped prisoner, probably wouldn't understand the message at all – but Dirty Dick and Maggie would, because they knew all about the robbery. And now Maggie will certainly try to find out where the stuff is.'

'Well, we must find it first!' said George, her eyes gleaming with excitement. 'We're here first, anyway. And tomorrow, as early as possible we'll begin to snoop round. What was the next clue in the message, Dick? After Two-Trees and Gloomy Water.'

'Saucy Jane,' said Dick.

'Sounds a silly sort of clue,' said Anne. 'Do you suppose Maggie and Jane are *both* in the secret?'

'Saucy Jane sounds more like a boat to me,' said Dick.

'Of *course*!' said George. 'A boat! Why not? There's a lake here, and I imagine that people don't build a house

104

beside a lake unless they want to go boating and bathing and fishing. I bet we shall find a boat called Saucy Jane tomorrow – and the stolen goods will be inside it.'

'Too easy!' said Dick. 'And not a very clever place either. Anyone could come across goods hidden in a boat. No – Saucy Jane is a clue, but we shan't find the stolen goods in her. And remember, there's that bit of paper as well. It must have something to do with the hiding-place too, I should think.'

'Where is it?' asked Julian. 'That wretched policeman! He tore it up. Have you still got the pieces, Dick?'

'Of course,' said Dick. He fished in his pocket and brought them out. 'Four little pieces! Anyone got some gummed paper?'

Nobody had – but George produced a small roll of plaster. Strips were cut and stuck behind the four portions of paper. Now it was whole again. They all examined it carefully.

'Look – four lines drawn, meeting in the centre,' said Julian. 'At the outer end of each line there's a word, so faintly written I can hardly read one of them. What's this one? "Tock Hill." And this next one is "Steeple". Whatever are the others?'

They made them out at last. ' "Chimney",' said Anne. 'That's the third.'

'And "Tall Stone" is the fourth,' said George. 'Whatever do they all mean? We shall never, never find out!'

'We'll sleep on it,' said Julian, cheerfully. 'It's wonderful what good ideas come in the night. It will be a very interesting little problem to solve tomorrow!'

CHAPTER THIRTEEN

A night in the cellar

THE PIECE of paper was carefully folded and this time Julian took it for safe keeping. 'I can't imagine what it means, but it's clearly important,' he said. 'We may quite suddenly come on something – or think of something – that will give us a clue to what the words and the lines mean on the paper.'

'We mustn't forget that dear Maggie has a copy of the paper too,' said Dick. 'She probably knows better than we do what it all means!'

'If she does, she will pay a visit to Two-Trees too,' said Anne. 'We ought to keep a look-out for her. Should we have to hide if we saw her?'

Julian considered this. 'No,' he said, 'I certainly don't think we should hide. Maggie can't *possibly* guess that we have had the message from Nailer, and the paper too. We had better just say we are on a hike and found this place and thought we would shelter here. All perfectly true.'

'And we can keep an eye on her, and see what she does if she comes!' said Dick, with a grin. 'Won't she be annoyed!'

'She wouldn't come alone,' said Julian, thoughtfully. 'I should think it quite likely that she would come with Dirty Dick! He didn't get the message, but she did – and probably part of her message was the statement that Dirty Dick would know everything too. So she would get in touch with him.'

'Yes – and be surprised that he hadn't got the message or the paper,' said George. 'Still, they'd think that the escaped fellow hadn't been able to get to Dirty Dick.'

'All very complicated,' said Anne, yawning. 'I can't follow any more arguments and explanations – I'm half asleep. How long are you going to be before you settle down?'

Dick yawned too. 'I'm coming now,' he said. 'My bed of bracken and heather looks inviting. It's not at all cold in here, is it?'

'The only thing I don't like is the thought of those cellars beyond this little underground room,' said Anne. 'I keep thinking that Maggie and her friends might be there, waiting to pounce on us when we are asleep.'

'You're silly,' said George, scornfully. '*Really* silly! Do you honestly suppose that Timmy would lie here quietly if there was anyone in those cellars? You know jolly well he would be barking his head off!'

'Yes. I know all that,' said Anne, snuggling down in her heathery bed. 'It's just my imagination. You haven't got any, George, so you don't bother about imaginary fears. I'm not *really* scared while Timmy is here. But I do think it's funny the way we always plunge into something peculiar when we're together.'

'Adventures always do come to some people,' said Dick.

A NIGHT IN THE CELLAR

'You've only got to read the lives of explorers and see how they simply *walk* into adventures all the time.'

'Yes, but I'm not an explorer,' said Anne. 'I'm an ordinary person, and I'd be just as pleased if things *didn't* keep happening to me.'

The others laughed. 'I don't expect anything much will happen this time,' said Julian, comfortingly. 'We go back to school on Tuesday and that's not far off. Not much time for anything to happen!'

He was wrong of course. Things can happen one after the other in a few minutes! Still, Anne cuddled down feeling happier. This was better than last night when she was all alone in that horrid little loft. Now she had all the others with her, Timmy too.

Anne and George had one big bed between them. They drew their two rugs over themselves, and put their blazers on top too. Nobody had undressed because Julian had said that they might be too cold in just their night things.

Timmy as usual put himself on George's feet. She moved them because he was heavy. He wormed his way up the bed and found a very comfortable place between the knees of the two girls. He gave a heavy sigh.

'That means he's planning to go to sleep!' said George. 'Are you quite comfortable, Anne?'

'Yes,' said Anne, sleepily. 'I like Timmy there. I feel safe!'

Julian was blowing out the candles. He left just one

burning. Then he got into his bed of bracken and heather beside Dick. He felt tired too.

The four slept like logs. Nobody moved except Timmy, who got up once or twice in the night and sniffed round inquiringly. He had heard a noise in the cellars. He stood at the closed door that led to the cellars and listened, his head on one side.

He sniffed at the crack. Then he went back to bed, satisfied. It was only a toad! Timmy knew the smell of toads. If toads liked to crawl about in the night, they were welcome to!

The second time he awoke he thought he heard something up in the kitchen above. He padded up the steps, his paws making a click-click-click as he went. He stood in the kitchen silently, his eyes gleaming like green lamps, as the moon shone on him.

An animal with a long bushy tail began to slink away outside the house. It was a fine fox. It had smelt unusual smells near the old ruin – the scent of people and of a dog, and it had come to find out what was happening.

It had slunk into the kitchen and then smelt the strong scent of Timmy in the room below. As quietly as a cat it had slunk out again – but Timmy had awakened!

Now the dog stood watching and waiting – but the fox had gone! Timmy sniffed its scent and padded to the door. He debated whether to bark and go after the fox.

The scent grew very faint, and Timmy decided not to make a fuss. He padded back to the steps that led down to the cellar room, and curled up on George's feet again. He was very heavy, but George was too tired to wake up and push him off. Timmy lay with one ear cocked for a while, and then went to sleep again, with his ear still cocked. He was a good sentinel!

It was dark in the cellar when the one candle went out. There was no daylight or sunshine to wake the children down in that dim little room, and they slept late.

Julian woke up first. He found his bed suddenly very hard, and he turned over to find a comfortable place. The heather and bracken had been flattened with his weight, and the floor below was very hard indeed! The movement woke him up, and he lay blinking in the darkness. Where was he?

He remembered at once and sat up. Dick woke too and yawned. 'Dick! It's half past eight!!' said Julian, looking at the luminous hands of his wrist-watch. 'We've slept for hours and hours!'

They rolled out of their heathery bed. Timmy leapt off George's feet and came over to them, his tail wagging gladly. He had been half-awake for a long time and was very glad to see Julian and Dick awake too, because he was thirsty.

The girls awoke – and soon there was a great deal of noise and activity going on. Anne and George washed at the big stone sink, the cold water making them squeal. Timmy lapped up a big bowlful of water gladly. The boys debated whether or not to have a splash in the lake. They felt very dirty.

Dick shivered at the thought. 'Still, I think we ought to,' he said. 'Come on, Ju!'

The two boys went down to the lake-side and leapt in. It was icy-cold! They swam out out strongly and came back glowing and shouting.

By the time they were back the girls had got breakfast in the cellar room. It was darker than the kitchen, but all of them disliked the look of the burnt, scorched rooms above. The bread and butter, potted meat, cake and chocolate went down well.

A NIGHT IN THE CELLAR

In the middle of the meal a sound came echoing into the old house – bells! Anne stopped eating, and her heart beat fast.

But they were not the clanging warning bells she had heard before!

'Church bells,' said Julian at once, seeing Anne's sudden look of fright. 'Lovely sound I always think!'

'Oh *yes*,' said Anne, thankfully. 'So it is. It's Sunday and people are going to church. I'd like to go too, on this lovely sunny October day.'

'We might walk across the moor to the nearest village if you like,' said Dick, looking at his watch. 'But we should be very late.'

It was decided that it was much too late. They pushed their plates aside and planned what to do that day.

'The first thing, of course, is to see if there's a boat-house and find out if there's a boat called *Saucy Jane*,' said Julian. 'Then we'd better try and puzzle out what that plan means. We could wander here and there and see if we can find Tall Stone – and I'll look at the map to see if Tock Hill is marked. That was on the plan too, wasn't it?'

'You boys go and get some more heather and bracken while we clear away and wash up,' said Anne. 'That is if you mean us to camp here another night.'

'Yes. I think we will,' said Julian. 'I think we may find things rather interesting here this weekend!'

Julian went out with Dick and they brought in a great deal more bedding. Everyone had complained that the hard

113

floor came through the amount of heather and bracken they had used the night before, and poor George was quite stiff.

The girls took the dirty things up to the big sink to wash them. There was nothing to dry them with but that didn't matter. They laid them on the old worn draining board to dry.

They wiped their hands on their hankies and then felt ready for exploring round outside. The boys were ready too.

With Timmy bounding here and there they went down to the lake. A path had once led down to it, with a low wall on each side. But now the wall was broken, moss had crept everywhere, and the path was choked with tufts of heather and even with small bushes of gorse.

The lake was as still and dark as ever. Some moorhens chugged across it quickly, disappearing under the water when they saw the children.

'Now, what about the boat-house?' said Dick at last. 'Is there one – or not?'

CHAPTER FOURTEEN

Where is the Saucy Jane?

THEY WALKED beside the lake as best they could. It was difficult because bushes and trees grew right down to the edge. It seemed as if there was no boat-house at all.

And then George came to a little backwater, leading off the lake. 'Look!' she called. 'Here's a sort of river running from the lake.'

'It's not a river. It's only a little backwater,' said Dick. 'Now we *may* find a boat-house somewhere here.'

They followed the backwater a little way, and then Julian gave an exclamation. 'There it is! But it's so covered up with ivy and brambles that you can hardly see it!'

They all looked where he pointed. They saw a long low building built right across the backwater, where it narrowed and came to an end. It was almost impossible to tell that it was a building, it was so overgrown.

'That's it!' said Dick, pleased. 'Now for the *Saucy Jane*!'

They scrambled through bushes and brambles to get to the entrance of the building. It had to be entered by the front, which was over the water and completely open. A broad ledge ran right round the boat-house inside, and the steps that went up to it from the bank outside were all broken away, completely rotted.

'Have to tread warily here,' said Julian. 'Let me go first.'

He tried the old wooden steps, but they gave way beneath him at once. 'Hopeless!' he said. 'Let's see if there's any other way into the boathouse.'

There wasn't – but at one side some of the wooden boards that made the wall of the boat-house were so rotten that they could be pulled away to make an opening. The boys pulled them down and then Julian squeezed through the opening into the dark, musty boat-house.

He found himself on the broad ledge that went round the great shed. Below him was the dark, quiet water with not even a ripple on it. He called to the others.

'Come along in! There's a wooden ledge to stand on here, and it's hardly rotted at all. It must be made of better wood.'

They all went through the opening and stood on the ledge, peering down. Their eyes had to get used to the darkness at first, because the only light came through the big entrance at the farther end – and that was obscured by big trails of ivy and other creepers hanging down from roof to water.

'There *are* boats here!' said Dick, excited. 'Tied up to posts. Look – there's one just below us. Let's hope one of them is the *Saucy Jane*!'

There were three boats. Two of them were half full of

116

water, and their bows were sunk right down. 'Must have got holes in them,' said Julian, peering about. He had got out his torch and was shining it all round the old boat-house.

Oars were strung along the walls. Dirty, pulpy masses of something lay on the shelves too – rotted cushions probably. A boat-hook stood in one corner. Ropes were in coils on a shelf. It was a dreary desolate sight, and Anne didn't like the strange echoes of their voices in the damp-smelling, lonely boat-house.

'Let's see if any of the boats are called *Saucy Jane*,' said Dick. He flashed his torch on to the nearest one. The name was almost gone.

'What is it?' said Dick, trying to decipher the faded letters. '*Merry* something.'

'*Meg*!' said Anne. '*Merry Meg*. Well, she may be a sister of *Saucy Jane*. What's the next boat's name?'

The torch shone steadily on to it. The name there was easier to read. They all read it at once.

'*Cheeky Charlie*!'

'Brother to *Merry Meg*!' said Dick. 'Well, all I can say is that these poor old boats look anything but merry or cheeky.'

'I'm sure the last one must be *Saucy Jane*!' said Anne, excited. 'I do hope it is!'

They went along the broad ledge and tried to read the name on the half-sunk boat there. 'It begins with C,' said George, disappointed. 'I'm sure it's C.'

WHERE IS THE SAUCY JANE?

Julian took out his handkerchief and dipped it in the water. He rubbed at the name to try and clean it and make it clearer.

It could be read then – but it wasn't *Saucy Jane*!

'*Careful Carrie!*' read the four, mournfully. 'Blow!'

'*Merry Meg, Cheeky Charlie, Careful Carrie,*' said Julian. 'Well, it's quite obvious that *Saucy Jane* belongs to the family of boats here – but where oh where is she?'

'Sunk out of sight?' suggested Dick.

'Don't think so,' said Julian. 'The water is pretty shallow in this boat-house – it's right at the very end of the little backwater, you see. I think we should be able to spot a boat sunk to the bottom. We can see the sandy bottom of the backwater quite clearly by the light of our torches.'

Just to make quite sure they walked carefully all round the broad wooden ledge and flashed their torches on the water that filled the boat-house. There was no completely sunken boat there at all.

'Well, that's that,' said Dick. 'The *Saucy Jane* is gone. Where? Why? And when?'

They flashed their torches round the walls of the boat-house once more. George's eye was caught by a large flat wooden thing standing upright on the ledge at one side of the house.

'What's that?' she said. 'Oh – a raft, isn't it? That's what those paddles are for, then, that I saw on the shelf above.'

They went and examined the raft. 'Yes – and in quite

good condition too,' said Julian. 'It would be rather fun to see if it would carry us on the water.'

'Ooooh *yes*!' said Anne, thrilled. 'That would be super. I always like rafts. I'd rather try that raft than any of those boats.'

'Well, there's only one boat that is possible to use,' said Julian. 'The others are obviously no good – they must have big holes in them to sink down like that.'

'Hadn't we better look into them carefully just to make sure there's no loot hidden there?' said Dick.

'If you like,' said Julian. 'But *I* think it's *Saucy Jane* that's got the loot – otherwise why mention it by name in that message?'

Dick felt that Julian was right. All the same he went to examine the three boats most methodically. But except for rotted and burst cushions and coils of rope there was nothing to be seen in the boats at all.

'Well – where's the *Saucy Jane*?' said Dick, puzzled. 'All the family are here but her. Can she be hidden anywhere on the banks of the lake?'

'*That's* an idea!' said Julian, who was trying to shift the big raft. 'That's a really good idea! I think we ought to explore all round the lake and see if we can find the *Saucy Jane* hidden anywhere.'

'Let's leave the raft for a bit then,' said George, feeling thrilled at the thought of possibly finding the *Saucy Jane* tucked away somewhere, all the loot hidden in her. 'Let's go now!'

WHERE IS THE SAUCY JANE?

They made their way round the wooden ledge to the opening they had made in the side of the boat-house, and jumped down. Timmy leapt down gladly. He hadn't liked the dark boat-house at all. He ran into the warm sunshine, wagging his tail.

'Now which side of the lake shall we go to first?' said Anne. 'The left or the right?'

They went down to the edge of the silent water and looked to left and right. They both seemed to be equally thick with bushes!

'It's going to be difficult to keep close to the edge of the water,' said Julian. 'Anyway, we'll try. The left side looks a bit easier. Come on!'

It was fairly easy at first to keep close to the water, and examine any tiny creek or look under overhanging bushes. But after about a quarter of a mile the undergrowth became so very thick and grew so close to the water's edge that it was quite impossible to force their way through it without completely ruining their clothes.

'I give up!' said Julian at last. 'I shall have no jersey left in a minute! These spiteful brambles! My hands are ripped to bits.'

'Yes – they *are* spiteful!' said Anne. 'I felt that too!'

Timmy was the only one really enjoying himself. He couldn't *imagine* why the four were scrambling through such thick undergrowth, but as it was just what he liked he was very pleased. He was disappointed when they decided to give up and go back.

'Shall we try the right hand side of the lake, do you think?' said Julian, as they went back, rather disheartened.

'No. Don't let's,' said Anne. 'It looks even worse than this side. It's only a waste of time. I'd rather go out on the raft!'

'Well – that would surely be a better way of exploring the banks of the lake than scrambling through prickly bushes, wouldn't it?' said George. 'We'd only need to paddle along slowly and squint into all the little creeks and under overhanging trees – it would be easy!'

'Of course,' said Dick. 'We were silly not to think of it

before. It would be a lovely way of spending the afternoon, anyway.'

They came through the trees and saw the ruined house in the distance. Timmy suddenly stopped. He gave a low growl, and all the others stopped too.

'What's up, Timmy?' said George in a low voice. 'What is it?'

Timmy growled again. The others cautiously retreated behind bushes and looked intently towards the house. They could see nothing out of the way. Nobody seemed to be about. Then what was Timmy growling at?

And then a woman came in sight, and with her was a man. They were talking earnestly together.

'Maggie! I bet it's Maggie!' said Julian.

'And the other is Dirty Dick,' said Dick. 'I recognise him – yes – it's Dirty Dick.'

CHAPTER FIFTEEN

Maggie – and Dirty Dick

THEY WATCHED the couple in the distance, and thought quickly. Julian had been expecting them, so he was not surprised. Dick was looking at Dirty Dick, recognising the broad, short man, with his hunched-up shoulders and shock of hair. He didn't like the look of him any more than when he had seen him up at the old cottage!

Anne and George didn't like the look of the woman either! She was wearing trousers and had a jacket draped round her shoulders. She was also wearing sun-glasses, and smoking a cigarette. She walked quickly and they could hear her voice. It was sharp and determined.

'So that's Maggie,' thought Julian. 'Well, I don't like her. She looks as hard as nails – a good companion for Nailer!'

He moved cautiously towards the other three. George had her hand on Timmy's collar, afraid that he might show himself.

'Listen,' said Julian. 'You're none of you to turn a hair! We'll just walk out into the open, talking cheerfully together and let them see us. If they ask us what we're doing, you all know what to say. Chatter nonsense as

124

much as you like – put them off and make them think we're a bunch of harmless kids. If there are any leading questions asked us – leave *me* to answer them. Ready?'

They nodded. Then Julian swung out from the bushes and walked into the open, calling to Dick. 'Here we are again – there's the old house! My word, it looks worse than ever this morning!'

George and Timmy came bounding out together, and Anne followed, her heart beating fast. She wasn't as good as the others at this sort of thing!

The man and the woman stopped abruptly when they saw the children. They said a few words to one another very rapidly. The man scowled.

The children went towards them, chattering all the time as Julian had ordered. The woman called sharply to them.

'Who are you?' What are you doing here?'

'Just hiking,' said Julian, stopping. 'It's our half-term.'

'What do you want to come *here* for then?' asked the woman. 'This is private property.'

'Oh no,' said Julian. 'It's only a burnt-out ruin. Anyone can come. We want to explore this strange lake – it looks exciting.'

The man and the woman looked at one another. It was clear that the idea of the children exploring the lake was surprising and annoying to them. The woman spoke again.

'You can't explore this lake. It's dangerous. People are forbidden to bathe in it or use a boat.'

'We weren't told that,' said Julian, looking astonished. 'We were told how to get here, and no one said the lake was forbidden. You've been told wrongly.'

'We want to watch the moorhens, you see,' put in Anne, suddenly seeing a moorhen on the water. 'We're fond of nature.'

'And we've been told there are deer near here,' said George.

'And wild ponies,' said Dick. 'We saw some yesterday. They were really lovely. Have you seen any?'

This sudden burst of chatter seemed to annoy the man and the woman more than Julian's answers. The man spoke roughly.

'Stop this nonsense. People aren't allowed here. Clear out before we make you!'

'Why are *you* here, then, if people aren't allowed?' asked Julian, and a hard tone came into his voice. 'Don't talk to us like that.'

'You clear off, I say!' cried the man, suddenly shouting loudly as he lost his temper. He took two or three steps towards them, looking very threatening indeed. George loosed her hold on Timmy's collar.

Timmy also took two or three steps forward. His hackles went up and he emitted a most fearsome growl. The man stopped suddenly, and then retreated.

'Take hold of that dog's collar,' he ordered. 'He looks savage.'

'Then he looks what he is,' said George. 'I'm not taking

127

hold of his collar while you're about. Don't think it!'

Timmy took two or three more steps forward, growling loudly, walking stiffly and menacingly. The woman called out at once.

'It's all right, children. My friend here just lost his temper for a moment. Call your dog back.'

'Not while you are about,' said George. 'How long are you staying?'

'What's that to do with you?' growled the man, but he didn't say any more because Timmy at once growled back.

'Let's go and have something to eat,' said Julian, loudly, to the others. 'After all, we have as much right to be here as these people have. We don't need to take any notice of them – and we shan't be in *their* way!'

The four children marched forward. Timmy was still loose. He barked savagely once or twice as he came close to the unpleasant couple, and they shrank back at once. Timmy was such a big dog and he looked so very powerful! They eyed the children angrily as they went by, and watched them go into the ruined house.

'On guard, Timmy,' said George, as soon as they were in, pointing to the ruined doorway. Timmy understood at once, and stood in the doorway, a menacing figure with hackles up and snarling mouth. The children went down to the cellar room. They looked round to see if anyone had been there while they were away, but nothing seemed to have been moved.

'They probably haven't even noticed the cellars,' said Julian. 'I hope there's plenty of bread left. I'm hungry. I wish to goodness we were going to have a dinner like the one we had yesterday! I say – what an unpleasant pair Maggie and Dick are!'

'Yes. Very,' said Dick. 'I can't bear Maggie. Horrid mean voice and hard face. Ugh!'

'I think Dirty Dick is worse,' said Anne. 'He looks like a gorilla or something with his broad hunched-up body. And WHY doesn't he cut his hair?'

'Fancies himself like that, I expect,' said George, cutting a loaf of bread. 'His surname ought to be Hairy. Or Tarzan. I'm jolly glad we've got Timmy.'

'So am I,' said Anne. 'Good old Timmy. He hated them, didn't he? I bet they won't come near the doorway with Timmy there!'

'I wonder where they are,' said Dick picking up a great hunk of bread and butter and potted meat. 'I'm going to look.'

He came back in half a minute. 'They've gone to the boat-house, I think,' he said. 'I just caught a sight of one of them moving in that direction. Looking for *Saucy Jane*, I expect.'

'Let's sit down and eat and talk over what we'll do next,' said Julian. 'And what we think *they* will do next! That's quite important. They may be able to read the clues on that paper better than we can. If we watch what they do it may give us a guide as to what *we* must do.'

'That's true,' said Dick. 'I imagine that the plan Nailer sent must mean something to Dirty Dick and Maggie, just as the message did.' He chewed at his bread, thinking hard, trying once more to fathom the meaning of that mysterious piece of paper.

'I think on the whole we will follow out our original plan for this afternoon,' said Julian, after a little silence. 'We'll get out that raft and go on the lake with it. It's a harmless-looking thing to do. We can examine the banks as we go – and if Maggie and Dick are out in a boat too, we can keep an eye on them as well.'

'Yes. Good idea,' said George. 'It's a heavenly afternoon anyway. I'd love to paddle about on the lake with that raft. I hope it's good and sound.'

'Sure to be,' said Dick. 'The wood it's made of is meant to last. Pass the cake, George – and *don't* save Timmy any. It's wasted on him.'

'It isn't!' said George. 'You know he loves it.'

'Yes. But I still say it's wasted on him,' said Dick. 'Good thing we got such an enormous cake! Are there any biscuits left?'

'Plenty,' said Anne. 'And chocolate too!'

'Good,' said Dick. 'I only hope our food will last us out. It won't if George has her usual colossal appetite.'

'What about yours?' said George, indignantly, rising every time to Dick's lazy teasing.

'Shut up, you two,' said Julian. 'I'm going to fill the

130

water jug and have some orangeade. Give me something to take to old Tim.'

They spent about half an hour over their lunch. Then they decided to go and tackle the raft in the boathouse, and see if they could possibly launch it on the lake. It would be heavy, they knew.

They left the old house and went off to the boat-house. Julian suddenly caught sight of something out on the lake.

'Look!' he said, 'they've got one of the boats out of the boat-house – the one that wasn't half-sunk, I suppose! Dirty Dick is rowing hard. I BET they're looking for the *Saucy Jane*!'

They all stood still and watched. Dick's heart sank. Would Maggie and Dirty Dick get there first, and find what he and the other three were looking for? Did they know where the *Saucy Jane* was?

'Come on,' said Julian. 'We'd better get going if we want to keep an eye on them. They may be rowing to where the *Saucy Jane* is hidden!'

They climbed in through the wooden side of the boat-house and went to the raft. Julian saw at once that one of the boats had gone – *Merry Meg*. It was the only boat that was fit to take.

The four began to manhandle the big raft. They took it to the edge of the ledge. It had rope-handles on each side which the children held on to.

'Now – ease her gently,' said Julian. 'Gently does it. Down she goes!'

131

And down she went, landing with a big splash in the water. She bobbed there gently, a strong, sound raft, eager to go out on the lake!

'Get the paddles,' said Julian. 'Then we'll be off.'

CHAPTER SIXTEEN

Out on the raft

THERE WERE four little paddles. Dick got them, and gave everyone one each. Timmy looked down solemnly at the raft. What was it? Surely he was not expected to ride on that bobbing, floating thing?

Julian was on the raft already, holding it steady for the others. He helped Anne on and then George stepped down. Dick came last – well, not quite last, because Timmy was not yet on.

'Come on, Tim!' said George. 'It's all right! It's not the kind of boat you're used to, but it acts in the same way. Come *on*, Timmy!'

Timmy jumped down and the raft bobbed violently. Anne sat down suddenly with a giggle. 'Oh dear – Timmy is so *sudden*! Keep still, Tim – there isn't enough room on this raft for you to walk all over it.'

Julian pushed the raft out of the boat-house. It knocked against the wooden ledge as it went, and then swung out on to the backwater outside. It floated very smoothly.

'Here we go!' said Julian, paddling deftly. 'I'll steer, Dick. None of you need to paddle till I say so. I can paddle and steer at the moment, till we get on to the lake itself.'

They were all sitting on the raft except Timmy, who was standing up. He was very interested in seeing the water flow past so quickly. *Was* this a boat then? He was used to boats – but in boats the water was never quite so near. Timmy put out a paw into the water. It was pleasantly cool and tickled him. He lay down with his nose almost in the water.

'You're a funny dog, Timmy!' said Anne. 'You won't get up too suddenly, will you, or you'll knock me overboard.'

Julian paddled down the little backwater and the raft swung out on to the lake itself. The children looked to see if there was any sign of Maggie and Dirty Dick.

'There they are!' said Julian. 'Out in the middle, rowing hard. Shall we follow them? If they know where the *Saucy Jane* is they'll lead us to it.'

'Yes. Follow them,' said Dick. 'Shall *we* paddle now? We'll have to be quick or we may lose them.'

They all paddled hard, and the raft suddenly swung to and fro in a most alarming manner.

'Hey, stop!' shouted Julian. 'You're all paddling against one another. We're going round in circles. Dick and Anne go one side and George the other. That's better. Watch how we're going, all of you, and stop paddling for a moment if the raft swings round too much.'

They soon got into the way of paddling so that the raft went straight ahead. It was fun. They got very hot and wished they could take off their jerseys. The sun was quite warm, and there was no wind at all – it was really a perfect October afternoon.

'They've stopped rowing,' said George, suddenly. 'They're looking at something – do you suppose they have got a bit of paper like the one we have, with the same marks, and are examining it? I *wish* I could see!'

They all stopped paddling and looked towards the boat in which Maggie and Dirty Dick sat. They were certainly examining something very carefully – their heads were close together. But they were too far away for the children to see if they were holding a piece of paper.

'Come on – we'll get as close to them as we can!' said Julian, beginning to paddle again. 'I expect it will make them absolutely mad to see us so close, but we can't help that!'

They paddled hard again, and at last came up to the boat. Timmy barked. Maggie and Dirty Dick at once looked round and saw the raft and the four children. They stared at them savagely.

'Hallo!' cried Dick, waving a paddle. 'We took the raft out. It goes well. Does your boat go all right?'

Maggie went red with rage. 'You'll get into trouble for taking that raft without permission,' she shouted.

'Whose permission did *you* ask when you took that boat?' shouted back Julian. 'Tell us and we'll ask their permission to use this raft!'

George laughed. Maggie scowled, and Dirty Dick looked as if he would like to throw his oars at them.

'Keep away from us!' he shouted. 'We don't want you kids spoiling our afternoon!'

'We like to be friendly!' called Dick, and made George laugh again.

Maggie and Dirty Dick had a hurried and angry conversation. They glared at the raft and then Maggie gave an order to Dirty Dick. He took up the oars again, and began to row, looking rather mutinous.

'Come on – follow,' said Julian, so the four began to paddle again following after the boat. 'Maybe we'll learn something now.'

But they didn't. Dirty Dick rowed the boat towards the west bank, and the raft followed. Then he swung out into the middle again, and again the raft followed, the children panting in their efforts to keep up.

Dirty Dick rowed right across to the east bank and stayed there till the children came up. Then he rowed off again.

'Having some nice exercise, aren't you?' called the woman in her harsh voice. 'So good for you all!'

The boat swung out to the middle of the lake again. Dick groaned. 'Blow! My arms are so tired I can hardly paddle. What are they doing?'

'I'm afraid they're just leading us on a wild goose chase,' said Julian, ruefully. 'They have evidently made up their minds that they won't look for the *Saucy Jane* while we're about – they're just tiring us out!'

'Well, if *that's* what they're doing I'm not playing!'

said Dick, and he put down his paddle and lay flat on his back, his knees drawn up, panting hard.

The others did the same. They were all tired. Timmy licked each one sympathetically and then sat down on George. She pushed him off so violently that he nearly fell into the water.

'Timmy! Right on my middle!' cried George, surprised and indignant. 'You great clumsy dog, you!'

Timmy licked her all over, shocked at being scolded by George. She was too exhausted to push him away.

'What's happened to the boat?' asked Anne at last. 'I'm too tired to sit up and see.'

Julian sat up, groaning. 'Oh, my back! Now where is that wretched boat? Oh, there it is – right away down the lake, making for the landing-place by the house – or for the boat-house probably. They've given up the search for the *Saucy Jane* for the time being anyway.'

'Thank goodness,' said Anne. 'Perhaps we can give it up too – till tomorrow anyhow! Stop snuffling down my neck, Timmy. What do you want us to do, Julian?'

'I think we'd better get back,' said Julian. 'It's too late now to start searching the banks of the lake – and anyway somehow I think it wouldn't be much use. The two in the boat didn't appear to be going anywhere near the banks – except when they began to play that trick on us to make us tired out!'

'Well, let's get back then,' said George. 'But I simply

138

must have a rest first. Timmy, I shall push you into the water if you keep sitting on my legs.'

There was a sudden splash. George sat up in alarm. Timmy was not on the raft!

He was swimming in the water, looking very pleased with himself.

'There! He thought he'd rather jump in than be pushed,' said Dick, grinning at George.

'*You* pushed him in!' said George, looking fierce.

'I didn't,' said Dick. 'He just took a header. He's having a jolly good time. I say – what about putting a rope round him and getting him to pull us to shore? It would save an awful lot of paddling.'

George was just about to say what she thought of *that* idea, when she caught Dick's sly grin. She kicked out at him.

'Don't keep baiting me, Dick. I'll push *you* in, in a minute.'

'Like to try?' asked Dick, at once. 'Come on. I'd like a wrestle to see who'd go into the water first.'

George, of course, always rose to a challenge. She never could resist one. She was up in a moment and fell on Dick, who very nearly went overboard at once.

'Shut up, you two!' said Julian, crossly. 'We haven't got a change of clothing, you know that. And I don't want to take you back with bronchitis or pneumonia. Stop it, George.'

George recognised the tone in his voice and she stopped. She ran her hand through her short curls and gave a sudden grin.

'All right, Teacher!' she said, and sat down meekly. She picked up her paddle.

Julian picked up his. 'We'll get back,' he said. 'The sun's sinking low. It seems to slide down the sky at a most remarkable speed in October.'

They took a very wet Timmy on board and began to

paddle back. Anne thought it was a truly lovely evening. She gazed dreamily round as she paddled. The lake was a wonderful dark blue, and the ripples they made turned to silver as they ran away from the raft. Two moorhens said 'crek-crek' and swam round the raft in curiosity, their heads bobbing like clockwork.

Anne gazed over the tops of the trees that grew at the lake-side. The sky was turning pink. Away in the distance, on a high slope about a mile away she saw something that interested her.

It looked like a high stone. She pointed at it. 'Look, Julian,' she said. 'What's that stone? Is it a boundary mark, or something? It must be very big.'

Julian looked where she was pointing. 'Where?' he said. 'Oh, that. I can't imagine what it is.'

'It looks like a very tall stone,' said Dick, suddenly catching sight of it too.

'A tall stone,' repeated Anne, wondering where she had heard that before. 'A tall . . . oh, of *course*! It was printed on that plan, wasn't it – on the piece of paper Dick was given. Tall Stone! Don't you remember?'

'Yes. So it was,' said Dick and he stared at the far-away stone monument with interest. Then as the raft swung onwards, high trees hid the stone. It was gone.

'Tall Stone,' said Julian. 'It may be only a coincidence, of course. It wants a bit of thinking about, though. Funny we should suddenly spot it.'

'Would the loot be buried there?' asked George,

doubtfully. Julian shook his head. 'Oh, no,' he said, 'it is probably hidden in some position explained by that mysterious map. Paddle up, everyone! We really must get back.'

CHAPTER SEVENTEEN

Tit for tat!

WHEN THEY arrived at the boat-house there was no sign of
Maggie or Dick. But their boat was in the shed, tied up in
front of the other two, where it had been before.

'They're back all right,' said Julian. 'I wonder where
they are. Don't let's drag this clumsy, heavy raft into the
boat-house. I don't feel as if I've any strength left in my
arms. Let's drag it under a bush and tie it there.'

They thought this a good idea. They pulled the raft up
to some thick bushes and tied it firmly to a root that was
sticking out of the ground.

Then they made their way to the ruined house, keeping
a sharp look-out for Maggie and Dick. There was still no
sign of them.

They went in, Timmy first. He didn't growl so they
knew it was safe. He led the way to the cellar steps. Then
he growled!

'What's up?' said Julian. 'Are they down there, Tim?'

Timmy ran straight down the steps into the cellar room.
He growled again, but it was not the fierce growl he always
gave when he wanted to warn that enemies or strangers
were near. It was an angry, annoyed growl as if something
was wrong.

'I expect dear Maggie and Dirty Dick have been down here and found out where our headquarters are!' said Julian, following Timmy down the steps. He switched on his torch.

The beds of heather and bracken were there as they had left them, and their macs and rugs and rucksacks. Nothing seemed to have been disturbed. Julian lit the candles on the mantelpiece and the dark little underground room came to life at once.

'What's the matter with Timmy?' asked George, coming down into the room. 'He's still growling. Timmy, what's up?'

'I expect he can smell that the others have been down here,' said Dick. 'Look at him sniffing all round. It's quite clear that *someone* has been here.'

'Anyone hungry?' asked Anne. 'I could do with some cake and biscuits.'

'Right,' said Julian, and opened the cupboard where they had put the food they had bought.

There was none there! Except for the crockery and one or two odds and ends that had been in the cupboard before, there was nothing. The bread had gone, the biscuits, the chocolate – everything!

'Blow!' said Julian, angrily. 'Look at that! The beasts! They've taken all our food – every bit. Not even a biscuit left. We were mad not to think they might do that!'

'Clever of them,' said Dick. 'They know we can't stay here long without food. It's a good way of chasing us out.

It's too late to go and get any tonight, anyway – and if we go tomorrow for some, they'll do what they have come to do in their own good time . . . when we're not here.'

Everyone felt distinctly down in the dumps. They were hungry and tired, and a good meal would have made all the difference. Anne sank down on her bed of heather and sighed.

'I wish I'd left some chocolate in my rucksack,' she said. 'But I didn't leave any there at all. And poor Tim – he's hungry too! Look at him sniffing in the cupboard and looking round at George. Tim, there's nothing for you. The cupboard is bare!'

'Where have those two wretches gone?' suddenly said Julian, fiercely. 'I'll tick them off! I'll tell them what I think of people who come and rifle cupboards and take away all the food.'

'Woof,' said Timmy, in full agreement.

Julian went angrily up the stairs. He wondered again where Maggie and Dirty Dick were. He went to the empty doorway and looked out. Then he saw where they were.

Two small tents had been put up under some thickly growing trees! So that's where the two were going to sleep. He debated whether or not to go and tell them what he thought of people who stole food. He decided that he would.

But when he got over to the tents with Timmy, there was no one there! Rugs were laid inside, and there was a primus stove and a kettle and other odds and ends. At the back of one tent was a pile of something, covered by a cloth.

Julian had a good look into each tent, and then went to see if he could find out where Maggie and Dirty Dick had gone. He saw them at last, walking through the trees. They must have gone for an evening stroll, he thought.

They didn't come back to the tents, but sat down by the lake. Julian gave up the thought of tackling them and went back to the others. Timmy was left behind, snuffling about happily.

'They've got tents,' Julian informed the others when he was back in the cellar room again. 'They're obviously

146

staying put till they've got what they came for. They aren't in the tents – they're out by the lake.'

'Where's Timmy?' asked George. 'You shouldn't have left him behind, Ju. They might do something to him.'

'Here he is!' said Julian, as a familiar noise of claws clattering on the floor came to their ears. Timmy came down the stone steps and ran to George.

'He's got something in his mouth!' said George, in surprise. Timmy dropped it into her lap. She gave a yell.

'It's a tin of shortbread! Where did he get it from?'

Julian began to laugh. 'He must have taken it from one of the tents!' he said. 'I saw something covered up with a cloth in one tent – their food, I imagine! Well, well – tit for tat – they took our food and now Timmy is taking theirs!'

'Fair exchange is no robbery,' grinned Dick. 'Serves them right! I say – Tim's gone again!'

He was back in a minute with something large and paper-covered. It was a big cake! The four roared with laughter. 'Timmy! You're a wonder! You really are!'

Timmy was pleased at this praise. Off he went again and brought back a cardboard box in which was a fine pork-pie. The children could hardly believe their eyes.

'It's a miracle!' said Anne. 'Just as I had made up my mind to starve for hours! A pork-pie of all things! Let's have some.'

'Well, I have no second thoughts about it,' said Julian,

firmly. 'They took our food and we deserve some of theirs. Good gracious – don't say Tim's gone again.'

He had! He was enjoying himself thoroughly. He arrived this time with a packet of ham, and the children couldn't *imagine* how he had stopped himself from eating some on the way.

'Fancy carrying it in his mouth and not even *tasting* a bit!' said Dick. 'Tim's a better person than I am. I'd just have to have had a lick.'

'I say – we ought to stop him now,' said Julian, as Timmy ran up the steps again, his tail wagging nineteen to the dozen. 'We're getting a bit too much in exchange!'

'Oh, do see what he brings back this time,' begged Anne. 'Then stop him.'

He came back carrying an old flour bag in which something had been packed. Timmy carried it cleverly by the neck so that nothing had fallen out. George undid the bag.

'Home-made scones – and buns,' she said. 'Timmy, you are very, very clever, and you shall have a wonderful supper. But you are not to go and take any more things, because we've got enough. See? No more. Lie down and be a good dog and eat your supper.'

Timmy was quite willing. He wolfed ham and scones and a slice of cake, and then he went up into the kitchen, jumped into the sink and lapped the water lying there. He then jumped down and went to the doorway to look out. He barked. Then he growled loudly.

TIT FOR TAT!

The children rushed up the stone steps at once. Outside, at a safe distance, was Dirty Dick.

'Have you been taking anything of ours?' he shouted.

'No more than you have been taking of ours!' shouted back Julian. 'Fair exchange, you know, and all that.'

'How dare you go into our tents?' raged the man, his shock of hair making him look very peculiar in the twilight.

'We didn't. The dog fetched and carried for us,' said Julian. 'And don't you come any nearer. He's just longing to fly at you! And I warn you, he'll be on guard tonight, so don't try any funny tricks. He's as strong and savage as a lion.'

'Grrrr,' said Timmy, so fiercely that the man started back in fright. He went off without another word, shaking with anger.

Julian and the others went back to finish a very delicious supper. Timmy went with them – but he planted himself at the top of the cellar steps.

'Not a bad place for him to be in tonight,' said Julian. 'I don't trust that couple an inch. We can give him one of our blazers to lie on. I say – this has boiled up into quite an adventure, hasn't it? It seems frightful to think we'll be back at school on Tuesday!'

'We *must* find the loot first!' said Anne. 'We really must. Let's get out that plan again, Ju. Let's make sure that Tall Stone is marked on it.'

TIT FOR TAT!

They got it out and put it on the table. They bent over it once more.

'Yes – Tall Stone is marked at the end of one of the lines,' said Julian. 'Tock Hill is at the end of the opposite line. Let's get the map and see if there *is* a Tock Hill.'

They got the map, and studied it. Anne suddenly put her finger down on it. 'There it is. On the opposite side of the lake from where we saw the Tall Stone. Tock Hill on one side. Tall Stone on the other. Surely that *means* something.'

'It does, of course,' said Julian. 'It is bearings given to show the whereabouts of the hidden goods. There are four bearings given – Tall Stone. Tock Hill. Chimney. And Steeple.'

'Listen!' said Dick, suddenly. 'LISTEN! *I* know how to read that map. It's easy.'

The others looked at him in surprise and doubt.

'Read it, then,' said Julian. 'Tell us what it all means. I don't believe you can!'

CHAPTER EIGHTEEN

A very exciting time

'LET'S TAKE all the clues we know,' said Dick, looking excited. 'Two-Trees. That's here. Gloomy Water. That's where the hidden stuff must be. *Saucy Jane*. It's a boat that contains the stuff, hidden somewhere on Gloomy Water.'

'Go on,' said Julian, as Dick paused to think.

'Maggie is the next clue – well she's here, probably an old friend of Nailer's,' said Dick. 'She knows all the clues too.'

He jabbed his finger at the piece of paper. 'Now for *these* clues. Listen! We saw Tall Stone when we were out on the lake, didn't we? Very well. There must be SOME spot on the lake where we can see not only Tall Stone, but also Tock Hill, Chimney and Steeple, whatever they are! There must be only one spot from which we can see all those four things at the same time – and *that's* the spot to hunt in for the treasure!'

There was an astonished silence after this. Julian drew a long breath and clapped Dick on the back.

'Of course! What idiots we were not to see it before. The *Saucy Jane* must be somewhere on – or in – the lake at the spot where all four clues are seen at the same time. We've only got to explore and find out!'

A VERY EXCITING TIME

'Yes – but don't forget that Maggie and Dirty Dick know what these clues mean too! They'll be there first if they possibly can!' said Dick. 'And what's more if they get the goods we can't do anything about it. We're not the police! They'll be off and away with their find and disappear completely.'

Everyone began to feel intensely excited. 'I think we'd better set off early tomorrow morning,' said Julian. 'As soon as it's light. Otherwise Maggie and Dick will get in first. I wish to goodness we had an alarm clock.'

'We'll go on the raft, and we'll paddle about till we see Tall Stone again – then we'll keep that in sight till we see Tock Hill, whatever that is,' said Dick. 'And once we've spotted that we'll keep both Tall Stone *and* Tock Hill in sight and paddle round to find out where we can see a steeple – and then a chimney. I should think that would be the one chimney left on Two-Trees house! Did you notice there is just one left, sticking up high?'

'Yes, I noticed,' said Anne. 'What a clever way to hide anything, Dick. Nobody could possibly know what the clues meant unless they knew something of the secret. This is *awfully* exciting!'

They talked about it for some time and then Julian said they really must try and go to sleep or they would never wake up early enough in the morning.

They settled down in their beds of heather and

bracken. Timmy lay on Julian's blazer on the top step of the stairs leading down to the cellar room. He seemed to think it was quite a good idea to sleep there that night.

They were all tired and they fell asleep very quickly. Nothing disturbed them in the night. The fox came again and looked into the old house, but Timmy didn't stir. He merely gave a small growl and the fox fled, his bushy tail spread behind him.

The morning came and daylight crept in at the burnt-out doorway and windows. Timmy stirred and went to the door. He looked towards the two tents. No one was about there. He went to the cellar steps and clattered down waking Dick and Julian at once.

'What's the time?' said Julian, remembering immediately that he was to wake early. 'Half past seven. Wake up, everyone! It's daylight. We've heaps to do!'

They washed hurriedly, combed out their hair, cleaned their teeth, and tried to brush-down their clothes. Anne got ready some snacks for them – ham, scones and a piece of shortbread each. They all had a drink of water and then they were ready to go.

There was no sign of anyone near the two tents. 'Good,' said Julian. 'We'll be there first!'

They dragged the raft out and got on to it, taking up the paddles. Then off they went, Timmy too, all feeling tremendously excited.

'We'll paddle out to where we think we were last night

when Anne caught sight of Tall Stone,' said Julian. So they paddled valiantly, though their arms were stiff with yesterday's paddling and it was really very painful to use the tired muscles all over again!

They paddled out to the middle of the lake and looked for Tall Stone. It didn't seem anywhere to be seen! They strained their eyes for it, but for a long time it was not to be spotted at all. Then Dick gave a cry. 'It's just come into sight. Look, when we passed those tall trees on the bank over there, Tall Stone came into view. It was behind them before that.'

'Good,' said Julian. 'Now I'm going to stop paddling and keep Tall Stone in sight. If it goes out of sight I'll tell you and you must back-paddle. Dick, can you possibly paddle and look out for something that could be Tock Hill on the opposite side? I daren't take my eyes off Tall Stone in case it disappears.'

'Right,' said Dick, and paddled while he looked earnestly for Tock Hill.

'Got it!' he said suddenly. 'It must be it! Look, over there – a funny little hill with a pointed top. Julian, can you still see Tall Stone?'

'Yes,' said Julian. 'Keep your eyes on Tock Hill. Now it's up to the girls. George, paddle away and see if you can spot Steeple.'

'I can see it now, already!' said George, and for one moment the boys took their eyes off Tall Stone and Tock Hill and looked where George pointed. They saw

155

the steeple of a faraway church glinting in the morning sun.

'Good, good, good,' said Julian. 'Now, Anne – look for Chimney – look down towards the end of the lake where the house is. Can you see its one chimney?'

'Not quite,' said Anne. 'Paddle just a bit to the left – the left, I said, George! Yes – yes, I can see the one chimney. Stop paddling everyone. We're here!'

They stopped paddling but the raft drifted on, and Anne lost the chimney again! They had to paddle back a bit until it came into sight. By that time George had lost her steeple!

At last all four things were in view at once, and the raft seemed to be still and unmoving on the quiet waters of the lake.

'I'm going to drop something to mark the place,' said Julian, still keeping his eyes desperately on Tall Stone. 'George, can you manage to watch Tall Stone and Steeple at the same time? I simply must look what I'm doing for the moment.'

'I'll try,' said George, and fixed her eyes first on Tall Stone, then on Steeple, then on Tall Stone again, hoping and praying that neither would slip out of sight if the raft moved on the water.

Julian was busy. He had taken his torch and his pocket-knife out of his pocket and had tied them together with string. 'I haven't enough string, Dick,' he said. 'You've got some, haven't you?'

Dick had, of course. He put his hand into his pocket, still keeping his eyes on Tock Hill and passed his string over to Julian.

Julian tied it to the end of the string that joined together the knife and torch. Then he dropped them into the water, letting out the string as they went down with their weight. The string slid through his hands. It stopped in a short while and Julian knew that the knife and torch had reached the bed of the lake.

He felt in his pockets again. He knew he had a cork somewhere that he had carved into a horse's head. He found it and tied the end of the string firmly round it. Then he dropped the cork thankfully into the water. It bobbed there, held by the string, which led right down to the knife and torch on the lake-bed below.

'It's done!' he said, with a sigh of relief. 'Take your eyes off everything! I've marked the place now, so we don't need to glue our eyes on the four bearings!'

He told them how he had tied together his knife and torch and dropped them on string to the bottom of the lake, and then had tied a cork to the other end, so that it would bob and show them the place.

They all looked at it. 'Jolly clever, Ju,' said Dick. 'But once we slide away from this spot, and it would be an easy thing to do, we'd find it jolly difficult to find that cork again! Hadn't we better tie something else to it?'

'I haven't got anything else that will float,' said Julian. 'Have you?'

'I have,' said George, and she handed him a little wooden box. 'I keep the five pence pieces I collect in that,' she said, putting the money into her pocket. 'You can have the box. It will be much easier to see than the cork.'

Julian tied the box to the cork. It was certainly a good deal easier to see! 'Fine!' he said. 'Now we're quite all right. We must be right over the loot!'

They all bent over the edge of the raft and looked down – and they saw a most surprising sight! Below them, resting on the bottom of the lake, was a boat! It lay there in the shadows of the water, its outline blurred by the ripples the raft made – but quite plainly it was a boat!

A VERY EXCITING TIME

'The *Saucy Jane*!' said Julian, peering down, feeling amazed and awed to think that they had read the bearings so correctly that they were actually over the *Saucy Jane* herself! 'The Nailer must have come here with the stolen goods – got out the *Saucy Jane* and rowed her to this spot. He must have taken his bearings very carefully indeed, and then holed the boat so that she sank down with the loot in her. Then I suppose he swam back to shore.'

'Most ingenious,' said Dick. 'Really, he must be a jolly clever fellow. But I say, Julian – how on earth are we going to get the boat up?'

'I can't imagine,' said Julian. 'I simply – can't – imagine! I hadn't even thought of that.'

Timmy suddenly began to growl. The four looked up quickly to see why.

They saw a boat coming over the water towards them – the *Merry Meg*, with Maggie and Dirty Dick in it. And the children felt quite certain that both were reading the bearings on their piece of paper in exactly the same way as they themselves had!

They were so engrossed in watching for Tall Stone, Tock Hill, Chimney and Steeple that they took no notice of the children at all. 'I don't think they guess for one moment that we've read the bearings and marked the place,' said Julian. 'How wild they'll be when they find we are right over the place they're looking for! Watch out for trouble!'

CHAPTER NINETEEN

Maggie and Dick are annoyed

THE BOAT in which Maggie and Dirty Dick were rowing went this way and that as the two searched for the same objects that the children had already spotted. The four watched them, and George put her hand on Timmy to stop him barking.

The boat came nearer and nearer. Maggie was trying to keep in view two or three of the bearings at once and her head twisted from side to side continually. The children grinned at one another. It had been hard enough for the four of them to keep all the bearings in view – it must be very difficult for Maggie, especially as Dirty Dick didn't seem to be helping very much.

They heard Maggie give sharp orders as the boat swung this way and that. Then it headed for them. Dirty Dick growled something to Maggie, who had her back to them, and she turned round sharply, losing the view of the things she was looking for.

Her face was full of anger when she saw the raft so near – and in the place where she wanted *her* boat to go! Afraid of completely losing the view of the things she was keeping her eyes on, she turned back again and hastily looked to see if Tock Hill, Tall Stone and Steeple

160

were still all to be seen together. She said something in a furious voice to Dirty Dick, and he nodded with a sour face.

The boat came nearer and they heard Maggie say, 'I think I can see it now – yes – a bit farther to the right, please.'

'She's spotted one Chimney now,' whispered Anne. 'I expect they've got all the bearings. Oh dear – the boat will bump right into us!'

It did! Dirty Dick rowed viciously at them and the bows of the boat gave them a terrific jolt. Anne would have fallen into the water if Julian hadn't grabbed at her.

He yelled at Dirty Dick. 'Look out, you ass! You nearly had us over! What on earth do you think you're doing?'

'Get out of the way then,' growled Dirty Dick. Timmy began to bark savagely, and the boat at once drew away from the raft.

'There's plenty of room on this lake,' shouted Julian. 'What do you want to come and disturb us for? We aren't doing any harm.'

'We're going to report you to the police,' called the woman, her face red with anger. 'Taking a raft that doesn't belong to you, sleeping in a house where you've no right to be – and stealing our food.'

'Don't talk nonsense,' cried Julian. 'And don't you dare to ram us again. If you do I'll send our dog after you. He's longing to come.'

'Grrrr!' said Timmy, and showed his magnificent set of gleaming white teeth. Dirty Dick muttered something quickly to Maggie. She turned round again and called to them.

'Now, look here, you kids – be sensible. My friend and I have come down here for a quiet weekend, and it isn't nice to find you four everywhere we go. Go back and keep out of our way and we won't report you at all. That's a fair bargain – we won't even say anything about your stealing our food.'

'We're going back when we think we will,' answered Julian. 'And no threats or bargains will make any difference to us.'

There was a silence. Then Maggie spoke hurriedly to Dirty Dick again. He nodded.

'Is this your half-term?' she called. 'When do you have to go back?'

'Tomorrow,' said Julian. 'You'll be rid of us then. But we're going to enjoy ourselves on this raft while we can.'

There was another hurried conference between the two. Then Dirty Dick rowed round a little, and Maggie began to peer down into the water. She suddenly looked up, nodded at Dirty Dick, and he rowed away again towards the end of the lake! Not another word did the couple say.

'I can see what they've decided to do,' said Julian, in a pleased voice. 'They think we'll be gone by tomorrow, so they'll wait till the coast is clear and then they'll come and collect the loot in peace. Did you see Maggie looking

163

down into the water to spot the boat? I was afraid she would also spot our mark – the cork and the box! But she didn't.'

'I don't know why you sound so pleased,' said George. 'We can't get the boat up, you know that – and *I* don't feel pleased that we'll have to leave tomorrow and let that horrid pair collect the loot. I imagine they'll have some clever grown-up way of pulling up the boat from the bed of the lake – which they will do when we've gone tomorrow.'

'You're not very bright today, George,' said Julian, watching the boat being rowed farther and farther away. 'I told them we'd be gone tomorrow, hoping they would clear off and wait – and leave us time to get the loot ourselves. I think we can!'

'How?' said three voices at once, and Timmy looked inquiringly at Julian too.

'Well, we don't need to pull up the *boat*,' said Julian. 'We only want the loot. What's to prevent us from going down and getting it? I'm quite prepared to strip and dive down to the bottom there and feel about for any sack or bag or box. If I find one I'll come up for air, borrow a bit of rope from the raft and go down again – tie the rope to the sack and you can haul it up to the surface!'

'Oh, Julian – it sounds so easy – but is it really?' said Anne. George and Dick considered the proposal carefully. They were most impressed by Julian's idea.

'Well, it may turn out to be much more difficult than it

sounds, but I'm jolly well going to try it,' said Julian, and began to strip off his jersey.

Anne felt the water. It was very cold to her warm hand. 'Ugh! I'd hate to dive down to the bottom of this horrid cold dark lake,' she said. 'I think you're brave, Ju.'

'Don't talk rubbish!' said Julian.

He was ready to go in now. He dived neatly into the water with hardly a splash. The other three craned over the edge of the raft to watch. They could see him down, deep down in the water, a ghostly figure. He stayed down such a long time that Anne got worried.

'He can't hold his breath all that time!' she said. 'He can't!'

But Julian could. He was one of the star swimmers and divers at his school, and this was easy to him. He came up again at last, and panted hard, trying to make up for holding his breath so long. The others waited patiently. At last his breathing grew more even and he grinned at them.

'Ah – that's better! Well – it's there!' he said, triumphantly.

'*Is* it!' said everyone, thrilled. 'Oh, Julian!'

'Yes. I dived right down to the boat – almost got there with the force of my dive – had to swim just a couple of strokes perhaps. And there was the poor old boat, rotting to bits. And in one end is a waterproof bag – almost a sack, it's so big. I ran my hands over it, and it's waterproof all right – so the loot must be packed in there.'

'Did it feel heavy?' asked Dick.

'I gave it a tug and couldn't move it,' said Julian. 'Either
it's wedged in somehow or is really heavy. Anyway we
can't fetch it out by diving down for it. I'll have to dive
down again, fix a rope to it, then come up – and we'll give
a heave-ho and up she'll come!'

Julian was shivering. Anne picked up the blazer she had
brought and gave it to him to dry himself with. Dick looked
hurriedly over the raft. There were certainly bits and pieces
of rope sticking out here and there, some of it half-rotten;
and a short length was tucked into a space between two
planks of the raft.

It was much too short though – and surely the other bits and pieces would never join to make a long enough rope?

'The bits of rope we've got won't do, Julian,' said Dick. Julian was drying himself and looking towards the end of the lake, where Two-Trees stood. He was frowning. The others looked too.

The boat had reached the bank there, and had been pulled up. One of the couple, the children couldn't see which, was standing up on the bank – and something was glinting in the sun, something he or she was holding!

'See that glint?' said Julian. 'Well, that's either Maggie or Dirty Dick using field-glasses. They're going to keep an eye on us while we're here – just to make sure we don't suddenly spot the boat, I suppose! They don't guess we've already found it. I bet they were worried when they saw I'd taken a header into the water just over the sunken boat!'

'Oh – so that's what the flash is,' said George. 'The glint of field-glasses! Yes – they're watching us. Blow! That will put an end to us trying to haul up the loot, Ju. They'd see it and wait for us!'

'Yes. No good trying for that now,' said Julian. 'Anyway, as Dick says, we've not got enough rope. We'll have to get some from the boat-house.'

'But when do you propose to get the bag out of the sunken boat?' asked Dick. 'They'll keep those field-glasses on us even if we go out again this afternoon.'

'There's only one time to go when they *won't* have their

167

glasses watching us,' said Julian, beginning to dress himself very rapidly, 'and that's tonight. We'll go tonight! My word – what an adventure!'

'Don't let's,' said Anne, in a small voice.

'There'll be a moon,' said George, excited.

'Smashing idea!' said Dick, thumping Julian on the back. 'Let's go back now so that they won't have any suspicions of us, and make our plans for tonight. And we'd better keep an eye on them too in case they row out to this spot themselves this afternoon.'

'They won't,' said Julian. 'They daren't run any risk of us spotting what they're doing. They will be sure to wait till we've gone.'

'And till the loot is gone!' said George with a laugh. 'I say – I do hope those two wretches haven't gone and taken our food again!'

'I hid it down in the cellars beyond our room – and locked the door leading there – and here's the key,' grinned Julian, holding up a large key.

'You never told us!' said George. 'Julian, you're a genius! How do you manage to think of things like that?'

'Oh – just brains!' said Julian, pretending to look modest, and then laughing. 'Come on – if I don't get warm quickly I'll have a most almighty chill!'

CHAPTER TWENTY

In the moonlight

THEY PADDLED rapidly away. Dick took a last glance back to make sure that the cork and the box were still bobbing on the water to mark the place where the sunken boat lay. Yes – they were still there.

'It'll be maddening if it's cloudy tonight and the moon doesn't come out,' said George, as they paddled. 'We shouldn't be able to see Tock Hill, Tall Stone and the rest – and we might paddle for ages in the dark without spotting our cork-and-box mark.'

'Don't cross your bridges before you come to them,' said Dick.

'I'm not,' said George. 'I was only just *hoping* that wouldn't happen.'

'It won't,' said Julian, looking at the sky. 'The weather's set fine again.'

As soon as Maggie saw the children coming back again, she and Dirty Dick disappeared into their tents. Julian grinned. 'They've heaved a sigh of relief and gone to have a snack,' he said. 'I could do with one myself.'

Everyone felt the same. Paddling was hard work, and the air on the lake was chilly – quite enough to give anyone a large appetite!

They pushed the raft into its hiding-place again. Then they made their way to the old house. They went down into the cellar room. Timmy growled and sniffed about again.

'I bet Maggie and Dirty Dick have been here, snooping round again,' said George. 'Looking for their pork-pie and ham! Good thing you locked it up, Ju!'

Julian unlocked the door into the cellars beyond, and brought out the food. 'A large toad was looking at it with great interest,' he said, as he brought it back. 'Timmy also looked at the toad with interest – but he's wary of toads by now. They taste much too nasty when pounced on!'

They took the meal up into the sunshine and enjoyed it. The orangeade was finished so they drank the cold clear water, pumping some vigorously.

'Do you know it's a quarter to three?' said Julian amazed. 'Where has the time gone? In a couple of hours or so it will be dark. Let me see – the moon will be well up about eleven o'clock. That's the time to go, I think.'

'Please don't let's,' said Anne. Julian put his arm round her.

'Now you know you don't mean that, Anne,' he said. 'You know you'll enjoy it all when the time comes. You couldn't bear to be left out of it! Could you?'

'No. I suppose I couldn't,' said Anne. 'But I *don't* like Maggie and Dirty Dick!'

'Nor do we,' said Julian, cheerfully. 'That's why we're going to beat them at their own game. We're on the side of the right, and it's worthwhile running into a bit of danger for that. Now let's see – perhaps we'd better just keep an eye on that couple till it's dark – just in *case* they try any funny tricks – and then we'll have a snooze, if we can, so as to be sure to be lively tonight.'

'There they are!' said Anne. As she spoke Maggie and her companion came out of their tents. They had a few words together and then walked off to the moorland.

'Taking their usual stroll, I suppose,' said Dick. 'Let's have a game of cricket. There's a bit of wood over there for a bat, and I've got a ball in my rucksack.'

'Good idea,' said Julian. 'I still feel a bit chilled from my bathe. Brrrrrr! That water was cold. I don't feel very thrilled at the thought of diving in tonight!'

'I'll do that,' said Dick, at once. 'My turn this time!'

'No. I know exactly where to spot the loot,' said Julian. 'I'll have to go down. But you can come down too, if you like, and help to tie the rope on to it.'

'Right,' said Dick. 'Now look out – I'm going to bowl!'

They enjoyed their game. The sun sank lower and lower, then it disappeared. A cloud came over the sky and darkness came quickly. George looked up at the sky anxiously.

'It's all right,' said Julian. 'It'll clear. Don't you worry!'

Before they went back into the house Julian and Dick slipped down to the boat-house for the coil of rope they would want that night. They found it quite easily enough and came back, pleased. It was quite a good strong rope, frayed only in one place.

Julian was right about the weather. The sky cleared again in about an hour, and the stars shone crisply. Good! Julian put Timmy on guard at the doorway. Then he and the others went into the dark cellar room and lit a couple of candles. They all snuggled down into their beds of heather.

'I shan't be able to snooze,' complained Anne. 'I feel much too excited.'

'Don't snooze then,' said Dick. 'Just have a rest and wake us up at the right time!'

Anne was the only one who didn't fall into a comfortable doze. She lay awake, thinking of this new adventure of theirs. Some children always had adventures and some didn't. Anne thought it would be much nicer to *read* about adventures than to have them. But then probably the ones who only read about them simply longed to have the adventures themselves! It was all very difficult.

Anne woke the others at ten to eleven. She shook George first, and then the boys. They were all in such a comfortable sleep that it was hard to wake them.

But soon they were up and about, whispering. 'Where's the rope? Good, here it is. Better put on blazers *and* macs. It'll be freezing on the lake. Everyone ready? Now – not a sound!'

Timmy had come to the cellar room as soon as he had heard them stirring. He knew he had to be quiet so he didn't give even one small bark. He was thrilled to find they were going out into the night.

172

The moon was well up now, and although it was not full, it was very bright. Small clouds swam across the sky, and every now and again the moon went behind one of them and the world became dark. But that was only for a minute or two, then out it came again, as brilliant as ever.

'Any sign of the others?' whispered Dick. Julian stood at the doorway and looked towards the tents. No – all was quiet there. Still, it would be better if he and the others crept round the side of the house and kept in the shadows.

'We don't want to run any risk of them spotting us now,' whispered Julian, giving his orders. 'Keep out of the moonlight, whatever you do. And see that Tim walks to heel, George.'

Keeping well in the shadows the five crept down to the lake-side. The water gleamed in the moonlight, and a bright moon-path ran all down it, lovely to see. The lake looked very dark and brooding. Anne wished it had a voice of some kind – even the little lap-lap-lap of waves at the edge. But there was none.

They pulled out the raft and threw the coil of rope on to it. Then they clambered on, enjoying its smooth bob-bob-bobbing as they paddled out on the water. They were off!

Timmy was thrilled. He kept licking first one of the four, then another. He loved going out in the night. The moon shone down on the little company and turned every little ripple to silver as the raft bobbed over the water.

'It's a heavenly night,' said Anne, looking round at the silent trees that lined the banks. 'The whole place is so quiet and peaceful.'

An owl immediately hooted very loudly indeed from the trees and Anne jumped violently.

'Now don't start all the owls hooting by talking about how quiet everything is,' teased Julian. 'I agree though that it really is a heavenly evening. How calm and mirror-like this lake is. I wonder if it ever produces a wave of any sort! Do you suppose it stays like this even in a storm?'

'It's a weird sort of lake,' said Dick. 'Look out, Timmy – that's my ear. Don't lick it all away. I say – anyone looking out for our four bearings?'

'Well, we know more or less where we've got to paddle

174

the raft to,' said Julian. 'We'll go in that direction and then see if we're spotting the bearings. I'm sure we're going right at the moment.'

They were. George soon saw Tall Stone, and then Tock Hill came into sight. It wasn't long before Steeple was seen too, shining in the moonlight.

'I bet the Nailer came and hid his loot out here on a moonlit night,' said Julian. 'All the bearings can be seen so very clearly – even Tall Stone. We really must find out sometime what it is. It looks like a great stone pointer of some sort, put up in memory of something or somebody.'

'There's the Chimney now,' said Anne. 'We have got them all in view – we should be near our mark.'

'We are!' said Dick, pointing to a little dark bobbing thing nearby. 'The cork and the box. How extremely clever we are! I really have a great admiration for the Five!'

'Idiot!' said Julian. 'Go on, strip now, Dick – we'll do our job straight away. Brrrrrrr! It's cold!'

Both boys stripped quickly, putting their clothes into a neat pile in the middle of the raft. 'Look after them, Anne,' said Julian. 'Got the rope, Dick? Come on, then, in we go. We can't see the boat now, the waters are so dark – but we know it's just below the cork and the box!'

The boys dived in one after the other. Splash! Splash! They were both beautiful divers. The raft rocked as they plunged in and Timmy nearly went in too.

Julian had dived in first. He opened his eyes under the water and found that he could see the sunken boat just

175

below him. With two strong strokes he reached it, and tugged at the waterproof bag there. Dick was beside him almost at once, the rope in his hands. The boys twisted it tightly round the top part of the bag.

Before they could finish the job they had to rise up to the surface to breathe. Dick couldn't hold his breath under water as long as Julian and he was up first, gasping painfully. Then Julian shot up and the night was full of great, painful breaths, as the boys gasped in the air they longed for.

The girls knew better than to ask anything just then. They waited anxiously till the boys' breathing grew easier. Julian turned and grinned at them.

'Everything's all right!' he said. 'Now – down we go again!'

CHAPTER TWENTY-ONE

The sack at last!

DOWN WENT the boys again and once more the raft jerked violently. The girls peered anxiously over the edge, waiting for them to return.

Julian and Dick were down at the sunken boat in a matter of a second or two. They finished the task of tying the rope to the waterproof bag. Julian gave it a hard jerk, hoping to free it if it were wedged tightly into the boat. He took the rest of the rope length in his hands in order to take it up to the surface.

Then, bursting for breath again, the two boys shot up to the raft, popping out of the water with loud gasps. They climbed on board.

They took a minute to get their breath and then Dick and Julian took the rope together. The girls watched, their hearts beating fast. Now was the test! Would that waterproof sack come up – or not?

The boys pulled strongly but without jerking. The raft slanted and Anne made a grab at the pile of clothes in the middle. Dick fell off into the water again.

He climbed back, spluttering. 'Have to pull more smoothly,' he said. 'I felt the sack give a bit, didn't you?'

THE SACK AT LAST!

Julian nodded. He was shivering with cold, but his eyes were shining with excitement. Anne put a macintosh round his shoulders and one round Dick's too. They never even noticed!

'Now – pull again,' said Julian. 'Steady does it – steady – steady! It's coming! Gosh, it's really coming. Pull, Dick, pull!'

As the heavy bag came up on the end of the rope, the raft slanted again, and the boys pushed themselves back to the other side of the raft, afraid of upsetting everyone into the water. Timmy began to bark excitedly.

'Be quiet, Timmy,' said George at once. She knew how easily sound travels over water, and she was afraid the couple in the tents might hear him.

'It's coming – it's there, look – just below the surface!' said Anne. 'One more pull, boys!'

But it was impossible to pull the heavy bag on board without upsetting the raft. As it was, the girls got very wet when the water splashed over the raft as it jerked and slanted.

'Look – let's paddle back to the shore and let the sack drag behind us,' said Julian, at last. 'We shall only upset the raft. Dress again, Dick, and we'll get back to the old house and open the sack in comfort. I'm so cold now that I can hardly feel my fingers.'

The boys dressed as quickly as they could. They were shivering, and were very glad to take up their paddles and work hard to get the raft back to shore. They soon felt a welcome warmth stealing through their bodies, and in ten minutes had stopped shivering. They felt very pleased with themselves indeed.

They looked back at the bulky object following them, dragging along just under the surface. What was in that bag? Excitement crept over all of them again, and the paddles struck through the water at top speed as all the four strained to get back as quickly as possible. Timmy felt the excitement too, and wagged his long tail without ceasing as he stood in the middle of the raft, watching the thing that bobbed along behind them.

They came at last to the end of the lake. Making as little noise as possible they dragged the raft under its usual bush. They did not want to leave it out on the bank in case Maggie and Dirty Dick saw that it had been used again, and started wondering.

Dick and Julian dragged the waterproof sack out of the water. They carried it between them as they went cautiously back to the house. It looked a most miserable, grotesque place with its burnt-out roof, doorways and windows – but the children didn't notice its forlorn appearance in the moonlight – they were far too excited!

They walked slowly up the overgrown path between the two broken-down walls, their feet making no sound on the soft mossy ground. They came to the doorway and dragged the bundle into the kitchen.

THE SACK AT LAST!

'Go and light the candles in the cellar room,' said Julian to George. 'I just want to make sure that that couple are not snooping anywhere about.'

George and Anne went to light the candles, flashing their torches before them down the stone steps. Julian and Dick stood at the open doorway, facing the moonlight, listening intently. Not a sound was to be heard, not a shadow moved!

They set Timmy on guard and left him there, dragging the dripping, heavy bundle across the stone floor of the kitchen. They bumped it down the cellar steps – and at last had it before them, ready to be opened!

Julian's fingers fumbled at the knots of the rope. George couldn't bear waiting. She took a pocket-knife and handed it to Julian.

'For goodness' sake, cut the rope!' she said. 'I simply can't wait another moment.'

Julian grinned. He cut the rope – and then he looked to see how to undo the waterproof wrapping.

'I see,' he said. 'It's been folded over and over the goods, and then sewn up to make a kind of bag. It must have kept the loot absolutely waterproof.'

'Buck *up*!' said George. 'I shall tear it open myself in a minute!'

Julian cut the strong stitches that closed the covering. They began to unwrap the bundle. There seemed to be yards and yards of waterproof covering! But at last it was off – and there, in the middle of the mass of waterproof,

181

were scores of little boxes – leather-covered boxes that everyone knew at once were jewel-boxes!

'It *is* jewellery then!' said Anne, and she opened a box. They all exclaimed in wonder.

A magnificent necklace glittered on black velvet. It shone and glinted and sparkled in the candlelight as if it were on fire. Even the two boys gazed without a word. Why – it was fit for a queen!

'It must be that wonderful necklace stolen from the Queen of Fallonia,' said George at last. 'I saw a picture of it in the papers. What diamonds!'

THE SACK AT LAST!

'Oooh – are they *diamonds*!' said Anne, in awe. 'Oh Julian – what a lot of money they must be worth! A hundred pounds, do you think?'

'A hundred thousand pounds more likely, Anne,' said Julian, soberly. 'My word – no wonder the Nailer hid these stolen goods carefully, in such an ingenious place. No wonder Maggie and Dirty Dick were longing to find them. Let's see what else there is.'

Every box contained precious stones of some kind – sapphire bracelets, ruby and diamond rings, a strange and wonderful opal necklace, earrings of such enormous diamonds that Anne was quite sure no one would be able to bear the weight of them!

'I would never, never dare to own jewellery like this,' said Anne. 'I should always be afraid of its being stolen. Did it all belong to the Queen of Fallonia?'

'No. Some to a princess who was visiting her,' said Julian. 'These jewels are worth a king's ransom. I just hate the thought of being in charge of them, even for a little while.'

'Well, it's better that we should have them, rather than Maggie or Dirty Dick,' said George. She held a string of diamonds in her hands and let them run through her fingers. How they sparkled! No one could have imagined that they had been at the bottom of a lake for a year or two!

'Now let's see,' said Julian, sitting down on the edge of the table. 'We're due back at school tomorrow afternoon, Tuesday – or is it Tuesday already? It must be past midnight – gosh, yes, it's almost half past two! Would you believe it?'

'I feel as if I'd believe anything,' said Anne, blinking at the glittering treasure on the table.

'We'd better start off fairly early tomorrow,' went on Julian. 'We've got to get these things to the police . . .'

'*Not* to that awful policeman we saw the other day!' said George, in horror.

'Of course not. I think our best course would be to ring up that nice Mr Gaston and tell him that we've got important news for the police and see which police station he recommends us to go to,' said Julian. 'He might even arrange a car for us, so that we don't need to take this stuff about in buses. I'm not particularly keen on carrying it about with me!'

'Have we got to carry all these boxes?' said George, in dismay.

'No. That would be asking for trouble if anyone spotted them,' said Julian. 'I fear we'll just have to wrap up the jewels in our hankies and stuff them down into the bottom of our rucksacks. We'll leave the boxes here. The police can collect them afterwards if they want to.'

It was all decided. The four divided up the glittering jewellery and wrapped it carefully into four handkerchiefs, one for each of them. They stuffed the hankies into their rucksacks.

'We'd better use them for pillows,' said Dick. 'Then they'll be quite safe.'

184

THE SACK AT LAST!

'What! These horrid rough bags!' said Anne. 'Why? Timmy's on guard, isn't he? I'll put mine beside me under the rug but I just won't put my head on it.'

Dick laughed. 'All right, Anne. Timmy won't let any robber through, I'm quite sure. Now – we start off first thing in the morning, do we, Julian?'

'Yes. As soon as we wake,' said Julian. 'We can't have much to eat. There're only a few biscuits and a bit of chocolate left.'

'I shan't mind,' said Anne. 'I'm so excited that at the moment I don't feel I'll ever eat anything again!'

'You'll change your mind tomorrow,' said Julian with a laugh. 'Now – to bed, everyone.'

They lay down on their heather and bracken, excited and pleased. What a weekend! And all because Dick and Anne had lost their way and Dick slept in the wrong barn!

'Good-night,' said Julian, yawning. 'I feel very very rich – richer than I'll ever be in my life again. Well – I'll enjoy the feeling while I can!'

CHAPTER TWENTY-TWO

An exciting finish

THEY AWOKE to hear Timmy barking. It was daylight already. Julian leapt up the steps to see what was the matter. He saw Maggie not very far away.

'Why do you keep such a fierce dog?' she called. 'I just came to see if you wanted to take any food with you. We'll give you some if you like.'

'It's *too* kind of you, all of a sudden!' said Julian. How anxious Maggie was to get rid of them! She would even give them food to get rid of them quickly. But Julian didn't want any food from Maggie or Dirty Dick!

'Do you want some, then?' asked the woman. She couldn't make Julian out. He looked a youngster, and yet his manner was anything but childish. She was rather afraid of him.

'No thanks,' said Julian. 'We're just about to go. Got to get back to school today, you know.'

'Well, you'd better hurry then,' said the woman. 'It's going to rain.'

Julian turned on his heel, grinning. It wasn't going to rain. Maggie would say anything to hurry them away! Still, that was just what Julian wanted – to get away as quickly as possible!

AN EXCITING FINISH

In ten minutes' time the four children were ready to go. Each had rucksack and mac on their backs – and each had jewels worth thousands of pounds in their charge! What a very extraordinary thing.

'It will be a lovely walk across the moors,' said Anne, as they went along. 'I feel like singing now everything's turned out all right. The only thing is – nobody at school will believe George or me when we tell them what's happened.'

'We shall probably be set a composition to do – "What did you do on your half-term?" ' said George. 'And Miss Peters will read ours and say "Quite well-written, but *rather* far-fetched, don't you think?" '

Everyone laughed. Timmy looked round with his tongue out and what George called 'his *smiling* face'. Then his 'smile' vanished, and he began to bark, facing to the rear of the children.

They looked round, startled. 'Gosh – it's Maggie and Dirty Dick – rushing along like fury!' said Dick. 'What's up? Are they sorry we've gone and want us back again?'

'They're trying to cut us off,' said Julian. 'Look – they've left the path and they're going to take a short cut to come across us. There is marshland all round, so we can't leave our own path. What idiots they are! Unless they know this bit of marsh-moor country they'll get bogged.'

Maggie and Dirty Dick were yelling and shouting in a

fury. Dirty Dick shook his fists, and leapt from tuft to tuft like a goat.

'They look as if they have gone quite mad,' said Anne, suddenly afraid. 'What's the matter with them?'

'I know!' said George. 'They've been into our cellar room – and they've found that waterproof covering and all those empty boxes. They've found out that we've got the goods!'

'Of course!' said Julian. 'We should have thrown all the boxes into the cellars beyond. No wonder they're in a fury. They've lost a fortune to us four!'

'What do they think they can do now, though?' said Dick. 'We've got Timmy. He'll certainly fly at them if they come too near. But Dirty Dick looks mad enough to fight even Timmy. Honestly, I think he's gone off his head.'

'I think he has,' said Julian, startled by the man's mad shouts and behaviour.

He looked at Anne, who had gone white. Julian felt sure that Timmy would go for Dirty Dick and bring him to the ground, and he didn't want Anne to see dog and man fighting savagely. There was no doubt that Dirty Dick was quite out of his mind with rage and disappointment.

Timmy began to bark fiercely. He snarled, and looked very savage. He could see that the man was spoiling for a fight with someone. All right – Timmy didn't mind!

'Let's hurry on,' said Julian. 'But no short cuts for us, mind – we'll keep strictly to the path. Maggie is in difficulties already.'

188

So she was. She was floundering ankle deep in marshy ground, yelling to Dirty Dick to help her. But he was too intent on cutting right across the children's path.

And then *he* got into difficulties too! He suddenly sank up to his knees! He tried to clamber out and reach a tuft of some sort. He missed his footing and went down again. He gave an anguished yell. 'My ankle! I've broken it! Maggie, come over here!'

But Maggie was having her own difficulties and paid no attention. The children stopped and looked at Dirty Dick. He was sitting on a tuft, nursing his foot, and even from where the children stood they could see that his face was deathly white. He certainly had done something to his ankle.

'Ought we to help him?' said Anne, trembling.

'Good gracious no!' said Julian. 'He may be pretending for all we know – though I don't think so. The chase is over, anyway. And if, as I think, Dirty Dick really has injured his ankle, he won't be able to get far out of that marsh – and nor will Maggie by the look of her – down she goes again, look! It may be that the police will find it very easy to pick up that unpleasant couple when they come along to look for them.'

'Nicely embedded in the marsh,' said Dick. 'Well, personally, I don't feel sorry for either of them. They're bad lots.'

They went on their way again, Timmy gloomy because he hadn't had a fight with Dirty Dick after all. They walked all the way to Reebles. It took them two hours.

'We'll go to the post-office, and telephone from there,' said Julian.

The old man was pleased to see them again. 'Had a nice time?' he said. 'Did you find Two-Trees?'

Julian left him talking to the others while he went to look up Mr Gaston's telephone number. He found it – and hoping devoutly that Mr Gaston wouldn't mind giving his help, he rang him up.

Mr Gaston answered the telephone himself. 'Hallo? Who? Oh, yes, of course I remember you. You want a bit of help? Well, what can I do for you?'

Julian told him. Mr Gaston listened in amazement.

'WHAT? You've found the Fallonia jewels! I can't believe it! In your rucksacks now, you say! Bless us all! You're not spoofing me, are you?'

Julian assured him that he wasn't. Mr Gaston could hardly believe his ears. 'Right. Right – of course I'll put you in touch with the police. We'd better go to Gathercombe – I know the inspector there, a fine fellow. Where are you? Oh yes, I know it. Wait there and I'll fetch you in my car – in about half an hour, say.'

He rang off and Julian went to find the others, delighted that he had thought of getting in touch with Mr Gaston. Some grown-ups were so jolly decent – and they knew exactly what to do. The other three were delighted too, when he told them.

'Well, I must say that although it's nice to have things happening to us, it's a sort of safe, comfortable feeling when we hand over to the grown-ups,' said George. 'Now I only want one thing – breakfast!'

'We'd better have a mixture of breakfast and lunch,' said Julian. 'It's so late.'

'Oh yes – let's have brunch!' said Anne, delighted. 'I love brunch.'

So they had some 'brunch' – sandwiches, buns, biscuits and ginger-beer, which they bought at a little shop down the road. And just as they were finishing, up swept Mr Gaston in an enormous car!

The four children grinned at him with pleasure. Julian introduced Anne and Dick. Timmy was thrilled to see him

191

again and offered him a polite paw, which Mr Gaston shook heartily.

'Nice manners your dog's got,' he said, and pressed down the accelerator. Whoooosh! Away they went at top speed, with Timmy sticking his head out of the window as he always did in a car.

They told their extraordinary story as they went. Mr Gaston was full of admiration for all they had done. 'You're a bunch of plucky kids!' he kept saying. 'My word, I wish you were mine!'

They came to the police station. Mr Gaston had already warned the inspector they were coming, and he was waiting for them.

'Come along into my private room,' he said. 'Now first of all – where are these jewels? Have you really got them with you? Let's have a look at them before you tell your story.'

The children undid their rucksacks – and out of the hankies inside they poured the shining, glittering jewellery on to the oak table.

The inspector whistled and exchanged a look with Mr Gaston. He picked up the diamond necklace.

'You've got them!' he said. 'The very jewels! And to think the police everywhere have been hunting for them for months and months and months. Where did you find them, youngsters?'

'It's rather a long story,' said Julian. He began to tell it, and he told it well, prompted by the others, when he forgot anything. Mr Gaston and the inspector listened with amazement on their faces. When Julian came to the bit where Dirty Dick and Maggie had been left floundering in the marshes, the inspector interrupted him.

'Wait! Would they still be there? They would? Right. Half a minute!'

He pressed a bell and a policeman appeared. 'Tell Johns to take his three men and the car, and go to the Green Marshes, near Gloomy Water,' ordered the inspector. 'He's to pick up two people floundering there – man and woman. Our old friends Dirty Dick and Maggie Martin! Look sharp!'

The policeman disappeared. Anne hugged herself. Now that awful couple would be put into safe custody for some time, thank goodness – till she had forgotten about them! Anne hadn't liked them a bit.

Julian's tale came to an end. The inspector looked across at the tousle-headed, dirty, untidy group and smiled. He held out his hand. 'Shake!' he said. 'All of you! You're the kind of kids we want in this country – plucky, sensible, responsible youngsters who use your brains and never give up! I'm proud to meet you!'

They all shook hands with him solemnly. Timmy held up his paw too, and the inspector grinned and shook that too.

'And now – what's your programme?' asked Mr Gaston, getting up.

'Well – we're supposed to be back at school by three

o'clock,' said Julian. 'But I don't think we can arrive looking like this. We'd get into awful rows! Is there a hotel where we can have a bath and clean ourselves up a bit?'

'You can do that here,' said the inspector. 'And if you like I'll run you back to your schools in the police car. We can't do too much for people who produce the Fallonia jewels out of rucksacks, you know. Bless us all – I can't believe it!'

Mr Gaston said good-bye and went, saying that he was very proud to have made friends with them. 'And don't you get stuck down any more rabbit-holes!' he said to Timmy, who woofed happily at him.

They bathed and washed every inch of themselves. They found their clothes neatly folded and brushed, and felt grateful. They brushed their hair and arrived looking very clean and tidy in the inspector's private room. He had a man there, inspecting the jewels and labelling them before he put them away into boxes.

'You'll be interested to know that we have picked up your couple,' he told them. 'The man had a broken ankle and couldn't stir a step. The woman was thigh deep in the marsh when we found her. They quite welcomed the police, they were so fed up with everything!'

'Oh *good!*' said the four, and Anne beamed with relief. That settled Maggie and Dirty Dick then!

'And these *are* the Fallonia jewels,' said the inspector. 'Not that I had any doubt of it. They are now being checked and labelled. I've no doubt the Queen of Fallonia and her titled friend will be extremely pleased to hear of your little exploit.'

A clock struck half past two. Julian looked at it. Half an hour only to get back in time. Would they do it?

'It's all right,' said the inspector, with his wide grin. 'Car's at the door. I'll come and see you off. You'll all be back at your schools in good time – and if anyone believes your tale I'll be surprised. Come along!'

He saw them into the car, Timmy too. 'Good-bye,' he said, and saluted them all smartly. 'I'm proud to have met you – good luck to you, Famous Five!'

Yes, good luck to you, Famous Five – and may you have many more adventures!

Five Have a Wonderful Time

CONTENTS

CHAPTER ONE

George is all alone

'I DO think it's *mean*,' said George, fiercely. 'Why can't I go when the others do? I've had two weeks at home, and haven't seen the others since school broke up. And now they're off for a wonderful fortnight and I'm not with them.'

'Don't be silly, George,' said her mother. 'You can go as soon as that cold of yours is better.'

'It's better now,' said George, scowling. 'Mother, you know it is!'

'That's enough, Georgina,' said her father, looking up from his newspaper. 'This is the third breakfast-time we've had this argument. Be quiet.'

George would never answer anyone when she was called Georgina – so, much as she would have liked to say something back, she pursed up her mouth and looked away.

Her mother laughed. 'Oh, George, dear! Don't look so terribly fierce. It was your own fault you got this cold – you *would* go and bathe and stay in far too long and after all, it's only the third week in April!'

'I always bathe in April,' said George, sulkily.

'I said "BE QUIET",' said her father, banging down his

201

paper on the table. 'One more word from you, George, and you won't go to your three cousins' at all.'

'Woof,' said Timmy, from under the table. He didn't like it when anyone spoke angrily to George.

'And don't *you* start arguing with me, either,' said George's father, poking Timmy with his toe, and scowling exactly like George.

His wife laughed again. 'Oh, be quiet, the two of you,' she said. 'George, be patient dear. I'll let you go off to your cousins as soon as ever I can – tomorrow, if you're good, and don't cough much today.'

'Oh, Mother – why didn't you say so before?' said George, her scowl disappearing like magic. 'I didn't cough once in the night. I'm perfectly all right today. Oh, if I can go off to Faynights Castle tomorrow, I *promise* I won't cough once today!'

'What's this about Faynights Castle?' demanded her father, looking up again. 'First I've heard of it!'

'Oh no, Quentin dear, I've told you at least three times,' said his wife. 'Julian, Dick and Anne have been lent two funny old caravans by a school friend. They are in a field near Faynights Castle.'

'Oh. So they're not *staying* in a castle, then,' said George's father. 'Can't have that. I won't have George coming home all high and mighty.'

'George couldn't *possibly* be high and mighty,' said his wife. 'It's as much as I can do to get her to keep her nails clean and wear clean jeans. Do be sensible,

Quentin. You know perfectly well that George and her cousins always like to go off on extraordinary holidays together.'

'And have adventures,' grinned George, who was in a very good temper indeed at the thought of going to join her cousins the next day.

'No. You're not to have any of those awful adventures this time,' said her mother. 'Anyway, I don't see how you can, staying in a peaceful place like the village of Faynights Castle, living in a couple of old caravans.'

'I wouldn't trust George anywhere,' said her husband. 'Give her just a *sniff* of an adventure, and she's after it. I never knew anyone like George. Thank goodness we've only got one child. I don't feel as if I could cope with two or three Georges.'

'There are plenty of people like George,' said his wife. 'Julian and Dick for instance. Always in the middle of something or other – with Anne tagging behind, longing for a peaceful life.'

'Well, I've had enough of this argument,' said George's father, pushing his chair out vigorously, and accidentally kicking Timmy under the table. He yelped.

'That dog's got no brains,' said the impatient man. 'Lies under the table at every meal and expects me to remember he's there! Well, I'm going to do some work.'

He went out of the room. The dining-room door banged. Then the study door banged. Then a window was shut with a bang. A fire was poked very vigorously.

There was the creak of an armchair as someone sat down in it heavily. Then there was silence.

'Now your father's lost to the world till lunchtime,' said George's mother. 'Dear, oh dear – I've told him at *least* three times about Faynights Castle, where your cousins are staying, bless him. Now, George, I do really think you can go tomorrow, dear – you look so much better today. You can get your things ready and I'll pack them this afternoon.'

'Thank you, Mother,' said George, giving her a sudden hug. 'Anyway, Father will be glad to have me out of the house for a bit! I'm too noisy for him!'

'You're a pair!' said her mother, remembering the slammed doors and other things. 'You're both a perfect nuisance at times, but I couldn't bear to do without you! Oh, Timmy, are you still under the table? I wish you wouldn't leave your tail about so! Did I hurt you?'

'Oh, he doesn't mind *you* treading on it, Mother,' said George, generously. 'I'm going to get my things ready this very minute. How do I get to Faynights Castle? By train?'

'Yes. I'll take you to Kirrin Station, and you can catch the ten-forty,' said her mother. 'You change at Limming Ho, and take the train that goes to Faynights. If you send a card to Julian, he'll get it tomorrow morning and will meet you.'

'I'll write it now,' said George, happily. 'Oh, Mother, I began to be afraid this awful cold would hang on all through the holidays! I shan't bathe again on such a cold day in April.'

204

GEORGE IS ALL ALONE

'You said that last year – and the year before that too,' said her mother. 'You have a very short memory, George!'

'Come on, Timmy!' said George, and the two of them went out of the door like a whirlwind. It slammed behind them, and the house shook.

At once the study door opened and an angry voice yelled loudly: 'Who's that slamming doors when I'm at work? Can't ANYBODY in this house shut a door quietly?'

George grinned as she fled upstairs. The biggest slammer-of-doors was her father, but he only heard the slams made by other people. George turned her writing-case inside out to find a postcard. She must post it at once or Julian

wouldn't get it – and it *would* be so nice to have all her three cousins meeting her!

'We're off tomorrow,' she told Timmy, who looked up at her and wagged his tail vigorously. 'Yes, you're coming too, of course – then the Five will all be together again. The Famous Five! You'll like that, won't you, Tim? So shall I!'

She scribbled the postcard and flew down to post it. Slam went the front door, and her father almost jumped out of his skin. He was a very clever and hardworking scientist, impatient, hot-tempered, kindly and very forgetful. How he wished his daughter was not so exactly like him, but was like his quiet, gentle little niece Anne!

George posted the card. It was short and to the point.

Cold gone. Coming tomorrow. Arriving 12.05 so make sure you all meet me and Timmy. Our tails are well up, I can tell you!

GEORGE.

George turned out her drawers and began to pick out the things she wanted to take with her. Her mother came to help. There was always an argument about packing, because George wanted to take as little as possible, and no warm things at all, and her mother had exactly opposite ideas.

However, between the two of them they managed to pack the suitcase full of quite sensible things. George refused as usual to take a dress of any sort.

'I wonder when you'll grow out of wanting to be a boy, and of acting like one!' said her mother, exasperated. 'All right, all right – take those awful old jeans if you want to, and that red jersey. But you *are* to pack those warm vests. I put them in once, and you took them out. And you must take a warm rug, Julian says. The caravans are not very warm in this weather.'

'I wonder what they're like,' said George, stuffing the vests in. 'They're funny, old-fashioned ones, Julian said in his letter. Perhaps they're like the ones the travellers have – not the modern, streamlined ones that are pulled along by cars.'

'You'll see tomorrow,' said her mother. 'Oh, George – you're coughing again!'

'Just the dust, that's all,' said George going purple in the face trying to hold back the tickle in her throat. She drank a glass of water in a hurry. It would be too dreadful if her mother said she wasn't to go after all!

However, her mother really did think that George was better. She had been in bed for a week, making a terrible fuss, and being a very difficult patient. Now, after being up for a few days she really seemed herself again.

'It will do her good to get down to Faynights and its good strong air,' thought her mother. 'She needs company again, too – she doesn't like having to be all alone, knowing the others are holidaying without her.'

George felt happy that evening. Only one more night

and she would be off to a fortnight's caravanning! If only the weather was good, what a fine time they would have!

Suddenly the telephone shrilled out. R-r-r-r-r-r-ring! R-r-r-r-r-ring!

George's mother went to answer it. 'Hallo!' she said. 'Oh – it's you, Julian. Is everything all right?'

George sped out into the hall at once. Oh, surely, surely, nothing had happened! Surely Julian wasn't ringing to tell her not to come! She listened breathlessly.

'What's that you say, Julian? I can't make out what you're talking about, dear. Yes, of course, your uncle is all right. Why shouldn't he be? No, he hasn't disappeared. Julian, what *are* you talking about?'

George listened impatiently. What *was* all this? But it turned out to be something quite ordinary, really. When at last her mother put down the receiver, she told George.

'Don't hop about like that, George. It's *quite* all right, you can go tomorrow. Julian was only ringing up to make sure that your father wasn't one of the scientists who have suddenly disappeared. Apparently in tonight's paper there is a short report about two that have completely vanished – and dear old Julian wanted to make sure your father was here safely!'

'As if Father would vanish!' said George, scornfully. 'Julian must be mad! It's just two more of those silly scientists who are disloyal to this country, and disappear to another country to sell our secrets! *I* could have told Julian that!'

208

CHAPTER TWO

All together again

NEXT MORNING, on a dewy hillside a good distance from Kirrin, where George lived, two boys leapt down the steps of a caravan, and went to one nearby. They rapped on the door.

'Anne! Are you awake? It's a heavenly day!'

'Of course I'm awake!' cried a voice. 'The door's unlocked. Come in. I'm getting breakfast.'

Julian and Dick pushed open the blue-painted door. Anne was standing at a little stove at one end of her caravan, boiling eggs in a saucepan.

'I can't look round,' she said. 'I'm timing them by my watch. One minute more to go.'

'The postman has just brought a card from George,' said Julian. 'She says her tail and Timmy's are both well up! I'm glad she's coming at last – and old Timmy too.'

'We'll all go and meet her,' said Anne, still with her eyes on her watch. 'Twenty seconds more.'

'We only came here ourselves three days ago,' said Dick. 'So she hasn't really missed much. Surely those eggs will be hard-boiled, Anne!'

Anne stopped looking at her watch. 'No, they won't. They'll be just right.' She scooped them out of the little saucepan with a big spoon. 'Put them in the egg-cups, Dick. There they are – just under your nose.'

Dick picked an egg up from the plate on which Anne had placed them. It was so hot that he dropped it with a yell, and it broke its shell. Yolk flowed out of it.

'DICK! You *saw* me take it out of boiling water!' said Anne. 'Now I've got to do another. It's a pity old Timmy isn't here. He'd soon have licked that broken egg up from the floor and saved me clearing up the mess.'

'We'll eat our breakfast sitting on the steps of your caravan, Anne,' said Julian. 'The sun's so lovely.'

So they all sat there, eating boiled eggs, well-buttered bread, with chunky, home-made marmalade afterwards, and then juicy apples. The sun shone down and Julian took off his coat.

Their two caravans were set on a sloping, grassy hillside. A tall hedge grew behind, and kept off the wind. Primroses ran in a pale gold streak under the hedge, and brilliant celandines shone in the sun, turning their polished faces towards it.

Not far off were three more caravans, but they were modern ones. The people staying in those were not yet up, and the doors were fast shut. The three children had had no chance of making friends with them.

On the opposite hill rose an old, ruined castle, whose great walls still defied the gales that sometimes blew over the hills. It had four towers. Three were very much broken, but the fourth looked almost complete. The windows were

slitholes, made centuries back when archers shot their arrows from them.

A very steep pathway led up to the castle. At the top of it was a gateway, enormously strong, built of big white blocks of stone. The gateway was now filled by a great screen of wrought-iron to prevent anyone entering, and the only entrance was by a small tower in which was a narrow door. Here there was a turnstile through which visitors might go to see the old castle.

A high, strong wall ran all round the castle, still standing after so many years. Bits of the top of it had fallen down the hill and lay half-buried in grass and weeds. It had once been a magnificent old castle, built on the high, steep hill for safety, a place from which the castle guards might see the country easily for miles around.

As Julian said, anyone up in one of the towers, or even on the wall, would be able to see enemies approaching from seven counties. There would be plenty of time to shut the great gate, man the walls, and get ready to withstand quite a long siege if necessary.

The three of them sat on the steps, lazing in the sun, when they had finished their breakfast. They looked at the ruined old castle, and watched the jackdaws circling round the four towers.

'There must be about a thousand jackdaws there,' said Dick. 'I wish we had field-glasses so that we could watch them. It would be as good as a circus. I love the way they all fly up together, and circle round and round and yet never bump into one another.'

'Do they nest in that old castle?' asked Anne.

'Oh, yes – they fill up the towers with big sticks,' said Dick, 'and put their nests on the top. I bet we'd find the ground beneath the towers strewn ankle-deep in sticks if we went to see.'

'Well, let's go one day when George is here,' said Anne. 'It only costs five pence to go in. I like old castles. I like the *feel* of old places.'

'So do I,' said Julian. 'I hope George brings the field-glasses she had for her birthday. We could take them up into the castle with us and see all round the countryside for miles and miles. We could count the seven counties!'

ALL TOGETHER AGAIN

'I must wash up,' said Anne, getting up. 'I must tidy the caravans too before George comes.'

'You don't really think old George will notice if they're tidy or not, do you?' said Dick. 'It will be a waste of your time, Anne!'

But Anne always enjoyed tidying things and putting them away in cupboards or on shelves. She liked having the two caravans to look after. She had just got used to them nicely and was looking forward to showing George round them.

She skipped over to the hedge and picked a great bunch of primroses. Back she went and divided them into two. She stuffed half into one little blue bowl, set their green crinkled leaves round them, and then put the other half into a second bowl.

'There – you go with the green and yellow curtains!' she said. She was soon very busy sweeping and dusting. She debated whether to send Dick to the stream to wash the breakfast things, and decided not to. Dick wasn't too good with crockery, and it was not theirs to break – it belonged to the owner of the caravans.

By the time it was half past eleven the caravans were spick and span. George's sheets and blankets were on the shelf above her bunk, which, in the daytime, let down neatly against the wall to make more room. Anne had a bunk on the opposite side.

'This is the kind of holiday I *like*,' said Anne to herself. 'Somewhere small to live, fields and hills just outside, picnicky meals – and not too much adventure!'

'What are you murmuring about, Anne?' said Dick peeping in at the window. 'Did I hear something about adventure? Are you looking for one already?'

'Good gracious no!' said Anne. 'It's the last thing I want! And the last thing we'll get too, in this quiet little place, thank goodness.'

Dick grinned. 'Well, you never know,' he said. 'Are you ready to come and meet George, Anne? It's about time we went.'

Anne went down the steps and joined Dick and Julian. 'Better lock the door,' said Dick. 'We've locked ours.' He locked Anne's door and the three set off down the grassy hillside to the stile that led into the lane below. The old castle on the opposite hill seemed to tower up higher and higher as they went down towards the village.

'It will be lovely to see Timmy again,' said Anne. 'And I'll be jolly glad to have George too, in my caravan. I didn't really *mind* being alone at night – but it's always nice to have George near me, and Timmy grunting in his sleep.'

'You want to sleep with Dick if you like grunts and snorts and moans,' said Julian. 'What *do* you dream about, Dick? You must have more nightmares than anyone else in the kingdom!'

'I *never* grunt or snort or moan,' said Dick indignantly. 'You want to hear yourself! Why . . .'

'Look – isn't that the train coming in – isn't that it curving round the line in the distance?' said Anne. 'It must

214

be! There's only one train in the morning here! We'd better run!'

They ran at top speed. The train drew in at the station just as they raced on to the platform. A head of short curly hair looked out from a window – and then another brown head just below it.

'George – and Timmy!' yelled Anne.

'Hallo!' shouted George, almost falling out of the door.

'WOOF!' barked Timmy, and leapt down to the platform almost on top of Dick. Down jumped George, her eyes shining. She hugged Anne, and gave Julian and Dick a punch each. 'I'm here!' she said. 'I felt awful knowing you were away camping without me. I gave poor old Mother a dreadful time.'

'I bet you did,' said Julian, and linked his arm in hers. 'Let me take that suitcase. We'll just slip into the village first and have a few ice-creams to celebrate. There's a shop here that has some jolly decent ones.'

'Good. I feel exactly like ice-creams,' said George, happily. 'Look, Timmy knows what you said. His tongue is hanging out for an ice-cream already. Timmy, aren't you pleased we're all together again?'

'Woof,' said Timmy, and licked Anne's hand for the twentieth time.

'I really ought to bring a towel with me when I meet Timmy,' said Anne. 'His licks are so very wet. Oh no, not *again*, Timmy – go and use your tongue on Julian!'

215

'I say, look – George *has* brought her field-glasses with her!' said Dick, suddenly noticing that the brown strap over George's shoulder did not belong to a camera but to a very fine leather case that held the new field-glasses. 'Good! We wanted to watch the jackdaws with them – and there are some herons down on the marsh too.'

'Well, I thought I *must* bring them,' said George. 'It's the first hols I've had a chance to use them. Mother wouldn't let me take them to school. I say – how much further is this ice-cream shop?'

'In the dairy here,' said Julian, marching her in. 'And I advise you to start off with vanilla, go on to strawberry and finish up with chocolate.'

'You do have good ideas!' said George. 'I hope you've got some money as well, if we're going to eat ice-creams at this rate. Mother didn't give me very much to spend.'

They sat down and ordered ice-creams. The plump little shop-woman smiled at them. She knew them by now. 'This is very good weather for you,' she said. 'Are there many caravanners up on Faynights Field?'

'No, not many,' said Julian, beginning his ice.

'Well, you're going to have a few more,' said the little plump lady. 'I hear there's some fair-folk coming – they usually camp up in your field. You'll have some fun if so.'

'Oh, good!' said Dick. 'We'll really be able to make a few friends then. We like fair-folk, don't we, Timmy?'

CHAPTER THREE

A pleasant morning

'Is THERE going to be a fair near here then?' asked George, starting on her strawberry ice. 'What sort of a fair? A circus or something?'

'No. Just a mixed-up show,' said the shop-woman. 'There's to be a fire-eater, and that'll bring the villagers to the show faster than anything. A fire-eater! Did you ever hear of such a thing? I wonder that anyone cares to make a living at that!'

'What else is there to be?' asked Anne. She didn't somehow fancy watching anyone eating fire!

'Well, there's a man who can get himself free in under two minutes, no matter how tightly he's tied up with rope,' said the woman. 'Fair miracle he must be! And there's a man called Mr India-rubber, because he can bend himself anywhere, and wriggle through drain-pipes and get in at a window if it's left open just a crack!'

'Gracious! He'd make a good burglar!' said George. 'I wish I was like india-rubber! Can this man bounce when he falls down?'

Everyone laughed. 'What else?' said Anne. 'This sounds very exciting.'

'There's a man with snakes,' said the plump little lady with a shudder. 'Snakes! Just fancy! I'd be afraid they would bite me. I'd run a mile if I saw a snake coming at me.'

'Are they poisonous snakes that he has, I wonder?' said Dick. 'I don't somehow fancy having a caravan next to ours with lashings of poisonous snakes crawling round.'

'Don't!' said Anne. 'I should go home at once.'

Another customer came in and the shop-woman had to leave the children and go to serve her. The four felt rather thrilled. What a bit of luck to have such exciting people in the same field as they were!

'A fire-eater!' said Dick. 'I've always wanted to see one. I bet he doesn't *really* eat fire! He'd burn the whole of his mouth and throat.'

'Has everyone finished?' asked Julian, getting some money out of his pocket. 'If so, we'll take George up to the field and show her our painted caravans. They aren't a bit like the ones we once went caravanning in, George – they are old-fashioned travellers' ones. You'll like them. Colourful and very picturesque.'

'Who lent you them?' asked George, as they left the shop. 'Some school friend, wasn't it?'

'Yes. He and his family always go and camp in their caravans in the Easter and summer hols,' said Julian. 'But this Easter they're going to France – and rather than leave them empty, they thought they'd lend them out – and we're the lucky ones!'

They walked up the lane and came to the stile. George looked up at the towering castle, gleaming in the sun on the hill opposite.

219

'Faynights Castle,' she said. 'Hundreds of years old! How I'd love to know all the things that happened there through the centuries. I do love old things. I vote we go and explore it.'

'We will. It only costs five pence,' said Dick. 'We'll all have a good five pence worth of castle. I wonder if there are any dungeons. Dark, damp, drear and dreadful!'

They went up the grassy hillside to the field where their caravans were. George exclaimed in delight. 'Oh! Are *those* our caravans? Aren't they lovely? They're just like the caravans the travellers use – only these look cleaner and brighter.'

'The red caravan, picked out with black and yellow, is ours,' said Dick. 'The blue one, picked out in black and yellow, is yours and Anne's.'

'Woof,' said Timmy at once.

'Oh, sorry – yours *too*, Timmy,' said Dick at once, and everyone chuckled. It was funny the way Timmy suddenly made a woofish remark, just as if he really understood every word that was said. George was quite certain he did, of course.

The caravans stood on high wheels. There was a window on each side. The door was at the front, and so were the steps, of course. Bright curtains hung at the windows, and a line of bold carving ran round the edges of the out-jutting roof.

'They are old traveller caravans painted and made really up to date,' said Julian. 'They're jolly comfortable inside too – bunks that fold down against the walls in the daytime

220

A PLEASANT MORNING

– a little sink for washing-up, though we usually use the stream, because it's such a bore to fetch water – a small larder, cupboards and shelves – cork carpet on the floor with warm rugs so that no draught comes through . . .'

'You sound as if you are trying to sell them to me!' said George, with a laugh. 'You needn't! I love them both, and I think they're miles nicer than the modern caravans down there. Somehow these seem *real*!'

'Oh, the others are real enough,' said Julian. 'And they've got more space – but space doesn't matter to us because we shall live outside most of the time.'

'Do we have a camp-fire?' asked George, eagerly. 'Oh, yes – I see we do. There's the ashy patch where you had your fire. Oh, Julian, do let's have a fire there at night and sit round it in the darkness!'

'With midges biting us and bats flapping all round,' said Dick. 'Yes, certainly we will! Come inside, George.'

'She's to come into my caravan first,' said Anne, and pushed George up the steps. George was really delighted.

She was very happy to think she was going to have a peaceful two weeks here with her three cousins and Timmy. She pulled her bunk up and down to see how it worked. She opened the larder and cupboard doors. Then she went to see the boys' caravan.

'How *tidy*!' she said, in surprise. 'I expected Anne's to be tidy – but yours is just as spick and span. Oh dear – I hope you haven't all turned over a new leaf and become models of neatness – *I* haven't!'

'Don't worry,' said Dick, with a grin. 'Anne has been at work – you know how she loves to put everything in its place. We don't need to worry about anything when she's about. Good old Anne!'

'All the same, George will have to help,' said Anne, firmly. 'We've all got to tidy up and cook and do things like that.'

George groaned. 'All right, Anne, I'll do my share – sometimes. I say – there won't be much room for Timmy on my bunk at nights, will there?'

'Well, he's not coming on mine,' said Anne. 'He can sleep on the floor on a rug. Can't you, Timmy?'

'Woof,' said Timmy, without wagging his tail at all. He looked very disapproving.

'There you are – he says he wouldn't *dream* of doing such a thing!' said George. 'He *always* sleeps on my feet.'

They went outside again. It really was a lovely day. The primroses opened more and more of their little yellow flowers, and a blackbird suddenly burst into a fluting song on the bough of a hawthorn tree in the hedge nearby.

'Did anyone get a paper in the village?' asked Dick. 'Oh, you did, Julian. Good. Let's have a look at the weather forecast. If it's good we might go for a long walk this afternoon. The sea is not really very far off.'

Julian took the folded paper from his pocket and threw it over to Dick. He sat down on the steps of the caravan and opened it.

He was looking for the paragraph giving the weather forecast when headlines caught his eye. He gave an exclamation.

'Hallo! Here's a bit more about those two vanished scientists, Julian!'

'Oh!' said George, remembering Julian's telephone call of the night before. 'Julian, whatever in the world made you think my father could be one of the vanished scientists? As if he would ever be disloyal to his country and take his secrets anywhere else!'

'Oh, I didn't think that,' said Julian, at once. 'Of *course* I didn't! I'd never think Uncle Quentin would do a thing like that. No – in yesterday's paper it just said that two of our most famous scientists had disappeared – and I thought perhaps they had been kidnapped. And as Uncle Quentin is really very famous, I just thought I'd ring up to make sure.'

'Oh,' said George. 'Well, as Mother hadn't heard a thing about them she was awfully astonished when you asked her if Father had disappeared. Especially as he was banging about just then in the study, looking for something he had lost.'

'Which he was sitting on as usual, I suppose,' said Dick with a grin. 'But listen to this – it doesn't look as if the two men have been kidnapped – it looks as if they just walked out and took important papers with them! Beasts! There's too much of that sort of thing nowadays, it seems to me!'

He read out a paragraph or two.

'Derek Terry-Kane and Jeffrey Pottersham have been missing for two days. They met at a friend's house to discuss a certain aspect of their work, and then left together to walk to the Underground. Since then they have not been seen.

'It has, however, been established that Terry-Kane had brought his passport up to date and had purchased tickets for flying to Paris. No news of his arrival there has been reported.'

'There! Just what I said to Mother!' exclaimed George. 'They've gone off to sell their secrets to another country. Why do we let them?'

'Uncle Quentin won't be pleased about that,' said Julian. 'Didn't he work with Terry-Kane at one time?'

'Yes, I believe he did,' said George. 'I'm jolly glad I'm not at home today – Father will be rampaging round like anything, telling Mother hundreds of times what he thinks about scientists who are traitors!'

'He certainly will,' said Julian. 'I don't blame him either. That's a thing I don't understand – to be a traitor to one's own country. It leaves a nasty taste in my mouth to think of it. Come on – let's think about dinner, Anne. What are we going to have?'

'Fried sausages and onions, potatoes, a tin of sliced peaches and I'll make a custard,' said Anne, at once.

'I'll fry the sausages,' said Dick. 'I'll light the fire out here and get the frying-pan. Anyone like their sausages split in the cooking?'

Everyone did. 'I like mine nice and *burnt*,' said George. 'How many do we have each? I've only had those ice-creams since breakfast.'

'There are twelve,' said Anne, giving Dick the bag. 'Three each. None for Timmy! But I've got a large, juicy bone for him. Julian, will you get me some water, please? There's the pail, over there. I want to peel the potatoes. George, can you possibly open the peaches without cutting yourself like you did last time?'

'Yes, Captain!' said George, with a grin. 'Ah – this is like old times. Good food, good company and a good time. Three cheers for Us!'

CHAPTER FOUR

The fair-folk arrive

THAT FIRST day they were all together was a lovely one. They enjoyed it thoroughly, especially George, who had fretted all by herself for two weeks at home. Timmy was very happy too. He tore after rabbits, most of them quite imaginary, up and down the field and in and out the hedges till he was tired out.

Then he would come and fling himself down by the four, panting like a steam-engine going uphill, his long pink tongue hanging out of his mouth.

'You make me feel hot just to *look* at you, Timmy,' said Anne, pushing him away. 'Look, George – he's so hot he's steaming! One of these days, Timmy, you'll blow up!'

They went for a walk in the afternoon, but didn't quite get to the sea. They saw it from a hill, sparkling blue in the distance. Little white yachts dotted the blue water like far-off swans with wings outspread. They had tea at a farm-house, watched by a couple of big-eyed farm children.

'Do you want to take some of my home-made jam with you?' asked the farmer's jolly, red-faced wife, when they paid her for their tea.

'Oh, yes, rather!' said Dick. 'And I suppose you couldn't sell us some of that fruit cake? We're camping in caravans in Faynights Field, just opposite the castle – so we're having picnic meals each day.'

'Yes, you can have a whole cake,' said the farmer's wife. 'I did my baking yesterday, so there's plenty. And would you like some ham? And I've some good pickled onions too.'

This was wonderful! They bought all the food very cheaply indeed, and carried it home gladly. Dick took off the lid of the pickled onions halfway back to the caravans, and sniffed.

'Better than any scent!' he said. 'Have a sniff, George.'

It didn't stop at sniffs, of course. Everyone took out a large pickled onion – except Timmy who backed away at once. Onions were one thing he really couldn't bear. Dick put back the lid.

'I think somebody else ought to carry the onions, not Dick,' said Anne. 'There won't be many left by the time we reach our caravans!'

When they climbed over the stile at the bottom of the field the sun was going down. The evening star had appeared in the sky and twinkled brightly. As they trudged up to their caravans Julian stopped and pointed.

'Hallo! Look! There are two more caravans here – rather like ours. I wonder if it's the fair-folk arriving.'

'And there's another one, see – coming up the lane,' said Dick. 'It will have to go to the field-gate because it can't come the way we do – over the stile. There it goes.'

'We shall soon have plenty of exciting neighbours!' said Anne, pleased. They went up to their own caravans and looked curiously at the one that stood near theirs. It was yellow, picked out with blue and black, and could have done with a new coat of paint. It was very like their own caravans, but looked much older.

There didn't seem to be anyone about the newly arrived vans. The doors and windows were shut. The four stood and looked curiously at them.

'There's a big box under the nearest caravan,' said Julian. 'I wonder what's in it!'

The box was long, shallow and wide. On the sides were round holes, punched into it at intervals. George went to the caravan and bent down to look at the box, wondering if there was anything alive in it.

Timmy went with her, sniffing at the holes in curiosity. He suddenly backed away, and barked loudly. George put her hand on his collar to drag him off but he wouldn't go with her. He barked without stopping!

A noise came from inside the box – a rustling, dry, sliding sort of noise that made Timmy bark even more frantically.

'Stop it, Timmy! Stop it!' said George, tugging at him. 'Julian, come and help me. There's something in that box that Timmy has never met before – goodness knows what – and he's half-puzzled and half-scared. He's barking defiance – and he'll never stop unless we drag him away!'

An angry voice came from the bottom of the field by the stile. 'Hey you! Take that dog away! What do you mean by poking into my business – upsetting my snakes!'

'Oooh – snakes!' said Anne, retiring quickly to her own caravan. 'George, it's snakes in there. Do get Timmy away.'

Julian and George managed to drag Timmy away, half-choking him with his collar, though he didn't seem to notice this at all. The angry voice was now just behind them. George turned and saw a little dark man, middle-aged, with gleaming black eyes. He was shaking his fist, still shouting.

'Sorry,' said George, pulling Timmy harder. 'Please stop shouting, or my dog will go for you.'

'Go for me! He will go for me! You keep a dangerous dog like that, which smells out my snakes and will go for me!' yelled the angry little man, dancing about like a boxer on his toes. 'Ahhhhhh! Wait till I let out my snakes – and then your dog will run and run, and will never be seen again!'

This was a most alarming threat. With an enormous heave, Julian, Dick and George at last got Timmy under control, dragged him up the steps of Anne's caravan, and shut the door on him. Anne tried to quieten him, while the other three went out to the angry little man again.

He had dragged out the big, shallow box, and had opened the lid. The three watched, fascinated. What snakes had he in there? Rattlesnakes? Cobras? They were all ready to run for their lives if the snakes were as angry as their owner.

A great head reared itself out of the box, and swung itself from side to side. Two unblinking dark eyes gleamed – and then a long, long body writhed out and glided up the man's legs, round his waist and round his neck. He fondled it, talking in a low, caressing voice.

George shivered. Julian and Dick watched in amazement. 'It's a python,' said Julian. 'My, what a monster. I've never seen one so close before. I wonder it doesn't wind itself round that fellow and squeeze him to death.'

'He's got hold of it near the tail,' said Dick, watching. 'Oh, look – there's another one!'

Sure enough a second python slid out of the box, coil upon gleaming coil. It too wreathed itself round its owner, making a loud hissing noise as it did so. Its body was thicker than Julian's calf.

Anne was watching out of her caravan window, hardly able to believe her eyes. She had never in her life seen snakes as big as these. She didn't even know what they were. She began to wish their caravans were miles and miles away.

The little man quieted his snakes at last. They almost hid him with their great coils! From each side of his neck came a snake's head, flat and shining.

Timmy was now watching out of the window also, his head beside Anne's. He was amazed to see the gliding snakes, and stopped barking at once. He got down from the window and went under the table. Timmy didn't think he liked the look of these new creatures at all!

The man fondled the snakes and then, still speaking to them lovingly, got them back into their box again. They glided in, and piled themselves inside, coil upon coil. The man shut down the lid and locked it.

Then he turned to the three watching children. 'You see

how upset you make my snakes?' he said. 'Now you keep away, you hear? And you keep your dog away too. Ah, you children! Interfering, poking your noses, staring! I do not like children and nor do my snakes. You KEEP AWAY, SEE?'

He shouted the last words so angrily that the three jumped. 'Look here,' said Julian, 'we only came to say we were sorry our dog barked like that. Dogs always bark at strange things they don't know or understand. It's only natural.'

'Dogs, too, I hate,' said the little man, going into his caravan. 'You will keep him away from here, especially when I have my snakes out, or one might give him too loving a squeeze. Ha!'

He disappeared into his van and the door shut firmly.

'Not so good,' said Julian. 'We seem to have made a bad start with the fair-folk – and I had hoped they would be friendly and let us into some of their secrets.'

'I don't like the last thing he said,' said George, worried. 'A "loving squeeze" by one of those pythons would be the end of Timmy. I shall certainly keep him away when I see that funny little man taking out his snakes. He really seemed to *love* them, didn't he?'

'He certainly did,' said Julian. 'Well, I wonder who lives in the second newly arrived caravan. I feel I hardly dare even to look at it in case it contains gorillas or elephants or hippos, or . . .'

'Don't be an idiot,' said George. 'Come on, it's getting

dark. Hallo, here comes the caravan we saw down in the lane just now!'

It came slowly up the grassy hillside, bumping as it went. On the side was painted a name in large, scarlet letters.

'Mister India-rubber.'

'Oh – the rubber man!' said George. 'Dick – is he the driver, do you think?'

They all stared at the driver. He was long and thin and droopy, and he looked as if he might burst into tears at any moment. His horse looked rather the same.

'Well – he *might* be Mr India-rubber,' said Julian. 'But certainly there doesn't seem to be much *bounce* in him! Look – he's getting down.'

The man got down with a supple, loose grace that didn't seem to fit his droopy body at all. He took the horse out of the shafts and set it loose in the field. It wandered away, pulling here and there at the grass, still looking as sad and droopy as its master.

'Bufflo!' suddenly yelled the man. 'You in?'

The door of the second caravan opened and a young man looked out – a huge young man with a mop of yellow hair, a bright red shirt and a broad smile.

'Hiya, Rubber!' he called. 'We got here first. Come along in – Skippy's got some food ready.'

Mr India-rubber walked sadly up the steps of Bufflo's caravan. The door shut.

'This is really rather exciting,' said Dick. 'An india-rubber man – Bufflo and Skippy, whoever they may be – and a man with tame snakes next to us. Whatever next!'

Anne called to them. 'Do come in. Timmy's whining like anything.'

They went up the steps of her caravan and found that Anne had got ready a light supper for them – a ham sandwich each, a piece of fruit cake and an orange.

'I'll have a pickled onion with my sandwich, please,' said Dick. 'I'll chop it up and put it in with the ham. What wonderful ideas I do have, to be sure!'

CHAPTER FIVE

Night and morning

As THEY had their supper they talked about the strange new arrivals. Timmy sat close to George, trying to tell her that he was sorry for causing such a disturbance. She patted him and scolded him at the same time.

'I quite understand that you don't like the snakes, Timmy – but when I tell you to stop barking and come away you MUST do as you're told! Do you understand?'

Timmy's tail dropped and he put his big head on George's knee. He gave a little whine.

'I don't think he'll ever go near that box again, now he's seen the snakes that came out of it,' said Anne. 'You should have seen how scared he was when he looked out of the window with me and saw them. He went and hid under the table.'

'It's a pity we've made a bad start with the fair-folk,' said Julian. 'I don't expect they like children much, because as a rule the kids would make themselves an awful nuisance – peering here and poking there.'

'I think I can hear more caravans arriving,' said George, and Timmy pricked up his ears and growled. 'Be quiet, Timmy. We're not the only ones allowed in this field!'

Dick went to the window and peered out into the twilight. He saw some large dark shapes in another part of the field, looming out of the darkness. A little camp-fire burned brightly in front of one, showing a small figure bending over it.

'These are jolly good sandwiches, Anne,' said Dick. 'What about another pickled onion, everyone?'

'No, Dick,' said Anne firmly. 'You've eaten your sandwich.'

'Well, I can eat a pickled onion *without* a sandwich,

236

can't I?' said Dick. 'Hand over, Anne.'

Anne wouldn't. 'I've hidden them,' she said. 'You want some for tomorrow, don't you? Don't be greedy, Dick. Have a biscuit if you're still hungry.'

'I meant to ask if we could have a camp-fire outside tonight,' said George, remembering. 'But somehow I feel so sleepy I think I'd nod off if I sat by it!'

'I feel sleepy too,' said Anne. 'Let's clear up, George, and snuggle into our bunks. The boys can go to their caravan and read or play games if they want to.'

Dick yawned. 'Well – I might read for a bit,' he said. 'I hope you've got enough water, Anne, for the various things you use it for – because I do NOT intend to stumble over this dark field to the stream, and fall over snakes and anything else the fair-folk may have strewn carelessly about the grass!'

'You don't think those snakes could get loose, do you?' said Anne, anxiously.

'Of course not!' said Julian. 'Anyway, Timmy will bark the place down if even a hedgehog comes roving by, so you don't need to worry about snakes!'

The boys said good night and went off to their own caravan. The girls saw a light suddenly shine out there, and shadows moved across the curtains drawn over the windows.

'Dick's lit their lamp,' said Anne. Theirs was already lit, and the caravan looked cosy and friendly. Anne showed George how to put up her bunk. It clicked into place, felt nice and firm and was most inviting-looking.

The girls made their beds in the bunks, putting in sheets and blankets and rugs. 'Where's my pillow?' asked George. 'Oh – it's a cushion in the daytime, is it? What a good idea!'

She and Anne took the covers off the two cushions in the chairs, and underneath were the pillow-cases over the pillows, ready for the night!

They undressed, washed in stream water in the little sink, cleaned their teeth and brushed their hair. 'Does the water go under the caravan when I pull the plug out of the sink?' said George. 'Here goes!'

The water gurgled out and splashed on the ground under the van. Timmy pricked up his ears and listened. He could see that he would have to get used to quite a lot of new noises here!

'Got your torch?' said Anne when at last they had both got into their bunks. 'I'm going to blow out the lamp. If you want anything in the night you'll have to put on your torch, George. Look at Timmy sitting on the floor still! He doesn't realise we've gone to bed! Tim – are you waiting for us to go upstairs?'

Timmy thumped his tail on the floor. That was just exactly what he *was* waiting for. When George went to bed she *always* went upstairs, whether she was at school or at home – and though he hadn't managed to discover any stairs in the caravan yet, he was sure that George knew where they were!

238

It took Timmy a few minutes to realise that George was going to sleep for the night in the bunk she had put up against the wall. Then, with one bound he was on top of her, and settled down on her legs. She gave a groan.

'Oh, Timmy – you *are* rough! Get off my legs – get further down – get into the curve of my knees.'

Timmy found the bunk too small to be really comfortable. However he managed to curl himself up in as small a space as possible, put his head down on one of George's knees, gave one of his heavy sighs, and fell asleep.

He had one ear open all the time, though – an ear for a rat that for some peculiar reason ran over the roof – an ear for a daring rabbit that nibbled the grass under the caravan – and a very alert ear for a big cockchafer that flew straight into the glass pane of the right-hand window, just above George's bunk.

Plang! It collided with the pane, and fell back, stunned. Timmy couldn't for the life of him think what it was, but soon fell asleep again, still with one ear open. The blackbird in the hawthorn tree woke him up early. It had thought of a perfectly new melody, and was trying it out very loudly and deliberately. A thrush nearby joined in.

'Mind how you do it, mind how you do it!' sang the thrush at the top of its voice. Timmy sat up and stretched. George woke up at once, because Timmy trod heavily on her middle.

She couldn't think where she was at first, then she remembered and smiled. Of course – in a caravan, with

Anne. How that blackbird sang – a better song than the thrush! Cows mooed in the distance, and the early morning sun slid in through the window and picked out the clock and the bowl of primroses.

Timmy settled down. If George wasn't going to get up neither was he! George shut her eyes and fell asleep again too. Outside, the camp began to awake. Caravan doors opened. Fires were lit. Somebody went down to the stream to get water.

The boys came banging at the door of the girls' caravan. 'Come on, sleepyheads! It's half past seven, and we're hungry!'

'Goodness!' said Anne, sitting up, bright-eyed with sleep. 'George! Wake up!'

It wasn't long before they were all sitting round a little fire, from which came a very nice smell. Dick was frying bacon and eggs, and the smell made everyone very hungry. Anne had boiled a kettle on her little stove, and made some tea. She came down the steps with a tray on which she had put the teapot and hot water.

'Anne always does things properly,' said Dick. 'Here, hold your plate out, Ju – your bacon's done. Take your nose out of the way, Timmy, you silly dog – you'll get it splashed with hot fat again. Do look after Timmy when I'm cooking, George. He's already wolfed one slice of bacon.'

'Well, it saved you cooking it,' said George. 'I say, aren't there a lot of caravans here now? They must have come last night.'

They stared round at the field. Besides the snakeman's caravan, and Bufflo's and Mr India-rubber's, there were four or five more.

One interested the children very much. It was a brilliant yellow with red flames painted on the sides. The name on it was 'Alfredo, the Fire-Eater'.

'I imagine him to be a great big fierce chap,' said Dick. 'A regular fire-eater, with a terribly ferocious temper, an enormous voice and a great stride when he walks.'

'He will probably be a skinny little fellow who trots along like a pony,' said Julian.

'There's someone coming out of his caravan now,' said George. 'Look.'

'It's a woman,' said Anne. 'His wife, I expect. How tiny she is – rather sweet. She looks Spanish, she's so dark.'

'*This* must be the fire-eater, coming behind her,' said George. 'Surely it is! And he's JUST like you imagined him, Dick. How clever of you!'

A great big fellow came down the steps behind his tiny wife. He certainly looked very fierce, for he had a lion-like mane of tawny hair, and a big red face with large, gleaming eyes. He took enormous strides as he went, and his little wife had to run to keep up with him.

'*Just* my idea of a fire-eater,' said Dick, pleased. 'I think we'll keep out of his way until we know if he also dislikes children, like the snake-man. What a tiny wife he has! I bet he makes her run around him, and wait on him hand and foot.'

'Well, he's fetching water from the stream for her, anyway,' said Anne. 'Two huge pails. My word, he really does look like a fire-eater, doesn't he?'

'There's somebody else, look,' said Dick. 'Now who would *he* be? Look at him going to the stream – he walks like a tiger or a cat – all slinky and powerful.'

'The man who can set himself free from ropes no matter how he's tied!' said Anne. 'I'm sure he is.'

It was most exciting to watch the new arrivals. They all seemed to know one another. They stopped to talk, they laughed, they visited one another's caravans, and finally three of the women set off together with baskets.

'Going off to shop,' said Anne. 'That's what *I* ought to do. Coming, George? There's a bus that goes down to the village in about ten minutes. We can easily clear up when we come back.'

'Right,' said George, and got up too. 'What are the boys going to do while we're gone?'

'Oh, fetch more water, find sticks for the fire, and see to their own bunks,' said Anne, airily.

'Are we *really*?' said Dick, grinning. 'Well, we might. On the other hand, we might not. Anyway, you two go, because food is getting rather low. A very serious thought, that! Anne, get me some more toothpaste, will you? And if you can spot some of those doughnuts at the dairy, bring a dozen back with you.'

'Yes – and see if you can get a tin of pineapple,' said Julian. 'Don't forget we want milk too.'

'If you want many more things you'll have to come and help us carry them,' said Anne. 'Anything else?'

'Call at the post office and see if there are any letters,' said Dick. 'And don't forget to buy a paper. We may as well find out if anything has happened in the outside world! Not that I feel I can take much interest in it at the moment.'

'Right,' said Anne. 'Come on, George – we shall miss that bus!' And off they went with Timmy at their heels.

CHAPTER SIX

Unfriendly folk

THE TWO boys decided they *would* fetch the water and stack up some firewood while the girls were gone. They 'made' their bunks too, by the simple process of dragging off all the clothes and bundling them on the shelf, and then letting down the bunks against the wall.

That done there didn't seem much else to do except wait for the girls. So they took a walk round the field. They kept a good distance from the snake-man, who was doing something peculiar to one of his pythons.

'It *looks* as if he's polishing it, but he surely can't be,' said Julian. 'I'd like to go near enough to watch but he's such a hot-tempered little fellow he might quite well set one of those enormous pythons on to us!'

The snake-man was sitting on a box, with one snake spread over his knee, some of its coils round one of his legs, the other coils round his waist. The head appeared to be under his armpit. The man was rubbing away hard at the snake's scaly body, and it really seemed as if the python was enjoying it!

Bufflo was doing something with a whip. It had a magnificent handle, set with semi-precious stones that caught the sun and glittered in many colours.

'Look at the lash,' said Julian. 'Yards and yards long! I'd like to see him crack it!'

Almost as if he heard him, Bufflo got to his feet, and swung the great whip in his hand. Then he raised it – and a moment later there was a sound exactly like a pistol-shot! The lash cracked as it was whipped through the air, and the two boys jumped, not expecting such a loud noise.

Bufflo cracked it again. Then he whistled and a small plump woman came to the steps of his caravan.

'You mended it yet?' she called.

'Perhaps,' said Bufflo. 'Get a cigarette, Skippy. Hurry!'

Skippy put her hand into the caravan, felt along a shelf, and brought out a packet of cigarettes. She didn't go down the steps, but stood there, holding out the cigarette between her finger and thumb.

Bufflo swung his whip. CRACK! The cigarette disappeared as if by magic! The boys stared in amazement. Surely the end of the lash hadn't whipped that cigarette from Skippy's fingers? It didn't seem possible.

'There it is,' said Bufflo, pointing some distance away. 'Hold it again, Skippy. I reckon this whip is okay now.'

Skippy picked up the cigarette and put it in her mouth!

'No!' called Bufflo. 'I ain't sure enough of this lash yet. You hold it like you did.'

Skippy took it out of her mouth and held out the cigarette in her finger and thumb once more.

CRACK! Like a pistol-shot the whip cracked again, and once more the cigarette disappeared.

'Aw, Bufflo – you've gone and broken it in half,' said Skippy, reproachfully, pointing to where it lay on the ground, neatly cut in half. 'That was real careless of you.'

Bufflo said nothing. He merely turned his back on Skippy, and set to work on his lash again, though what he was doing neither of the boys could make out. They went a little nearer to see.

Bufflo had his back to them but he must have heard them coming. 'You clear out,' he said, hardly raising his voice. 'No kids allowed round here. Clear out – or I'll crack my whip and take the top hairs off your head!'

Julian and Dick felt perfectly certain he would be able to carry out his threat, and they retreated with as much dignity as they could. 'I suppose the snake-man told him what a disturbance old Timmy made yesterday with the snakes,' said Dick. 'I hope it won't spoil things for us with all the fair-folk.'

They went across the field and on the way met Mr India-rubber. They couldn't help staring at him. He honestly looked as if he were made of rubber – he was a curious grey, the grey of an ordinary school rubber, and his skin looked rubbery too.

He scowled at the two boys. 'Clear out,' he said. 'No kids allowed in our field.'

Julian was annoyed. 'It's our field as much as yours,' he said. 'We've got a couple of caravans here – those over there.'

'Well, this has always *been* our field,' said Mr India-rubber. 'So you clear out to the next one.'

'We haven't any horses to pull our caravans, even if we wanted to go, which we don't,' retorted Julian, angrily. 'Anyway, why should you object to us? We'd like to be friendly. We shan't do you any harm, or make a nuisance of ourselves.'

'Us-folk and you-folk don't mix,' said the man, obstinately. 'We don't want you here – nor them posh caravans down there, neither,' and he pointed to the three modern caravans in one corner of the field. 'This has always been *our* field.'

'Don't let's argue about it,' said Dick, who had been looking at the man with the greatest curiosity. 'Are you really so rubbery that you can wriggle in and out of pipes and things? Do you –'

But he didn't have time to finish his question because the rubber-man flung himself down on the ground, did a few strange contortions, flicked himself between the boys' legs – and there they both were, flat on the ground! The rubber-man was walking off, looking quite pleased with himself.

'Well!' said Dick, feeling a bump on his head. 'I tried to grab his legs and they honestly felt like rubber! I say – what a pity these people resent us being in their field. It's not going to be very pleasant to have them all banded against us. Not fair either. I should *like* to be friendly.'

'Well, perhaps it's just a case of us-folk and you-folk,' said Julian. 'There's a lot of that kind of feeling about these days, and it's so silly. We're all the same under the skin. We've always got on well with anyone before.'

They hardly liked to go near the other caravans, though they longed to have a closer view of Alfredo the Fire-Eater.

'He looked so *exactly* like what I imagined a fire-eater ought to be,' said Dick. 'I should think he's probably chief of all the fair-folk here – if they've got a chief.'

'Look – here he comes!' said Julian. And sure enough, round the corner came Alfredo, running fast. He came towards the boys, and Julian at first thought that he was coming to chase them away. He didn't mean to run from Alfredo, but it wasn't very pleasant standing still, either, with this enormous fellow racing towards them, his cheeks as red as fire, his great mane of hair flopping up and down.

And then they saw why Alfredo was running! After him came his tiny little dark wife. She was shrieking at him in a foreign language, and was chasing him with a saucepan!

Alfredo lumbered by the two boys, looking scared out of his life. He went down to the stile, leapt over it and disappeared down the lane.

The little dark woman watched him go. When he turned to look round she waved the saucepan at him.

'Big bad one!' she cried. 'You burn breakfast again! Again, again! I bang you with saucepan, big bad one. Come, Alfredo, come!'

248

But Alfredo had no intention of coming. The angry little woman turned to the two boys. 'He burn breakfast,' she said. 'He no watch, he burn always.'

'It seems odd for a fire-eater to burn something he's cooking,' said Julian. 'Though, on second thoughts, perhaps it's not!'

'Poof! Fire-eating, it is easy!' said Alfredo's hot-tempered little wife. 'Cooking is not so easy. It needs brains and eyes and hands. But Fredo, he has no brains, his hands are clumsy – he can only eat fire, and what use is that?'

'Well – I suppose he makes money by it,' said Dick, amused.

'He is my big bad one,' said the little woman. She turned to go and then turned back again with a sudden smile. 'But he is very good sometimes,' she said.

She went back to her caravan. The boys looked at one another. 'Poor Alfredo,' said Dick. 'He looks as brave as a lion, and he's certainly a giant of a man – but he's as timid as a mouse. Fancy running away from that tiny little woman.'

'Well, I'm not so sure I wouldn't too, if she came bounding over the field after me, brandishing that dangerous-looking saucepan,' said Julian. 'Ah – who's this?'

The man that Anne had thought might be the one who could set himself free when bound with ropes was coming up from the stile. He walked easily and lightly, really very like a cat. Julian glanced at his hands – they were small but looked very strong. Yes – he could certainly undo knots with hands like that. They gazed at him curiously.

'No kids allowed here,' said the man, as he came up.

'Sorry, but we're caravanners too,' said Dick. 'I say – are you the fellow that can undo ropes when he's tied up in them?'

'Could be,' said the man, and walked on. He turned round suddenly. 'Like me to tie *you* up?' he called. 'I've a good mind to try. Don't you try interfering with us, or I'll do it!'

'Dear me – what a nice, pleasant lot they are!' said Julian. 'Quite different from the other circus folk we've known. I begin to feel we shan't make friends as fast as I thought!'

'We'd better be careful, I think,' said Dick. 'They seem to resent us, goodness knows why. They may make things jolly unpleasant. Don't let's snoop round any more this morning. Let's keep away from them till they get a bit used to us. Then perhaps they'll be more friendly.'

'We'll go and meet the girls,' said Julian. So they went down to the stile and walked to the bus-stop. The bus came panting up the hill at that very moment, and the girls stepped off, with the three fair-women behind them.

The girls joined the boys. 'We've done a lot of shopping,' said Anne. 'Our baskets are awfully heavy. Thanks, Julian, if you'll carry mine. Dick can take George's. Did you see those women who got off with us?'

'Yes,' said Julian. 'Why?'

'Well, we tried to talk to them but they were very unfriendly,' said Anne. 'We felt quite uncomfortable. And Timmy growled like anything, of course, which made things worse. I don't think he liked the smell of them.'

'*We* didn't get on too well either, with the rest of the fair-folk,' said Julian. 'In fact I can't say that Dick and I were a success at all. All they wanted us to do was to clear out.'

'I got a paper for you,' said Anne, 'and George found a letter at the post office from her mother. It's addressed to all of us so we didn't open it. We'll read it when we get to the caravans.'

'I *hope* it's nearly time for dinner,' said George. 'What do *you* think, Timmy?'

Timmy knew the word dinner! He gave a joyful bark and led the way. Dinner? There couldn't be a better idea!

CHAPTER SEVEN

A letter – a walk – and a shock

GEORGE OPENED her mother's letter when they had finished their meal. Everyone voted that it was a truly wizard lunch – two hard-boiled eggs each, fresh lettuce, tomatoes, mustard and cress, and potatoes baked in the fire in their jackets – followed by what Julian had asked for – slices of tinned pineapple, very sweet and juicy.

'Very nice,' said Julian, lying back in the sun. 'Anne, you're a jolly good housekeeper. Now, George, let's hear what Aunt Fanny has got to say in her letter.'

George unfolded the notepaper and smoothed it out. 'It's to all of us,' she said.

'DEAR GEORGE, ANNE, JULIAN AND DICK,

'I hope George arrived safely and that you all met her. I am really writing to remind George that it is her grandmother's birthday on Saturday, and she must write to her. I forgot to remind George before she went, so thought I must quickly send a letter.

'George, your father is very much upset to read about those two missing scientists. He knows Derek Terry-Kane very well, and worked with him for some time. He says he is absolutely sure that he isn't a traitor to his country; he thinks he has been spirited away somewhere, and Jeffrey Pottersham too – probably in a plane miles away by now, in a country that will force them to give up their secrets. It's just as well you went off today, because this afternoon your father is striding about all over the place, talking nineteen to the dozen, and banging every door he comes to, bless him.

'If you write, please don't mention scientists, as I am hoping he will calm down soon. He really is very upset, and keeps on saying, "What is the world coming to?" when he knows quite well that it's coming to exactly what the scientists plan it to come to.

'Have a good time, all of you, and DON'T forget to write to your grandmother, George!

'Your loving,

Mother (Aunt Fanny).'

'I can just see Father striding about like a – like a . . .'

'Fire-eater,' said Julian with a grin, as George stopped for a word. 'He'll drive Aunt Fanny into chasing him around with a saucepan one day! Funny business about these scientists though, isn't it? After all, Terry-Kane *had* planned to leave the country – got his aeroplane ticket and everything – so although your father believes in him, George, it honestly looks a bit fishy, doesn't it?'

'Anything in the paper about it?' asked Dick, and shook it open. 'Yes – here we are:

MISSING SCIENTISTS

It is now certain that Jeffrey Pottersham was in the pay of a country unfriendly to us, and was planning to join Terry-Kane on his journey abroad. Nothing has been heard of the two men, although reports that they have been seen in many places abroad have been received.

'That rather settles it,' said Julian. 'Two Really Bad Eggs. Look – here are their photographs.'

The four leant over the paper, looking at the pictures of the two men. 'Well, I should have thought *anyone* would recognise Terry-Kane if they saw him,' said Anne. 'Those big, thick, arched eyebrows, and that enormous forehead. If I saw anyone with eyebrows like that I'd think they weren't real!'

'He'll shave them off,' said Dick. 'Then he'll look completely different. Probably stick them on his upper lip upside down and use them for moustaches!'

'Don't be silly,' said George, with a giggle. 'The other fellow is very ordinary-looking, except for his dome of a head. Pity none of us four have got great foreheads – I suppose we must be rather stupid people!'

'We're not so bad,' said Julian. 'We've had to use our brains many times in all our adventures – and we haven't come off so badly!'

'Let's clear up and then go for a walk again,' said Anne. 'If we don't I shall fall asleep. This sun is so gloriously hot, it's really cooking me.'

'Yes – we'd better go for a walk,' said Julian, getting up. 'Shall we go and see the castle, do you think? Or shall we leave that for another day?'

'Leave it,' said Anne. 'I honestly don't feel like clambering up that steep hill just now. I think the morning would be a better time!'

They cleared up and then locked the two caravans and set out. Julian looked back. Some of the fair-folk were sitting together, eating a meal. They watched the children in silence. It wasn't very pleasant somehow.

'They don't exactly love us, do they?' said Dick. 'Now you listen, Timmy – don't you go accepting any titbits from people here, see?'

'Oh, Dick!' said George, in alarm, 'you surely don't think they would harm Timmy?'

'No, I don't really,' said Dick. 'But we might as well be careful. As the rubber-man pointed out to us this morning, us-folk and his-folk think differently about some things. It just can't be helped. But I do wish they'd let us be friendly. I don't like this kind of thing.'

'Well, anyway I shall keep Timmy to heel all the time,' said George, making up her mind firmly. 'Timmy, to heel!' Please understand that as long as we are in the caravan field you must walk to heel! *Do* you understand?'

'Woof-woof,' said Timmy, and immediately kept so close to George's ankles that his nose kept bumping into them.

They decided to catch the bus to Tinkers' Green, and then walk from there to the sea. They would have time to get there and back before dark. The bus was waiting at the corner, and they ran to catch it. It was about two miles to Tinkers' Green, which was a dear little village, with a proper green and a duck-pond with white ducks swimming on it.

'Shall we have an ice-cream?' suggested Dick as they came to a grocer's shop with an ice-cream sign outside it.

'No,' said Julian firmly. 'We've just had an enormous lunch, and we'll save up ice-cream for tea-time. We shall never get down to the sea if we sit and eat ice-creams half the afternoon!'

It was a lovely walk, down violet-studded lanes, and then over a heathery common with clumps of primroses in the hollows – and even a few very very early bluebells, much to Anne's delight.

'There's the sea! Oh, what a dear little bay!' said Anne,

257

in delight. 'And isn't it blue – as blue as cornflowers. We could almost bathe.'

'You wouldn't like it if you did,' said Julian. 'The sea would be as cold as ice! Come on – let's get down to the little jetty and have a look at the fishing-boats.'

They went down to the sun-warmed stone jetty and began talking to the fishermen there. Some were sitting in the sun mending their nets, and were very willing to talk.

'How nice to have a bit of friendliness shown us instead of the stares and rudeness of the fair-folk!' said Dick to Julian, who nodded and agreed.

A fisherman took them on his boat, and explained a lot of things they already knew and some they didn't. It was nice to sit and listen to his broad speech, and to watch his bright blue eyes as he talked. He was as brown as an oak-apple.

'Could we ever hire a boat here if we wanted to?' asked Julian. 'Is there one we could manage by ourselves? We are quite good at sailing.'

'Old Joseph there has a boat he could hire out if you wanted one,' said the man they were talking to. 'He hired it out the other day, and I expect he'd hire it out to you too if you think you can really manage it.'

'Thanks. We'll ask him, if we ever decided to go out,' said Julian. He looked at his watch. 'We'd better go and get some tea somewhere. We want to be home before dark. We're camping over at Faynights Castle.'

'Oh ay?' said the fisherman. 'You've got the fair-folk there now, haven't you? They were here two weeks since.

258

My, that fire-eater is a fair treat, he is! And that rope-man
– well! I tell you this – I tied him up in my fishing-line –
you can see it here, strong as two ropes it is! I tied him up
with all the knots I know – and in under a minute he stood
up and the line fell off him, knots and all!'

'Ay, that is so,' said the old fellow called Joseph. 'A
wonder he is, that man. So is the rubber fellow. He called

for a drain-pipe, narrow as this, see? And he wriggled through it, quick as an eel. Fair scared me, it did, to see him wriggling out of the other end.'

'We'll go and see them perform when they begin their show,' said Julian. 'At the moment they're not very friendly towards us. They don't like us being in their field.'

'They keeps themselves to themselves,' said Joseph. 'They had a heap of trouble at the place they were in before they came to us – someone set the police on them, and now they won't make friends with anyone.'

'Well, we must go,' said Julian, and they said goodbye to the friendly fishermen and went. They stopped and had tea at a little tea-shop, and then made their way home. 'Anyone want to take the bus?' said Julian. 'We can easily get home before dark if we walk – but if the girls are tired we'll bus from Tinkers' Green.'

'Of *course* we're not tired!' said George, indignantly. 'Have you *ever* known me say I'm tired, Julian?'

'All right, all right – it was just a bit of politeness on my part,' said Julian. 'Come on – let's get going.'

The way was longer than they had thought. It was getting dark when they got to the stile that led into the caravan field. They climbed over it and made their way slowly to their corner.

And then they suddenly stopped and stared. They looked all round and stared again.

Their two caravans were gone! They could see the places

where they had stood, and where their fire had been. But no caravans stood there now!

'*Well!*' said Julian, astounded. 'This beats everything! Are we dreaming? I can't see a sign of our caravans anywhere!'

'Yes – but – *how* could they go?' said Anne, almost stammering in her surprise. 'I mean – we had no horses to pull them away anywhere! They couldn't go just by themselves.'

There was a silence. The four were completely bewildered. How could two large, solid caravans disappear into thin air?

'Look – there are wheel-marks in the grass,' said Dick suddenly. 'See – our caravans went this way – come on, follow. Down the hillside, look!'

In the greatest astonishment the four children and Timmy followed the wheel-marks. Julian glanced back once, feeling that they were being watched. But not one of the fair-folk was to be seen. Perhaps they are watching silently behind their caravan curtains, Julian thought, uncomfortably.

The wheel-marks went right down the field and reached the gate. It was shut now, but it must have been opened for the two caravans, because there were marks in the grass by the gate, marks that passed through it and then were lost in the lane.

'What are we to do?' said Anne, scared. 'They're gone! We've nowhere to sleep. Oh, Julian – what are we going to *do*?'

CHAPTER EIGHT

Where are the caravans?

FOR ONCE in a way Julian was quite at a loss what to do! It looked as if someone had stolen the two caravans – taken them right away somewhere!

'I suppose we'd better ring up the police,' he said. 'They'll watch out for the two caravans, and arrest the thieves. But that won't help us much for tonight! We've got to find somewhere to sleep.'

'I think we ought to go and tackle one or two of the fair-folk,' said Dick. 'Even if they have got nothing to do with the theft they *must* have seen the caravans being taken away.'

'Yes. I think you're right,' said Julian. 'They must know *something* about it. George, you stay here with Anne, in case the fair people are rude. We'll take Timmy – he may be useful!'

George didn't want to stay behind – but she could see that Anne did! So she stayed with her, straining her eyes after the two boys as they went back up the hill with Timmy close behind.

'Don't let's go to the snake-man,' said Dick. 'He might be playing with his snakes in his caravan!'

'What possible game can you play with snakes?' said Julian. 'Or are you thinking of snakes and ladders?'

'Funny joke,' said Dick, politely. 'Look – there's somebody by a camp-fire – Bufflo, I think. No, it's Alfredo. Well, we know he isn't as fierce as he looks – let's tackle *him* about the caravans.'

They went up to the big fire-eater, who was sitting smoking by the fire. He didn't hear them coming and jumped violently when Julian spoke to him.

'Mr Alfredo,' began Julian, 'could you tell us where our two caravans have gone? We found them missing when we got back just now.'

'Ask Bufflo,' said Alfredo, gruffly, not looking at them.

'But don't *you* know anything about them?' persisted Julian.

'Ask Bufflo,' said Alfredo, blowing out clouds of smoke.

Julian and Dick turned away, annoyed, and went over to Bufflo's caravan. It was shut. They knocked on the door, and Bufflo appeared, his mop of golden hair gleaming in the lamplight.

'Mr Bufflo,' began Julian politely again, 'Mr Alfredo told us to come and ask you about our caravans, which are missing, and . . .'

'Ask the rubber-man,' said Bufflo, shortly, and slammed the door. Julian was angry. He knocked again. The window opened and Skippy, Bufflo's little wife, looked out.

'You go and ask Mr India-rubber,' she called, and shut the window with what sounded suspiciously like a giggle.

'Is this a silly trick they're playing on us?' said Dick fiercely.

'Looks like it,' said Julian. 'Well, we'll try the rubber-man. Come on. He's the last one we'll try, though!'

They went to the rubber-man's caravan, and rapped smartly on the door. 'Who's there?' came the voice of Mr India-rubber.

'Come out – we want to ask you something,' said Julian.

'Who's there?' said the rubber-man again.

'You know jolly well who we are,' said Julian, raising his voice. 'Our caravans have been stolen, and we want to find out who took them. If you won't give us any help, we're going to telephone the police.'

The door opened and the rubber-man stood on the top of the steps, looking down at Julian. 'Nobody has stolen them,' he said. 'Nobody at all. You go and ask the snake-man.'

'If you think we're going round asking every single person in this camp, you're mistaken!' said Julian, angrily. 'I don't *want* to go to the police – we wanted to be friends with you fair-folk, not enemies. This is all very silly. If the caravans *are* stolen we've no choice but to go to the police – and I don't imagine you want them after you again! We know they were put on to you a few weeks back.'

'You know too much,' said the rubber-man, in a very surly voice. 'Your caravans are *not* stolen. I will show you where they are.'

He came lightly down the steps of his caravan and walked in front of the two boys in the half-darkness. He went across the grassy hillside, making for where the children's caravans had stood.

'Where are you taking us?' called Julian. 'We know the vans are not there! Please don't act the idiot – there's been enough of that already.'

The man said nothing, but walked on. The boys and Timmy could do nothing but follow. Timmy was not happy. He kept up a continuous low growling, like far-off thunder. The rubber-man took not the slightest notice. Julian wondered idly if he didn't fear dogs because they wouldn't be able to bite rubber!

The man took them to the hedge that ran at one side of the field, beyond where the two caravans had stood. Julian began to feel exasperated. He knew perfectly well that the two vans had been taken down to the field-gate and out into the lane – then why was this fellow leading them in the opposite direction?

The rubber-man forced his way through the hedge, and the boys followed – and there, just the other side, two big, dark shapes loomed up in the twilight – the caravans!

'Well!' said Julian, taken aback. 'What *was* the idea of putting the caravans here, in the next field?'

'Us-folk and you-folk don't mix,' said the man. 'We don't like kids messing about. Three weeks ago we had a canary-man, with over a hundred canaries that gave a show with him – and some kids opened all the cages one night and set them loose.'

'Oh,' said Julian. 'They'd die, of course, if they were set loose – they don't know how to look for their own food. That was bad luck. But *we* don't do things like that.'

'No kids allowed with us now,' said the rubberman. 'That's why we put horses into your vans, took them down to the field-gate, and up into the next field – and here they are. We thought you'd be back in the daylight and would see them.'

'Well, it's nice to find you can be chatty, all of a sudden,' said Julian. 'Don't growl any more, Timmy. It's all right. We've found our vans!'

The rubber-man disappeared without another word. They heard him squeezing easily through the hedge. Julian took out the key to his caravan, went up the steps and opened the door. He rummaged about and found his torch. He switched it on and shone it round. Nothing had been disturbed.

'Well – so that's that,' he said. 'Just a bit of spite on the part of the fair-folk, I suppose – punishing us for what those horrid kids did to the canaries. I must say it was a shame to open those cages – half the poor little creatures must have died. I don't *like* birds put in cages – but canaries can't live in this country unless they are looked after, it's cruel to let them go loose, and starve.'

'I agree with you,' said Dick. They were now walking down the hillside to a gap in the hedge through which the vans must have been pulled up the hill. George and Anne would be most relieved to hear they had found the caravans!

Julian gave a whistle, and George answered it at once. 'We're still here, Julian! What's happened?'

'We've got the caravans,' shouted back Julian, cheerily. 'They're in this field.'

The girls joined them at once, most surprised to hear this news. Julian explained.

'The fair-folk really have got a hate on against children,' he said. 'Apparently they had a canary-man, whose show consisted of singing canaries – and some kids set all the birds loose one night – so half of them died. And now the fair-folk won't have children anywhere near them.'

'I suppose the snake-man is afraid of us setting his snakes loose,' said Dick, with a chuckle. 'Well, thank goodness we've found the vans. I had a feeling we might have to sleep in a haystack tonight!'

'I wouldn't have minded that,' said George. 'I like haystacks.'

'We'll light a fire and cook something,' said Julian. 'I feel hungry after all this upset.'

'I don't,' said Anne. 'I hate feeling that the fair-folk won't be friends. It's silly of them. We're not used to that.'

'Yes – but they're rather like children themselves,' said Julian. 'Somebody does something unkind to them, so they get sulky, and wait for a chance to hit back – and then someone set the police on them, too, don't forget – they're very touchy at the moment, I imagine.'

'Well, it's a pity,' said George, watching Dick light a camp-fire very efficiently. 'I was looking forward to having a good time with them. Do you suppose the farmer will mind us being here?'

'Oh – I never thought of that.' said Julian. 'This may not be a camping field. I hope to goodness we don't have an angry farmer shouting at us tomorrow!'

'And, oh dear, we are so far away from the stream now,' said Anne. 'It's on the other side of the field where we were – and we do badly want water.'

'We'll have to do without it tonight,' said Dick firmly. 'I don't want the top of my hair taken off by Bufflo, or a rope tying up my legs, thrown by the rope-man, or a snake wriggling after me. I bet those fair-folk will be on the watch for us to fetch water. This is all very silly.'

WHERE ARE THE CARAVANS?

They had rather a solemn meal. Things had suddenly begun to seem rather complicated. They *couldn't* go to the police about such a silly thing – nor did they want to. But if the farmer wanted to turn them out of this field, how could they go back to their first camping place? Nobody wanted to live in a camp surrounded by enemies!

'We'll sleep on it,' said Julian, at last. 'Don't worry, you girls. We'll find a way out of this problem. We are pretty good at getting out of difficulties. Never say die!'

'Woof,' said Timmy, agreeing heartily. George patted him.

'That's one of *your* mottoes, isn't it, Timmy?' she said.

'And another motto of his is "Let sleeping dogs lie",' said Dick, with a broad grin. 'He hates being woken up when he's having a nice nap, dreaming of millions of rabbits to catch!'

'Well, talking of naps, what about getting into our bunks?' said Julian, with a yawn. 'We've had a good long walk today, and I'm tired. I'm going to lie in my bunk and read.'

Everyone thought this a very good idea. They cleared up the supper things, and the girls said good night to the boys. They went into the caravan with Timmy.

'I do hope this holiday isn't going to be a failure,' said Anne, as she got into her bunk. George gave one of her snorts.

'A failure! You wait and see! I've a feeling it will turn out to be *super*.'

269

CHAPTER NINE

A great surprise

IT DIDN'T seem as if George's feeling that the holiday was going to be 'super' was at all correct the next morning. A loud rapping came on the door of the boys' caravan before they were even awake!

Then a large red face looked in at the window, startling Julian considerably.

'Who gave you permission to camp here?' said the face, looking as black as thunder.

Julian went to the door in his pyjamas. 'Do you own this field?' he said, politely. 'Well, we were camping in the next field, and . . .'

'That's let for campers and caravanners,' said the man, who was dressed like a farmer. 'This isn't.'

'As I said, we were in the next field,' repeated Julian, 'and for some reason the fair-folk there didn't like us – and when we were out they brought our caravans here! As we've no horses to take them away, we couldn't do anything else but stay!'

'Well, you *can't* stay,' said the farmer. 'I don't let out this field. I use it for my cows. You'll have to go today, or I'll put your caravans out into the road.'

'Yes, but look here . . .' began Julian, and then stopped.

The farmer had walked off, a determined figure in riding-breeches and tweed coat. The girls opened their window and called to Julian.

'We heard what he said. Isn't he mean? *Now* what are we going to do?'

'We're going to get up and have breakfast,' said Julian. 'And then I'm going to give the fair-folk one more chance – they'll have to lend us two horses – and pull us back into our rightful place. Otherwise I very much fear I shall have to get help from the police!'

'Oh, dear,' said Anne. 'I do hate this kind of thing. We were having such a lovely time before the fair people

271

arrived. But it seems quite impossible to get them to be friends with us.'

'Quite,' said Julian. 'I'm not so sure *I* want to be friendly now, either. I'd rather give up this holiday altogether and go back home than have continual trouble going on round us! Dick and I will go and tackle the fair-folk after breakfast.'

Breakfast was just as solemn as supper had been. Julian was rather silent. He was thinking what was best to say to the sullen folk in the next field. 'You must take Timmy with you,' said George, voicing the thoughts of everyone.

Julian and Dick set off with Timmy about half past eight. All the fair people were up and about, and the smoke of their fires rose up in the morning air.

Julian thought he would go and tackle the fire-eater, so the two boys went towards his caravan. The other fair people looked up, and one by one left their vans or their fires and closed round the boys. Timmy bared his teeth and growled.

'Mr Alfredo,' began Julian, 'the farmer is turning us out of that field. We must come back here. We want you to lend us two horses for our vans.'

A ripple of laughter spread through the listening people. Mr Alfredo answered politely, with a large smile on his face. 'What a pity! We don't hire out our horses!'

'I don't want to hire them from you,' said Julian, patiently. 'It's up to you to let us have them to bring back our vans. Otherwise – well, I shall *have* to go and ask the police for help. Those caravans don't belong to us, you know.'

There was an angry murmur from the listening crowd. Timmy growled more loudly. One or two of the fair-folk stepped back hurriedly when they heard him.

CRACK! Julian turned quickly. The fair people ran back, and the two boys found that they were facing Bufflo, who, with a large and unpleasant grin on his face, was swinging his whip in his hand.

CRACK! Julian jumped violently, for a few hairs from the top of his head were suddenly whisked off into the air – the end of the lash had neatly cut them away!

The crowd laughed loudly. Timmy bared his white teeth, and snarled.

Dick put his hand down on the dog's collar. 'Do that again and I shan't be able to hold the dog!' he called, warningly.

Julian stood there, at a loss to know what to do next. He couldn't *bear* turning tail and going off to the accompaniment of jeers and howls. He was so full of rage that he couldn't say a word.

And then something happened. Something so utterly unexpected that nobody did anything at all except let it happen!

A boyish figure came running up the grass hillside – someone very like George, with short curly hair and a very freckled face – someone dressed, however, in a short grey skirt, and not in jeans, like George.

She came racing up, yelling at the top of her voice. 'Dick! DICK! Hey, DICK!'

Dick turned and stared in amazement.

'Why – it's Jo! JO! The traveller girl who once got mixed up with us in an adventure! Julian, it's Jo!'

There was no doubt about it at all. It *was* Jo! She came tearing up, her face glowing with the utmost delight and flung herself excitedly on Dick. She had always liked him best.

'Dick! I didn't know *you* were here! Julian! Are the others here too? Oh, Timmy, dear old Timmy! Dick, are you camping here? Oh, this is really too marvellous to be true!'

Jo seemed to be about to fling herself on Dick again, and he fended her off. 'Jo! Where in the world have you come from?'

'Well, you see,' said Jo, 'I've got school holidays like you – and I thought I'd go and visit you at Kirrin Cottage. So I did. But you had all gone away together. That was yesterday.'

'Go on,' said Dick, as Jo stopped, out of breath.

'Well, I didn't want to go back home again straight-away,' said Jo. 'So I thought I'd pay a visit to my uncle – he's my mother's brother – and I knew he was camping here so I hitch-hiked all the way yesterday, and came late last night.'

'Well, I'm blessed,' said Julian. 'And who is your uncle, may I ask?'

'Oh Alfredo – the Fire-Eater,' was Jo's astonishing reply. 'Didn't you know? Oh, Dick! Oh, Julian! Can I stay here while you're here? Do, DO say I can! You haven't forgotten me, have you?'

'Of course not,' said Dick, thinking that nobody could

possibly forget this wild little girl, with her mad ways and her staunch affection.

Then for the first time Jo realised that something was going on! What was this crowd doing round Julian and Dick?

She looked round, and immediately sensed that the fair people were not friendly to the two boys – although the main expression on their faces now was one of astonishment!

How did Jo know these boys? they wondered. How was it she was so very friendly with them? They were puzzled and suspicious.

'Uncle Alfredo, where are you?' demanded Jo, looking all round. 'Oh, there you are! Uncle, these are my very best friends – and so are the girls too, wherever they are. I'll tell you all about them, and how nice they were to me! I'll tell everybody!'

'Well,' said Julian, feeling rather embarrassed at what Jo might reveal, 'well, you tell them, Jo, and I'll just pop back and break the news to George and Anne. They *will* be surprised to find you are here – and that Alfredo is your uncle!'

The two boys and Timmy turned to go. The little crowd opened to let them pass. It closed up again round the excited Jo, whose high voice the boys could hear all the way across the field.

'Well, well, well!' said Dick, as they got through the hedge. 'What an astonishing thing! I couldn't believe my eyes when young Jo appeared, could you? I hope George won't mind. She was always rather jealous of Jo and the things she could do.'

The two girls were amazed at the boys' news. George was not too pleased. She preferred Jo at a distance rather than near. She liked and admired her but rather unwillingly. Jo was too like George herself for George to give her complete friendliness!

'Well, fancy *Jo*, Jo herself being here!' said Anne, smiling. 'Oh, Julian – it was a good thing she arrived when she did! I don't like that bit about Bufflo cracking his whip at you. He might have made you bald on the top!'

'Oh, it was only a few hairs,' said Julian. 'But it gave me quite a shock. And I think it gave the fair people a shock too when Jo arrived like a little hurricane, yelling at the top of her voice, and flinging herself on poor old Dick. She almost knocked him over!'

'She's not a bad kid,' said Dick, 'but she never stops to think. I wonder if the people she stays with know where she's gone. I wouldn't be a bit surprised if she just disappeared without a word.'

'Like the two scientists,' said Julian, with a grin. 'Gosh, I can't get over it! Jo was the very last person I would expect here.'

'Well, not really, if you think a bit,' said Anne. 'Her father is a traveller, isn't he – and her mother was in a circus, she told us so. She trained dogs, don't you remember, Julian? So it's quite natural for Jo to have

277

relations like the fair people. But just fancy having a fire-eater for an uncle!'

'Yes – I'd forgotten that Jo's mother was in a circus,' said Julian. 'I expect she's got relations all over the country! I wonder what she's telling them about us.'

'She's singing *Dick's* praises anyway,' said George. 'She always thought the world of Dick. Perhaps the fair people won't be *quite* so unfriendly if they know that Jo is fond of us.'

'Well, we're in a bit of a fix,' said Dick. 'We can't stay in this field, or the farmer will be after us again – and I can't see the fair people lending us their horses – and without horses we can't leave this field!'

'We could ask the farmer to lend us his horses,' suggested Anne.

'We'd have to pay him, though, and I don't see why we should,' said Julian. 'After all, it isn't *our* fault that our caravans were moved here.'

'I think this is a horrid and unfriendly place,' said Anne. 'And I don't want to stay here another day. I'm not enjoying it a bit.'

'Cheer up!' said Dick. 'Never say die!'

'Woof,' said Timmy.

'Look – someone's coming through that gap in the hedge down there by the lane,' said George, pointing. 'It's Jo!'

'Yes – and my goodness me, she's got a couple of horses with her!' cried Dick. 'Good old Jo! She's got Alfredo's horses!'

CHAPTER TEN

Back with the fair-folk again

THE FOUR of them, with Timmy capering behind, ran to meet Jo. She beamed at everyone.

'Hallo, Anne, hallo, George! Pleased to meet you again. This isn't half a surprise!'

'Jo! How did you get those horses?' said Dick, taking one by the bridle.

'Easy,' grinned Jo. 'I just told Uncle Fredo all about you – what wonders you were – and all you did for me – and wasn't I shocked when I heard they'd turned you out of your field! I let go then! I told them just what I thought of them, treating my best friends like that!'

'Did you really, Jo?' said George, doubtfully.

'Didn't you hear me?' demanded Jo. 'I yelled like anything at Uncle Fredo, and then his wife, my Aunt Anita, she yelled at him too – and then we both yelled at everyone.'

'It must have been quite a yelling match,' said Julian. 'And the result was that you got your way, and got the horses to take back our caravans, Jo?'

'Well, when Aunt Anita told me they'd taken your caravans into the next field and left them there, and wouldn't lend you horses to bring them back, I told them

279

all a few things,' said Jo. 'I said – no, I'd better not tell you what I said. I wasn't very polite.'

'I bet you weren't,' said Dick, who had already had a little experience of Jo's wild tongue the year before.

'And when I told them how my father went to prison, and you got me a home with somebody nice who looks after me, they were sorry they'd treated you roughly,' said Jo. 'And so I told Uncle Fredo I was going to catch two horses and bring your caravans back into the field again.'

'I see,' said Julian. 'And the fair-folk just let you?'

'Oh, yes,' said Jo. 'So let's hitch them in, Julian, and go back at once. Isn't that the farmer coming over there?'

It was, and he looked pretty grim. Julian hurriedly put one horse into the shafts of the girls' caravan, and Dick backed the other horse into the shafts of the second caravan. The farmer came up and watched.

'So you thought you'd get horses after all, did you?' he said. 'I thought you would. Telling me a lot of poppycock about being stranded here and not being able to get away!'

'Grrrrrrr,' said Timmy at once, but he was the only one who made any reply!

'Gee-up!' said Jo, taking the reins of the horse pulling the girls' caravan. 'Hup there! Git along, will you?'

The horse got along, and Jo wickedly drove him so near to the farmer that he had to move back in a hurry. He growled something at her. Timmy, appearing round the caravan, growled back. The farmer stood back further, and watched the two caravans going down the hillside, out through the wide gap in the hedge, and down the lane.

They came to the field-gate and Anne opened it. In went the horses, straining now, because they were going uphill,

and the vans were heavy. At last they arrived in the corner where the vans had stood before. Julian backed them over the same bit of ground.

He unhitched the horses, and threw the reins of the second horse to Dick. 'We'll take them back ourselves,' he said.

So the two boys walked the horses over to Alfredo, who was pegging up some washing on a line. It seemed a most unsuitable thing for a fire-eater to do, but Alfredo didn't seem to mind.

'Mr Alfredo, thank you for lending us the horses,' said Julian, in his politest tones. 'Shall we tie them up anywhere, or set them loose?'

Alfredo turned round, and took some pegs out of his large mouth. He looked rather ashamed.

'Set them loose,' he said. He hesitated before he put the pegs back into his mouth. 'We didn't know you were friends with my niece.' he said. 'She told us all about you. You should have told us you knew her.'

'And how could he do that when he didn't know she was your niece?' shouted Mrs Alfredo from the caravan door. 'Fredo, you have no brains, not a single brain do you have. Ahhhhhh! Now you drop my best blouse on the ground!'

She ran out at top speed, and Alfredo stared in alarm. Fortunately she had no saucepan with her this time. She turned to the two amused boys.

'Alfredo is sorry he took your caravans away,' she said. 'Are you not, Fredo?'

BACK WITH THE FAIR-FOLK AGAIN

'Well! It was *you* who . . .' began Alfredo, with a look of astonishment. But he wasn't allowed to finish. His dark little wife gave him a violent nudge, and spoke again herself, her words tumbling over one another.

'Pay no attention to this big bad man! He has no brains. He can only eat fire, and that is a poor thing to do! Now, Jo, she has brains. Now, are you not glad that you are back again in your corner?'

'I should have felt gladder if you had all been friendly to us,' said Julian. 'I'm afraid we don't feel like stopping here any longer, though. We shall probably leave tomorrow.'

'Now there, Fredo, see what you have done! You have chased away these nice children!' cried Mrs Alfredo. 'They have manners, these boys, a thing you know nothing about, Fredo. You should learn from them, Fredo, you should . . .'

Fredo took some pegs from his mouth to make an indignant answer, but his wife suddenly gave a shriek and ran to her caravan. 'Something burns! Something burns!'

Alfredo gave a hearty laugh, a loud guffaw that surprised the boys. 'Ha! She bakes today, and burns her cake! She has no brains, that woman! No brains at all!'

Julian and Dick turned to go. Alfredo spoke to them in a low voice. 'You can stay here now, here in this field. You are Jo's friend. That is enough for us.'

'It may be,' said Julian. 'But it's not quite enough for *us*, I'm afraid. We shall leave tomorrow.'

The boys went back to the caravans. Jo sat on the grass with George and Anne, eagerly telling them of her life with a very nice family. 'But they won't let me wear jeans or be a boy,' she ended sadly. 'That's why I wear a skirt now. Could you lend me some jeans, George?'

'No, I couldn't,' said George, firmly. Jo was quite enough like her as it was, without wearing jeans! 'Well, you seem to have turned over a new leaf, Jo. Can you read and write yet?'

'Almost,' said Jo, and turned her eyes away. She found lessons very difficult, for she had never been to school when she lived with her traveller father. She looked back again with bright eyes. 'Can I stay with you?' she said. 'My foster-mother would let me, I know – if it was you I was with.'

'Didn't you tell her you were coming here?' said Dick. 'That was unkind, Jo.'

'I never thought,' said Jo. 'You send her a card for me, Dick.'

'Send one yourself,' said George at once. 'You said you could write.'

Jo took no notice of that remark. '*Can* I stay with you?' she said. 'I won't sleep in the caravans, I'll doss down underneath. I always did that when the weather was fine, and I lived with my dad in his caravan. It would be a change for me now not to live in a house. I like lots of things in houses, though I never thought I would – but I shall always like sleeping rough best.'

284

'Well – you *could* stay here with us, if we were going to stay,' said Julian. 'But I don't much feel inclined to, now we've had such an unfriendly welcome from everyone.'

'I'll tell everyone to be kind to you,' said Jo at once, and got up as if she meant to go then and there to force everyone into kindness!

Dick pushed her down. 'No. We'll stay here one more day and night, and make up our minds tomorrow. What do you say, Julian?'

'Right,' said Julian. He looked at his watch. 'Let's go and celebrate Jo's coming with a few ice-creams. And I expect you two girls have got some shopping to do, haven't you?'

'Yes,' said Anne, and fetched the shopping bags. They set off down the hill, the five of them and Timmy. As they passed the snake-man he called out cheerily to them: 'Good morning! Nice day, isn't it?'

After the surliness and sulkiness the children had got from the fair-folk up till then, this came as a surprise. Anne smiled, but the boys and George merely nodded and passed by. They were not so forgiving as Anne!

They passed the rubber-man, bringing back water. Behind him came the rope-man. Both of them nodded to the children, and the sad-looking rubber-man actually gave a brief grin.

Then they saw Bufflo, practising with his whip – crack-crack-crack! He came over to them. 'If you'd like a crack

285

with my whip, you're welcome any time,' he said to Julian.

'Thanks,' said Julian, politely but stiffly. 'But we're probably leaving tomorrow.'

'Keep your hair on!' said Bufflo, feeling snubbed.

'I would if you'd let me,' said Julian at once, rubbing his hand over the top of his head where Bufflo had stripped off a few up-standing hairs.

'Ho, ho!' guffawed Bufflo and then stopped abruptly, afraid he had given offence. Julian grinned at him. He rather liked Bufflo, with his mop of yellow hair and lazy drawl.

'You stay on with us,' said Bufflo. 'I'll lend you a whip.'

'We're probably leaving tomorrow,' repeated Julian. He nodded to him, and went on with the others.

'I'm beginning to feel I'd rather like to stay after all,' said George. 'It makes such a difference if people are friendly.'

'Well, we're not staying,' said Julian, shortly. 'I've practically made up my mind – but we'll just wait till tomorrow. It's a – matter of pride with me. You girls don't understand quite how I feel about the whole thing.'

They didn't. Dick understood, though, and he agreed with Julian. They went on down to the village and made their way to the ice-cream shop.

They had a very pleasant day. They had a wonderful lunch on the grass by their caravans – and to their surprise Mrs Alfredo presented them with a sponge sandwich she had made. Anne thanked her very much indeed to make up for a certain stiffness in the thanks of the two boys.

'You *might* have said a bit more,' she said reproachfully to them. 'She really is a kind little woman. Honestly I wouldn't mind staying on now.'

But Julian was curiously obstinate about it. He shook his head. 'We go tomorrow,' he said. 'Unless something unexpected happens to *make* us stay. And it won't.'

But Julian was quite wrong. Something unexpected *did* happen. Something really very peculiar indeed.

CHAPTER ELEVEN

A very strange thing

THE UNEXPECTED happening came that evening after tea. They had all had rather a late tea, and a very nice one. Bread and butter and honey – new doughnuts from the dairy – and the sponge cake that Mrs Alfredo had presented them with, which had a very rich filling indeed.

'I can't eat a thing more,' said George, 'that sponge cake was too rich for words. I don't even feel as if I can get up and clear away – so don't start suggesting it, Anne.'

'I'm not,' said Anne. 'There's plenty of time. It's a heavenly evening – let's sit for a while. There goes that blackbird again. He has a different tune every time he sings.'

'That's what I like about blackbirds,' said Dick, lazily. 'They're proper composers. They make up their own tunes – not like the chaffinch who just carols the same old song again and again and again. Honestly there was one this morning that said it fifty times without stopping.'

'Chip-chip-chip, cherry-erry-erry, chippee-OO-EE-Ar!' shouted a chaffinch, rattling it all off as if he had learnt it by heart. 'Chip-chip-chip . . .'

'There he goes again,' said Dick. 'If he doesn't say that,

he shouts "pink-pink-pink" as if he'd got that colour on the brain. Look at him over there – isn't he a beauty?'

He certainly was. He flew down to the grass beside the children and began to peck up the crumbs, even venturing on to Anne's knee once. She sat still, really thrilled.

Timmy growled, and the chaffinch flew off. 'Silly, Timmy,' said George. 'Jealous of a chaffinch! Oh, look, Dick – are those herons flying down to the marsh on the east side of the castle hill?'

'Yes, said Dick, sitting up. 'Where are your field-glasses, George? We could see the big birds beautifully through them.'

George fetched them from her caravan. She handed them to Dick. He focused them on the marsh. 'Yes – four herons – gosh, what long legs they've got, haven't they? They are wading happily about – now one's struck down at something with its great beak. What's it got? Yes, it's a frog. I can see its back legs!'

'You can't!' said George, taking the field-glasses from him. 'You're a fibber. The glasses aren't powerful enough to see a frog's legs all that way off!'

But they *were* powerful enough. They were really magnificent ones, far too good for George, who wasn't very careful with valuable things.

She was just in time to see the poor frog's legs disappearing into the big strong beak of the heron. Then something frightened the birds, and before the others could have a look at them they had all flapped away.

'How slowly they flap their wings,' said Dick. 'They must surely flap them more slowly than any other bird. Give me the glasses again, George. I'll have a squint at the jackdaws. There are thousands of them flying again over the castle – their evening jaunt, I suppose.'

He put them to his eyes, and moved the glasses to and fro, watching the endless whirl and swoop of the black jackdaws. The sound of their many voices came loudly over the evening air. 'Chack-chack-chack-chack!'

Dick saw some fly down to the only complete tower of the castle. He lowered the glasses to follow them. One jackdaw flew down to the sill of the slit-window near the top of the tower, and Dick followed its flight. It rested for half a second on the sill and then flew off as if frightened.

And then Dick saw something that made his heart suddenly jump. His glasses were trained on the window-slit and he saw something most astonishing there! He gazed as if he couldn't believe his eyes.

Then he spoke in a low voice to Julian.

'Ju! Take the glasses, will you? Train them on the window-slit near the top of the only complete tower – and tell me if you see what I see. Quick!'

Julian held out his hand in astonishment for the glasses. The others stared in surprise. What could Dick have seen? Julian put the glasses to his eyes and focused them on the window Dick had been looking at. He stared hard.

'Yes. Yes, I can. What an extraordinary thing. It must be an effect of the light, I think.'

By this time the others were in such a state of curiosity that they couldn't bear it. George snatched the glasses from Julian. 'Let *me* see!' she said, quite fiercely. She trained them on to the window. She gazed and gazed and gazed.

Then she lowered the glasses and stared at Julian and Dick. 'Are you being funny?' she said. 'There's nothing there – nothing but an empty window!'

Anne snatched the glasses from her just before Dick tried to take them again. She too trained them on the window. But there was absolutely nothing there to see.

'There's nothing,' said Anne, disgusted, and Dick took the glasses from her at once, focusing them once more on the window. He lowered them.

'It's gone,' he said to Julian. 'Nothing there now.'

'DICK! If you don't tell us what you saw we'll roll you down the hill,' said George, crossly. 'Are you making something up? *What* did you see?'

'Well,' said Dick, looking at Julian. '*I* saw a face. A face not far from the window, staring out. What did you see, Ju?'

'The same,' said Julian. 'It made me feel pretty peculiar, too.'

'A *face*!' said George, Anne and Jo all together. 'What do you mean?'

'Well – just what we said,' replied Dick. 'A face – with eyes and nose and mouth.'

'But nobody lives in the castle. It's a ruin,' said George. 'Was it someone exploring, do you think?'

Julian looked at his watch. 'No, it couldn't have been a visitor, I'm sure – the castle shuts at half past five and it's gone six. Anyway – it looked a – a – sort of *desperate* face!'

'Yes. I thought so too,' said Dick. 'It's – well, it's very peculiar, isn't it, Julian? There may be some kind of ordinary explanation for it, but I can't help feeling there's something *odd* about it.'

A VERY STRANGE THING

'Was it a man's face?' asked George. 'Or a woman's?'

'A man's, I think,' said Dick. 'I couldn't see any hair against the darkness inside the window. Or clothes. But it *looked* a man's face. Did you notice the eyebrows, Ju?'

'Yes, I did,' said Julian. 'They were very pronounced, weren't they?'

This rang a bell with George! 'Eyebrows!' she said at once. 'Don't you remember – the picture of that scientist, Terry-Kane, showed that he had thick black eyebrows – you said he'd shave them off and use them upside down for moustaches, don't you remember, Dick?'

'Yes. I do remember,' said Dick, and looked at Julian. Julian shook his head. 'I didn't recognise the likeness,' he said, 'but after all it's a very long way away. It is only because George's glasses are so extraordinarily good that we managed to spot a face looking out of a window so very far away. Actually I think there will be an ordinary explanation – it's just that we were so startled – and that made us think it was very strange.'

'I *wish* I'd seen the face,' sighed George. 'They're my glasses, too – and I never saw the face!'

'Well, you can keep on looking and see if it comes back,' said Dick, handing over the glassess. 'It may do.'

So Anne, George, and Jo took turn and turn about, gazing earnestly through the field-glasses – but they saw no face. In the end it got so dark that it was quite difficult to make out the tower, let alone the window or a face!

'I tell you what we might do,' said Julian. 'We could go

293

and see over the castle ourselves tomorrow. And we could go up into that tower. Then we should certainly see if there's a face there.'

'But I thought we were leaving tomorrow,' said Dick.

'Oh – yes, we did think of leaving, didn't we?' said Julian, who had quite forgotten this idea of his in his excitement. 'Well – I don't feel as if we can go before we've explored that castle, and found the explanation of the face.'

'Of *course* we can't,' said George. 'Fancy seeing a thing like that and rushing off without finding out about it. I couldn't possibly.'

'*I'm* going to stay anyhow,' announced Jo. 'I could stop with my Uncle Alfredo, if you go, and I'll let you know if the face comes again – if George will leave me her glasses.'

'Well, I shan't,' said George, with much determination. 'If I go, my glasses go with me. But I'm not going. You *will* stay now, won't you, Julian?'

'We'll stay and find out about the face,' said Julian. 'I honestly feel awfully puzzled about it. Hallo, who's this coming?'

A big figure loomed up in the twilight. It was Alfredo, the fire-eater. 'Jo! Are you there?' he said. 'Your aunt invites you to supper – and all your friends too. Come along.'

There was a pause. Anne looked expectantly across at Julian. Was he still going to be high-and-mighty and proud? She hoped not.

'Thanks,' said Julian, at last. 'We'd be pleased to come. Do you mean now?'

'That would be nice,' said Alfredo, with a little bow. 'I fire-eat for you? Anything you say!'

This was too tempting to resist. Everyone got up at once and followed the big Alfredo over the hillside to his caravan. Outside there was a really good fire, and on it was a big black pot that gave out a wonderful smell.

'Supper is not quite ready,' said Alfredo. The five children were relieved. After their big tea they didn't feel ready even for a meal that smelt as good as the one in the pot! They sat down by it.

'Will you really eat fire for us?' asked Anne. 'How do you do it?'

'Ah, very difficult!' said Alfredo. 'I do it only if you promise me not to try it by yourselves. You would not like blisters all over your mouth inside, would you?'

Everyone felt certain that they wouldn't. 'I don't want you to have blisters in *your* mouth, either,' added Anne.

Alfredo looked shocked. 'I am a very good fire-eater,' he assured her. 'No good ones ever make blisters in their mouths. Now – you sit still and I will fetch my torch and eat fire for you.'

Someone else sat down beside them. It was Bufflo. He grinned at them. Skippy came and sat down too. Then the snake-man came up, and he sat down on the opposite side of the fire.

Alfredo came back carrying a few things in his hands. 'Quite a family circle!' he said. 'Now watch – I will eat fire for you!'

CHAPTER TWELVE

Fire-eating and other things!

ALFREDO SAT down on the grass, some way back from the fire. He set a little metal bowl in front of him, that smelt of petrol. He held up two things to show the children.

'His torches,' said Mrs Alfredo, proudly. 'He eats fire from them.'

Alfredo called out something to the snake-man, dipping his two torches into the bowl. They were not alight yet, and to the children they looked like very large button-hooks, with a wad of wool caught in the hook part.

The snake-man leant forward and took a burning twig out of the fire. With a deft throw he pitched it right into the metal bowl. Immediately it set light to the petrol there, and flames shot up in the darkness.

Alfredo had held his torches out of the way, but now he thrust first one and then another into the burning petrol in the bowl.

They flared alight at once, and red flames shot up as he held one in each hand. His eyes gleamed in the brilliant light, and the five children sat still, spell-bound.

Then Alfredo leaned back his head – back and back – and opened his great mouth wide. He put one of the lighted torches into it, and closed his mouth over it, so that his

296

cheeks gleamed a strange and unbelievable red from the flames inside his mouth. Anne gave a little scream and George gasped. The two boys held their breath. Only Jo watched unconcerned. She had seen her uncle do this many times before!

Alfredo opened his mouth, and flames rushed out of it, gushing like a fiery waterfall. What with the other torch flaring in his left hand, the burning petrol in the bowl, the torch in his right hand and the flames from his mouth, it really was an extraordinary scene!

He did the same with the other torch, and once more his cheeks glowed like a lamp. Then fire came from his mouth again, and was blown this way and that by the night breeze.

Alfredo closed his mouth. He swallowed. Then he looked round, opened his mouth to show that he no longer had any flames there, and smiled broadly.

'Ah – you like to see me eat fire?' he said, and put out his torches. The bowl was no longer flaming, and now only the fire light lit the scene.

'It's marvellous,' said Julian, with great admiration. 'But don't you burn your mouth?'

'What me? No, never!' laughed Alfredo. 'At first maybe, yes – when I begin years and years ago. But now, no. It would be a shameful thing to burn my mouth – I would hang my head, and go away.'

'But – how is it you *don't* burn your mouth?' asked Dick, puzzled.

Alfredo refused to give any explanation. That was part of the mystery of his act and he wasn't going to give it away.

'*I* can fire-eat too,' announced Jo, casually and most unexpectedly. 'Here, Uncle, let me have one of your torches.'

'You! You will do nothing of the sort!' roared Alfredo. 'Do you want to burn to bits?'

'No. And I shan't either,' said Jo. 'I've watched you and I know just how it's done. I've tried it.'

'Fibber!' said George at once.

'Now you listen to me,' began Alfredo again. 'If you fire-eat I will whip you till you beg me for mercy. I will . . .'

'Now, Fredo,' said his wife, 'you'll do nothing of the sort. I'll deal with Jo if she starts any nonsense here. As for fire-eating – well, if there's to be anyone else fire-eating here, *I* will do it, I, your wife.'

'You will *not* fire-eat,' said Alfredo obstinately, evidently afraid that his hot-tempered little wife might try to do it.

Anne suddenly gave a scream of fright. A long, thick body glided between her and Julian – one of the snakeman's pythons! He had brought one with him, and the children hadn't known. Jo caught hold of it and held on for dear life.

'Let him be,' said the snake-man. 'He will come back to me. He wants a run.'

'Let me hold him for a bit,' begged Jo. 'He feels so smooth and cold. I like snakes.'

Julian put out his hand gingerly and touched the great snake. It did feel unexpectedly smooth, and quite cool. How extraordinary! It looked so scaly and rough.

The snake slithered all the way up Jo and then began to pour itself down her back. 'Now, don't you let him get his

tail round you,' warned the snake-man. 'I've told you that before.'

'I'll wear him round my neck,' said Jo, and proceeded to pull the snake's long body until in the end he hung round her neck like a scarf. George watched in unwilling admiration. Anne had removed herself as far from Jo as possible. The boys gazed in astonishment, and felt a new respect for the little traveller girl.

Someone struck up a soft melody on a guitar. It was Skippy, Bufflo's wife. She hummed a sad little song that had a gay little chorus in which all the fair-folk joined. Practically all the camp had come along now, and there were quite a few the children hadn't seen before.

FIRE-EATING AND OTHER THINGS!

It was exciting sitting there round the glowing fire, listening to the thrum of the guitar, and the sound of Skippy's low, clear voice – sitting near a fire-eater too, and within arm's length of a snake who also seemed to be enjoying the music! He swayed about in time to the chorus, and then suddenly poured himself all down the front of Jo, and glided like magic to his master, the snake-man.

'Ah, my beauty,' said the funny little man, and let the python slide between his hands, its coils pulsing powerfully as it went. 'You like the music, my beauty?'

'He really loves his snake,' whispered Anne to George. 'How can he?'

Alfredo's wife got up. 'It is time to go,' she told the audience. 'Alfredo needs his supper. Is it not so, my big bad man?'

Alfredo agreed that it was so. He placed the heavy iron pot over the glowing fire again, and in a few seconds such a glorious smell came from it that all the five children began to sniff expectantly.

'Where's Timmy?' said George, suddenly. He was nowhere to be seen!

'He crept away with his tail down when he saw the snake,' said Jo. 'I saw him go. Timmy, come back! It's all right! Timmy, Timmy!'

'I'll call him, thank you,' said George. 'He's *my* dog. Timmy!'

Timmy came, his tail still down. George fondled him and so did Jo. He licked them both in turn. George tried to drag him away from Jo. She didn't like Timmy to show affection for the little traveller girl – but he always did! He loved her.

The supper was lovely. '*What* is in your pot?' asked Dick, accepting a second helping. 'I've never tasted such a delicious stew in my life.'

'Chicken, duck, beef, bacon, rabbit, hare, hedgehog, onions, turnips . . .' began Alfredo's wife. 'I put there everything that comes. It cooks and I stir, it cooks and I stir. Perhaps a partridge goes in one day, and a pheasant the next, and . . .'

'Hold your tongue, wife,' growled Alfredo, who knew quite well that the farmers round about might well ask questions about some of the things in that stew.

'You tell me to hold my tongue!' cried little Mrs Alfredo angrily, flourishing a spoon. 'You tell me that!'

'Woof,' said Timmy, receiving some nice tasty drops on his nose, and licking them off. 'Woof!' He got up and went towards the spoon, hoping for a few more.

'Oh, Aunt Nita, do give Timmy a spoonful out of the stew,' begged Jo, and to Timmy's great joy he got a big plateful all to himself. He could hardly believe it!

'Thank you very much for a very nice supper,' said Julian, feeling that it really was time to go. He got up and the others followed his example.

'And thank you for fire-eating for us, Alfredo,' said George. 'It doesn't seem to have spoilt your appetite!'

'Poof!' said Alfredo, as if such a thing would never

enter his head. 'Jo – are you going to stay with us again tonight? You are welcome.'

'I'd just like an old rug, that's all, Aunt Nita,' said Jo. 'I'm going to sleep under George's caravan.'

'You can sleep on the floor inside, if you like,' said George. But Jo shook her head.

'No. I've had enough of sleeping indoors for a bit. I want to sleep out. Under the caravan will be a fine place for me. Travellers often sleep there when the weather is warm.'

They went back over the dark hillside. A few stars were out, but the moon was not yet up. 'That was a jolly interesting evening,' said Dick. 'I enjoyed it. I like your aunt and uncle, Jo.'

Jo was delighted. She always loved praise from Dick. She went under the girls' caravan, and rolled herself up in the rug. She had been taught to clean her teeth and wash and do her hair, by the foster-mother she had lived with for some months – but all that was forgotten now that she was leading a traveller's life again!

'In a day or two she'll be the filthy, dirty, tangly-haired, rude girl she was when we first knew her,' said George, combing out her own hair extra well. 'I'm glad we're going to stay here after all, aren't you, Anne? I really do think the fair people are friendly towards us now.'

'Thanks to Jo,' said Anne. George said nothing. She didn't like being under obligation to Jo! She finished preparing herself for bed and got into her bunk.

'I wish *we'd* seen that face at the window, don't you, Anne?' she said. 'I do wonder whose it was – and why it was there, looking out.'

'I don't think I want to talk about faces at windows just now,' said Anne, getting into her bunk. 'Let's change the subject.' She blew out the lamp and settled down. They talked for a few minutes, and then George heard something outside the caravan. What could it be? Timmy raised his head and gave a little growl.

George looked at the window opposite. A lone star shone through it – and then something came in front of the star, blotted it out, and pressed itself against the glass pane. Timmy growled again, but not very loudly. Was it someone he knew?'

George flashed on her torch, and immediately saw what it was. She gave a little giggle. Then she called to Anne.

'Anne! Anne! Quick, there's a face at the window. Anne, wake up!'

'I'm not asleep,' said Anne's voice, and she sat up, scared. 'What face? Where? You're not just frightening me, are you?'

'No – there it is, look!' said George and shone her torch at the window. A big, long, dark-brown face looked in, and Anne gave a shriek. Then she laughed. 'You beast, George – it's only Alfredo's horse. Oh, you *did* give me a fright. I've a good mind to pull you out of your bunk on to the floor. Go away, you silly staring horse – shoo, go away!'

CHAPTER THIRTEEN

Off to the castle

NEXT MORNING, as they had breakfast, the children discussed the face at the castle window again. They had levelled the field-glasses time and again at the window, but there was nothing to be seen.

'Let's go and see over the castle as soon as it opens,' said Dick. 'But mind – nobody is to mention faces at windows – you hear me, Jo? You're the one who can't keep your tongue still sometimes.'

Jo flared up. 'I'm not! I can keep a secret!'

'All right, fire-eater,' said Dick with a grin. He looked at his watch. 'It's too soon to go yet.'

'I'll go and help Mr Slither with his snakes,' said Jo. 'Anyone else coming?'

'Mr Slither! What a marvellous name for a man who keeps snakes,' said Dick. 'I don't mind coming to watch, but I'm not keen on the way they pour themselves up and down people.'

They all went to Mr Slither's caravan except Anne, who said she would much rather clear up the breakfast things.

The snake-man had both his snakes out of their box. 'He *is* polishing them,' said George, sitting down near by. 'See how he makes their brown bodies shine.'

'Here, Jo – you mop Beauty for me,' said Mr Slither. 'The stuff is in that bottle over there. He's got those nasty little mites again under his scales. Mop him with that stuff and that will soon get rid of them.'

Jo seemed to know what to do. She got a rag, tipped up the bottle of yellow stuff and began to pat one of the snakes gently, letting the lotion soak round his scales.

George, not to be outdone, offered to help in the polishing of the other snake. 'You hold him then,' said Mr Slither, and slid the snake over to George. He got up and went into his caravan. George hadn't quite bargained for this. The snake lay across her knees, and then began to wind round her body. 'Don't you let him get a hold of you with his tail,' Jo warned her.

The boys soon got tired of seeing Jo and George vying with one another over the pythons, and went off to where Bufflo was practising spinning rope-rings. He spun loop after loop of rope, making wonderful patterns in the air with it. He grinned at the boys.

'Like a try?' he said. But neither of them could do anything with the rope at all.

'Let's see you snap off something with the whip-lash,' said Dick. 'I think you're a marvel at that.'

'What do you want me to hit?' asked Bufflo, picking up his magnificent whip. 'The topmost leaves on that bush?'

'Yes,' said Dick. Bufflo looked at them, swung his whip once or twice, lifted it – and cracked it.

Like magic the topmost leaves disappeared off the bush.

The boys gazed in admiration. 'Now pick off that daisy-head over there,' said Julian, pointing.

Crack! The daisy-head vanished. 'That's easy,' said Bufflo. 'Look, you hold a pencil or something in your hand, one of you. I'll pick it out without touching your fingers!'

Julian hesitated. But Dick dived his hand into his pocket and brought out a red pencil, not very long. He held out his hand, with the pencil between finger and thumb. Bufflo looked at it with half-closed eyes, as if measuring the distance. He raised his whip.

Crack! The tip-end of the lash curled itself round the pencil and pulled it clean out of Dick's hand. It flew up into the air, and Bufflo reached out his hand and caught it!

'Jolly good,' said Dick, lost in admiration. 'Does it take long to learn a thing like that?'

'Matter of twenty years or so,' said Bufflo. 'But you want to begin when you're a nipper – about three years old, say. My pa taught me – and if I didn't learn fast enough he'd take the skin off the tips of my ears with his whip-lash! You soon learn if you know that's going to happen to you!'

The boys gazed at Bufflo's big ears. They certainly did look a bit rough at the edges!

'I throw knives too,' said Bufflo, basking in the boys' admiration. 'I put Skippy up against a board, and throw knives all round her – so that when she walks away from the board at the end, there's her shape all outlined in knives. Like to see me?'

307

'Well, no, not now,' said Julian, looking at his watch. 'We're going to see over the castle. Have you ever seen over it, Bufflo?'

'No. Who wants to waste time going over a ruined old castle?' said Bufflo, scornfully. 'Not me!'

He went off to his caravan, spinning rope-rings as he went with an ease that Dick couldn't help envying from the bottom of his heart. What a pity he hadn't begun to learn these things early enough. He was afraid he would never be really good at them now. He was too old!

'George! Jo! It's time we went,' called Julian. 'Put down those snakes, and come along. Anne! Are you ready?'

Mr Slither went to collect his snakes. They glided over him in delight, and he ran his hands over their smooth, gleaming bodies.

'I must wash my hands before I go,' said George. 'They're a bit snaky. Coming, Jo?'

Jo didn't really see why it was necessary to wash snaky hands, but she went with George to the stream and they rinsed them thoroughly. George wiped her hands on a rather dirty hanky, and Jo wiped hers on a much dirtier skirt. She looked at George's jeans enviously. What a pity to have to wear skirts!

They didn't lock up the caravans. Julian felt sure that the fair-folk were now really friendly to them, and would not take anything from them themselves, nor permit anyone else to do so. They all walked down the hillside, Timmy bounding along joyfully, under the impression that he was going to take them for a nice long walk.

They climbed over the stile, walked up the lane a little way, and came to the wooden gate that opened on to the steep path up to the castle. Now that it was so near to them it looked almost as if it might fall on top of them!

They went up the path and came to the small tower in which was the little door giving entrance to the castle. An old woman was there, looking a little like a witch. If she had had green eyes Anne would most certainly have set her down as a descendant of a witch! But she had eyes like black beads. She had no teeth at all and it was difficult to understand what she said.

'Five, please,' said Julian, giving her twenty-five pence.

'You can't take the dog in,' said the old woman, mumbling so much that they couldn't make out what she said. She pointed to the dog and repeated her remark again, shaking her head all the time.

'Oh – can't we really take our dog?' said George. 'He won't do any harm.'

The old woman pointed to a set of rules: 'DOGS NOT ALLOWED IN.'

'All right. We'll leave him outside then,' said George, crossly. 'What a silly rule! Timmy, stay here. We won't be long.'

Timmy put his tail down. He didn't approve of this. But he knew that he was not allowed into certain places, such as churches, and he imagined this place must be an enormous church – the kind of place into which George

310

so often disappeared on Sundays. He lay down in a sunny corner.

The five children went in through the clicking turnstile. They opened the door beyond and went into the castle grounds. The door shut behind them.

'Wait – we ought to get a guide-book,' said Julian. 'I want to know something about that tower.'

He went back and bought one for another five pence. They stood in the great castle yard and looked at the book. It gave the history of the old place – a history of peace and war, quarrels and truces, family feuds, marriages and all the other things that make up history.

'It would be an exciting story if it was written up properly,' said Julian. 'Look – here's the plan. There *are* dungeons!'

'Not open to the public,' quoted Dick, in disappointment. 'What a pity.'

'It was once a very strong and powerful castle,' said Julian, looking at the plan. 'It always had the strong wall that is still round it – and the castle itself is built in the middle of a great courtyard that runs all round. It says the walls of the castle itself are eight feet thick. Eight feet thick! No wonder most of it is still standing!'

They looked at the silent ruins in awe. The castle towered up, broken here and there, with sometimes a whole wall missing, and with all the doorways misshapen.

'There were four towers, of course,' said Julian, still with his nose glued to the guide-book. 'It says three are

311

almost completely ruined now – but the fourth one is in fairly good condition, though the stone stairway that led up to the top has fallen in.'

'Well then – you couldn't have seen a face at that window,' said George, looking up at the fourth tower. 'If the stairway has fallen in, no one could get up there.'

'Hm. We'll see how much fallen in it is,' said Julian. 'It may be dangerous to the public, and perhaps we'll find a notice warning us off – but it might be quite climbable in places.'

'Shall we go up it if so?' said Jo, her eyes shining. 'What shall we do if we find the Face?'

'We'll wait till we find it first!' said Julian. He shut the guide-book and put it into his pocket. 'Well, we seem to be the only people here. Let's get going. We'll walk round the courtyard first.'

They walked round the courtyard that surrounded the castle. It was strewn with great white stones that had fallen from the walls of the castle itself. In one place a whole wall had fallen in, and they could see the inside of the castle, dark and forbidding.

They came round to the front of it again. 'Let's go in at the front door – if you can call that great stone archway that,' said Julian. 'I say – can't you imagine knights on horseback riding round this courtyard, impatient to be off to some tournament, their horses' hoofs clip-clopping all the time?'

'Yes!' said Dick. 'I can just imagine it!'

312

They went in at the arched entrance, and wandered through room after room with stone floors and walls, and with small slit-like windows that gave very little light indeed.

'They had no glass for panes in those days,' said Dick. 'I bet they were glad on cold windy days that the windows were so tiny. Brrrrrrr! This must have been a terribly cold place to live in.'

'The floors used to be covered with rushes, and tapestry was hung on the walls,' said Anne, remembering a history lesson. 'Julian – let's go and look for the stairway to that tower now. Do let's! I'm longing to find out whether there really *is* a face up in that tower!'

CHAPTER FOURTEEN

Faynights Castle

'CHACK-CHACK-CHACK! Chack-chack-chack!' The jack-daws circled round the old castle, calling to one another in their cheerful, friendly voices. The five children looked up and watched them.

'You can see the grey at the backs of their necks,' said Dick. 'I wonder how many years jackdaws have lived round and about this castle.'

'I suppose the sticks lying all over this courtyard must have been dropped by them,' said Julian. 'They make their nests of big twigs – really, they must drop as many as they use! Just look at that pile over there!'

'Very wasteful of them!' said Dick. 'I wish they would come and drop some near our caravan to save me going to get firewood each day for the fire!'

They were standing at the great archway that made the entrance to the castle. Anne grew impatient. 'Do let's look at the towers now,' she said.

They went to the nearest one, but it was almost impossible to realise that it *had* been a tower. It was just a great heap of fallen stones, piled one on top of another.

They went to the only good tower. They had hoped to find some remains of a stone stairway, but to their great disappointment they could not even look up into the tower! One of the inner walls had fallen in, and the floor was piled up, completely blocked. There was no sign of a stairway. Either it too had fallen in, or it was covered by the stones of the ruined wall.

Julian was astonished. It was obvious that nobody could possibly climb up the tower from the inside! Then how in the world could there have been a face at the tower window? He began to feel rather uncomfortable. Was it a real face? If not, what could it have been?

'This is odd,' said Dick, thinking the same as Julian, and pointing to the heaped-up stones on the ground floor of the tower. 'It does look absolutely impossible for anyone to get up into the top of the tower. Well – what about that face then?'

'Let's go and ask that old woman if there *is* any way at all of getting up into the tower,' said Julian. 'She might know.'

So they left the castle, walked across the courtyard, back to the little tower in the outer wall that guarded the big gateway. The old woman was sitting by the turnstile, knitting.

'Could you tell us, please, if there is any way of getting up into the tower over there?' asked Julian

The old woman answered something, but it was difficult to understand a word she said. However, as she shook her head vigorously, it was plain that there *was* no way up to the tower. It was very puzzling.

'Is there a better plan of the castle than this?' asked Julian, showing his guide-book. 'A plan of the dungeons for instance – and a plan of the towers as they once were, before they were ruined?'

The old lady said something that sounded like 'Society of Reservation of something-or-other.'

'What did you say?' asked Julian, patiently.

The witch-like woman was evidently getting tired of these questions. She opened a big book that showed the amount of people and fees paid, and looked down it. She put her finger on something written there, and showed it to Julian.

'Society for Preservation of Old Buildings,' he read. 'Oh – did somebody come from them lately? Would they know more than it says in the guide-book?'

'Yes,' said the old woman. 'Two men came. They spent all day here – last Thursday. You ask that Society what you want to know – not me. I only take the money.'

She sounded quite intelligible all of a sudden. Then she relapsed into mumbles again, and no one could understand a word.

'Anyway, she's told us what we want to know,' said Julian. 'We'll telephone the Society and ask them if they can tell us any more about the castle. There may be secret passages and things not shown in the guide-book at all.'

'How exciting!' said George, thrilled. 'I say, let's go back to that tower and look at the *outside* of it. It might be climbable there.'

They went back to see – but it *wasn't* climbable. Although the stones it was built of were uneven enough to form slight foot-holds and hand-holds it would be much too dangerous for anyone to try to climb up – even the cat-footed Jo. For one thing it would not be possible to tell which stones were loose and crumbling until the climber caught hold – and then down he would go!

All the same, Jo was willing to try. 'I might be able to do it,' she said, slipping off one of her shoes.

'Put your shoe on,' said Dick at once. 'You are NOT

going to try any tricks of that sort. There isn't even ivy for you to cling to.'

Jo put back her shoe sulkily, looking astonishingly like George as she scowled. And then, to everyone's enormous astonishment, who should come bounding up to them but Timmy!

'Timmy! Wherever have you come from?' said George, in surprise. 'There's no way in except through the turnstile – and the door behind it is shut. We shut it ourselves! *How* did you get in?

'Woof,' said Timmy, trying to explain. He ran to the good tower, made his way over the blocks of stone lying about and stopped by a small space between three or four of the fallen stones. 'Woof,' he said again, and pawed at one of the stones.

'He came out there,' said George. She tugged at a big stone, but she couldn't move it an inch, of course. 'I don't know how in the world Timmy squeezed himself out of this space – it doesn't look big enough for a rabbit. Certainly none of *us* could get inside!'

'What puzzles *me*,' said Julian, 'is how Timmy got in from the outside. We left him right outside the castle – so he must have run round the outer wall somewhere and found a small hole. He must have squeezed into that.'

'Yes. That's right,' said Dick. 'We know the walls are eight feet thick, so he must have found a place where a bit of it had broken at the bottom, and forced his way in. But

318

– would there be a hole right through the whole thickness of eight feet?'

This was really puzzling. They all looked at Timmy, and he wagged his tail expectantly. Then he barked loudly and capered round as if he wanted a game.

The door behind the turnstile opened at once and the old lady appeared. 'How did that dog get here?' she called. 'He's to go out at once!'

'We don't know how he got in,' said Dick. 'Is there a hole in the outer wall?'

'No,' said the old woman. 'Not one. You must have let that dog in when I wasn't looking. He's to go out. And you too. You've been here long enough.'

'We may as well go,' said Julian. 'We've seen all there is to see – or all that we are *allowed* to see. I'm quite sure there is some way of getting up into that tower although the stairway is in ruins. I'm going to ring up the Society for the Preservation of Old Buildings and ask them to put me in touch with the fellows who examined the castle last week. They must have been experts.'

'Yes. They would probably have a complete plan,' said Dick. 'Secret passages, dungeons, hidden rooms and all – if there are any!'

They took Timmy by the collar, and went out through the turnstiles, click-click-click. 'I feel like having a couple of doughnuts at the dairy,' said George. 'And some lemonade. Anyone else feel the same?'

Everyone did, including Timmy, who barked at once.

'Timmy's silly over those doughnuts,' said George. 'He just wolfs them down.'

'It's a great waste,' said Anne. 'He ate four last time – more than anyone else had.'

They walked down to the village. 'You go and order what we want,' said Julian, 'and I'll just go and look up this Society. It may have an office somewhere in this district.'

He went to the post office to use the telephone there, and the rest of them trooped in at the door of the bright little dairy. The plump shop-woman welcomed them beamingly. She considered them her best customers, and they certainly were.

They were each on their second doughnut when Julian came back. 'Any news?' asked Dick.

'Yes,' said Julian. 'Peculiar news, though. I found the address of the Society – they've got a branch about fifty miles from here – that deals with all the old buildings for a radius of a hundred miles. I asked if they had any recent booklet about the castle.'

He stopped to take a doughnut, and bit into it. The others waited patiently while he chewed.

'They said they hadn't. The last time they had checked over Faynights Castle was two years ago.'

'But – but what about those two men who came from the Society last week, then?' said George.

'Yes. That's what *I* said,' answered Julian, taking another bite. 'And here's the peculiar bit. They said they

320

didn't know what I was talking about, nobody had been sent there from the Society, and who was I, anyhow?'

'Hmm!' said Dick, thinking hard. 'Then – those men were examining and exploring the castle for their own reasons!'

'I agree,' said Julian. 'And I can't help thinking that the face at the window and those two men have something to do with one another. It's quite clear that the men had nothing whatever to do with any official society – they merely gave it as an excuse because they wanted to find out what kind of hiding-place the castle had.'

The others stared at him, feeling a familiar excitement rising in them – what George called the 'adventure feeling'.

'Then there *was* a real face at that tower window, and there *is* a way of getting up there,' said Anne.

'Yes,' said Julian. 'I know it sounds very far-fetched, but I do think there is just a possibility that those two scientists have gone there. I don't know if you read it in the paper, but one of them, Jeffrey Pottersham, has written a book on famous ruins. He would know all about Faynights Castle, because it's a very well-known one. If they wanted to hide somewhere till the hue and cry had died down, and then escape to another country, well . . .'

'They could hide in the tower, and then quietly slip out from the castle one night, go down to the sea, and hire a fishing-boat!' cried Dick, taking the words out of Julian's mouth. 'They'd be across the Channel in no time.'

'Yes. That's what I'd worked out too,' said Julian. 'I rather think I'll telephone Uncle Quentin about this. I'll describe the face as well as I can to him. I feel this is all rather too important to manage quite on our own. Those men may have extremely important secrets.'

'It's an adventure again,' said Jo, her face serious, but her eyes very bright. 'Oh – I'm *glad* I'm in it too!'

CHAPTER FIFTEEN

An interesting day

EVERYONE BEGAN to feel distinctly excited. 'I think I'll catch the bus into the next town,' said Julian. 'The telephone-box here is too easily overheard. I'd rather go to a kiosk somewhere in a street, where nobody can hear what I'm saying.'

'All right. You go,' said Dick. 'We'll do some shopping and go back to the caravans. I wonder what Uncle Quentin will say!'

Julian went off to the bus-stop. The others wandered in and out of the few village shops, doing their shopping. Tomatoes, lettuces, mustard and cress, sausage rolls, fruit cake, tins of fruit, and plenty of creamy milk in big quart bottles.

They met some of the fair-folk in the street, and everyone was very friendly indeed. Mrs Alfredo was there with an enormous basket, nearly as big as herself. She beamed and called across to them.

'You see I have to do my shopping myself! That big bad man is too lazy to do it for me. And he has no brains. I tell him to bring back meat and he brings fish, I tell him to buy cabbage and he brings lettuce. He has no brains!'

The children laughed. It was strange to find great big

323

Alfredo, a real fire-eater, ordered about and grumbled at by his tiny little wife.

'It's a change to find them all so friendly,' said George, pleased. 'Long may it last. There's the snake-man, Mr Slither – he hasn't got his snakes with him, though.'

'He'd have the whole village to himself if he did!' said Anne. 'I wonder what he buys to feed his snakes on.'

'They're only fed once a fortnight,' said Jo. 'They swallow . . .'

'No, don't tell me,' said Anne, hastily. 'I don't really want to know. Look, there's Skippy.'

Skippy waved cheerily. She carried bags filled to bursting too. The fair-folk certainly did themselves well.

'They must make a lot of money,' said Anne.

'Well, they spend it when they have it,' said Jo. 'They never save. It's either a good time for them or a very bad time. They must have had a good run at the last show-place – they all seem very rich!'

They went back to the camp and spent a very interesting day, because the fair-folk, eager to make up for their unfriendly behaviour, made them all very welcome. Alfredo explained his fire-eating a little more, and showed how he put wads of cotton wool at the hook-end of his torches, and then soaked them in petrol to flare easily.

The rubber-man obligingly wriggled in and out of the wheel-spokes of his caravan, a most amazing feat. He also doubled himself up, and twisted his arms and legs together in such a peculiar manner that he seemed to be more like a four-tentacled octopus than a human being.

He offered to teach Dick how to do this, but Dick couldn't even bend himself properly double. He was disappointed because he couldn't help thinking what a marvellous trick it would be to perform in the playing-field at school.

Mr Slither gave them a most entertaining talk about snakes, and ended up with some information about poisonous snakes that he said they might find very useful indeed.

'Take rattlers now,' he said, 'or mambas, or any poisonous snake. If you want to catch one to tame, don't go after it with a stick, or pin it to the ground. That frightens it and you can't do anything with it.'

'What do you have to do then?' asked George.

'Well, you want to watch their forked tongues,' said Mr Slither, earnestly. 'You know how they put them out, and make them quiver and shake?'

'Yes,' said everyone.

'Well, now, if a poisonous snake makes its tongue go all stiff without a quiver in it, just be careful,' said Mr Slither, solemnly. 'Don't you touch it then. But if its tongue is nice and quivery, just slide your arms along its body, and it will let you pick it up.' He went through the motions he described, picking up a pretend snake and letting its body slither through his arms. It was fascinating to watch, but very weird.

325

'Thanks most awfully,' said Dick. 'Whenever I pick up poisonous snakes, I'll do exactly as you say.'

The others laughed. Dick sounded as if he went about picking up poisonous snakes every day! Mr Slither was pleased to have such an appreciative audience. George and Anne, however, had firmly made up their minds that they were not going even to *look* at a snake's tongue if it put it out – they were going to run for miles!

There were a few more fair-folk there that the children didn't know much about – Dacca, the tap-dancer, who put on high boots and tap-danced for the children on the top step of her caravan – Pearl, who was an acrobat and could walk on wire-rope, dance on it, and turn somersaults over it, landing back safely each time – and others who belonged to the show but only helped with the crowds and the various turns.

Jo didn't know them all, but she was soon so much one of them that the children began to wonder if she would ever go back to her foster-mother again!

'She's exactly like them all now,' said George. 'Cheerful and dirty, slap-dash and generous, lazy and yet hardworking too! Bufflo practises for hours at his rope-spinning, but he lies about for hours too. They're strange folk, but I really do like them very much.'

The others agreed with her heartily. They had their lunch without Julian, because he hadn't come back. Why was he so long? He only had to telephone his uncle!

He came back at last. 'Sorry I'm so late,' he said, 'but

326

first of all I couldn't get any answer at all, so I waited a bit in case Aunt Fanny and Uncle Quentin were out – and I had lunch while I waited. Then I telephoned again, and Aunt Fanny was in, but Uncle Quentin had gone to London and wouldn't be back till night.'

'To London!' said George, astonished. 'He hardly ever goes to London.'

'Apparently he went up about these two missing scientists,' said Julian. 'He's so certain that his friend Terry-Kane isn't a traitor, and he went up to tell the authorities so. Well, I couldn't wait till night, of course.'

'Didn't you report our news then?' said Dick, disappointed.

'Yes. But I had to tell Aunt Fanny,' said Julian. 'She said she would repeat it all to Uncle Quentin when he came back tonight. It's a pity I couldn't get hold of him and find out what he thinks. I asked Aunt Fanny to tell him to write to me at once.'

After tea they sat on the hillside again, basking in the sun. It really was wonderful weather for them. Julian looked over to the ruined castle opposite. He fixed his eyes on the tower where they had seen the face. It was so far away that he could only just make out the window-slit.

'Get your glasses, George,' he said. 'We may as well have another squint at the window. It was about this time that we saw the face.'

George fetched them. She would not give them to Julian first though – she put them to her own eyes and gazed at the window. At first she saw nothing – and then, quite suddenly, a face appeared at the window! George was so astonished that she cried out.

Julian snatched the glasses from her. He focused them on the window and saw the face at once. Yes – the same as yesterday – eyebrows and all!

Dick took the glasses, and then each of them in turn gazed at the strange face. It did not move at all, as far as they could see, but simply stared. Then, when Anne was looking at it, it suddenly disappeared and did not come back again.

'Well – we *didn't* imagine it yesterday then,' said Julian. 'It's there all right. And where there's a face, there should be a body. Er – did any of you think that the face had a – a sort of – despairing expression?'

'Yes,' said Dick and the others agreed. 'I thought so yesterday, too,' said Dick. 'Do you suppose the fellow, whoever he is, is being kept prisoner up there?'

'It looks like it,' said Julian. 'But how in the world did he get there? It's a marvellous place to put him, of course. Nobody would ever dream of a hiding-place like that – and if it hadn't been for us looking at the jackdaws through very fine field-glasses, we'd never have seen him looking out. It was a chance in a thousand that we saw him.'

'In a *million*,' said Dick. 'Look here, Ju – I think we ought to go up to the castle and yell up to the fellow – he might be able to yell back, or throw a message out.'

'He would have thrown out a message before now if he'd been able to,' said Julian. 'As for yelling, he'd have to lean right out of that thick-walled window to make himself heard. He's right at the back of it, remember, and the slit is very deep.'

'Can't we go and find out something?' said George, who was longing to take some action. 'After all, Timmy got in somewhere, and we might be able to as well.'

'That's quite an idea,' said Julian. 'Timmy *did* find a way in – and it may be the way that leads up to the top of the tower.'

'Let's go then,' said George at once.

'Not now,' said Julian. 'We'd be seen if we scrambled about on the hill outside the castle walls. We'd have to go at night. We could go when the moon comes up.'

A shiver of excitement ran through the whole five. Timmy thumped his tail on the ground. He had been listening all the time, just as if he understood.

'We'll take you too, Timmy,' said George, 'just in case we run into any trouble.'

'We shan't get into trouble,' said Julian. 'We're only going to explore – and I don't think for a minute we'll find much, because I'm sure we shan't be able to get up into the tower. But I expect you all feel like I do – you can't leave this mystery of the face at the window alone – you want to *do* something about it, even if it's only scrambling round the old walls at night.'

'Yes. That's *exactly* how I feel,' said George. 'I wouldn't

329

be able to go to sleep tonight, I know. Oh, Julian – isn't this exciting?'

'Very,' said Julian. 'I'm glad we didn't leave today, after all! We should have, if we hadn't seen that face at the window.'

The sun went down and the air grew rather cold. They went into the boys' caravan and played cards, not feeling at all sleepy. Jo was very bad at cards, and soon stopped playing. She sat watching, her arm round Timmy's neck.

They had a supper of sausage rolls and tinned strawberries. 'It's a pity they don't have meals like this at school,' said Dick. 'No trouble to prepare, and most delicious to eat. Julian – is it time to go?'

'Yes,' said Julian. 'Put on warm things – and we'll set off! Here's to a really adventurous night!'

CHAPTER SIXTEEN

Secret ways

THEY WAITED till the moon went behind a cloud, and then, like moving shadows, made their way down the hillside as fast as they could. They did not want any of the fair-folk to see them. They clambered over the stile and went up the lane. They made their way up the steep path to the castle, but when they came to the little tower where the turnstile was they went off to the right, and walked round the foot of the great, thick walls.

It was difficult to walk there, because the slope of the hill was so steep. Timmy went with them, excited at this unexpected walk.

'Now, Timmy, listen – we want you to show us how you got in,' said George. 'Are you listening, Timmy? Go in, Timmy, go in where you went this morning.'

Timmy waved his long tail, panted, and let his tongue hang out in the way he did when he wanted to show he was being as helpful as he could. He ran in front, sniffing.

Then he suddenly stopped and looked back. He gave a little whine. The others hurried to him.

The moon most annoyingly went behind a cloud. Julian took out his torch and shone it where Timmy stood. The dog stood there, looking very pleased.

'Well, what is there to be pleased about, Timmy?' said
Julian, puzzled. 'There's no hole there – nowhere you

could possibly have got in. What are you trying to show us?'

Timmy gave a little bark. Then suddenly leapt about four feet up the uneven stones of the wall, and disappeared!

'Hey – where's he gone?' said Julian, startled. He flashed his torch up. 'I say, look! There's a stone missing up there, quite a big block – and Timmy's gone in at the hole.'

'There's the block – fallen down the hillside,' said Dick, pointing to a big white stone, roughly square in shape. 'But how has Timmy gone in, Ju? This wall is frightfully thick, and even if one stone falls out, there must be plenty more behind!'

Julian climbed up. He came to the space where the great fallen stone had been and flashed his torch there. 'I say – this is interesting!' he called. 'The wall is hollow just here. Timmy's gone into the hollow!'

At once a surge of excitement went through the whole lot. 'Can we get in and follow Timmy?' called George. 'Shout to him, Julian, and see where he is.'

Julian called into the hollow. 'Timmy! Timmy, where are you?'

A distant, rather muffled bark answered him, and then Timmy's eyes suddenly gleamed up at Julian. The dog was standing down in the small hollow behind the fallen stone. 'He's here,' called back Julian. 'I tell you what I think we've hit on. When this enormous wall was built, a space was left inside – either to save stones, or to make a hidden passage, I don't know which. And that fallen stone has exposed a bit of the hollow. Shall we explore?'

'Oh, *yes*,' came the answer at once. Julian climbed down into the middle of the wall. He flashed his torch into the space he was standing in. 'Yes,' he called, 'it's a kind of passage. It's small, though. We'll have to bend almost double to get along it. Anne, you come next, then I can help you.'

'Will the air be all right?' called Dick into the passage.

'It smells a bit musty,' said Julian. 'But if it really *is* a passage, there must be secret air-holes somewhere to keep the air fresh in here. That's right, Anne – you hang on to me. Jo, you come next, then George, then Dick.'

Soon they were all in the curious passage, which ran along in the centre of the wall. It certainly was very small. They all got tired of going along bent double. It was pitch dark too, and although they all had torches, except Jo, it was very difficult to see.

Anne hung on to Julian's jacket for dear life. She wasn't enjoying this very much, but she wouldn't have been left out of it for anything.

Julian suddenly stopped, and everyone bumped into the one in front. 'What's up?' called Dick, from the back.

'Steps here!' shouted back Julian. 'Steps going down very very steeply – almost like a stone ladder. Be careful, everybody!'

The steps were certainly steep. 'Better go down

backwards,' decided Julian. 'Then we can have handholds as well as foot-holds. Anne, wait till I'm down and I'll help you.'

The steps went down for about ten feet. Julian got down safely, then Anne turned herself round and went down backwards too, as if she were on a ladder instead of on stairs. It was much easier that way.

At the bottom was another passage, wider and higher, for which everyone was devoutly thankful. 'Where does *this* lead to?' said Julian, stopping to think. 'This passage is at right angles to the wall – we've left the wall now – we're going underneath part of the courtyard, I should think.'

'I bet we're not far from that tower,' called Dick. 'I say – I do hope this leads to the tower.'

Nobody could possibly tell where it was going to lead to! Anyway, it seemed to run quite straight, and after about eighty feet of it, Julian stopped again.

'Steps up again!' he called. 'Just as steep as the others. I think we may be going up into the inside of the castle walls. This is possibly a secret way into one of the old rooms of the castle.'

They went carefully up the steep stone steps and found themselves, not in a passage, but in a very small room that appeared to be hollowed out of the wall of the castle itself. Julian stopped in surprise, and everyone crowded into the tiny room. It really wasn't much larger than a big cupboard. A narrow bench stood at one side, with a shelf above it. An old pitcher stood on the shelf, with a broken lip, and on the bench was a small dagger, rusty and broken.

'I *say*! Look here! This is a secret room – like they used to have in old places, so that someone might hide if necessary,' said Julian. 'We're inside one of the walls of the castle itself – perhaps the wall of an old bedroom!'

'And there's the old pitcher that had water in,' said George. 'And a dagger. Who hid here – and how long ago?'

Dick flashed his torch round to see if he could spot anything else. He gave a sudden exclamation, and kept his torch fixed on a corner of the room.

'What is it?' said Julian.

'Paper – red and blue silver paper,' said Dick. 'Chocolate wrapping! How many times have we bought this kind of chocolate, wrapped in silver paper patterned with red and blue!'

He picked it up and straightened it out. Yes – there was the name of the chocolate firm on it!

Everyone was silent. This could only mean one thing. *Someone* had been in this room lately – someone who ate chocolate – someone who had thrown down the wrapping never expecting it to be found!

'Well,' said Julian, breaking the silence. 'This *is* surprising. Someone else knows this way in. Where does it lead to? Up to that tower, I imagine!'

'Hadn't we better be careful?' said Dick, lowering his voice. 'I mean – whoever was here might quite well be wandering about somewhere near.'

'Yes. Perhaps we'd better go back,' said Julian, thinking of the girls.

'No,' said George, in a fierce whisper. 'Let's go on. We can be very cautious.'

A passage led from the strange hidden room. It went along on the level for a little way, and then they arrived at a spiral stairway that ran straight upwards like a corkscrew.

At the top they came to a small, very narrow door. It had a great, old-fashioned iron ring for a handle.

Julian stood hesitating. Should he open it or not? He stood for half a minute, trying to make up his mind. He whispered back to the others. 'I've come to a little door. Shall I open it?'

'Yes,' came back the answering whispers. Julian cautiously took hold of the iron ring. He turned it, and it made no noise. He wondered if the door was locked on the other side. But it wasn't. It opened silently.

Julian looked through it, expecting to see a room, but there wasn't one. Instead he found himself on a small gallery that seemed to run all the way round the inside of the tower. The moon shone in through a slit-window, and Julian could just make out that he must be looking down from a gallery into the darkness of a tower room on the second or third floor of the tower – the third, probably.

He pulled Anne out and the other three followed. There was no sound to be heard. Julian whispered to the others.

337

'We've come out on to a gallery, which overlooks one of the rooms inside the tower. It may be a second-floor room, because we know that the ceiling of the first floor has fallen in. Or perhaps it's even the third floor.'

'Must be the third,' said Dick. 'We're pretty high.' His whisper went all round the gallery and came back to them. He had spoken more loudly than Julian. It made them jump.

'How do we get higher still?' whispered George.

'Is there any way up from this gallery?'

'We'll walk round it and see,' said Julian. 'Be as quiet as you can. I don't *think* there's anyone here, but you never know. And watch your step, in case the stone isn't sound – it's very crumbly here and there.'

Julian led the way round the curious little gallery. Had this tower room been used for old plays or mimes? Was the gallery for spectators? He wished he could turn back the years and lean over the gallery to see what had been going on in the room below, when the castle was full of people.

About three-quarters of the way round the gallery a little flight of steps led downwards into the room below. But just beyond where the steps began there was another door set in the wall, very like the one they had just come through.

It too had an iron ring for a handle. Julian turned it slowly. It didn't open. Was it locked? There was a great key standing in the iron lock, and Julian turned it. But still the door didn't open. Then he saw that it was bolted.

The bolt was securely pushed home. So somebody was a prisoner on the other side! Was it the man who owned the Face? Julian turned and whispered very softly in Anne's ear.

'There's a door here bolted on my side. Looks as if we're coming to the Face. Tell George to send Timmy right up to me.'

Anne whispered to George, and George pushed Timmy forward. He squeezed past Anne's legs and stood by Julian, sensing the sudden excitement.

'We're probably coming to stairs that lead up to the top tower room, where that window is with the Face,' thought Julian, as he slid back the bolt very cautiously. He pushed the door, and it opened. He stood listening, his torch switched off. Then he switched it on.

Just as he had thought, another stone stairway led up steeply. At the top must be the prisoner, whoever he was.

'We'll go up,' said Julian softly. 'Quiet, everybody!'

CHAPTER SEVENTEEN

Excitement and shocks

TIMMY STRAINED forward, but Julian had his hand on the dog's collar. He went up the stone stairway, very steep and narrow. The others followed with hardly a sound. All of them but Jo had on their rubber shoes; she had bare feet. Timmy made the most noise, because his claws clicked on the stone.

At the top was another door. From behind it came a curious noise – guttural and growling. Timmy growled in his throat. At first Julian couldn't think what the noise was. Then he suddenly knew.

'Somebody snoring! Well, that's lucky. I can take a peep in and see who it is. We must be at the top of the tower now.'

The door in front of him was not locked. He pushed it open and looked inside, his hand still on Timmy's collar.

The moonlight struck through a narrow window and fell on the face of a sleeping man. Julian stared at it in rising excitement. Those eyebrows! Yes – this was the man whose face had appeared at the window!

'And I know who he is too – it *is* Terry-Kane!' thought Julian, moving like a shadow into the room. 'He's exactly like the picture we saw in the papers. Perhaps the other man is here too.'

He looked cautiously round the room but could see no one else, although it was possible there might be someone in the darkest shadows. He listened.

There was only the snoring of the man lying in the moonlight. He could not hear the breathing of anyone else. With his hand still on Timmy's collar he switched on his torch and swept it round the tower room, its beam piercing the black corners.

No one was there except the one man – and, with a sudden shock, Julian saw that he was tied with ropes! His arms were bound behind him and his legs were tied together too. If this was Terry-Kane then his uncle must be right. The man was no traitor – he had been kidnapped and was a prisoner.

Everyone was now in the room, staring at the sleeping man. He had his mouth open, and he still snored loudly.

'What are you going to do, Julian?' whispered George. 'Wake him up?'

Julian nodded. He went over to the sleeping man and shook him by the shoulder. He woke up at once and stared in amazement at Julian, who was full in the moonlight. He struggled up to a sitting position.

'Who are you?' he said. 'How did you get here – and who are those over in the shadows there?'

'Listen – are you Mr Terry-Kane?' asked Julian.

'Yes. I am. But who are you?'

FIVE HAVE A WONDERFUL TIME

'We are staying on the hill opposite the castle,' said
Julian. 'And we saw your face at the window, through our
field-glasses. So we came to find you.'

'But – but how do you know who I am?' said the man, still amazed.

'We read about you in the papers,' said Julian. 'And we saw your picture. We couldn't help noticing your eyebrows, sir – we even saw them through the glasses.'

'Look here – can you undo me?' said the man, eagerly. 'I must escape. Tomorrow night my enemies are smuggling me out of here, into a car and down to the sea – and a boat is being hired to take me across to the Continent. They want me to tell them what I know about my latest experiments. I shan't, of course – but life wouldn't be at all pleasant for me!'

'I'll cut the ropes,' said Julian, and he took out his pocket-knife. He cut the knots that tied Terry-Kane's wrists together and then freed his legs. Timmy stood and watched, ready to pounce if the man did anything fierce!

'That's better,' said the man, stretching his arms out.

'How did you manage to get to the window?' asked Julian, watching the man rub his arms and knees.

'Each evening one of the men who brought me here comes to bring me food and drink,' said Terry-Kane. 'He undoes my hands so that I can feed myself. He sits and smokes while I eat, taking no notice of me. I drag myself over to the window to have a breath of fresh air. I can't stay there long because I am soon tied up again, of course. I can't imagine how anyone could see my face at this deep-set slit-window!'

343

'It was our field-glasses,' said Julian. 'They are such fine ones. It's a good thing you *did* get to the window for a breath of air or we'd never have found you!'

'Julian – I can hear a noise,' said Jo, suddenly. She had ears like a cat, able to pick up the slightest sound.

'Where?' said Julian, turning sharply.

'Downstairs,' whispered Jo. 'Wait – I'll go and see.'

She slipped out of the door and down the steep little stairs. She came to the door at the bottom, the one that led into the gallery.

Yes – someone was coming! Coming along the gallery too. Jo thought quickly. If she darted back up the stairs to warn the others, this newcomer might go up there too, and they would all be caught. He could bolt the door at the top and would have six prisoners instead of one! She decided to crouch down on the floor of the gallery a little beyond the door that led upwards.

Footsteps came loudly along the gallery and up to the door. Then the stranger obviously found the door unbolted, and stopped in consternation. He stood perfectly still, listening. Jo thought he really must be able to hear her heart beating, it was thumping so loudly. She didn't dare to call out to try and warn the others – if she did they would walk straight into his arms!

And then Jo heard Julian's voice calling quietly down the stone stairs. 'Jo! Jo! Where are you?' And then, oh dear, she thought she could hear Julian coming down the stairs to find her. 'Don't come, Julian,' she said under her breath. 'Don't come.'

But Julian came right down – and behind him came Terry-Kane and Dick, with the girls following with Timmy, on their way to escaping.

The stranger down at the door was even more amazed to hear voices and footsteps. He slammed the door suddenly and rammed the stout bolt home. The footsteps on the stairs stopped in alarm.

'Hey, Jo! Is that you?' called Julian's voice. 'Open the door!'

The stranger spoke angrily. 'The door's bolted. Who are you?'

There was a silence – then Terry-Kane answered. 'So you're back again, Pottersham! Open that door at once.'

Oho! thought Julian, so the other scientist is here too – Jeffrey Pottersham. He must have got Terry-Kane here by kidnapping him. What can have happened to Jo?

The man at the door stood there as if he didn't quite know what to do. Jo crouched down in the gallery and listened intently. The man spoke again.

'Who set you free? Who's that with you?'

'Now, listen, Pottersham,' said Terry-Kane's voice. 'I've had enough of this nonsense. You must be out of your mind, acting like this! Doping me, and kidnapping me, telling me we're going to go off by fishing-boat to the Continent, and the rest of it! There are four children here, who saw my face at the window and came to investigate, and . . .'

'*Children!*' said Pottersham, taken aback. 'What, in the middle of the night! How did they get up to this tower? I'm the only one that knows the way in.'

'Pottersham, open the door!' shouted Terry-Kane, furiously. He gave it a kick, but the old door was sturdy and strong.

'You can go back to the tower, all of you,' said Pottersham. 'I'm going off to get fresh orders. It looks as if we'll have to take those kids with us, Terry-Kane – they'll be sorry they saw your face at the window. They won't like life where we're going!'

Pottersham turned and went back the way he had come. Jo guessed that he knew the same way in as they had happened on. She waited until she felt that it was perfectly safe, and then she ran to the door again. She hammered on it.

'Dick! Dick! Come down. Where are you?' She heard an answering shout from up the stairs behind the door, and then Dick came running down.

'Jo! Unbolt the door, quick!'

Jo unbolted it – but it wouldn't open. Julian had now come down too, and he called to Jo: 'Turn the key, Jo. It may be locked too.'

'Julian, the key's gone!' cried Jo, and she tugged in vain at the door. 'He must have locked it as well as bolted it – and he's taken the key. Oh, how can I get you out?'

EXCITEMENT AND SHOCKS

'You can't,' said Dick. 'Still, *you're* free, Jo. You can go and tell the police. Buck up, now. You know the way, don't you?'

'I haven't got a torch,' said Jo.

'Oh dear – well, we can't possibly get one of ours out to you,' said Dick. 'You'd better wait till morning, then, Jo. You may lose yourself down in those dark passages. Yes – wait till morning.'

'The passages will still be dark!' said poor Jo. 'I'd better go now.'

'No – you're to wait till morning,' said Julian, fearing that Jo might wander off in the strange passages, and be lost for ever! She might even find herself down in the dungeons. Horrible thought.

'All right,' said Jo. 'I'll wait till morning. I'll curl up on the gallery here. It's quite warm.'

'It will be very hard!' said Dick. 'We'll go back to the room upstairs, Jo. Call us if you want us. What a blessing you're free!'

Jo curled up on the gallery, but she couldn't sleep. For one thing the floor was very hard, and the stone was very very cold. She suddenly thought of the little room where they had seen the pitcher, the dagger and the chocolate wrapping-paper. That would be a far better place to sleep! She could lie on the bench!

She stood up and thought out the way. All she had to do was to go round the gallery till she came to the little door that opened on to the corkscrew staircase leading from the gallery to the little hidden room.

She made her way cautiously to the door. She felt for the iron ring, turned it and opened the door. It was very, very dark, and she could see nothing at all in front of her. She put out her foot carefully. Was she at the top of the spiral staircase?

She found that she was. She held out her hands on either side, touching the stone walls of the curious little stairway, and went slowly down, step by step.

'Oh dear – am I going the right way? The stairs seem to be going on so long!' thought Jo. 'I don't like it – but I MUST go on!'

CHAPTER EIGHTEEN

Jo has an adventure on her own

JO CAME to the end of the spiral stairway at last. She found herself on the level once more, and remembered the little straight passage that led to the secret room from the stairway. Good, good, good! Now she would soon be in the room and could lie down on the bench.

She went through the doorway of the secret room without knowing it, because it was so dark. She groped her way along, and suddenly felt the edge of the bench.

'Here at last,' she said thankfully, out loud.

And then poor Jo got a dreadful shock! A pair of strong arms went round her and held her fast! She screamed and struggled, her heart beating in wild alarm. Who was it? Oh, if only she had a light!

And then a torch was switched on, and held to her face. 'Oho! You must be Jo, I suppose,' said Pottersham's voice. 'I wondered who you were when one of those kids yelled out for you! I thought you must be wandering somewhere about. I guessed you'd come this way, and I sat on the bench and waited for you.'

'Let me go,' said Jo fiercely and struggled like a wild cat. The man only held her all the more tightly. He was very strong.

Jo suddenly put down her face and bit his hand. He gave a shout and loosened his hold. Jo was almost free when he caught her again, and shook her like a rat. 'You little wild cat! Don't you do that again!'

Jo did it again, even more fiercely, and the man dropped her on to the ground, nursing his hand. Jo made for the entrance of the room, but again the man was too quick and she found herself held again.

'I'll tie you up,' said the man, furiously. 'I'll rope you so that you won't be able to move! And I'll leave you here in the dark till I come back again.'

He took a rope from round his waist and proceeded to tie Jo up so thoroughly that she could hardly move. Her hands were behind her back, her legs were tied at the knees and ankles. She rolled about the floor, calling the man all the names she knew.

'Well, you're safe for the time being,' said Pottersham, sucking his bitten hand. 'Now I'm going. I wish you joy of the hard cold floor and the darkness, you savage little wild cat!'

Jo heard his footsteps going in the distance. She could have kicked herself for not having guessed he might have been lying in wait for her. Now she couldn't get help for the others. In fact, she was much worse off than they were because she was tied up, and they weren't.

Poor Jo! She dozed off, exhausted by the night's excitement and her fierce struggle. She lay against the wall, so uncomfortable that she kept waking from her doze every few minutes.

And then a thought came into her head. She remembered the rope-man, all tied up in length after length of knotted rope. She had watched him set himself free so many times. Could any of his tricks help her now?

'The rope-man would be able to get himself free of this rope in two minutes!' she thought, and began to wriggle and struggle again. But she was not the rope-man, and after about an hour she was so exhausted again that she went into a doze once more.

When she awoke, she felt better. She forced herself into a sitting position, and made herself think clearly and slowly.

'Work one knot free first,' she said to herself, remembering what the rope-man had told her. 'At first you won't know which knot is best. When you know that you will always be able to free yourself in two minutes. But find that one knot first!'

She said all this to herself as she tried to find a knot that might be worked loose. At last one seemed a little looser than the others. It was one that bound her left wrist to her right. She twisted her wrist round and got her thumb to the knot. She picked and pulled and at last it loosened a little. She had more control over that hand now. If only she had a knife somewhere! She could manage to get it between her finger and thumb now and perhaps use it to cut another knot.

She suddenly lost her patience and flung her head back on the bench, straining and pulling at the rope. She knocked against something and it fell to the stone floor with a clatter. Jo wondered what it was – and then she knew.

'That dagger! The old, rusty dagger! Oh, if I could find it I might do something with it!'

She swung herself round on the floor till she felt the dagger under her. She rolled over on her back and tried to pick it up with her free finger and thumb, and at last she managed to hold it.

She sat up, bent forward and did her best to force the rusty dagger up and down a little on the rope that tied her hands behind her. She could hardly move it at all because her hands were still so tightly tied. But she persevered.

She grew so tired that she had to give it up for a long while. Then she tried again, then had another long rest. The third time she was lucky! The rope suddenly frayed and broke! She pulled her hands hard, found them looser and picked at a knot.

It took Jo a long time to free her hands, but she did it at last. She couldn't manage to undo her legs at first, because her hands were trembling so much. But after another long rest she undid the tight knots, and shook her legs free. 'Well, thank goodness I learnt a few hints from the rope-man,' she said, out loud. 'I'd never have got free if I hadn't!'

She wondered what the time was. It was pitch dark in the little room, of course. She stood up and was surprised to find that her legs were shaky. She staggered a few steps and then sat down again. But her legs soon felt better and she stood up once more. 'Now to find my way out,' she said. 'How I wish I had a torch!'

She went carefully down the flight of stone steps that

led down from the room, and then came to the wide passage that ran under the courtyard. She went along it, glad it was level, and then came once again to stone steps that led upwards. Up she climbed, knowing that she was going the right way, although she was in the dark.

Now she came to the small passage where she had to bend almost double, the one that ran through the centre of the thick outer walls. Jo heaved a sigh of relief. Surely she would soon come to where the stone had fallen out and would be able to see daylight!

She saw daylight before she came to the place where the stone was missing. She saw it some way in front of her, a misty little patch that made her wonder what it was at first. Then she knew.

'Daylight! Oh, thank goodness!' She stumbled along to it and climbed up to the hole from which the stone had fallen. She sat there, drinking in the sunlight. It was bright and warm and very comforting.

After the darkness of the passages Jo felt quite dazed. Then she suddenly realised how very high the sun was in the sky! Goodness, it must be afternoon!

She looked cautiously out of the hole in the wall. Now that she was so near freedom she didn't want to be caught by anyone watching out for her! There was nobody. Jo leapt down from the hole and ran down the steep hillside. She went as sure-footed as a goat, leaping along till she came to the lane. She crossed it and made her way to the caravan-field.

She was just about to go over the stile when she stopped. Julian had said she was to go to the police. But Jo, like the other traveller folk, was afraid of the police. No traveller ever asked the police for help. Jo felt herself shrivelling up inside when she thought of talking to big policemen.

'No. I'll go to Uncle Fredo,' she thought. 'He will know what to do. I will tell him about it.'

She was going up the field when she saw someone strange there! Who was it? Could it be that horrid man who had tied her up? She had not seen him at all clearly,

355

and she was afraid it might be. She saw that he was talking urgently to some of the fair-folk. They were listening politely, but Jo could see that they thought he was rather mad.

She went a bit nearer, and found that he was asking where Julian and the rest were. He was becoming very angry with the fair-people because they assured him that they did not know where the children had gone.

'It's the man they called Pottersham,' said Jo to herself, and dived under a caravan. 'He's come to find out how much we've told anyone about that Face.'

She hid till he had gone away down the hillside to the lane, very red in the face, and shouting out that he would get the police.

Jo crawled out, and the fair-folk crowded round her at once. 'Where have you been? Where are the others? That man wanted to know all about you. He sounds quite mad!'

'He's a *bad* man,' said Jo. 'I'll tell you all about him – and where the others are. We've got to rescue them!'

Whereupon Jo launched into her story with the greatest zest, beginning in the middle, then going back to the beginning, putting in things she had forgotten, and thoroughly muddling everyone. When she ended they all stared at her in excitement. They didn't really know what it was all about but they had certainly gathered a few things.

'You mean to say that those kids are locked up in that

tower over there?' said Alfredo, amazed. 'And a spy is with them!'

'No – *he's* not a spy – he's a good man,' explained Jo. 'What they call a scientist, very, very, clever.'

'That man who left just now, he said he was a – a scientist,' said Skippy, stumbling over the unfamiliar word.

'Well, he's a *bad* man,' said Jo, firmly. 'He is probably a spy. He kidnapped the good man, up in the tower there, to take him away to another country. And he tied me up too, like I told you. See my wrists and ankles?'

She displayed them, cut and bruised. The fair-folk looked at them in silence. Then Bufflo cracked his whip and made everyone jump.

'We will rescue them!' he said. 'This is no police job. It is our job.'

'I say, look – that scientist comes back,' said Skippy suddenly. And sure enough, there he was, coming hurriedly up the field to ask some more questions!

'We will get him,' muttered Bufflo. All the fair-folk waited in silence for the man to come up. Then they closed round him solidly and began to walk up the hill. The man was taken with them. He couldn't help himself! He was walked behind a caravan, and before the crowd had come apart again he was on the ground, neatly roped by the rope-man!

'Well, we've got *you*,' said the rope-man. 'And now we'll get on to the next bit of business!'

CHAPTER NINETEEN

Jo joins in

THE 'SCIENTIST', as Skippy persisted in calling him, was put into an empty caravan with windows and doors shut, because he shouted so loudly. When the snake-man opened the door and slid in one of his pythons the scientist stopped shouting at once and lay extremely still.

The snake-man opened the door and his python glided out again. But the man in the caravan had learnt his lesson. Not another sound came from him!

Then everyone in the camp held a conference. There was no hurry about it at all, because it had been decided that nothing should be done before night-time.

'If we make a rescue in the daylight, then the police will come,' said Alfredo. 'They will interfere. They will not believe a word we say. They never do.'

'How shall we rescue them?' said Skippy. 'Do we go through these strange passages and up steep stone stairs? It does not sound nice to me.'

'It isn't at all nice,' Jo assured her. 'And anyway it wouldn't be sensible. The door leading to the tower room is locked, I told you. And that man has got the key.'

'Ah!' said Bufflo, springing up at once. 'You didn't tell us that before! He has the key? Then I will get it from him!'

358

'I didn't think of that,' said Jo, watching Bufflo leap up the caravan steps.

He came out in a minute or two and joined them again. 'He has no key on him,' he said. 'He says he never had. He says we are all mad, and he will get the police.'

'He will find it hard to get the police just yet,' said Mrs Alfredo, and gave a high little laugh. 'He has thrown away the key – or given it to a friend, perhaps?'

'Well, it's settled we can't get in through the door that leads to the tower room, then,' said the snakeman, who seemed to have a better grasp of things than the others. 'Right. Is there any other way into the room?'

'Only by the window,' said Jo. 'That slit-window there, see? Too high for any ladder, of course. Anyway, we've got to get into the courtyard first. We'll have to climb over the high castle wall.'

'That is easy,' said the rubber-man. 'I can climb any wall. But not, perhaps, one so high as the tower wall.'

'Can anyone get into or out of the slit of a window?' asked Bufflo, screwing up his eyes to look at the tower.

'Oh, yes – it's bigger than you think,' said Jo. 'It's very *deep* – the walls are so thick, you see – though I don't think they are so thick up there as they are down below. But Bufflo, how can anyone get up to that window?'

'It can be done,' said Bufflo. 'That is not so difficult! You can lend us a peg-rope, Jekky?' he said to the rope-man.

'Yes,' said Jekky. Jo knew what that was – a thick rope with pegs thrust through the strands to act as footholds.

'But how will you get the peg-rope up?' said Jo, puzzled.

'It can be done,' said Bufflo again, and the talking went on. Jo suddenly began to feel terribly hungry and got up to get herself a meal. When she got back to the conference everything was apparently settled.

'We set off tonight as soon as darkness comes,' Bufflo told her. 'You will not come, Jo. This is man's business.'

'Of course I'm coming!' said Jo, amazed that anyone should think she wasn't. 'They're my friends, aren't they? I'm coming all right!'

'You are not,' said Bufflo, and Jo immediately made up her mind to disappear before the men set off and hide somewhere so that she might follow them.

By this time it was about six o'clock. Bufflo and the rope-man disappeared into Jekky's caravan and became very busy there. Jo went peeping in at the door to see what they were doing but they ordered her out.

'This is not your business any more,' they said, and turned her out when she refused to go.

When darkness came, a little company set out from the camp. They had searched for Jo to make sure she was not coming, but she had disappeared. Bufflo led the way down the hill, looking extremely fat because he was wound about with a great deal of peg-rope. Then came Mr Slither with one of his pythons draped round him. Then the rubber-man with Mr Alfredo.

Bufflo also carried his whip though nobody quite knew why. Anyway, Bufflo always did carry a whip, it was part of him, so nobody questioned him about it.

Behind them, like a little shadow, slipped Jo. What were they going to do? She had watched the tower-window for the last two hours, and when darkness came she saw a light there – a light that shone on and off, on and off.

'That's Dick or Julian signalling,' she thought. 'They will have wondered why I haven't brought help sometime today. They don't know that I was captured and tied up! I'll have something to tell them when we're all together again!'

The little company went over the stile, into the lane and up the path to the castle. They came to the wall. The rubber-man took a jump at it, and literally seemed to run up it, fling himself on to the top, roll over and disappear!

'He's over,' said Bufflo. 'What it is to be made of rubber! I don't believe that fellow ever feels hurt!'

There was a low whistle from the other side of the wall. Bufflo unwound a thin rope from his waist, tied a stone to it and flung it over. The rope slithered after the stone and over the wall like a long thin worm.

Thud! They heard the stone fall on the ground on the other side. Another low whistle told them that the rubber-man had it. Bufflo then undid the peg-rope from his waist, and he and the others held out its length between them, standing one behind the other. One end was fastened to the thin rope whose other end held the stone.

The rubber-man, on the other side of the wall, began to pull on the thin rope. When all the slack was taken in, the peg-rope began to go up the wall too, because it was tied to the thin rope and had to follow it! Up went the peg-rope and up, looking like a great thick caterpillar with tufts sticking out of its sides.

Jo watched. Yes, that was clever. A good and easy way of getting over the thick high wall. But to get the peg-rope up to the slit-window would not be so easy.

A whistle came again. Bufflo let go the peg-rope, and it swung flat against his side of the wall. He tugged it. It was firm. Evidently the rubber-man had tied it fast to something. It was safe to go up. It would bear anyone's weight without slipping down the wall.

Bufflo went up first, using the pegs as foot-holds and pulling himself up by the rope between the pegs. Each of the men was quick and deft in the way he climbed. Jo waited till the last one had started up, and then leapt for the rope too!

Up she went like a cat and landed beside Bufflo on the other side of the wall. He was astounded and gave her a cuff. She dodged away, and stood aside, watching. She wondered how the men intended to reach the topmost window of the high tower. Perhaps she would be of some help. If only she could be!

The four men stood in the moonlight, looking up at the tower. They talked in low tones, while the rubber-man undid the thin rope from the peg-rope, and neatly coiled it into loops. The peg-rope was left on the wall.

Jo heard a car going up the lane at the bottom of the castle hill. She heard it stop and back somewhere. Part of her attention was on the four men and the other part on the car.

The car stopped its engine. There was no further sound. Jo forgot it for a few minutes, and then was on the alert again – was that voices she heard somewhere? She listened intently. The sound came again on the night air – a low murmur that came nearer.

Jo held her breath – could that horrid man – what was his name – Pottersham – could he have arranged for his equally horrid friends to fetch Mr Terry-Kane and all the children out of the tower that night, and take them off to the coast? Perhaps they had already hired a fishing-boat from Joseph the old fisherman, and they would all be away and never heard of again!

So the thoughts ran in Jo's alert mind. Mr Pottersham would have had plenty of time to get fresh orders, and arrange everything before he had gone to the camp and got himself locked up in a caravan! Oh dear – dare she go and warn her Uncle Alfredo, where he stood in the moonlight, holding a little conference with the others?

'He'll cuff me as soon as I go near,' thought Jo, rubbing her left ear, which still stung from Bufflo's cuff. 'They won't listen to me, I know. Still, I'll try.'

She went up to the group of men cautiously. She saw Bufflo take out a dagger-knife from his belt, and tie it to the end of the thin rope that the rubber-man held. She guessed in a moment what he was about to do, and ran to him.

'No, Bufflo, no! Don't throw that knife up – you'll hurt someone – you might wound one of them! No, Bufflo, no!'

'Clear out,' said Bufflo, angrily and raised his hand to slap her. She dodged away.

She went round the group to her uncle. 'Uncle Fredo,' she said, beseechingly, 'listen. I can hear voices – I think those . . .'

Alfredo pushed her away roughly. 'Will you stop this, Jo? Do you want a good whipping? You behave like a buzzing fly!'

Mr Slither called her. 'See here, Jo – if you want to be useful, hold Beauty for me. He will be in the way in a minute.'

He draped the great snake over her shoulders, and Beauty hissed loudly. He began to coil himself round Jo, and she caught hold of his tail. She liked Beauty, but just at that moment she didn't want him at all!

She stood back and watched what Bufflo was going to do. She knew, of course, and her heart beat fearfully. He was going to throw his knife through that high slit-window, a thing that surely only Bufflo, with his unerring aim, could possibly do!

'But if he gets it through the window, it may stick into one of the four up there – or into Mr Terry-Kane,' she thought, in a panic. 'It might wound Dick – or Timmy! Oh, I wish Bufflo wouldn't do it!'

She heard low voices again – this time they came from just the other side of the wall! Men were going to follow those secret passages, and go right up to the tower room! Jo knew they were! They would be there before Bufflo and the others had followed out their rescue plan. She pictured the four children being dragged down the stairs, and Terry-Kane, too. Would Timmy defend them? He would – but the men would certainly deal with him. They knew there was a dog there, because Timmy had barked the night before.

'Oh, dear,' thought Jo, in despair. 'I must do something! But what can I DO?'

CHAPTER TWENTY

A lot of excitement

JO SUDDENLY made up her mind. She would follow the men through those passages, and see if she could warn the others by shouting when she came near enough to the tower room. She would help them *somehow*. Bufflo and the others would be too late to save them now.

Jo ran to the wall. She was up the peg-rope left there and down the other side in a trice. She made her way to where the missing stone left the gap in the old wall.

Beauty, the python, was surprised to find himself pulled off and thrown on the ground, just before Jo ran for the wall. He wasn't used to that sort of treatment. He lay there, coiling and uncoiling himself. Where had that nice girl gone? Beauty liked Jo – she knew how to treat him!

He glided after her. He too went up the wall and over, quite easily, though he did not need to use the peg-rope like Jo. He glided after Jo quickly. It was amazing to see his speed when he really wanted to be quick!

He came to the hole in the wall. Ah, he liked holes. He glided in after Jo. He caught up with her just as she had reached the end of the small passage, through which she had had to walk bent double. He pushed against her legs and then twined himself round her.

She gave a small scream, and then realised what it was. 'Beauty! You'll get into trouble with Mr Slither, coming after me like this. Go back! Stop twining yourself round me – I've got important things to do.'

But Beauty was not like Timmy. He obeyed only when he thought he would, and he was not going to obey this time!

'All right – come with me if you want to,' said Jo, at last, having in vain tried to push the great snake back. 'You'll be company, I suppose. Stop hissing like that, Beauty! You sound like an engine letting off steam in this narrow passage.'

Soon Jo had gone down the steep steps that led to the level passage under the courtyard. Beauty slithered down them too, rather surprised at the sudden drop. Along the wider passage they went, Beauty now in front, and Jo sometimes tripping over his powerful tail.

Up steps again, and into the thick wall of the castle itself. Something shining ahead made Jo suddenly stop. She listened but heard nothing. She went forward cautiously and found that in the little secret room was a small lantern, left there probably by one of the men in front.

She saw the rusty dagger lying on the floor where she had left it the night before and grinned. The rope was there too, that she had untied from her arms and legs.

Jo went on, along the passage that led to the spiral stairway. Now she thought she could hear something. She climbed the steep stairs, cross with Beauty because he

368

pushed by her and almost sent her headlong down them. She came to the door that opened on to the little gallery. Dare she open it? Suppose the men were just outside?

She opened it slowly. It was pitch dark on the other side, of course, but Jo knew she was about to step out on the little gallery. Beauty suddenly slithered up her and coiled himself lovingly round her. Jo could not make the snake uncoil, and she stepped out on the small gallery with Beauty firmly wrapped about her.

And then, what a noise she heard! She stood quite aghast. Whatever could be going on? She heard excited voices – surely one was Bufflo's? And was that crack a pistol-shot?

What had happened down below in the courtyard when Jo had disappeared over the wall with Beauty? None of the men noticed her go. They were all too intent on their plan.

Bufflo was to use his gift for knife-throwing – but in quite a different way from usual! He was to throw the knife high into the air, and make it curve in through the slit-window at the top of the tower!

Bufflo was an expert at knife-throwing, or, indeed, at any kind of throwing. He stood there in the courtyard, looking up at the high window. He half-closed his eyes, getting the distance and the direction fixed in his mind. The moon suddenly went in, and he lowered his hand. He could not throw accurately in the dark!

The moon sailed out again, quite brilliant. Bufflo lost no time. Once more he took aim, his eyes narrowed – and then the knife flew high into the air, gleaming as it went – taking behind it a long tail of very thin rope.

It struck the sill of the slit-window and fell back. Bufflo caught it deftly. The moonlight showed plainly that the knife was not sharp-pointed – Bufflo had filed off the point, and it was now quite blunt. Jo need not have worried about someone in the tower being hurt by a sharp dagger!

A LOT OF EXCITEMENT

Once more Bufflo took aim, and once more the knife sailed up, swift as a swallow, shining silver as it went. This time it fell cleanly in at the window-opening, slithered all the way across the stone ledge inside, and fell to the floor of the tower room with a thud.

It caused the greatest astonishment there. Mr Terry-Kane, the four children and Timmy were all huddled together for warmth in one corner. They were hungry and cold. No one had brought them food, and they had nothing to keep them warm except a rug belonging to Terry-Kane. All that day they had been in the tower room, sometimes looking from the window, sometimes shouting all together at the tops of their voices. But nobody heard them, and nobody saw them.

'Why doesn't Jo bring help?' they had said a hundred times that long, long day. They didn't know that poor Jo was spending hours trying to free herself from the knots round her legs and wrists.

They had looked out of the window at the camp on the opposite hill, where the fair-folk went about their business, looking like ants on the far-off green slope. Was Jo there? It was too far-off to make out anyone for certain.

When darkness came Julian had flashed his torch from the window on and off – on and off. Then, cold and miserable, they had all huddled together, with Timmy licking first one and then another, not at all understanding why they should stay in this one room.

'Timmy will be so thirsty,' said George. 'He keeps

licking round his mouth in the way he does when he wants a drink.'

'Well, I feel like licking round *my* mouth too,' said Dick.

They were half-asleep when the knife came thudding into the room. Timmy leapt up at once and barked madly. He stood and stared at the knife that lay gleaming in the moonlight, and barked without stopping.

'A knife!' said George, in amazement. 'A knife with a string tied on the end!'

'It's blunt,' said Julian, picking it up. 'The tip has been filed off. What's the meaning of it? And why the string tied to it?'

'Be careful that another knife doesn't come through,' warned Terry-Kane.

'It won't,' said Julian. 'I think this is something to do with Jo. She hasn't gone to the police. She has got the fair-folk to help us. This is Bufflo's knife, I'm sure!'

They were all round him, examining it now. 'I'm going to the window,' said Julian. 'I'll look right out into the courtyard. Hold my legs, Dick.'

He climbed up on the stone sill and crawled a little forward through the deep-set slit. He came to the outer edge of the window and looked down. Dick hung on to his legs, afraid that the sill might crumble away and Julian would fall.

'I can see four people down in the courtyard,' said Julian. 'Oh, good – one is Alfredo, one is Bufflo – and I can't make out the other two. AHOY down there!'

A LOT OF EXCITEMENT

The four men below were standing looking up intently. They saw Julian's head appear outside the window, and waved to him.

'Pull in the rope!' shouted Bufflo. He had now tied the end of a second peg-rope to the thin rope, and he and the others lifted it so that it might run easily up the wall.

Julian slid back into the tower room. He was excited. 'This string on the knife runs down the wall and is tied to a thicker rope,' he said. 'I'll pull it up – and up will come a rope that we can climb down!'

He pulled on the string, and more and more of it appeared through the window. Then Julian felt a heavier weight and he guessed the thicker rope was coming up. Now he had to pull more slowly. Dick helped him.

Over the window-sill, in at the window, appeared the first length of the peg-rope. The children had never seen one like it before, they were used to the more ordinary rope-ladder. But Terry-Kane knew what it was.

'A peg-rope,' he said. 'Circus people and fair-people make them – they are lighter and easier to manage than rope-ladders. We'll have to fix the end to something really strong, so that it will hold our weight.'

Anne looked at the peg-rope in dismay. She didn't at all like the idea of climbing down that, swinging on it all the way down the high stone wall of the tower! But the others looked at it with pleasure and excitement – a way of escape – a good, strong rope to climb down out of this hateful cold room!

Terry-Kane looked about for something to fasten the rope to. In the wall at one side was a great iron ring, embedded in the stone. What it had been used for once upon a time nobody could imagine – but certainly it would be of great use now!

There were no pegs in the first yard or so of the rope. Terry-Kane and Julian cut off the string that had pulled it up, and then dragged it right through until the first peg stopped it. Then they twisted the rope-end round upon itself and made great strong knots that could not slip.

Julian took hold of the rope, and leant back hard on it, pulling it with all his strength. 'It would hold a dozen of us at once!' he said, pleased. 'Shall I go first, sir? I can help everyone else down then, if I'm at the bottom. Dick and you can see to the girls when they climb out.'

'What about Timmy?' asked George, at once.

'We'll wrap him up in the rug, tie him firmly and lower him down on the string,' said Dick. 'It's very strong string – thin rope, really.'

'I'll go down now,' said Julian, and went to the window. Then he stopped. Someone was clattering up the stone steps that led to the tower. Someone was at the door! Who could it be?

CHAPTER TWENTY-ONE

In the tower room

THE DOOR was flung open, and a man stood there, panting. Behind him came three others.

'Pottersham!' said Terry-Kane. 'So you're back!'

'Yes. I'm back,' said the panting man.

Timmy began to bark and try to escape from George's hand. He showed his teeth and all his hackles rose up on his neck. He looked a very savage dog indeed.

Pottersham backed away. He didn't like the look of Timmy at all! 'If you let that dog go, I'll shoot him,' he said, and as if by magic a gun appeared in his right hand.

George tried her hardest to restrain the furious Timmy, and called to Julian to help her. 'Julian, hold him as well. He'll fling himself on that man, he's so angry.'

Julian went to help. Between them they forced the furious dog back into a corner, where George tried in vain to pacify him. She was terrified that he might be shot.

'You can't behave like this, Pottersham,' began Terry-Kane, but he was cut short.

'We've no time to lose. We're taking you, Terry-Kane, and one of the kids. We can use him for a hostage if too much fuss is made about your disappearance. We'll take this boy,' and he grabbed at Dick. Dick gave him a punch

375

on the jaw immediately, thanking his stars that he had learnt boxing at school. But he at once found himself on the floor! These men were not standing for any nonsense. They were in a hurry!

'Get him,' said Pottersham, to one of the men behind him, and Dick was pounced on. Then Terry-Kane was taken too, and his arms held behind him.

'What about these other kids?' he said, angrily. 'You're surely not going to lock them up in this room and leave them.'

'Yes, we are,' said Pottersham. 'We're leaving a note for the old turnstile woman to tell her they're up here. Let the police rescue them if they can!'

'You always were a . . .' began Terry-Kane, and then ducked to avoid a blow.

Timmy barked madly all the time, and almost choked himself trying to get away from George and Julian. He was mad with rage, and when he saw Dick being roughly treated he very nearly did manage to get loose. 'Take them,' ordered Pottersham. 'And hurry. Go on – down the steps with them.'

The three men forced Terry-Kane and Dick to the stone stairs – and then everyone shot round in astonishment! A loud voice suddenly came from the window!

Anne gasped. Bufflo was there! He hadn't been able to understand why nobody came down the peg-rope, so he had come up to find out. And to his enormous surprise there appeared to be quite an upset going on!

'Hey there! WHAT'S UP?' he yelled, and slid into the room, looking most out of place with his mop of yellow hair, bright checked shirt and whip!

'BUFFLO!' shouted all four of the children, and Timmy changed his angry bark to a welcoming one. Terry-Kane

377

looked on in astonishment, his arms still pinioned behind him.

'Who in the world is this?' shouted Pottersham, alarmed at Bufflo's sudden appearance through the window. 'How did he get through there?'

Bufflo eyed the gun in Pottersham's hand and lazily cracked his small whip once or twice. 'Put that thing away,' he said, in his drawling voice. 'You ought to know better than to wave a thing like that about when there's kids around. Go on – put it away!'

He cracked his whip again. Pottersham pointed the gun at him angrily. And then a most amazing thing happened.

The gun disappeared from Pottersham's hand, flew right up into the air, and was neatly caught by Bufflo! And all by the crack of a whip!

Crack! Just that – and the gun had been flicked from his hand by the powerful lash-end – and had stung Pottersham's fingers so much he was now howling in pain and bending double to nurse his injured hand.

Terry-Kane gasped. What a neat trick – but how dangerous! The gun might have gone off. Now the tables were indeed turned, for it was Bufflo who held the gun, not Pottersham. And Pottersham looked very pale indeed!

He stared as if he hardly knew what to do. 'Let go of them,' ordered Bufflo, nodding his head towards Terry-Kane and Dick. The three men released them and stood back.

'Seems as if we got to get the police after all,' remarked Bufflo, in a perfectly ordinary voice, as if these happenings were not at all unusual. 'You can let that dog go now, if you want, Julian.'

'No! NO!' cried Pottersham in terror – and at that moment the moon went behind a cloud, and the tower room was plunged in darkness – except for the lantern that Pottersham had set down on the floor when he had first arrived.

He saw one slight chance for himself and the others. He suddenly kicked the lantern, which flew into the air and hit Bufflo, then went out, and left the entire place in pitch darkness. Bufflo did not dare to fire. He might hit the wrong person!

'Set the dog loose!' he roared – but it was too late. By the time Timmy had got to the door, it was slammed shut – and the bolt was shot home on the other side! There was the sound of hurried steps slipping and stumbling down the stone stairway in the dark.

'Hrrr!' said Bufflo, when the moon came out again, and showed him the astonished and dismayed faces of the five in the room. 'We slipped up somewhere, didn't we? They've gone!'

'Yes. But without *us*,' said Terry-Kane, letting Dick untie his arms. 'They've probably gone down through those passages. They'll be out before we've escaped ourselves, more's the pity. And now we've got to try this rope-trick down the tower wall, seeing that the door is locked!'

'Come on, then,' said Julian. 'Let's go before anything else happens.' He went to the window, slid to the outer

379

edge, and took hold of the rope. It was perfectly easy to climb down, though it wasn't very pleasant to look below him into the courtyard. It seemed so very far away.

Anne went next, very much afraid, but not showing it. She was quite a good climber so she didn't find the rope difficult. She was very, very glad when she at last stood safely beside Julian.

Then came George, with a bit of news. 'I can't think what's happening to the four men,' she said. 'They still seem to be about – and they're yelling like anything. It sounds as if they are rushing round that gallery that runs along the walls of the tower room below.'

'Well, let them,' said Julian. 'If they stay there long enough, we'll have time to go to the hole in the outer wall, and wait for them to come out one by one! That would be very, very nice.'

'Timmy's coming now,' said George. 'I've wrapped him up well in that rug and tied it all round him, and put a kind of rope-harness on him. Dick's going to lower him down. We doubled the rope to make sure it would hold. Look – here he comes! Poor darling Timmy! He can't think what in the world is happening!'

Timmy came down slowly, swinging a little, and bumping into the stone wall now and again. He gave a little yelp each time, and George was sure he would be covered with bruises! She watched in great suspense as he came lower and lower.

'Timmy ought to be used to this sort of thing by now,'

said Julian. 'He's had plenty of it in the adventures he's shared with us. Hey there, Tim! Slowly does it! Good dog, then! I guess you're glad to be standing on firm ground again!'

Timmy certainly was. He allowed himself to be untied from his rug by George, and then tried a few steps to see if the ground was really firm beneath his feet. He leapt up at George joyfully, very glad to be out in the open air again.

'Here comes Dick,' said Julian. The peg-rope swayed a little, and Alfredo went to hold it steady. He and the rubber-man and Mr Slither were now extremely concerned about something, so concerned that they had hardly a word to say to Julian and George and Anne.

They had suddenly missed Jo and the snake! The snakeman didn't care tuppence about Jo – but he did care about his precious, beloved, magnificent python! He had already hunted all round the courtyard for it.

'If Jo's taken it back to camp with her, I'll pull her hair off!' muttered the snake-man, unhappily, and Julian looked at him in astonishment. What *was* he muttering about?

Terry-Kane came next, and last of all, Bufflo, who seemed to slide down in a most remarkable way, not using the pegs at all. He leapt down beside them, grinning.

'There's a tremendous upset up aloft!' he said. 'Yelling and shouting and scampering about. What do you suppose is the matter with those fellows? We'll be able to get them nicely, if we go to the hole in the wall. They'll be out there soon, I reckon. Come on!'

382

CHAPTER TWENTY-TWO

Beauty and Jo enjoy themselves

SOMETHING CERTAINLY had happened to upset Pottersham and his three friends. After the door of the tower room had been slammed and bolted, the men had gone clattering down the stone steps. They had come to the door that led into the gallery, and had opened it and gone out on to the gallery itself.

But before they could find the spiral staircase a little way along, Pottersham had tripped over something – something that hissed like an engine letting off steam, and had wound itself round his legs.

He yelled, and struck out at whatever it was. At first he had thought it was a man lying in wait for him, who had pounced at his legs – but he knew it wasn't a man now. No man could hiss like that!

One of the men shone a torch down to see what was the matter with Pottersham. What he saw made him yell and almost drop the torch.

'A snake! A snake bigger than any I've ever seen! It's got you, Pottersham!'

'Help me, man, help me!' shouted Pottersham, hitting down at the snake as hard as he could. 'It's squeezing my legs together in its coils.'

The other men ran to help him. As soon as they began to tug, Beauty uncoiled and glided off into the shadows.

'Where's the horrible thing gone?' panted Pottersham.

'It nearly crushed my legs to powder! Quick, let's go before it comes back. Where in the world did it come from?'

They took a few steps – but the snake was lying in wait for them! It tripped them all up by gliding in and out of their legs, and then began to coil itself round one of the men's waists.

Such a shouting and yelling and howling began then! If ever there were frightened men, those four were! No matter where they went, that snake seemed to be there, coiling and uncoiling, gliding, writhing, squeezing!

It was Jo who had set the python on to them, of course. Jo had stayed in the gallery while all the disturbance upstairs had been going on, Beauty draped round her neck. The girl tried in vain to make out what was happening.

And then she had heard a door slam, a bolt shot home, and men's feet pouring down the stone stairs! She guessed it must be the four whose voices she had heard earlier in the evening, the men who had gone through the passage.

'Beauty! Now it's *your* turn to do something,' said Jo, and she pulled the snake off her shoulders. He poured himself down her and flowed on to the ground in one beautiful movement. He glided towards the men, who were now coming out of the gallery. After that, the python had the time of his life. The more the men howled the more excited the big snake became.

Jo was huddled in a corner, laughing till the tears ran down her cheeks. She knew the snake was quite harmless unless he gave one of the men too tight a squeeze. She couldn't see what was going on, but she could hear.

'Oh dear – there's another one down!' she thought, as she heard one of the men tripped up by Beauty. 'And there goes another! I shall die of laughing. Good old Beauty! He's never allowed to behave like this in the usual way. He *must* be enjoying himself!'

At last the men could bear it no more. 'Come up to that tower room!' yelled Pottersham. 'I'm not going back through those dark passages with snakes after me. There must be dozens of them here. We'll be bitten soon!'

Jo laughed out loud. Dozens of them! Well, probably Beauty did seem like a dozen snakes to the bewildered men falling over one another in the dark. But Beauty would not bite – he was not poisonous.

Somehow the men got up into the tower room, and left the snake behind. Beauty was tired of the game now, and went to Jo when the girl called to him. She draped him round her neck, and listened.

The door up in the tower room had slammed. Jo slipped up the steps, felt for the door-bolt in the darkness and neatly and quietly pulled it across. Now, unless the men liked to risk going down the peg-rope, which she guessed Bufflo had put up against the wall to rescue the others, they were nicely trapped. And if they *did* go down the rope they would be sure to find a few people waiting for them at the bottom!

'Come on, Beauty, let's go,' said Jo, and went down the

steps, wishing she had a torch. She remembered the little lantern that had been left in the hidden room, and felt more cheerful. She would be able to take that with her down all those dark passages. Good!

Beauty slithered in front of her. He knew the way all right! They came to the little room, and Jo thankfully picked up the lantern. She looked down at the big python and he stared up at her with gleaming, unwinking eyes. His long body coiled and uncoiled, shining brown and polished in the light.

'I wouldn't mind you for a pet, if you were a bit smaller,' Jo told him. 'I don't know why people don't like snakes. Oh, Beauty – it makes me laugh to think of the way you treated those men!'

She chuckled as she went along the secret ways, holding the lantern high, except when she came to the last passage of all, and had to walk bent double. Beauty waited for her when she came to the hole in the wall. He had heard noises outside.

Jo climbed out first, and was immensely surprised to find herself pounced on and held. She wriggled and shouted and struggled, and finally bit the hand that was holding her.

Then a torch was shone on her and a shout went up. 'It's Jo! Jo, where have you been? And look here, if you bite like that I'll scrag you!'

'Bufflo! I'm sorry – but what did you want to go and pounce on me for?' cried Jo. The moon suddenly came out

and lit up the scene. She saw Julian and the rest there, coming up eagerly.

'Jo! Are you all right?' said her uncle. 'We were worried about you. Where have you been?'

Jo took no notice. She ran up to Dick and the others. 'You escaped!' she cried. 'Did you all get safely down the peg-rope?'

'There's no time to tell about that now,' said Bufflo, watching the hole in the wall. 'What about those fellows? We're waiting for them here. Did you hear anything of them, Jo?'

'Oh, yes. I followed them. Oh, Bufflo, it was so funny . . .' said Jo, and began to laugh. Bufflo shook her, but she couldn't stop. And then who should come gliding out through the hole but Beauty!

Mr Slither saw him at once and gave a yell. 'Beauty! Jo, did you take him with you? You wicked girl! Come here, my Beauty!'

The snake glided to him and wound himself lovingly round him.

'I'm not wicked,' said Jo, indignantly. 'Beauty wanted to come with me and he did – and oh, he got mixed up with all those men, and . . .'

She went off into peals of laughter again. Dick grinned in sympathy. Jo was very funny when she couldn't stop laughing.

Alfredo shook her roughly and made her stop. 'Tell us what you know about those men,' he commanded. 'Are they coming out this way? Where are they?'

'Oh – the men,' said Jo, wiping her eyes and trying to stop laughing. 'They're all right. Beauty chased them back to the tower room, and I bolted them in. They're still there, I expect – unless they dare to get down the peg-rope, which I bet they won't!'

Bufflo gave a short laugh. 'You did well, Jo,' he said. 'You and Beauty!'

He gave a sharp order to Alfredo and the rubber-man, who went back over the wall and into the courtyard to watch if the men slid down the peg-rope.

'I think it would be a good idea to get the police now,' said Terry-Kane, beginning to feel that he must be in some kind of extraordinary dream, with peg-ropes and whips and knives and snakes turning up in such a peculiar manner. 'That fellow Pottersham is dangerous. He's a traitor, and must be caught before he gives away all that he knows about the work he and I have been doing.'

'Right,' said Bufflo. 'We've got another fellow locked up too – in an empty caravan.'

'But – didn't he escape, then?' said Jo, surprised. 'I thought that man Pottersham, who's up in the tower room now, was the one we locked up.'

'The one we locked up is *still* locked up,' said Bufflo grimly.

'But who is *he*, then?' said Terry-Kane, bewildered.

'We'll soon find out,' said Bufflo. 'Come on, let's get going now. It's very late, you kids must be dying of hunger, somebody ought to go to the police, and I want to get back to camp.'

'Alfredo and the rubber-man will keep guard on the peg-rope,' said Mr Slither, still fondling Beauty. 'There is no need to stay here any longer.'

So down the hill they went, talking nineteen to the dozen. Terry-Kane went off to the police station and to telephone what he vaguely called 'the high-up authorities'. The five children began to think hungrily of something to eat and drink! Timmy ran to the stream as soon as they reached the field and began to lap thirstily.

'Let's just find out if you know the fellow we've got locked up in this caravan,' said Bufflo, when they got to the camp. 'He seems the only unexplained bit so far.'

He unlocked the caravan, and called loudly: 'Come on out. We want to know who you are!' He held up a lamp, and the man inside came slowly to the door.

There was a shout of amazement from all the children. 'Uncle Quentin!' cried Julian, Dick and Anne. 'Father!' shouted George. 'What ARE you doing here?'

CHAPTER TWENTY-THREE

Having a wonderful time!

THERE WAS a minute or two of silence. Everyone was most astonished. To think that George's father had been locked up like that! It had been Jo's mistake, of course – she had been so sure he was Mr Pottersham.

'Julian,' said Uncle Quentin, very much on his dignity, and also very angry, 'I must ask you to go and get the police here. I was set on and locked up in this caravan for no reason at all.'

Bufflo began to look most disturbed. He turned on Jo.

'Why didn't you tell us he was George's father?' he said.

'I didn't know it *was*,' said Jo. 'I've never seen him, and anyhow I thought . . .'

'It doesn't matter what you thought,' said Uncle Quentin, looking at the dirty little girl in disgust. 'I insist on the police being fetched.'

'Uncle Quentin, I'm sure it's all been a mistake,' said Julian, 'and anyway Mr Terry-Kane has gone to the police himself.'

His uncle stared at him as if he couldn't believe his ears. '*Terry-Kane?* Where is he? What has happened? Is he found?'

'Yes. It's rather a long story,' said Julian. 'It all began when we saw that face at the window. I told Aunt Fanny all about that, Uncle, and she said she would tell you when you got back from London. Well – it *was* Mr Terry-Kane at the window!'

'I thought so! I told your Aunt Fanny I had a feeling it was!' said his uncle. 'That's why I came as soon as ever I could – but you were none of you here. What happened to you?'

'Well, that's part of the story, Uncle,' said Julian, patiently. 'But I say, do you mind if we have something to eat? We're practically dead from starvation – haven't had anything since yesterday!'

That ended the interview for the time being! Mrs Alfredo bustled about, and soon there was a perfectly glorious meal set in front of the five half-starved children. They sat round a camp-fire and ate and ate and ate.

Mrs Alfredo practically emptied her big pot for them. Timmy was surrounded by plates of scraps and big bones brought by every member of the camp! Almost every minute someone loomed up out of the darkness with a plate of something or other either for the hungry children, or for Timmy.

At last they really could eat no more, and Julian began to tell their extraordinary story. Dick took it up, and George added quite a few bits. Jo interrupted continually and even Timmy put in a few barks. Only Anne said nothing. She was leaning against her uncle, fast asleep.

394

HAVING A WONDERFUL TIME!

'I never heard such a tale in my life,' said Uncle Quentin, continually. 'Never! Fancy that fellow Pottersham going off with Terry-Kane like that. I *knew* Terry-Kane was all right – *he* wouldn't let his country down. Now, Pottersham I never did like. Well, go on.'

The fair-folk were as enthralled as Uncle Quentin with the tale. They came closer and closer as the story of the secret passages, the hidden room, the stone stairways and the rest was unfolded.

They got very excited when they learnt how Bufflo had appeared in the tower room and had flicked the gun out of Pottersham's hand. Uncle Quentin threw back his head and roared when he heard that bit.

'What a shock for that fellow!' he said. 'I'd like to have seen his face. Well, well – I never heard such a tale in my life!'

And then it was Jo's turn to tell how she had followed the four men into the secret passages, and had set Beauty, the python, on to the men. She began to laugh again as she told her tale, and soon all the fair-folk were laughing in sympathy, rocking to and fro, with tears streaming down their faces.

Only Uncle Quentin looked rather solemn at this point. He remembered how he had felt when, because of his shouting, the fair-folk had sent the python into his caravan, and almost frightened him out of his life.

'Mr Slither, please do get Beauty,' begged Jo. 'He ought to listen to his part of the story. He was wonderful. He enjoyed it all too. I'm sure he would have laughed if only snakes *could* laugh.'

Poor Uncle Quentin didn't like to object when the snake-man fetched his beloved python – in fact, he fetched both of them, and they had never had such a fuss made of them before. They were patted and rubbed and pulled about in a way they both seemed to enjoy hugely.

'Let me hold Beauty, Mr Slither,' said Jo, at last, and she draped him round her neck like a long, shiny scarf. Uncle Quentin looked as if he was going to be sick. He would certainly have got up and gone away if it hadn't been that his favourite niece Anne was fast asleep against his shoulder.

'What extraordinary people George seems to be friends with,' he thought. 'I suppose they are all right – but really! What with whips and knives and snakes I must say I find all this very peculiar.'

'Somebody's coming up the field,' said Jo, suddenly. 'It's – yes, it's Mr Terry-Kane, and he's got three policemen with him.'

Immediately almost all the fair-folk melted away into the darkness. They knew quite well why the police had come – not for them, but because of Mr Pottersham and his unpleasant friends. But all the same they wanted nothing to do with the three burly policemen walking up the hill with Terry-Kane.

Uncle Quentin leapt to his feet as soon as he saw Terry-

Kane. He ran to meet him joyfully, and pumped his arm up and down, up and down, shaking hands so vigorously that Terry-Kane felt quite exhausted.

'My dear fellow,' said Uncle Quentin, 'I'm so glad you're safe. I told everyone you weren't a traitor, and never could be – everyone! I went up to London and told them. I'm glad you're all right.'

'Well – it's thanks to these children,' said Terry-Kane, who looked very tired. 'I expect you've heard the peculiar and most extraordinary tale of the Face at the Window.'

'Yes – it's all so extraordinary that I shouldn't believe it if I read it in a book,' said Uncle Quentin. 'And yet it all happened! My dear fellow, you must be very tired!'

'I am,' said Terry-Kane. 'But I'm not going to lie down and sleep until those other fellows are safely under lock and key – Pottersham and his fine friends! Do you mind if I leave you for a bit, and go off to the castle again? We simply must catch those fellows. I came to ask if one of the children could go with us, because I hear we have to creep through all kinds of passages and galleries and up spiral stairways and goodness knows what.'

'But – didn't *you* go that way when Pottersham first took you there and hid you in that room?' asked Dick, surprised.

'Yes. I must have gone that way,' said Mr Terry-Kane. 'But I was blindfolded and half-doped with something they had made me drink. I've no idea of the way. Of

397

course, Pottersham knew every inch – he's written books about all these old castles, you know – nobody knows more about them and their secrets than he does. He certainly put his knowledge to good use this week!'

'I'll go with you,' said Jo. 'I've been up and down those passages four times now. I know them by heart! The others have only been once.'

'Yes, you go,' said Bufflo.

'Take Timmy,' said George most generously, for usually she would never let Timmy go with Jo.

'Or take a snake,' suggested Dick, with a grin.

'I won't take anything,' said Jo. 'I'll be all right with three big policemen! So long as they're not after *me*, I like them!'

She didn't really, but she couldn't help boasting a little. She set off with Terry-Kane and the three policemen, strutting a little, and feeling quite a heroine.

The others all went to their caravans, tired out. Uncle Quentin sat by the camp-fire, waiting for the arrival of Pottersham and his three friends.

'Good night,' said Julian to the girls. 'I'd like to wait till the crowd come back – complete with the rubber-man and Alfredo – but I shall fall asleep standing on my feet in a minute. I say, wasn't that a smashing supper?'

'Super!' said the others. 'Well – see you tomorrow.'

They all slept very late the next day. Jo was back long before they awoke, very anxious to tell them how they had captured Pottersham and the others, and how they had been marched off to the police station, with her following all the way. But Mrs Alfredo would not let her wake the four children up.

However, they did awake at last, and got up eagerly, remembering all the exciting moments of the day before. Soon they were jumping down the steps of the two caravans, eager to hear the latest news.

'Hallo, Father!' shouted George, seeing him not far off.

'Hallo, Uncle Quentin! Hallo, Jo!' called the others, and soon heard the latest bits of information from Jo who was very proud of being in at the finish.

'But they didn't put up any fight at all,' she said, rather disappointed. 'I think Beauty scared all the fight out of them last night – they just gave in without a word.'

'Now you children!' called Mrs Alfredo, 'I have kept a little breakfast for you. You like to come?'

They did like to come! Jo went too, though she had already had one breakfast. Uncle Quentin went to sit down with them. He gazed around amazed at all the goings-on of the camp.

Bufflo was doing some remarkable rope-spinning and whip-cracking. The rubber-man was wriggling in and out of the wheel-spokes of his caravan without stopping. Mr Slither was polishing his snakes. Dacca was step-dancing on a board, click-click-clickity-click.

Alfredo came up with his buttonhook-like torches, and his metal bowl. 'I give you a treat,' he announced to Uncle Quentin. 'You would like to see me fire-eat?'

Uncle Quentin stared at him as if he thought he had gone raving mad.

'He's a fire-eater, Uncle,' explained Dick.

'Oh. No, thank you, my good man. I would rather not see you eat fire,' said Uncle Quentin, politely but very firmly. Alfredo was most disappointed. He had meant to give this man a real treat to make up for locking him into the caravan! He went away sadly, and Mrs Alfredo screamed after him.

'You foolish man. Who wants to see you fire-eat? You have no brains. You are a big, silly bad man. You keep away with your fire-eating!' She disappeared into her caravan, and Uncle Quentin looked after her, astonished at her sudden outburst.

'This is really a very extraordinary place,' he said. 'And *most* extraordinary people. I'm going back home today, George. Wouldn't you all like to come with me? I don't really feel it's the right thing for you to get mixed up in so many funny doings.'

'Oh *no*, Father,' said George, in horror. 'Go home when we've only just settled in! Of *course* not. None of us wants to leave – do we, Julian?' she said, looking round beseechingly at him.

Julian answered at once. 'George is right, Uncle. We're just beginning to enjoy ourselves here. I think we're *all* agreed on that!'

'We are,' said everyone, and Timmy thumped his tail hard and gave a very loud 'WOOF'.

'Very well,' said Uncle Quentin, getting up. 'I must go, I suppose. I'll catch the bus down to the station. Come down with me.'

They went to see him off on the bus. It came up well on time and he got in.

'Good-bye,' he said. 'What message shall I give your mother, George? She'll expect to hear something from the five of you.'

'Well,' shouted everyone, as the bus rumbled off, 'well – just tell her the FIVE ARE HAVING A WONDERFUL TIME! Good-bye, Uncle Quentin, good-bye!'

Five go Down to the Sea

CONTENTS

CHAPTER ONE

The holiday begins

'BLOW! I'VE got a puncture!' said Dick. 'My tyre's going flat. Worst time it could possibly happen!'

Julian glanced down at Dick's back tyre. Then he looked at his watch. 'You've just got time to pump it up and hope for the best,' he said. 'We've got seven minutes before the train goes.'

Dick jumped off and took his pump. The others got off their bicycles, too, and stood round, watching to see if the tyre blew up well or not.

They were on their way to Kirrin Station to catch the train, bicycles and all. Their luggage had gone on in advance, and they thought they had left plenty of time to ride to the station, get their bicycles labelled and put in the luggage van, and catch the train comfortably.

'We *can't* miss the train!' said George, putting on her best scowl. She always hated it when things went wrong.

'We can. Easiest thing in the world!' said Julian, grinning at George's fierce face. 'What do *you* say, Timmy?'

Timmy barked sharply, as if to say he certainly agreed. He licked George's hand and she patted him. The scowl left her face as she saw Dick's tyre coming up well. They'd just do it! Dick felt his tyre, gave a sigh of relief, and put his pump back in its place.

'Phew! That was hot work,' he said, mounting his bicycle. 'Hope it will last till we get to the station. I was afraid you'd have to go without me.'

'Oh, *no*,' said Anne. 'We'd have caught the next train. Come on, Timmy!'

The four cousins and Timmy the dog raced on towards the station. They cycled into the station yard just as the signal went up to show the train was due. The porter came towards them, his big round face red and smiling.

'I sent your luggage off for you,' he said. 'Not much between you, I must say – just one small trunk!'

'Well, we don't wear much on holidays,' said Julian. 'Can you label our bikes quickly for us? I see the train is due.'

The porter began to label the four bicycles. He didn't hurry. He wouldn't let the train go off again till he had done his job, that was certain. There it was now, coming round the bend.

'You going off to Cornwall, I see?' said the porter. 'And to Tremannon, too. You want to be careful of bathing there. That's a fierce coast and a hungry sea.'

'Oh, do you know it?' said Anne, surprised. 'Is it a nice place?'

'Nice? Well, I dunno about that,' said the porter, raising his voice as the train came rumbling in. 'I used to go out in my uncle's fishing-boat all round there, and it's wild and lonely. I shouldn't have thought it was much of a place for a holiday – no pier, no ice-cream sellers, no concert parties, no cinema, no . . .'

'Good,' said Julian. 'We can do without all those, thank you. We mean to bathe, and hire a boat, and fish, and bike all round about. That's *our* kind of holiday!'

'Woof!' said Timmy, wagging his tail.

'Yes, and yours too,' said George, rubbing his big head. 'Come on, we'd better get into a carriage.'

'I'll see to your bikes,' said the porter. 'Have a good holiday, and if you see my uncle tell him you know me.

His name's same as mine, John Polpenny.'

' "By Tre, Pol and Pen, you may know the Cornishmen",' quoted Julian, getting into a carriage with the others. 'Thanks, John. We'll look up your uncle if we can!'

They each took a corner seat, and Timmy went to the opposite door, put his feet up on the ledge and his nose out of the window. He meant to stand like that all the way! He loved the rush of air past his nose.

'Timmy, come down,' said George.

Timmy took no notice. He was happy. It was holidays again, and he was with everybody he loved. They were going away together. There might be rabbits to chase. Timmy had never yet caught a rabbit, but he went on hoping!

'Now, we're off again!' said Julian, settling into his corner. 'Gosh, how I do like the beginnings of a holiday, getting ready, looking at maps, planning how to get there, and then at last setting off!'

'On a lovely fine day like this!' said Anne. 'George, how did your mother hear of Tremannon Farm?'

'Well, it was Father who heard about it, really,' said George. 'You know Father's got a lot of scientist friends who like to go off to lonely places and work out all kinds of ideas in peace and quiet. Well, one of them went to Tremannon Farm because he heard it was one of the quietest places in the country. Father said his friend went there all skin and bone and came back as fat as a Christmas goose, and Mother said that sounded *just* the place for us to go these hols!'

'She's right!' said Dick. 'I feel a bit skin-and-bonish myself after slaving at school for three months. I could do with fattening up!'

They all laughed. 'You may *feel* skin-and-bonish, but you don't look it,' said Julian. 'You want a bit of exercise to take your fat off. We'll get it, too. We'll walk and bike and bathe and climb . . .'

'And eat,' said George. 'Timmy, you must be polite to farm dogs, or you'll have a bad time.'

'And you must remember that when you go out to play, you'll have to ask the other dogs' permission before you can chase their rabbits,' said Dick solemnly.

Timmy thumped his tail against Dick's knees and opened his mouth to let his tongue hang out. He looked exactly as if he were laughing.

'That's right. Grin at my jokes,' said Dick. 'I'm glad you're coming, Tim, it would be awful without you.'

'He always *has* come with us, on every holiday,' said George. 'And he's shared in every single adventure we've ever had.'

'Good old Timmy,' said Julian. 'Well, he may share in one this time, too. You never know.'

'I'm not going to have any adventures this time,' said Anne in a firm voice. 'I just want a holiday, nothing more. Let's have a jolly good time, and not go on looking for anything strange or mysterious or adventurous.'

'Right,' said Julian. 'Adventures are *off* this time.

Definitely off. And if anything does turn up, we pooh-pooh it and walk off. Is that agreed?'

'Yes,' said Anne.

'All right,' said George, doubtfully.

'Fine,' said Dick.

Julian looked surprised. 'Gosh, you're a poor lot, I must say. Well, I'll fall in with you, if you're all agreed. Even if we find ourselves right in the very middle of Goodness Knows What, we say "No, thank you" and walk away. That's agreed.'

'Well,' began George, 'I'm not sure if . . .' But what she wasn't sure about nobody knew because Timmy chose that moment to fall off the seat. He yelped as he hit the floor with a bang, and immediately went back to his post at the window, putting his head right out.

'We'll have to get him in and shut the windows,' said George. 'He might get something in his eye.'

'No, I'm not going to cook slowly to a cinder in this hot carriage with all the windows shut, not even for the sake of Timmy's eyes,' said Julian, firmly. 'If you can't make him obey you and come inside, he can jolly well get something in his eye.'

However, the problem was solved very quickly because at that moment the train gave a most unearthly shriek and disappeared headlong into utter blackness. Timmy, astounded, fell back into the carriage and tried to get on to George's knee, terrified.

'Don't be a baby, Timmy,' said George. 'It's only a tunnel!

Ju, haul him off me. It's too hot to try and nurse a heavy dog like Timmy. Stop it, Timmy, I tell you it's only a *tunnel*!'

The journey seemed very long. The carriage was so hot, and they had to change twice. Timmy panted loudly and hung his tongue out; George begged the porters for water at each changing place.

They had their lunch with them, but somehow they weren't hungry. They got dirtier and dirtier, and thirstier and thirstier, for they very quickly drank the orangeade they had brought with them.

'Phew!' said Julian, fanning himself with a magazine. 'What wouldn't I give for a bathe? Timmy, don't pant all over me. You make me feel hotter still.'

'What time do we get there?' asked Anne.

'Well, we have to get out at Polwilly Halt,' said Julian. 'That's the nearest place to Tremannon Farm. We bike from there. With luck, we should be there by tea-time.'

'We ought to have brought masses more to drink,' said Dick. 'I feel like a man who's been lost in a sun-scorched desert for weeks.'

They were all extremely glad when they at last arrived at Polwilly Halt. At first they didn't think it was a halt, but it was. It was nothing but a tiny wooden stage built beside the railway. The children sat and waited. They hadn't even seen the little wooden stage or the small sign that said 'Polwilly Halt'.

The sound of impatient feet came along the little platform. The guard's perspiring face appeared at the window.

413

'Well? Didn't you want to get out here? You going to sit there all day?'

'Gosh! Is this Polwilly?' said Julian, leaping up. 'Sorry. We didn't know it was a halt. We'll be out in half a tick.'

The train started off almost before they had banged the door. They stood there on the funny little staging, all alone save for their four bicycles at the other end. The little halt seemed lonely and lost, set in the midst of rolling fields and rounded hills. Not a building was in sight!

But not far off to the west George's sharp eyes saw something lovely. She pulled Julian's arm. 'Look, the sea! Over there, between the hills, in the dip. Can't you see it? I'm sure it's the sea. What a heavenly blue.'

'It's always that gorgeous blue on the Cornish coast,' said Dick. 'Ah, I feel better when I see that. Come on, let's get our bikes and find our way to Tremannon Farm. If I don't get something to drink soon I shall certainly hang my tongue out, like Timmy.'

They went to get their bikes. Dick felt his back tyre. It was a bit soft, but not too bad. He could easily pump it up again. 'How far is it to Tremannon Farm?' he asked.

Julian looked at his notes. '"Get out at Polwilly Halt. Then bike four miles to Tremannon Farm, along narrow lanes. Tremannon Village is about one mile before you get to the farm." Not too bad. We might get some lemonade, or even an ice-cream, in the village.'

'Woof, woof,' said Timmy, who knew the word ice-cream very well indeed.

'Poor Tim!' said Anne. 'He'll be so hot running beside our bikes. We'd better go slowly.'

'Well, if anyone thinks I'm going to tear along, he can think again,' said Dick. 'I'll go as slowly as you like, Anne!'

They set off with Timmy down a funny little lane, deepset between high hedges. They went slowly for Timmy's sake. He panted along valiantly. Good old Timmy! He would never give up as long as he was with the four children.

It was about five o'clock and a very lovely evening. They met nobody at all, not even a slow old farm cart. It was even too hot for the birds to sing. No wind blew. There seemed a curious silence and loneliness everywhere.

Julian looked back at the other three with a grin. 'Adventure is in the air! I feel it. We're all set for adventure! But no, we'll turn our backs on it and say: "Away with you!" That's agreed!'

CHAPTER TWO

Tremannon Farm

IT CERTAINLY was a lovely ride to Tremannon Farm. Poppies blew by the wayside in hundreds, and honeysuckle threw its scent out from the hedges as they passed. The corn stood high in the fields, touched with gold already, and splashed with the scarlet of the poppies.

They came to Tremannon Village at last. It was really nothing but a winding street, set with a few shops and houses, and beyond that, straggling out, were other houses. Farther off, set in the hills, were a few farmhouses, their grey stone walls gleaming in the sun.

The four children found the general store and went in. 'Any ice-cream?' said Julian hopefully. But there was none. What a blow! There was orangeade and lemonade, however, quite cool through being kept down in the cellar of the store.

'Are you the folks that old Mrs Penruthlan is having in?' said the village shopkeeper. 'She's expecting you. Foreigners, aren't you?'

'Well, not exactly,' said Julian, remembering that to many Cornish folk anyone was a foreigner who did not belong to Cornwall. 'My mother had a great-aunt who

416

lived in Cornwall all her life. So we're not *exactly* "foreigners", are we?'

'You're foreigners all right,' said the bent little shopkeeper, looking at Julian with bird-like eyes. 'Your talk is foreign-like, too. Like that man Mrs Penruthlan had before. We reckoned he was mad, though he was harmless enough.'

'Really?' said Julian, pouring himself out a third lemonade. 'Well, he was a scientist, and if you're going to be a really *good* one you have to be a bit mad, you know. At least, so I've heard. Golly, this lemonade is good. Can I have another bottle, please?'

The old woman suddenly laughed, sounding just like an amused hen. 'Well, well, Marty Penruthlan's got a fine meal ready for you, but seems like you won't be able to eat a thing, not with all that lemonade splashing about in your innards!'

'Don't say you can hear the splashing,' said Julian earnestly. 'Very bad manners, that! Foreigners' manners, I'm sure. Well, how much do we owe you? That was jolly good lemonade.'

He paid the bill and they all mounted their bicycles once more, having been given minute directions as to how to get to the farm. Timmy set off with them, feeling much refreshed, having drunk steadily for four minutes without stopping.

'I should think you've had about as much water as would fill a horse-trough, Timmy,' Julian told him. 'My word, if this weather holds we're going to get really brown!'

It was an uphill ride to Tremannon Farm, but they got

there at last. As they cycled through the open gates, a fusillade of barks greeted them, and four large dogs came flying to meet them. Timmy put up his hackles at once and growled warningly. He went completely stiff, and stood there glaring.

A woman came out behind the dogs, her face one large smile. 'Now, Ben; now, Bouncer! Here, Nellie, here! Bad dog, Willy! It's all right, children, that's their way of saying "Welcome to Tremannon Farm!"'

The dogs now stood in a ring round the four children, their tongues out, three collies and one small black Scottie. Timmy eyed them one by one. George had her hand on his collar, just in case he should feel foolhardy all of a sudden and imagine he could take on all four dogs single-handed.

But he didn't. He behaved like a perfect gentleman! His tail wagged politely, and his hackles went down. The little Scottie ran up to him and sniffed his nose. Timmy sniffed back, his tail wagging more vigorously.

Then the three sheepdogs ran up, beautiful collies with plumy tails, and the children heaved sighs of relief to see that the farm dogs evidently were not going to regard Timmy as a 'foreigner'!

'They're all right now,' said Mrs Penruthlan. 'They've introduced themselves to one another. Now come along with me. You must be tired and dirty – and hungry and thirsty. I've high tea waiting for you.'

She didn't talk in the Cornish way. She was pleased to

FIVE GO DOWN TO THE SEA

see them and gave them a grand welcome. She took them
upstairs to a bathroom, big but primitive. There was one
tap only and that was for cold water. It ran very slowly
indeed!

But it was really cold, and was lovely and soft to wash
in. The tired children cleaned themselves and combed their
hair.

They had two bedrooms between them, one for the
girls and one for the boys. They were rather small, with
little windows that gave a meagre amount of light, so
that the rooms looked dark even in the bright evening
sunshine.

They were bare little rooms, with two beds in each,
one chair, one chest of drawers, one cupboard and two
small rugs. Nothing else! But, oh! the views out of the
windows!

Miles and miles of countryside, set with cornfields,
pasture land, tall hedges and glimpses of winding lanes;
heather was out on some of the hills, blazing purple in the
sun; and, gleaming in the distance was the dark blue
brilliance of the Cornish sea. Lovely!

'We'll bike to the sea as soon as we can,' said Dick,
trying to flatten the few hairs that would stick up straight
on the top of his head. 'There are caves on this coast.
We'll explore them. I wonder if Mrs Penruthlan would
give us picnic lunches so that we can go off for the day
when we want to.'

'Sure to,' said Julian. 'She's a pet. I've never felt so

welcome in my life. Are we ready? Come on down, then. I'm beginning to feel very empty indeed.'

The high tea that awaited them was truly magnificent. A huge ham gleaming as pink as Timmy's tongue; a salad fit for a king. In fact, as Dick said, fit for *several* kings, it was so enormous. It had in it everything that anyone could possibly want.

'Lettuce, tomatoes, onions, radishes, mustard and cress, carrot grated up – this *is* carrot, isn't it, Mrs Penruthlan?' said Dick. 'And lashings of hard-boiled eggs.'

There was an enormous tureen of new potatoes, all gleaming with melted butter, scattered with parsley. There was a big bottle of home-made salad cream.

'Look at that cream cheese, too,' marvelled Dick, quite overcome. 'And that fruit cake. And are those drop-scones, or what? Are we supposed to have something of everything, Mrs Penruthlan?'

'Oh, yes,' said the plump little woman, smiling at Dick's pleasure. 'And there's a cherry tart made with our own cherries, and our own cream with it. I know what hungry children are. I've had seven of my own, all married and gone away. So I have to make do with other people's when I can get them.'

'I'm jolly glad you happened to get hold of *us*,' said Dick, beginning on ham and salad. 'Well, we'll keep you busy, Mrs Penruthlan. We've all got big appetites!'

'Ah, I've not met any children yet that could eat like mine,' said Mrs Penruthlan, sounding really sorry. 'Same as I've not met any man that can eat like Mr Penruthlan. He's a fine eater, he is. He'll be in soon.'

'I hope we shall leave enough for him,' said Anne, looking at the ham and the half-empty salad dish. 'No wonder my uncle's friend, the man who came to stay here, went away as fat as butter, Mrs Penruthlan.'

'Oh, the poor man!' said their hostess, who was now filling up their glasses with rich, creamy milk. 'Thin as my husband's old rake, he was, and all his bones showing and creaking. He said "No" to this and "No" to that, but I took no notice of him at all. If he didn't eat his dinner, I'd take his tray away and tidy it up, and then in ten minutes I'd take it back again and say: "Dinner-time, sir, and I hope you're hungry!" And he'd start all over again, and maybe that time he'd really tuck in!'

'But didn't he know you'd already taken him his dinner-tray once?' said Julian, astonished. 'Goodness, he *must* have been a dreamer.'

'I took his tray in three times once,' said Mrs Penruthlan. 'So you be careful in case I do the same kind of thing to you!'

'I should love it!' grinned Julian. 'Yes, please, I'd like some more ham. *And* more salad.'

Footsteps came outside the room, on the stone floor of the hall. The door opened and the farmer himself came in. The children stared at him in awe.

He was a strange and magnificent figure of a man – tall, well over six feet, broadly built, and extremely dark. His

422

mane of hair was black and curly, and his eyes were as black as his hair.

'This is Mr Penruthlan,' said his wife, and the children stood up to shake hands, feeling half afraid of this dark giant.

He nodded his head and shook hands. His hand was enormous, and was covered with hairs so thick and black that it was like fur. Anne felt that it would be quite nice and soft to stroke, like a cat's back!

He didn't say a word, but sat down and let his wife serve him. 'Well, Mr Penruthlan,' she said, 'and how's the cow getting along?'

'Ah,' said the farmer, taking a plate of ham. The children gazed at the slices in awe, seven or eight of them. Goodness!

'Oh, I'm glad she's all right,' said Mrs Penruthlan, stacking up some dirty plates. 'And is the calf a dear little thing – and what's the colour?'

'Ah,' said Mr Penruthlan, nodding his head.

'Red and white, like its mother! That's good, isn't it?' said his wife, who seemed to have a miraculous way of interpreting his 'Ahs'. 'What shall we call it?'

Everybody badly wanted to say 'Ah', but nobody dared. However, Mr Penruthlan didn't say 'Ah' that time, but something that sounded like 'Ock'.

'Yes, we'll call it Buttercup, then,' said his wife, nodding her head. 'You always have such good ideas, Mr Penruthlan.'

It sounded odd to hear her call her husband by his surname like that, and yet, somehow, the children couldn't imagine this giant of a fellow even *owning* a name like Jack or Jim. They went on with their own meal, enjoying every minute of it, watching Mr Penruthlan shovel in great mouthfuls, and working his way quickly through every dish. Mrs Penruthlan saw them watching him.

'He's a grand eater, isn't he?' she said, proudly. 'So were all my children. When they were at home, I was kept really busy, but now, with only Mr Penruthlan to feed, I feel quite lost. That's why I like people here. You'll tell me if you don't have enough to eat, won't you?'

They all laughed, and Timmy barked. He had had a wonderful meal, too; it was the remains of Mrs Penruthlan's big stock-pot, and was very tasty indeed. He had also got the largest bone he had ever had in his life. The only thing that really worried the well-fed Timmy now was, where could he put the bone out of the way of the farm dogs?

Mr Penruthlan suddenly made a peculiar noise and began undoing a trouser pocket at the back. 'Oo-ah!' he said, and brought out a dirty, folded piece of paper. He handed it to his wife, who unfolded it and read it. She looked up at the children, smiling.

'Now, *here's* a bit of excitement!' she said. 'The Barnies will be along this week! You'll love them.'

'What *are* the Barnies?' asked George, puzzled at Mrs Penruthlan's evident pleasure and excitement.

'Oh, they're travelling players that wander round the countryside and play and act in our big barns,' said Mrs Penruthlan. 'We've no cinemas for miles, you know, so the Barnies are always very welcome.'

'Oh, you call them Barnies because they use your barns for their shows,' said Anne, seeing light. 'Yes, we shall love to see them, Mrs Penruthlan. Will they play in *your* barn?'

'Yes. We'll have all the village here when the Barnies come,' said Mrs Penruthlan, her cheeks going red with delight. 'And maybe people from Trelin Village, too. Now, there's a treat for you!'

'Ah,' said Mr Penruthlan, and nodded his great head. Evidently he liked the Barnies, too. He gave a sudden laugh and said something short and quite incomprehensible.

'He says you'll like Clopper the horse,' said his wife, laughing. 'The things he does! The way he sits down and crosses his legs. Well, you wait and see. That horse!'

This sounded rather astonishing. A horse that sat down and crossed its legs? Julian winked at Dick. They would most certainly see the Barnies!

CHAPTER THREE

The first evening

AFTER THEIR wonderful high tea the four children didn't really feel like doing very much. Dick thought he ought to mend his puncture, but wasn't sure that he could bend over properly!

Mrs Penruthlan began to stack the dishes and clear away. George and Anne offered to help her. 'Well, that's kind of you, Anne and Georgina,' said the farmer's wife. 'But you're tired tonight. You can give me a hand some other time. By the way, which of you is which?'

'I'm Anne,' said Anne.

'And I'm George, not Georgina,' said George. 'So please don't call me that. I hate it. I always wanted to be a boy, so I only like to be called George.'

'What she really means is that she won't answer unless you *do* call her George,' said Anne. 'Well, if you really are sure you don't need our help, we'll go out with the boys.'

So out they went, George really looking far more like a boy than a girl, with her grey jeans and shirt and her short, curly hair and freckled face. She put her hands in her pockets and tried to walk like Dick!

Dick soon found his puncture and mended it. Mr Penruthlan came by with some straw for his cow and new calf. The boys watched him in awe, for he was carrying almost a wagon load of straw tied up in bales! What strength he had! He nodded to them and passed without a word.

'Why doesn't he talk?' wondered Dick. 'I suppose all his seven children take after their talkative mother, and he never had a chance to get a word in. And it's too late now, he's forgotten how to!'

They laughed. 'What a giant of a man,' said Julian. 'I hope I grow as big as that.'

'I don't, I'd hate to have my bare feet poking out of the bottom of the bed every night,' said Dick. 'There. I've finished that puncture. See the nail that made it? I must have run over it on the way to the station this morning.'

'Do look at Timmy,' said Julian. 'He's having the time of his life with those farm dogs, acting just like a puppy!'

So he was, bounding here and there, rushing round the dogs and then rushing away, jumping on first one and then another, till they all went down in an excited, yapping scrum, the little Scottie doing his best to keep up with everything!

'Timmy's going to have a good time here,' said Dick. 'And he'll soon lose his beautiful waistline if he eats as well as we do!'

'We'll take him on long bike rides,' said Julian. 'He can't grow much tummy if he runs for miles!'

The girls came up just then. A few feet behind trotted an odd little boy, bare-footed, shock-headed and very dirty.

'Who's this?' said Dick.

'I don't know,' said George. 'He suddenly appeared behind us and has been following us ever since. He just won't go away!'

The boy wore a ragged pair of jeans and an old pullover. He was black-eyed and burnt dark-brown by the sun. He stood a few feet away and stared.

'Who are you?' said Dick. The boy went back a few steps in fright. He shook his head.

'I said, who are you?' said Dick again. 'Or, if you prefer it another way, what's your name?'

'Yan,' said the boy.

'Yan?' said Dick. 'That's a funny name.'

'He probably means *Jan*,' said George.

The boy nodded. 'Yes. Yan,' he said.

'All right, Jan. You can go now,' said Anne.

'I want to stay,' said the boy solemnly.

And stay he did, following them about everywhere, gazing at all they did with the utmost curiosity, as if he had never in his life seen children before!

'He's like a mosquito,' said Dick. 'Always buzzing around. I'm getting tired of it. Hey, Yan!'

'Yes?'

'Clear out now! Understand? Get away, go, run off, vamoose, bunk, scoot!' explained Dick sternly. Yan stared.

Mrs Penruthlan came out and heard all this. 'Jan bothering you?' she said. 'He's as full of curiosity as a cat.

429

Go home, Jan. Take this to your old grandad. And here's some for you.'

Jan came up eagerly and took the packet of food Mrs Penruthlan held out to him, and the slice of cake. He ran off without a word, his bare feet making no sound.

'Who is he?' asked George. 'What a little scarecrow!'

'He's a poor little thing,' said the farmer's wife. 'He's got no kith or kin except for his old great-grandad, and there's more than eighty years between them! The old man is our shepherd. Do you see that hill over there, well, he's got a hut on the other side, and there he lives, winter and summer alike, and that child with him.'

'Surely he ought to go to school?' said Julian. 'Perhaps he does?'

'No,' said Mrs Penruthlan. 'He plays truant nearly all the time. You ought to go and talk to his old great-grandad. His father was one of the Wreckers on this coast, and he can tell you some strange stories about those dreadful days.'

'We'll certainly go and talk to him,' said Dick. 'I'd forgotten that this Cornish coast was the haunt of Wreckers. They shone false lights to bring ships in close to shore, so that they would be smashed to pieces on the rocks, didn't they?'

'Yes, and then they robbed the poor, groaning ship when she was helpless,' said Mrs Penruthlan. 'And it's said they paid no heed to the drowning folk, either. Those were wicked days.'

THE FIRST EVENING

'How far is it to cycle to the sea?' said George. 'I can see it from my bedroom window.'

'Oh, it won't take you more than ten minutes,' said the farmer's wife. 'Go tomorrow, if you like. You all look very tired now. Why don't you take a short walk and go to bed? I'll have a snack ready for you when you come in.'

'Oh, we couldn't *possibly* eat any more tonight, thank you,' said Dick, hurriedly. 'But the walk is quite a good idea. We'd like to see round the farm.'

Mrs Penruthlan left them, and Dick looked round at the others. 'A snack!' he said. 'I never thought I'd groan at the thought. But I bet Mr Penruthlan will want a jolly good snack when he comes in. Come on, let's go up by those sheds.'

They went off together, Timmy following behind with his four friends, their tails wagging amiably. It was still a lovely evening, and a cool breeze came down from the hills, making it lovelier still. The children wandered round, enjoying the familiar farm sights, the ducks on the pond, a few hens still clucking round, the grey sheep dotting the hills. Cows were peacefully grazing and an old farm horse came to a gate to stare at them.

They rubbed his velvety nose, and he bent down to sniff at Timmy, whom he didn't know. Timmy sniffed solemnly back.

They went into the barns and looked around, big, dark, sweet-smelling places, stored with many things. Dick was sure that the biggest one would be the one used by the Barnies. What fun!

'I bet they'll be pretty awful, but good fun, all the same,' he said. 'It must be grand to wander round the countryside with all your belongings done up in a parcel or two, and then amaze the country people with your songs and dances and acting. I wouldn't mind trying it myself! I'm pretty good at a spot of conjuring, for instance!'

'Yes, you are,' said Anne. 'Wouldn't it be fun if we could give a little show too, if the Barnies would let us join them just for one evening?'

'We wouldn't be allowed to because we're "foreigners",' said Dick grinning. 'I say, what's that, over there, behind that sack?'

Timmy at once went over to see, and stood there barking. The others went over to look.

'It's that kid Yan again,' said Julian in disgust. He pulled the boy out from his hiding place. 'What are you following us around for, you little idiot?' he demanded. 'We don't like it. See? Go and find your old grandad before you eat all the food Mrs Penruthlan gave you. Go on now.'

He pushed the boy out of the barn, and watched him go into the next field. 'That's got rid of him,' he said. 'I think he's a bit simple. We'll go and see that grandad of his one day and see if he really *has* got anything interesting to say about the old Wreckers.'

'Let's go back now,' said Dick, yawning. 'I've seen enough of this place to know I'm going to like it a lot. I'm going to like my bed tonight too. Coming, Ju?'

They all felt the same as Dick. His yawn had set them
yawning too, and they thought longingly of bed. They

made their way back to the farm, followed closely by Timmy at their heels, and the other four dogs a respectful distance away.

They said good night to the two Penruthlans, who were sitting peacefully listening to their radio. Mrs Penruthlan wanted to come up with them but they wouldn't let her.

They said good night to the farmer, who grunted 'Ah!' without even looking at them, and went on listening to the radio programme. Then up the stairs they went, and into their rooms.

When Julian was in bed and almost asleep he heard a scrabbling noise outside his window. He half-opened his eyes, and listened. He hoped it wasn't rats! If it was, Anne would probably hear them too, and be scared, and Timmy would hear them and bark the place down!

The scrabbling noise came again. Julian spoke softly to Dick. 'Dick! Are you awake? Did you hear that noise at the window?'

No answer. Dick was sound asleep, dreaming that he had a puncture in his foot and couldn't walk till it was mended! Julian lay and listened. Yes, there it was again, and now surely there was someone trying to peep in at the tiny window?

He slid out of bed and went to the side of the window.

Thick ivy grew outside. Somebody was still there for Julian could see the leaves shaking.

He put his head suddenly out of the window, and a scared face, quite close to his, stared in fright.

THE FIRST EVENING

'Yan! What do you think you're doing?' said Julian, fiercely. 'I'll get very angry with you if you go on like this, staring and peeping! What's so strange about us?'

Yan was terrified. He suddenly slithered down the ivy like a cat, landed with a slight thud on the ground and then ran off into the twilight at top speed.

'I hope he's not going to follow us around all the time,' thought Julian, getting into bed again. 'I'll teach him a lesson if he does. Blow him! Now he's made me wide awake!'

But it wasn't long before Julian was sleeping as soundly as Dick. Neither of them stirred until a cock outside their window decided that it was time the whole world woke up, and crowed at the top of his voice.

'Cock-a-doodle-DOO!'

The boys woke with a jump. The early sun streamed into the room, and Julian glanced at his watch. How early it was! And yet he could hear movements downstairs that told him Mrs Penruthlan was up and about, and so was her giant of a husband.

He fell asleep again, and was awakened by a loud knock at his door, and Mrs Penruthlan's voice. 'It's half past seven, and breakfast will be on the table for you at eight. Wake up!'

How lovely to wake in a strange place at the beginning of a holiday, to think of bathing and biking and picnicking and eating and drinking, forgetting all about exams and rules and punishments! The four children and Timmy

435

stretched themselves and stared at the sunshine outside. What a day!

Downstairs breakfast awaited them. 'Super!' said Dick, eyeing the bacon and fried eggs, the cold ham, and the home-made jam and marmalade. 'Mrs Penruthlan, your seven children must have been very sorry to marry and leave home. I feel, if I'd been one of them, I'd have stayed with you for the rest of my life!'

CHAPTER FOUR

Down in the cove

THE FIRST three days at Tremannon Farm were lazy uneventful days, full of sunshine, good food, dogs – and of little Yan.

He really was a perfect nuisance. The four children seemed to have a real fascination for him, and he trailed them everywhere, following them bare-footed. He turned up behind hedges, along lanes, at their picnicking places, his dark eyes watching them intently.

'What's the good of telling him to go?' groaned Julian. 'He disappears behind one hedge and appears out of another. You'd think he'd get bored, doing this shadowing business all the time. What's the point of it, anyway?'

'No point,' said George. 'Just curiosity. What I can't understand is why Timmy puts up with him. You'd think he'd bark or growl or something, but he's quite silly with Yan, lets him play with him, and roll him over as if he was a mad puppy.'

'Well, I'm going to find this great-grandad of his tomorrow, and tell him to keep Yan with him,' said Julian. 'He's maddening. I feel I want to swot him like a gnat, always buzzing round us. Gosh, there he is again!'

So he was. A pair of dark eyes were gazing round a tree-trunk, half hidden by a sheaf of leaves. Timmy bounded up to him in glee, and made such a fuss of Yan that George was quite disgusted.

'Timmy! Come here!' she called, imperiously. 'Don't you understand that you ought to chase Yan away when he comes and not encourage him? I'm ashamed of you!'

Timmy put his tail down and went to her. He sat down beside her with a bump. Dick laughed.

'He's sulking! He won't look at you, George! He's turning his head away on purpose!'

DOWN IN THE COVE

Julian chased Yan away, threatening him with all sorts of things if he caught him, but the boy was as fast as a hare, and seemed suddenly to disappear into thin air. He had a wonderful way of vanishing, and an equally remarkable way of appearing again.

'I don't like that kid,' said Julian. 'He makes me shiver down my back whenever I see him suddenly peeping somewhere.'

'He can't be a bad kid, though, because Timmy likes him so much,' said Anne, who had great faith in Timmy's judgement. 'Timmy never likes anyone horrid.'

'Well, he's made a mistake this time, then,' said George, who was cross with Timmy. 'He's being very stupid. I'm not pleased with you, Timmy!'

'Let's go down to the sea and bathe,' said Dick. 'We'll go on our bikes and Yan won't be able to pop up and watch us there.'

They took their bicycles and rode off to the coast. Mrs Penruthlan made them sandwiches and gave them fruit cake and drinks to take with them. They saw Yan watching them from behind a hedge as they went.

They took the road to the sea. It was no more than a narrow lane, and wound about like a stream, twisting and turning so that they couldn't get up any speed at all.

'Look – the sea!' cried Dick as they rounded one last bend. The lane had run down between two high, rocky cliffs, and in front of them was a cove into which raced enormous breakers, throwing spray high into the air.

They left their bicycles at the top of the cove, and went behind some big rocks to change into bathing things. When they came out, Julian looked at the sea. It was calm beyond the rocks, but over these the waters raged fiercely and it was impossible to venture in.

They walked a little way round the cliffs, and came to a great pool lying in a rock hollow. 'Just the thing!' cried George and plunged in. 'Gosh, it's cold!'

It should have been hot from the sun, but every now and again an extra large wave broke right into the pool itself, bringing in cooler water. It was fun when that happened. The four of them swam to their hearts' content, and Timmy had a fine time too.

They picnicked on the rocks, with spray flying round them, and then went to explore round the foot of the cliffs.

'This is exciting,' said George. 'Caves, and more caves, and yet more caves! And cove after cove, all as lovely as the one before. I suppose when the tide's in, all these coves are shoulder-high in water.'

'My word, yes,' said Julian, who was keeping a very sharp eye indeed on the tide. 'And a good many of these caves would be flooded too. No wonder Mrs Penruthlan warned us so solemnly about the tides here! I wouldn't want to try and climb up these cliffs if we were caught!'

Anne looked up and shivered. They were so very steep and high. They frowned down at her as if to say 'We stand no nonsense from anyone! So look after yourself!'

'Well, I'm blessed! Look there, isn't that the tiresome

little wretch of a Yan?' said Dick, suddenly. He pointed to a rock covered with seaweed. Peeping from behind it was Yan!

'He must have run all the way here, and found us,' said Julian in disgust. 'Well, we'll leave him here. It's time we went. The tide's coming in. It'll serve him right to find us gone as soon as he arrives. He must be mad!'

'Do you think he knows about the tide?' said Anne, looking worried. 'I mean, knows that it's coming in and might catch him?'

'Of course he knows!' said Julian. 'Don't be silly. But we'll wait and have our tea at the top part of the cove, if you like. That's the only way back, if he wants to escape the tide, short of climbing the cliff, which no one would be mad enough to try!'

They had put aside some cake and biscuits for their tea, and they found a good picnicking place at the top of the cove where they had left their bicycles. They settled down to munch the solid fruit cake that Mrs Penruthlan had given them. There was no doubt about it, she was a wonderful cook!

The tide swept in at a great rate, and soon the noise of enormous waves pounding on the rocks grew louder. 'Yan hasn't appeared yet,' said Anne. 'Do you think he's all right?'

'He must be having a good old wetting if he's still there,' said Dick. 'I think we'd better go and see. Much as I dislike him I don't want him to be drowned.'

The two boys went down the cove as far as they could, peering round the cliff to where they had seen Yan hiding. But how different it all looked now!

'Gosh, the beach is gone already!' said Julian, startled. 'I can see how easily anyone could get caught by the tide now, see that last wave, it swept right into that cave we explored!'

'What's happened to Yan?' said Dick. 'He's nowhere to be seen. He didn't come out of the cove; we've been sitting there all the time. Where is he?'

Dick spoke urgently, and Julian began to feel scared too. He hesitated. Should they wade over the rocks a little way? The next wave decided him. It would be folly to do any such thing! Another wave like that and both he and Dick would be flung off the rock they were standing on!

'Look out, here comes an even bigger one!' yelled Julian, and the two boys leapt off their rock and raced back up the cove. Even so, the wave lapped right up to their feet.

They went back to the girls. 'Can't see him anywhere,' said Julian, speaking more cheerfully than he felt. 'The whole beach is covered with the tide now, more than covered. The lower caves are full too.'

'He – he won't be drowned, will he?' said Anne, fearfully.

'Oh, I expect he can look after himself,' said Julian. 'He's used to this coast. Come on, it's time we went.'

They all rode off, Timmy running beside their bicycles.

Nobody said anything. They couldn't help feeling worried about Yan. Whatever could have happened to him?

They arrived at the farm and put their bicycles away. They went in to find Mrs Penruthlan. They told her about Yan, and how he had disappeared.

'You don't think he might have been swept off his feet and drowned, do you?' asked Anne.

Mrs Penruthlan laughed. 'Good gracious, no! That boy knows his way about the countryside and the seashore blindfold. He's cleverer than you think. He never misses anything! He's a poor little thing, but he looks after himself all right!'

This was rather comforting. Perhaps Yan would turn up again, with his dark eyes fixed unblinking on them!

After a high tea as good as any they had had, they went for a walk down the honeysuckle-scented lanes, accompanied as usual by the five dogs. They sat on a stile, and Dick handed round some barley sugar.

'Look!' said George suddenly. 'Do you see what I see? Look!' She nodded her head towards an oak tree in the hedge, not far off. The others stared up into it.

Two dark eyes stared back. Yan! He had followed them as usual, and had hidden himself to watch them. Anne was so tremendously relieved to see him that she called to him in delight.

'Oh, Yan! Have a barley sugar?'

Yan slithered down the tree at top speed and came up. He held out his hand for the barley sugar. For the first time he smiled, and his dirty, sullen face lit up enchantingly. Anne stared at him. Why, he was all right after all! His eyes shone and twinkled, and a dimple came in each cheek.

'Here you are, here's a couple more sweets for you,' Dick said, very glad to see that the small boy hadn't been drowned. Yan almost snatched them from him! It was plain that he very, very seldom had any sweets! Timmy was making a fuss of him as usual. He lay down on his back and rolled over Yan's feet. He licked his fingers, and jumped up at him, almost knocking the boy down. Yan laughed and fell on Timmy, rolling over and over with him. Julian, Dick and Anne watched and laughed.

But George was not pleased. Timmy was her dog, and she didn't like him to make a fuss of anyone she disapproved of. She was glad that Yan was safe but she still didn't like him! So she scowled, and Julian nudged Dick to make him see the scowl. George saw him and scowled worse than ever.

'You'll be sorry you gave him sweets,' she said. 'He'll be round us worse than ever now.'

Yan came up after a minute or two, sucking all three sweets at once, so that his right cheek was very swollen indeed.

'Come and see my grandad,' he said, earnestly, talking even worse than usual because of the sweets. 'I've told him about you all. He'll tell you many things.'

He stared at them all seriously. 'Grandad likes sweets too,' he added, solemnly. 'Yes. Yes, he does.'

Julian laughed. 'All right. We'll come and see him tomorrow afternoon. Now you clear off or you won't get any more sweets. Understand?'

'Yes,' said Yan, nodding his head. He took the three sweets out of his mouth, looked at them to see how much he had sucked them, and then put them back again.

'Clear off now,' said Julian again. 'But wait a bit, I've just thought; how did you get away from that beach this afternoon? Did you climb that cliff?'

'No,' said Yan, shifting his sweets to the other cheek. 'I came the Wreckers' Way. My grandad showed me.'

He was off and away before anyone could ask him another question. The four looked at one another. 'Did you hear that?' said Julian. 'He went the Wreckers' Way. What's that, do you suppose? We must have been on one of the beaches the Wreckers used long, long ago.'

'Yes. But how did he get off that beach, and away into safety?' said Dick. 'I'd like to know more about the Wreckers' Way! I certainly think we'd better pay a visit to old Great-Grandad tomorrow. He might have some very interesting things to tell us.'

'Well, we'll go and see him,' said George, getting up. 'But just you remember what I said. Yan will pester us more than ever now we've encouraged him.'

'Oh well, he doesn't seem such a bad kid after all,' said Dick, remembering that sudden smile and the eager acceptance of a few sweets. 'And if he persuades Grandad to let us into the secret of Wreckers' Way, we might have some fun doing a bit of exploring. Don't you think so, Ju?'

'It might even lead to an adventure,' said Julian, laughing at Anne's serious face. 'Cheer up, Anne. I can't even *smell* an adventure in Tremannon. I'm just pulling your leg!'

'I think you're wrong,' said Anne. 'If *you* can't smell one somewhere, I can. I don't want to, but I can!'

CHAPTER FIVE

Yan – and his grandad

THE NEXT day was Sunday. It made no difference to the time that the two Penruthlans got up, however. As Mrs Penruthlan said, the cows and horses, hens and ducks didn't approve of late Sunday breakfasts! They wanted attending to at exactly the same time each day!

'Will you be going to church?' asked Mrs Penruthlan. 'It's a beautiful walk across the fields to Tremannou Church, and you'd like Parson. He's a good man, he is.'

'Yes, we're all going,' said Julian. 'We can tie Timmy up outside. He's used to that. And we thought we'd go up and see your old shepherd this afternoon, Mrs Penruthlan, and see what tales he has to tell.'

'Yan will show you the way,' said the farmer's wife, bustling off to her cooking. 'I'll get you a fine Sunday dinner. Do you like fresh fruit salad with cream?'

'You bet!' said everyone at once.

'Can't we help you to do something?' said Anne. 'I've just seen all the peas you're going to shell. Piles of them! And don't you want help with those redcurrants? I love getting the currants off their stalks with a fork!'

'Well, you'll have a few odd minutes before you go

448

to church, I expect,' said Mrs Penruthlan, looking pleased. 'It *would* be a bit of help today. But the boys needn't help.'

'I like that!' said George, indignantly. 'How unfair! Why shouldn't they, just because they're boys?'

'Don't fly off the handle, George,' grinned Dick. 'We're going to help, don't worry. We like podding peas too! You're not going to have all the treats!'

Dick had a very neat way of turning the tables on George when he saw her flying into a tantrum. She smiled unwillingly. She was always jealous of the boys because she so badly wanted to be one herself, and wasn't! She hitched up her jeans, and went to get a pan of peas to shell.

Soon the noise of the popping of pods was to be heard, a very pleasant noise, Anne thought. The four of them sat on the big kitchen step, out in the sun, with Timmy sitting beside them, watching with interest. He didn't stay with them long though.

Up came his four friends, the little Scottie trotting valiantly behind, trying to keep up with the longer legs of the others. 'Woof!' said the biggest collie. Timmy wagged his tail politely, but didn't stir.

'Woof!' said the collie again, and pranced around invitingly.

'Timmy! He says "Will you come and play?" ' said George. 'Aren't you going? You aren't the least help with shelling peas, and you keep breathing down my neck.'

Timmy gave George a flying lick and leapt off the step joyfully. He pounced on the Scottie, rolled him over, and then took on all three collies at once. They were big, strong dogs, but no match for Timmy!

'Look at him,' said George, proudly. 'He can manage the whole lot single-handed.'

'Single-footed!' said Dick. 'He's faster than even that biggest collie and stronger than the whole lot. Good old Tim. He's come in jolly useful in some of our adventures!'

'I've no doubt he will again,' said Julian. 'I'd rather have one Timmy than two police-dogs.'

'I should think his ears are burning, the way we're talking about him!' said Anne. 'Oh, sorry, Dick, that pod popped unexpectedly!'

'That's the second lot of peas you've shot all over me,' said Dick, scrabbling inside his shirt. 'I *must* just find one that went down my neck, or I shall be fidgeting all through church.'

'You always do,' said Anne. 'Look – isn't that Yan?'

It was! He came sidling up, looking as dirty as ever, and gave them a quick smile that once more entirely changed his sullen little face. He held out his hand, palm upwards, and said something.

'What's he saying?' said Dick. 'Oh, he's asking for a sweet.'

'Don't give him one,' said Julian, quickly. 'Don't turn him into a little beggar. Make him *work* for a sweet this

time. Yan, if you want a sweet, you can help pod these peas.'

Mrs Penruthlan appeared at once. 'But see he washes those filthy hands first,' she commanded, and disappeared again. Yan looked at his hands, then put them under his armpits.

'Go and wash them,' said Julian. But Yan shook his head, and sat down a little way away from them.

'All right. Don't wash your hands. Don't shell the peas. Don't have a sweet,' said George.

Yan scowled at George. He didn't seem to like her any more than she liked him. He waited till someone split a pod, and a few peas shot out on the ground instead of into the dish. Then he darted at them, picked them up and ate them. He was as quick as a cat.

'My grandad says come and see him,' announced Yan. 'I'll take you.'

'Right,' said Julian. 'We'll come this afternoon. We'll get Mrs Penruthlan to pack us up a basket, and we'll have a tea in the hills. You can share it if you wash your hands and face.'

'I shouldn't think he's ever washed himself in his life,' said George. 'Oh, here's Timmy come back. I *will* not have him fawn round that dirty little boy. Here, Timmy!'

But Timmy darted to Yan with the greatest delight and pawed at him to come and have a game. They began to roll over and over like two puppies.

'If you're going to church, you'd better get ready,' said Mrs Penruthlan, appearing again, this time with arms floured up to the elbow. 'My, what a lot of peas you've done for me!'

'I wish I had time to do the redcurrants,' said Anne. 'We've practically finished the peas, anyway, Mrs Penruthlan. We've done thousands, I should think!'

'Ah, Mr Penruthlan is very fond of peas,' said the farmer's wife. 'He can eat a whole tureen at one sitting.'

She disappeared again. The children went to get

ready for church, and then off they went. It certainly was a lovely walk over the fields, with honeysuckle trailing everywhere!

The church was small and old and lovely. Yan went with them, trailing behind, right to the church door. When he saw George tying Timmy up to a railing, he sat down beside him and looked pleased. George didn't look pleased, however. Now Timmy and Yan would play about together all the time she was in church! How annoying!

The church was cool and dark, except for three lovely stained-glass windows through which the sun poured, its brilliance dimmed by the colours of the glass. 'Parson' was as nice as Mrs Penruthlan had said, a simple friendly person whose words were listened to by everyone, from an old, old woman bent almost double in a corner to a solemn-eyed five-year-old clutching her mother's hand.

It was dazzling to come out into the sun again from the cool dimness of the church. Timmy barked a welcome. Yan was still there, sitting with his arm round Timmy's neck. He gave them his sudden smile, and untied Timmy, who promptly went mad and tore out of the churchyard at sixty miles an hour. He always did that when he had been tied up.

'Come and see Grandad,' said Yan to Dick, and pulled at his arm.

'This afternoon,' said Dick. 'You can show us the way. Come after dinner.'

So, after the children had had a dinner of cold boiled beef and carrots, with a dumpling each, and 'lashings' of peas and new potatoes, followed by a truly magnificent fruit salad and cream, Yan appeared at the door to take them to see his grandad.

'Did you see the amount of peas that Mr Penruthlan got through?' said Anne, in awe. 'I should think he really *did* manage a tureen all to himself. I wish he'd say something besides "Ah" and "Ock" and the other peculiar sounds he makes. Conversation is awfully difficult with him.'

'Is Yan taking you up to Grandad?' called Mrs Penruthlan. 'I'll put a few cakes in the basket for him, too, then, and for Grandad.'

'*Don't* make us up a big tea,' begged Dick. 'We only want a snack, just to keep us going till high tea.'

But all the same the basket was quite heavy when Mrs Penruthlan had finished packing it!

It was a long walk over the fields to the shepherd's hut. Yan led the way proudly. They crossed the fields and climbed stiles, walked up narrow cart-paths, and at last came to a cone-shaped hill on which sheep grazed peacefully. Half-grown lambs, wearing their woolly coats, unlike the shorn sheep, gambolled here and there – then remembered that they were nearly grown up, and walked sedately.

The old shepherd was sitting outside his hut, smoking a clay pipe. He wasn't very big, and he seemed shrivelled up, like an apple stored too long. But there was still sweetness in him, and the children liked him at once. He had Yan's sudden smile, that lit up eyes that were still as blue as the summer sky above.

His face had a thousand wrinkles that creased and ran into one another when he smiled. His shaggy eyebrows, curly beard and hair were all grey, as grey as the woolly coats of the sheep he had lived with all his life.

'You're welcome,' he said, in his slow Cornish voice. 'Yan told me about you.'

'We've brought our tea to share with you,' said Dick. 'We'll have it later on. Is it true that your father was one of the Wreckers in the old days?'

The old fellow nodded his head. Julian got out a bag of boiled sweets, and offered them to the old man. He took one eagerly. Yan edged up at once and was given one too.

Judging by the crunching that went on old Grandad still had plenty of teeth! When the sweet had gone, he began to talk. He talked slowly and simply, almost as Yan might have done, and sometimes paused to find a word he wanted.

Living with sheep all his life doesn't make for easy talking, thought Julian, interested in this old man with the wise, keen eyes. He must be much more at home with sheep than with human beings.

Grandad certainly had some interesting things to tell them, dreadful things, Anne thought.

'You've seen the rocks down on Tremannon coast,'

began Grandad. 'Wicked rocks they are, hungry for ships and men. Many a ship has been wrecked on purpose! Ay, you can look disbelieving-like, but it's true.'

'How did they get wrecked on purpose?' asked Dick. 'Were they lured here by a false light, or something?'

The old man lowered his voice as if he was afraid of being overheard.

'Way back up the coast, more than a hundred years ago, there was a light set to guide the ships that sail round here,' said Grandad. 'They were to sail towards that light, and then hug the coast and avoid the rocks that stood out to sea. They were safe then. But, on wild nights, a light was set two miles farther down the coast, to bemuse lost ships, and drag them to the rocks round Tremannon coves.'

'How wicked!' said Anne and George together. 'How *could* men do that?'

'It's amazing what men will do,' said Grandad, nodding his head. 'Take my old dad now – a kind man he was and went to church, and took me with him. But he was the one that set the false light burning every time, and sent men to watch the ship coming in on the rocks – crashing over them and breaking into pieces.'

'Did you – did you ever see a ship crashing to its death?' asked Dick, imagining the groaning of the sailing ships, and the groaning of the men flung into the raging sea.

'Ay, I did,' said Grandad, his eyes taking on a very faraway look. 'I was sent to the cove with the men, and had to hold a lantern to bemuse the ship again when she

456

came to the rocks. Poor thing, she groaned like a live thing when she ran into those wicked rocks, and split into pieces. And the next day I went to the cove to help get the goods that were scattered all around the cove. There were lots drowned that night, and . . .'

'Don't tell us about that,' said Dick, feeling sick. 'Where did they flash the false light from? From these hills, or from the cliff somewhere?'

'I'll show you where my dad flashed it from,' said Grandad, and he got up slowly. 'There's only one place on these hills where you could see the light flashing. The Wreckers had to find somewhere well hidden, so that their wicked light couldn't be seen from inland, or the police would stop it, but it could be seen plainly by any ship on the sea near this coast!'

He took them round his hill, and then pointed towards the coast. Set between two hills there the roof of a house could just be seen, and from it rose a tower. It could only be seen from that one spot! Dick took a few steps to each side of it, and at once the house disappeared behind one or other of the hills on each side of it.

'I was the only one who ever knew the false light could be seen from inland,' said Grandad, pointing with his pipe-stem towards the far-off square tower. 'I was watching lambs one night up here, and I saw the light flashing. 'And I heard there was a ship wrecked down in Tremannon cove that night so I reckoned it was the Wreckers at work.'

'Did you often see the light flashing over there, when

you watched the sheep?' asked George.

'Oh yes, many a time,' said the shepherd. 'And always on wild, stormy nights, when ships were labouring along, and in trouble, looking for some light to guide them into shore. Then a light would flare out over there, and I'd say to myself "Now may the Good God help those sailors tonight, for it's sure that nobody else will!"'

'How horrible!' said George, quite appalled at such wickedness. 'You must be glad that you never see that false light shining there on stormy nights now!'

Grandad looked at George, and his eyes were scared and strange. He lowered his voice and spoke to George as if she were a boy.

'Young man,' he said, 'that light still flares on dark and stormy nights. The place is a ruin, and jackdaws build in the tower. But three times this year I've seen that light again! Come a stormy night it'll flare again! I know it in my bones, I know it in my bones!'

CHAPTER SIX

A strange tale

THE FOUR children shivered suddenly in the hot sun, as they listened to the shepherd's strange words. Were they true? Did the Wreckers' light still flash in the old tower on wild and stormy nights? But why should it? Surely no Wreckers any longer did their dreadful work on this lonely rocky coast?

Dick voiced the thoughts of the others. 'But surely there are no wrecks on this coast now? Isn't there a good lighthouse farther up, to warn ships to keep right out to sea?'

Grandad nodded his grey head. 'Yes. There's a light-house, and there's not been a wreck along this coast for more years than I can remember. But I tell you that light flares up just as it used to do. I see it with my own eyes, and there's nothing wrong with them yet!'

'I've seen it too,' put in Yan, suddenly.

Grandad looked at Yan, annoyed. 'You hold your tongue,' he commanded. 'You've never seen the light. You sleep like a babe at night.'

'I've seen it,' said Yan, obstinately, and moved out of Grandad's way quickly as the old man raised his hand to cuff the small boy.

Dick changed the subject. 'Grandad, do you know anything about the Wreckers' Way?' he asked. 'Is it a secret way to get down to the coves from inland? Was it used by the Wreckers?'

Grandad frowned. 'That's a secret,' he said shortly. 'My dad showed it to me, and I swore I would never tell. We all had to swear and promise that.'

'But Yan here said that you taught the way to him,' said Dick, puzzled.

Yan promptly removed himself from the company and disappeared round a clump of bushes. His old great-grandad glared round at the disappearing boy.

'Yan! That boy! He doesn't know anything about the Wreckers' Way. It's lost and forgotten by every man living. I'm the last one left who knows of it. Yan! He's dreaming! Maybe he's heard tell of an old Wreckers' Way, but that's all.'

'Oh!' said Dick, disappointed. He had hoped that Grandad would tell them the old way, and then they could go and explore it. Perhaps they could go and search for it, anyhow! It would be fun to do that.

Julian came back to the question of the light flashing from the old tower by the coast. He was puzzled. 'Who could possibly flash that light?' he said to Grandad. 'You say the place is a ruin. Are you sure it wasn't lightning you saw? You said it came on a wild and stormy night.'

'It wasn't lightning,' said the old man shortly. 'I first saw that light near ninety years ago, and I tell you I saw it again three times this year, same place, same light, same weather! And if you told me it wasn't flashed by mortal hands, I'd believe you.'

There was a silence after this extraordinary statement. Anne looked over towards the far-off tower that showed just between the two distant hills. How strange that this spot where they were standing was the only place from which the tower could be seen from inland. The Wreckers had been clever to choose a spot like that to flash a light from. No one but old Grandad up on the hills could possibly have seen the light and guessed what was going on, no one but the callous Wreckers themselves.

Grandad delved deep into more memories stored in his mind. He poured them out, tales of the old days, strange unbelievable stories. One was about an old woman who was said to be a witch. The things she did!

The four stared at the old shepherd, marvelling to think they were, in a way, linked with the witches, the Wreckers and the killers of long-ago days, through this old, old man.

Yan appeared again as soon as Julian opened the tea-basket. They had now gone back to the hut, and sat outside in the sunshine, surrounded by nibbling sheep. One or two of the half-grown lambs came up, looking hot in their unshorn woolly coats. They nosed round the old shepherd, and he rubbed their woolly noses.

'These are lambs I fed from a bottle,' he explained. 'They always remember. Go away now, Woolly. Cake's wasted on you.'

A STRANGE TALE

Yan wolfed quite half the tea. He gave Anne a quick grin of pure pleasure, showing both his dimples at once. She smiled back. She liked this funny little boy now, and felt sorry for him. She was sure that his old Grandad didn't give him enough to eat!

The church bells began to ring, and the sun was now sliding down the sky. 'We must go,' said Julian, reluctantly. 'It's quite a long walk back. Thanks for a most interesting afternoon, Grandad. I expect you'll be glad to be rid of us now, and smoke your pipe in peace with your sheep around you.'

'Ay, I will,' said Grandad, truthfully. 'I'm one for my own company, and I like to think my own thoughts. Long thoughts they are, too, going back nearly a hundred years. If I want to talk, I talk to my sheep. It's rare and wonderful how they listen.'

The children laughed, but Grandad was quite solemn, and meant every word he said. They packed up the basket, and said goodbye to the old man.

'Well, what do you think he meant when he talked about the light still flashing in the old tower?' said Dick, as they went over the hills back to the farm. 'What an extraordinary thing to say. Was it true, do you suppose?'

'There's only one way to find out!' said George, her eyes dancing. 'Wait for a wild and stormy night and go and see!'

'But what about our agreement?' said Julian, solemnly. 'If anything exciting seems about to happen we turn our backs on it. That's what we decided. Don't you remember?'

'Pooh!' said George.

'We ought to keep the agreement,' said Anne, doubtfully. She knew quite well that the others didn't think so!

'Look! Who are all these people?' said Dick, suddenly. They were just climbing over a stile to cross a lane to another field.

They sat on the stile and stared. Some carts were going by, open wagons, their canvas tops folded down. They were the most old-fashioned carts the children had ever seen, not in the least like travellers' caravans.

Ten or eleven people were with the wagons, dressed in the clothes of other days! Some rode in the wagons and some walked. Some were middle-aged, some were young, but they all looked cheerful and bright.

The children stared. After Grandad's tales of long ago these old-time folk seemed just right! For a few moments Anne felt herself back in Grandad's time, when he was a boy. He must have seen people dressed like these!

'Who are they?' she said, wonderingly. And then the children saw red lettering painted on the biggest cart:

THE BARNIES

'Oh! It's the Barnies! Don't you remember Mrs Penruthlan telling us about them?' said Anne. 'The strolling players,

who play to the country folk around, in the barns. What fun!'

The Barnies waved to the watching children. One man, dressed in velvet and lace, with a sword at his side, and a wig of curly hair, threw a leaflet or two to them. They read them with interest.

THE BARNIES ARE COMING

They will sing, they will dance, they will fiddle.
They will perform plays of all kinds.
Edith Wells, the nightingale singer.
Bonnie Carter, the old-time dancer.
Janie Coster and her fiddle.
John Walters, finest tenor in the world.
George Roth – he'll make you laugh!
And Others.
We also present Clopper, the Funniest Horse in
   the World!

THE BARNIES ARE COMING

'This'll be fun! said George, pleased. She called out to the passing wagons: 'Will you be playing at Tremannon Farm?'

'Oh, yes!' called a man with bright, merry eyes. 'We always play there. You staying there?'

'Yes,' said George. 'We'll look out for you all. Where are you going now?'

'To Poltelly Farm for the night,' called the man. 'We'll be at Tremannon soon.'

The wagons passed, and the cheerful, oddly dressed players went out of sight. 'Good,' said Dick. 'Their show may not be first-rate, but it's sure to be funny. They looked a merry lot.'

'All but the man driving the front cart. Did you see him?' said Anne. 'He looked pretty grim, I thought.'

Nobody else had noticed him. 'He was probably the owner of the Barnies,' said Dick. 'And has got all the organisation on his shoulders. Well, come on. Where's Timmy?'

They looked round for him, and George frowned. Yan had followed them as usual, and Timmy was playing with him. Bother Yan! Was he going to trail them all day and everyday?

They went back to the peaceful farmhouse. Hens were still clucking around and ducks were quacking. A horse stamped somewhere near by, and the grunting of pigs came on the air. It all looked quite perfect.

Footsteps came through the farmyard, and Mr Penruthlan came by. He grunted at them and went into a barn.

Anne spoke in almost a whisper. 'I can imagine *him* living in the olden days and being a Wrecker. I can really!'

'Yes! I know what you mean,' said Dick. 'He's so fierce-looking and determined. What's the word I want? *Ruthless!* I'm sure he would have made a good Wrecker!

'Do you suppose there *are* any Wreckers now, and that

light really *is* flashed to make ships go on the rocks?' said George.

'Well, I shouldn't have thought there were any Wreckers in *this* country, anyway,' said Dick. 'I can't imagine that such a thing would be tolerated for an instant. But if that light *is* flashed, what is it flashed for?'

'Old Grandad said there hadn't been any wrecks on this coast for ages,' said Julian. 'I think really that the old man is wandering a bit in his mind about that light!'

'But Yan said he had seen it, too,' said Anne.

'I'm not sure that Yan's as truthful as he might be!' said Julian.

'Why did Grandad say that the light isn't flashed by mortal hands now?' asked George. 'It must be! I can't imagine any other hands working it! He surely doesn't think that his father is still doing it?'

There was a pause. 'We could easily find out if we popped over to that tower and had a look at it,' said Dick.

There was another pause. 'I thought we said we wouldn't go poking about in anything mysterious,' said Anne.

'This isn't really mysterious,' argued Dick. 'It's just a story an old man remembers, and I really *can't* believe that that light still flashes on a wild stormy night. Grandad must have seen lightning or something. Why don't we settle the matter for good and all and go and explore the old house with the tower?'

'I should like to,' said George firmly. 'I never was keen on this "Keep away from anything unusual" idea we suddenly had. We've got Timmy with us – we can't possibly come to any harm!'

'All right,' said Anne, with a sigh. 'I give up. We'll go if you want to.'

'Good old Anne,' said Dick, giving her a friendly slap on the back. 'But *you* needn't come, you know. Why don't you stay behind and hear our story when we come back?'

'Certainly *not*,' said Anne, quite cross. 'I may not want to go as much as you do, but I'm not going to be left out of anything, so don't think it!'

'All right. It's settled then,' said Julian. 'We take our opportunity and go as soon as we can. Tomorrow, perhaps.'

Mrs Penruthlan came to the door and called them. 'Your high tea is ready. You must be hungry. Come along indoors.'

The sun suddenly went in. Julian looked up at the sky in surprise. 'My word, look at those black clouds!' he said. 'There's a storm coming! Well, I thought there might be, it's been so terribly hot all day!'

'A storm!' said George. 'That light flashes on wild and stormy nights! Oh, Julian, do you think it will flash tonight? Can't we – *can't* we go and see?'

CHAPTER SEVEN

Out in the night

BEFORE THE children had finished their high tea, the big kitchen-sitting-room was quite dark. Thunder clouds had moved up from the west, gathering together silently, frowning and sinister. Then, from far off, came the first rumble of thunder.

The little Scottie came and cowered against Mrs Penruthlan's skirts. He hated storms. The farmer's wife comforted him, and her big husband gave a little unexpected snort of laughter. He said something that sounded like 'oose'.

'He's *not* as timid as a mouse,' said his wife, who was really marvellous at interpreting her husband's peculiar noises. 'He just doesn't like the thunder. He never did. He can sleep with us in our room tonight.'

There were a few more sounds from Mr Penruthlan to which his wife listened anxiously. 'Very well, if you have to get up and see to Jenny the horse in the night, I'll see Benny doesn't bark the house down,' she said. She turned to the children. 'Don't worry if you hear him barking,' she said. 'It will only be Mr Penruthlan stirring.'

The thunder crashed and rumbled again, this time a little nearer, and then lightning flashed. Then down came

470

the rain. How it poured! It rattled and clattered on the roof in enormous drops, and then settled down into a steady downpour.

The four children got out their cards and played games by the light of the oil lamp. There was no electricity at Tremannon. Timmy sat with his head on George's knee. He didn't mind the thunder but he didn't particularly like it.

'Well, I think we'd better go to bed,' said Julian at last. He knew that the Penruthlans liked to go to bed early because they got up so early, and as they did not go upstairs until after the children did, Julian saw to it that they, too, went early.

They said good night and went up to their bare little rooms. The windows were still open and the small curtains drawn back, so that the hills, lit now and again by lightning, showed up clearly. The children went and stood there, watching. They all loved a storm, especially Dick. There was something powerful and most majestic about this kind of storm, sweeping over hills and sea, rumbling all round, and tearing the sky in half with flashes of lightning.

'Julian, is it possible to go up to that place the shepherd showed us and see if the light flashes tonight?' said George. 'You only laughed when I asked you before.'

'Well, I laugh again!' said Julian. 'Of course not! We'd be drenched, and I don't fancy being out in this lightning on those exposed hills, either.'

471

'All right,' said George. 'Anyway, I don't feel *quite* such an urge to go now that it's so pitch dark.'

'Just as well,' said Julian. 'Come on, Dick, let's go to bed.'

The storm went on for some time, rumbling all round the hills again, as if it were going round in a circle. The girls fell asleep, but the boys tossed about, feeling hot and sticky.

'Dick,' said Julian, suddenly, 'let's get up and go out. It's stopped raining. Let's go and see if that light is flashing tonight. It should be just the night for it, according to old Grandad.'

'Right,' said Dick, and sat up, feeling for his clothes. 'I simply can't go to sleep, even though I felt really sleepy when I undressed.'

They pulled on as few clothes as possible, for the night was still thundery and hot. Julian took his torch and Dick hunted for his.

'Got it,' he said at last. 'Are you ready? Come on, then. Let's tiptoe past the Penruthlans' door, or we may wake that Scottie dog! He's sleeping there tonight, don't forget.'

They tiptoed along the passage, past the Penruthlans' door and down the stairs. One stair creaked rather alarmingly, and they stopped in dismay, wondering if Ben the Scottie would break out into a storm of barking.

But he didn't. Good! Down they went again, switching on their torches to see the way. They came to the bottom of the stairs. 'Shall we go out by the front door or back door, Ju?' whispered Dick.

472

'Back,' said Julian. 'The front door's so heavy to open. Come on.'

So they went down the passage to the back door that led out from the kitchen. It was locked and bolted, but the two boys opened it without too much noise.

They stepped out into the night. The rain had now stopped, but the sky was still dark and overclouded. The thunder rumbled away in the distance. A wind had got up and blew coolly against the boys' faces.

'Nice cool breeze,' whispered Dick. 'Now – do we go

through the farmyard? Is that the shortest way to the stile we have to climb over into that first field?'

'Yes, I think so,' said Julian. They made their way across the silent farmyard, where, in the daytime, such a lot of noise went on, clucking, quacking, grunting, clip-clopping, and shouting!

Now it was dark and deserted. They passed the barns and the stables. A little 'hrrrrrrumphing' came from one of the stables. 'That's Jenny, the horse that's not well,' said Julian, stopping. 'Let's just have a look at her and see if she's all right. She was lying down feeling very sorry for herself when I saw her last.'

They flashed their torch over the top half of the stable door, which was pulled back to let in air. They looked in with interest.

Jenny was no longer lying down. She was standing up, munching something. Goodness, she must be quite all right again! She whinnied to the two boys.

They left her and went on. They came to the stile and climbed over. The rain began drizzling again, and if the boys had not had their torches with them they would not have been able to see a step in front of them, it was so dark.

'I say, Ju – did you hear that?' said Dick, stopping suddenly.

'No. What?' said Julian, listening.

'Well, it sounded like a cough,' said Dick.

'One of the sheep,' suggested Julian. 'I heard one old sheep coughing just like Uncle Quentin does sometimes, sort of hollow and mournful.'

'No. It wasn't a sheep,' said Dick. 'Anyway, there aren't any in this field.'

'You imagined it,' said Julian. 'I bet there's nobody idiotic enough to be out on a night like this, except ourselves!'

They went on cautiously over the field. The thunder began again, a little nearer. Then came a flash, and again the thunder. Dick stopped dead once more and clutched Julian's arm.

'There's somebody a good way in front of us, the lightning just lit him up for half a second. He was climbing over that stile, the one we're making for. Who do you suppose it is on a night like this?'

'He's apparently going the same way that we are,' said Julian. 'Well, I suppose if we saw *him* he's quite likely to have seen *us*!'

'Not unless he was looking backwards,' said Dick. 'Come on, let's see where he's going.'

They went on cautiously towards the stile. They came to it and climbed over. And then a hand suddenly clutched hold of Dick's shoulder!

He jumped almost out of his skin! The hand gripped him so hard and so fiercely that Dick shouted in pain and tried to wriggle away from the powerful grip.

Julian felt a hand lunge at him, too, but dodged and pressed himself into the hedge. He switched off his torch at once and stood quite still, his heart thumping.

OUT IN THE NIGHT

'Let me go!' shouted Dick, wriggling like an eel. His shirt was almost torn off his back in his struggles. He kicked out at the man's ankles and for one moment his captor loosened his grasp. That was enough for Dick. He ripped himself away and left his shirt in the man's hand!

He ran up the lane into which the stile had led and flung himself under a bush in the darkness, panting. He heard his captor coming along, muttering, and Dick pressed himself farther into the bush. A torchlight swept the ground near him, but missed him.

Dick waited till the footsteps had gone and then crawled out. He went quietly down the lane. 'Julian!' he whispered, and jumped as a voice answered almost in his ear, just above his head!

'I'm here. Are you all right?'

Dick looked up into the darkness of a tree, but could see nothing. 'I've dropped my torch somewhere,' he said. 'Where are you, Ju? Up in the tree?'

A hand groped out and felt his head. 'Here I am, on the first branch,' said Julian. 'I hid in the hedge first and then climbed up here. I daren't put on my torch in case that fellow's anywhere around and sees it.'

'He's gone up the lane,' said Dick. 'My word, he nearly wrenched my shoulder off. Half my shirt's gone! Who was he? Did you see?'

'No. I didn't,' said Julian, clambering down. 'Let's find your torch before we go home. It's too good to lose. It must be by that stile.'

477

They went to look. Julian still didn't like to put on his torch, so that it was more a question of *feeling* for Dick's torch, not looking! Dick suddenly trod on it and picked it up thankfully.

'Listen, there's that fellow coming back again. I'm sure!' said Dick. 'I heard the same dry little cough! What shall we do?'

'Well, I don't now feel like going up to the shepherd's hill to see if that light is flashing from the tower,' said Julian. 'I vote we hide and follow this chap to see where he goes. I don't think anyone who is wandering out tonight can be up to any good.'

'Yes. Good idea,' said Dick. 'Squash into the hedge again. Blow, there are nettles here! Just my luck.'

The footsteps came nearer, and the cough came again. 'I seem to know that cough,' whispered Dick. 'Sh!' said Julian.

The man came up to the stile, and they heard him climbing over it. After a short time both boys followed cautiously. They couldn't hear the man's footsteps across the grass, but the sky had cleared a little and they could just make out a moving shadow ahead of them.

They followed him at a distance, holding their breath whenever they kicked against a stone or cracked a twig beneath their feet. Now and again they heard the cough.

'He's making for the farm,' whispered Julian. He could just see the outline of the big barns against the sky. 'Do

478

you think he's one of the labourers? They live in cottages round about.'

The man came to the farmyard and walked through it, trying to make as little sound as possible. The boys followed. He went round the barns and into the little garden that Mrs Penruthlan tended herself. Still the boys followed.

Round to the front door went the man, and the boys held their breath. Was he going to burgle the farm-house? They tiptoed nearer. There came the sound of a soft click, and then of bolts being shot home! After that there was silence.

'He's gone in,' said Julian in amazement.

'Don't you know who it was? Can't you guess now?' said Dick. 'We both ought to have known when we heard that cough! It was Mr Penruthlan! No wonder he almost dislocated my shoulder with his strong hand!'

'*Mr Penruthlan* – gosh, yes, you're right,' said Julian, astonished, almost forgetting to speak in a whisper. 'We didn't notice that the front door was undone because we went out the back way. So it was him we followed. How silly! But what was he doing out on the hills? He didn't go to see the horse, she wasn't ill.'

'Perhaps he likes a walk at night,' suggested Dick. 'Come on, let's go in ourselves. I feel a bit chilly with practically no shirt on!'

They crept round to the back door. It was still open, thank goodness! They went inside, bolted and locked it, and tiptoed upstairs. They heaved sighs of relief when they were safely in their room again.

'Switch on your torch, Julian, and see if my shoulder is bruised,' said Dick. 'It feels jolly painful.'

Julian flashed his torch on Dick's shoulder. He gave a low whistle. 'My word, you've got a wonderful bruise all down your right shoulder. He must have given you an awful wrench.'

'He did,' said poor Dick. 'Well, I can't say we had a very successful time. We followed our host through the night, got caught by him, and then followed him all the way back here. *Not* very clever!'

'Well, never mind, I bet no light flashed in that tower,' said Julian, getting into bed. 'We haven't lost much by not going all the way to see!'

CHAPTER EIGHT

Here come the Barnies!

THE TWO boys looked curiously at Mr Penruthlan the next morning. It seemed strange to think of their little adventure the night before with him, and *he* didn't even know it was them he had tried to catch! He gave the curious little dry cough again, and Julian nudged Dick and grinned.

Mrs Penruthlan was beaming at the head of the breakfast table as usual. 'The storm soon died down, didn't it?'

Mr Penruthlan got up, said: 'Ah, ock, oooh!' or something that sounded like that, and went out.

'What did he say?' asked Anne curiously. She could *not* think how anyone could possibly understand Mr Penruthlan's extraordinary speech. Julian had said that he thought he must talk in shorthand!

'He said he might not be back for dinner,' said Mrs Penruthlan. 'I hope he'll get some somewhere. He had his breakfast at half past six, and that's very early. I'm glad he came in and had a cup of your breakfast tea now. The poor man had a very bad night, I'm sorry to say.'

The boys pricked up their ears. 'What happened?' asked Julian at once.

'Oh, he had to get up and go and spend two hours with poor Jenny,' said Mrs Penruthlan. 'I woke when he left,

481

but luckily Benny didn't bark, and it wasn't till two hours later he came back, he'd been sitting with the horse all that time, poor man.'

Julian and Dick did not feel at all sympathetic. They knew quite well where Mr Penruthlan had been, not with the horse, that was certain! Anyway, Jenny hadn't been ill when they had looked at her in the night. What a lot of untruths!

They were puzzled. Why should Mr Penruthlan deceive his wife and tell her what wasn't true? What had he been doing that he didn't even want *her* to know?

They told the girls everything immediately after breakfast, when they went to pick currants, raspberries and plums for a fruit salad. Anne and George listened in surprise.

'You never told us you were going,' said George, reproachfully. 'I'd like to have come with you.'

'I always thought Mr Penruthlan looked sort of strange and – and *sinister*,' said Anne. 'I'm sure he's up to no good. What a pity. His wife is so very nice.'

They went on picking the endless redcurrants. Anne suddenly got the feeling that somebody was hiding somewhere near. She looked round uncomfortably. Yes, there was someone in the tall raspberry canes, she was sure! She watched.

It was Yan, of course. She might have guessed! He flashed his smile at her and came towards her. He liked Anne best of all! He held out his hand.

'No, I've no sweets,' said Anne. 'How did you get on last night in the storm, Yan? Were you frightened?'

Yan shook his head. Then he came nearer and spoke softly.

'I saw the light last night!'

Anne stared at him, astonished. What light?

'You don't mean – the light that flashes in that old hidden tower?' she said.

He nodded. Anne went quickly to Julian and Dick, who were picking whitecurrants and eating just about as many as they put into the basket!

'Julian! Dick! Yan says he saw that light flashing last night, the one in the tower!'

'Gosh!' said the boys together. They turned to Yan, who had followed Anne. 'You saw that light?' said Julian.

Yan nodded. 'Big light. Very big,' he said. 'Like – like a fire.'

'Shining from the tower?' said Dick, and Yan nodded again.

'Did your grandad see it?' asked Dick.

Yan nodded. 'He saw it, too.'

'Are you telling the truth?' demanded Julian, wondering how far he could believe Yan.

Yan nodded again.

'What time was this?' asked Dick. But that Yan couldn't tell him. He had no watch, and if he had had, he wouldn't have been able to use it. He couldn't tell the time.

'Blow!' said Julian to Dick. 'We missed it. If Yan's telling the truth we would have seen that light last night.'

'Yes. Well, we'll go tonight and watch for it,' said Dick, determined. 'It's a wild enough day, all wind and scurrying clouds. If that light is used at night in weather like this, we'll be able to see it again. But I'm blessed if I can understand why the Wreckers' tower should be used nowadays. No ship would take any notice of an odd light like that when they've got the lighthouse signalling hard all the time!'

'I'll come, too,' nodded Yan, who had overheard this.

'No, you won't,' said Julian. 'You stay with Grandad. He'll wonder where you are if you're not there.'

It began to rain. 'Blow!' said George. 'I do hope the weather hasn't broken up. It's been so gorgeous. It's quite cold today with this tearing wind. Come on, let's go in, Anne. We've got enough now to feed an army, I should think!'

They all went in, just as the rain came down properly. Mrs Penruthlan greeted them in excitement.

'The Barnies want our barn for tomorrow night!' she said. 'They're giving their first show in our barn, and after that they go to another place. Would you like to help clear out the barn and get ready?'

'You bet!' said Julian. 'We'll go now. There's a lot of stuff to clear out. Where shall we put it? In the other barn?'

The Barnies arrived in about twenty minutes and went straight to the barn, which they had been lent several times before for their shows. They were pleased to see the children and were glad of their help.

They were no longer dressed in fancy clothes, as they had been when the children had seen them on the Sunday evening. They were practically all dressed in slacks, the women, too, ready for the hard work of clearing the barn and setting up a simple stage and background.

Julian caught sight of a horse's head being carried in by a little nimble fellow who pranced along with it comically.

'What's that for?' he said. 'Oh, is that Clopper's head?

485

The horse that can sit down and cross its legs?'

'That's right,' said the little fellow. 'I'm in charge of it. Never let it out of my sight! Guv'nor's orders!'

'Who's the Guv'nor?' asked Julian. 'The fellow over there?' He nodded to a grim-faced man who was supervising the moving of some bales of straw.

'That's him,' said the little man with a grin. 'His lordship himself! What do you think of my horse?'

Julian looked at the horse's head. It was beautifully made and had a most comical look in its eye. Its mouth could open and shut, and so could its big eyes.

'I'm only the hind legs,' said the little man regretfully. 'But I work his tail, too. Mr Binks over there is his front legs, and works his head, the horse's head, I mean. You should see old Clopper when he performs! My, there isn't a horse like him in the world. He can do everything short of fly!'

'Where are his back and front legs – and – er – his body part?' asked Dick, coming up and looking with great interest at the horse's head.

'Over there,' said the little man. 'By the way, my name's Sid. What's yours, and how is it you're here?'

Julian introduced himself and Dick, and explained that they were helping because they were staying at the farm. He caught hold of a bale of straw, thinking it was about time he did some work.

'Like to give me a hand?' he asked.

Sid shook his head.

'Sorry. Orders are I'm not to put this horse's head down anywhere. Where I go, it goes! I can tell you, Clopper and I are quite attached to one another!'

'Why? Is it so valuable?' asked Dick.

'It's not so much that,' said Sid. 'It's just that Clopper's so popular, you know. And he's important. You see, whenever we think the show's flopping a bit, we bring Clopper on, and then we get the laughs and the claps, and the audience is in a good temper. Oh, Clopper's saved the show many times. He's a jolly good horse.'

Mr Binks came up. He was bigger than Sid and much stronger. He grinned at the two boys. 'Admiring old Clopper?' he said. 'Did Sid tell you about the time Clopper's head dropped off the wagon and we didn't miss him till we were miles away? My word, what a state the Guv'nor was in! Said we couldn't give a show without Clopper, and nearly gave us all the sack!'

'We're important, we are,' said Sid, throwing out his chest and doing a funny little strut with the horse's head in front of him. 'Me and Binks and Clopper – there'd be no show without us!'

'Don't you put that horse down even for a moment,' warned Mr Binks. 'The Guv'nor's got his eye on you, Sid. Look, he's calling you.'

Sid went over to the Guv'nor, looking rather alarmed. He carried the horse's head safely under his arm.

The grim-faced man said a few sharp words and Sid nodded. Julian went up to him when he came back. 'Let me feel how heavy the horse's head is,' he said. 'I've often wondered, when I've seen something like this on the stage.'

Sid immediately put the horse under his other arm, and glared at Julian, looking around quickly to see if the Guv'nor had heard.

'That's a stupid thing to ask me,' he said. 'After I've told you I'm not allowed to put the horse down! And didn't the Guv'nor just this minute say to me "Keep away from those kids, you know what tricks they're up to. They'll have that horse away from you if you're not careful." See? Do you want me to lose my job?'

Julian laughed. 'Don't be silly. You wouldn't lose your job for that! When are you and Mr Binks going to do a bit of practice? We want to see you!'

'Oh well, we could manage that all right,' said Sid, calming down. 'Here, Binks. Bit of practice wanted. Get the legs.'

Binks and Sid went to a cleared space in the big barn and proceeded to clothe themselves in the horse's canvas skin and legs. Sid showed the boys how he worked the tail with one of his hands when he wanted to.

Binks put on the head and the front legs. His head only went into the neck of the horse, no farther. He was able to use his hands for pulling strings to open the horse's mouth and work its rolling eyes.

Sid got his legs in the horse's back legs, bent over and put his head and arms over towards Binks, so making the

horse's back. Somebody came up and zipped up the two halves of the horse's 'skin'.

'Oh! What a jolly good horse!' said Dick, delighted. It looked a lively, comical, extremely supple beast, and the two men inside at once proceeded to make it do ridiculous things. It marched – left-right, left-right, left-right. It did a little tap-dance with its front feet, which then remained perfectly still, and then the back feet did the same little tap-dance.

The back feet got themselves entangled and fell over, and the horse's head looked round at itself in astonishment.

All four children were now watching, and Yan was peeping in at the door. They roared with laughter at the ridiculous horse.

It took its tail in its mouth and marched round and round itself. It stood up on its hind legs only. It jumped like a kangaroo, and made peculiar noises. The whole company stood and watched and even the grim-faced Guv'nor had to smile.

Then it sat down on its hind legs and crossed its front ones in the air, looking round comically. It then gave an enormous yawn that showed dozens of large teeth.

'Oh, don't do any more!' cried Anne, who was weak with laughing. 'Don't! Oh, I can quite well see how important you are, Clopper! You'll be the best part of the show!'

It was a mad, happy morning, for the Barnies were full of chatter and jokes and laughter. Sid and Binks took off their horse garments, and then Sid went about as before, the horse's head, grinning comically, tucked safely under his arm.

Mrs Penruthlan called the children in to dinner. Yan ran after Julian, and caught hold of his arm.

'I saw that light,' he said, urgently. 'Come and see it tonight. Don't forget. I saw that light!'

Julian *had* forgotten it in the excitement of the morning. He grinned down at the small boy.

'All right, all right. I won't forget. We're coming along tonight, but you're not coming, Yan, so get that out of your head! Look, here's a sweet for you. Now, scoot!'

CHAPTER NINE

The light in the tower

BY THE end of the day the big barn was quite transformed! It had been cleared of all straw, sacks of corn, bags of fertiliser and odd machines that had been stored in it. It looked enormous now, and the Barnies were very pleased with it.

'We've been here plenty of times,' they told the children. 'It's the best barn in the district. We don't get the best audience, though, because it's rather a lonely spot here, and there are only two villages near enough to send people to see us. Still, we have a good time, and Mrs Penruthlan gives us a marvellous supper afterwards!'

'I bet she does!' said Dick, grinning. 'I bet that's why you come to this lonely spot, too, to taste Mrs Penruthlan's cooking. I don't blame you. I'd come a good few miles myself!'

A stage had been set up, made of long boards, supported on barrels. A back-cloth had been unrolled and hung over the wooden wall of the barn at the back of the stage. It showed a country scene, and had been painted by the company themselves, bit by bit.

'That's my bit,' said Sid, showing Dick a horse standing in one of the fields painted on the back-cloth. 'I had to put old Clopper in! See him?'

492

THE LIGHT IN THE TOWER

The Barnies had plenty of scenery, which they were used to changing several times during their performance. This was all home-made too, and they were very proud of it, especially some that represented a castle with a tower.

The tower reminded the boys of the one Yan had said he had seen flashing a light the night before. They looked at one another secretly, and Julian nodded slightly. They would certainly watch to see that light themselves. Then they would know for certain whether Grandad and Yan were telling the truth.

Julian wondered if they would have to look out for Mr Penruthlan again that night. Jenny the horse was quite better now, if she had ever been ill, and was out in the fields again. So Mr Penruthlan had no excuse for creeping about the countryside at night again!

Neither of the boys could *imagine* what had taken him out the night before, on such a wild night too! Was he meeting somebody? He hadn't had time to go up to see the shepherd about anything, and there wouldn't have been much point in that anyway. He had seen Grandad in the morning already.

Mrs Penruthlan came to see the barn now that it was almost ready for the show the next night. She looked red and excited. This was a grand time for her, the Barnies in her barn, the villagers all coming up the next night, a grand supper to be held afterwards. What an excitement!

She was very busy in her kitchen, cooking, cooking, cooking! Her enormous larder was already full of the most appetising-looking pies, tarts, hams and cheeses. The children took turns at looking into it and sniffing in delight. Mrs Penruthlan laughed at them and shooed them out.

'You'll have to help me tomorrow,' she said. 'Shelling peas, scraping potatoes, stringing beans, picking currants and raspberries, and you'll find hundreds of wild strawberries in the copse too, which can go to add a flavour to the fruit salad.'

'We shall love to help,' said Anne. 'All this is grand fun!

But surely you aren't going to do all the supper single-handed, Mrs Penruthlan?'

'Oh, one or two of the villagers will stay behind to help me serve it,' said the plump little farmer's wife, who looked as happy as could be in the midst of so much hard work. 'Anyway, I'll be up at five o'clock tomorrow morning. I'll have plenty of time!'

'You'd better go to bed early tonight then!' said George.

'We all will,' said Mrs Penruthlan. 'We'll be up early and abed late tomorrow, and we'll need some sleep tonight. It's no trouble to get Mr Penruthlan to bed early. He's always ready to go!'

The children felt sure he would be ready to go early that night because he had spent so much time out in the storm the night before! Julian and Dick were tired too, but they were quite determined to go up to the shepherd's hill and find the place where they could watch and see if that light really did flash out!

They had a high tea as usual, at which Mr Penruthlan was present. He ate solidly and solemnly, not saying a word except something that sounded like 'Ooahah, ooh.'

'Well, I'm glad you like the pie, Mr Penruthlan,' said his wife. 'Though I say it myself, it's a good one.'

It really was wonderful the way she understood her husband's speech. It was also very strange to hear her speak to her husband as if he was someone to whom she had to be polite, and call Mister! Anne wondered if she called him Mr Penruthlan when they were alone together.

She looked at him earnestly. What a dark giant he was – and how he ate!

He looked up and saw Anne watching him. He nodded at her and said 'Ah! Oooh, ock, ukker.' It might have been a foreign language for all Anne could understand! She looked startled and didn't know what to say.

'Now, Mr Penruthlan, don't you tease the child!' said his wife. 'She doesn't know what to answer. Do you, Anne?'

'Well – I – er – I didn't really catch what he said,' said Anne, going scarlet.

'There now, Mr Penruthlan – see how badly you talk without your teeth in!' said the farmer's wife scoldingly. 'Haven't I told you you should wear your teeth when you want to make conversation! *I* understand you all right, but others don't. It must sound just a mumble to them!'

Mr Penruthlan frowned and muttered something. The children all stared at him, dumbfounded to hear that he had no teeth. Goodness gracious – HOW did he manage to eat all he did, then? He seemed to chew and munch and crunch, and yet he had no teeth!

'So that's why he speaks so oddly,' thought Dick, amused. 'But fancy eating as much as he does, with no teeth in his head! Goodness, what would he eat if he *had* got all his teeth?'

Mrs Penruthlan changed the conversation because it was clear that her husband was annoyed with her. She talked brightly about the Barnies.

'That horse Clopper! You wait till you see him prance on to the stage, and fall off it. You'll see Mr Penruthlan almost fall out of his seat he laughs so much. He loves that horse. He's seen it a dozen times, and it tickles him to death.'

'I think it's jolly funny myself,' said Julian. 'I've always thought I'd like to put on an act like that at our end-of-term concert at school. Dick and I could do it all right. I wish Sid and Mr Binks would let us try.'

The meal was finished at last. Most of the dishes were empty, and Mrs Penruthlan looked pleased. 'There now – you've done really well,' she said. 'That's what I do like to see, people finishing up everything put before them.'

'It's easy when it's food *you* put before us,' said George. 'Isn't it, Timmy? I bet Timmy wishes he lived here always, Mrs Penruthlan! I'm sure he keeps telling your dogs how lucky they are!'

After the washing-up, in which everyone but Mr Penruthlan helped, they went to sit down for a while, and read. But the farmer kept giving such enormous yawns that he set everyone else yawning too, and Mrs Penruthlan began to laugh.

'Come on, to bed, all of you!' she said. 'I've never heard so many yawns in my life! Poor Mr Penruthlan. He's tired out with sitting up with Jenny the horse half the night.'

The children exchanged glances. They knew better!

Everyone went up to bed, and the children laughed to hear Mr Penruthlan still yawning loudly in his room. Julian looked out of his window. It was a dark, blustery night, with sudden spurts of sharp rain. The wind howled and Julian almost thought he could hear the great waves crashing on the rocks in the nearest coves! How enormous they would be in this wind!

'A good night for Wreckers, if there were any nowadays!' he said to Dick. 'Not much chance for any ship that went too near those coves tonight! They'd be on the rocks, and dashed to pieces in half an hour! The beach would be strewn with thousands of pieces of wreckage the next day.'

'We'd better wait a bit before we go,' said Dick. 'It's really very early. On a bright sunny evening the hills would still be full of daylight, but this stormy evening is very dark. Let's light our torches and read.'

The wind became even stronger, and grew almost to a gale. It made a howling noise round the old farmhouse, and sounded angry and in pain. Not a very nice night to go out on the hills!

'We'll go now, I think,' said Julian, at last. 'It's quite dark, and getting late. Come on.'

They hadn't undressed, so they went down the stairs at once, and out of the back door as before, closing it silently behind them. They made their way through the farmyard, not daring to shine their torches till they were well away from the house.

They had had a quick look at the front door, when they had stood in the hall. It was locked and bolted!

498

THE LIGHT IN THE TOWER

Mr Penruthlan was not out tonight, that was certain.

They walked steadily through the gale, gasping when it caught them full in the face. They each had their warm jerseys on, for it was quite cold, and the wind blew all the time.

Across the fields. Over one stile after another. Across more fields. The boys stopped once or twice to make sure they were right. They were relieved when they came to the great flock of sheep, and knew they must be near the shepherd's hut.

'There's the hut,' whispered Julian, at last. 'You can just see its dark outline. We must go quietly now.'

They stole by the hut. Not a sound came from inside, and no candle-light showed through the cracks. Old Grandad must be fast asleep! Julian pictured Yan curled up with him on their bed of old sheepskins.

The boys went quietly along. Now, they must make for the spot from which the old tower could be seen, and it must be the *exact* spot, for the tower could be seen from nowhere else.

They couldn't find it, or, if they *had* found it, and were standing on it, they were unable to see the tower far off in the darkness.

'If it didn't happen to be flashing a light, we wouldn't know if we were looking in the right direction or not!' said Julian. 'We'd never see it in the dark. Why didn't we think of that? Somehow I thought we'd see the tower whether it was lit up or not. We're asses.'

THE LIGHT IN THE TOWER

They wandered about a little, continually looking in the direction where they thought the tower should be but saw nothing at all. What a waste of a long walk!

Then Julian suddenly gave an exclamation. 'Who's that? I saw someone there! Who is it?'

Dick jumped. What was this now? Then someone sidled up against them both, and a voice spoke timidly.

'It's me, Yan!'

'Good gracious! You turn up everywhere!' said Julian. 'I suppose you were watching out for us.'

'Yes. Come with me,' said Yan, and tugged at Julian's arm. The two boys went with him, a few yards to the right, then higher up the hill. Then Yan stopped.

The boys saw the distant light at once. There was no doubt about it at all! It flashed continually, rather like a small lighthouse light. Each time it flashed they could see the faint outline of the tower.

'It seems to be some kind of signal,' said Julian. 'Flash – flash-flash-flash – flash-flash – flash. My word, how weird. Who's doing it, and why? Surely there are no Wreckers nowadays!'

'Grandad says it's his old dad,' said Yan, in an awed voiced. Julian laughed.

'Don't be silly! All the same, it's a bit of a mystery, isn't it, Dick? *Could* any ship out at sea be deceived and come near to the shore, and be wrecked? It's a wicked night, just the night for great waves to pound a ship to pieces if it came near this coast.'

'Yes. Well, we shall hear tomorrow if there *has* been a wreck,' said Dick soberly. 'I hope there won't be. I can't bear thinking of it, anyway. Surely, *surely* there aren't Wreckers here now!'

'If there are, they will be creeping down the hidden Wreckers' Way, wherever it is,' said Julian. 'And watching for the ship to crash to pieces. Then they will collect sacks upon sacks of booty and creep away back.'

Dick felt a chill of horror. 'Shut up, Ju!' he said, sharply. 'Don't talk like that. Now, what are we going to do about that light?'

'I'll tell you,' said Julian, firmly. 'We're going to find that tower and see what's going on. That's what we're going to do! And as soon as ever we can too, maybe tomorrow!'

CHAPTER TEN

Getting ready for the show

JULIAN AND Dick watched the light for a little longer, and then turned to go back to the farm. The wind was so strong and so cold that even on that summer's night they found themselves shivering.

'I'm glad you found us, Yan,' said Dick, putting an arm round the small, shivering boy. 'Thanks for your help. We're going to explore the old tower. Would you like to show us the way to it?'

Yan shivered all the more, from fright as much as cold. 'No. I'm frightened,' he said. 'I'm frightened of that tower now.'

'All right, Yan,' said Dick. 'You needn't come. It *is* pretty peculiar, I must admit. Now, go back to your hut.'

Yan shot off in the dark like a scared rabbit. The boys made their way home, not very cautiously, for they felt sure they were the only people out at night. But when they come to the farmyard they saw something that made them stop suddenly.

'There's a light in the big barn!' whispered Dick. 'It's gone, no, there it is again. It's somebody with a torch, flashing it on and off. Who is it?'

'One of the Barnies, perhaps,' whispered back Julian.

503

'Let's go and see. We know the Barnies are sleeping in the near-by sheds tonight.'

They tiptoed to the barn and looked through a crack. They saw nothing at first. Then a torch flashed, shedding its light on some of the properties of the Barnies, stacked in a corner, scenery, dresses, coats, and other things.

'Somebody's going through the pockets!' said Julian, indignantly. 'Look at that! A thief!'

'Who is it?' said Dick. 'One of the Barnies pick-pocketing?'

For a moment or two the torch lit up the back of the intruder's hand in the barn, and the boys stifled an exclamation. They knew that hand! It was covered with black hairs almost as thick as fur!

'Mr Penruthlan!' whispered Dick. 'Yes, I see it's him now. Look at his enormous shadow. What's he doing? He must be mad, walking about at night on the hills, stealing into the barn, going through pockets. Look what he's doing now! Looking in the drawers of that chest the Barnies are going to use in one of their scenes. Yes, he's mad!'

Julian felt most uncomfortable. He didn't like spying on his host like this. What a strange man he was! He told untruths, he crept about at night, he went through people's pockets. Yes, he must be mad! Did Mrs Penruthlan know? She couldn't know, or she would be unhappy, and she really seemed the most cheerful happy little person in the world!

'Come on,' said Julian, in Dick's ear. 'He's going through everything! Though what he expects to find in the Barnies' stage clothes and properties, I don't know. He's weird! Come on, I really don't want to spot him taking something, stealing it. It would be so awkward if we had to say we saw him stealing.'

They left the barn and went back to the farmhouse, creeping in once more at the back door. They looked at the front door. It was shut, but no longer locked or bolted.

505

The boys went upstairs, puzzled. What a strange night! The howling wind, the flashing light, the furtive man in the barn, they didn't know what to make of it!

'Let's wake the girls and tell them,' said Julian. 'I feel as if I can't wait till the morning.'

George was awake and so was Timmy. Timmy had heard them going out, and had lain awake waiting for them to come back. He had stirred and had awakened George. She was quite prepared to hear a whisper at the door!

'Anne! George! We've got some news!' whispered Julian. Timmy gave a little welcoming whine and leapt off the bed. Soon Anne was awake, too, and the girls were listening in amazement to the boys' news.

They were almost as surprised to hear about Mr Penruthlan in the barn as to hear about the light actually flashing in the tower.

'So it *was* true what old Grandad said, then?' whispered Anne. 'He *had* seen the light again. I do think it's weird, all this. Julian, you don't think we'll hear of a wreck tomorrow, do you? I couldn't bear it!'

'Nor could I,' said George, listening to the wind howling outside. 'Fancy being wrecked on a night like this, and being dashed on the rocks by those pounding waves. I feel as if we ought to rush off to the coves here and now and see if we can do any rescuing!'

'We wouldn't be much use,' said Dick. 'I doubt if we could even get near the cove on a night like this. The waves would run right up to the road that leads down to it.'

They talked and talked about everything. Then George yawned. 'We'd better stop,' she said. 'We'll never wake up tomorrow morning. We can't go and explore that tower tomorrow, Julian. The Barnies will be here, and we've promised Mrs Penruthlan to help her.'

'It'll have to be next day, then,' said Julian. 'But I'm determined to go. Yan said he wouldn't show us the way. He said he was too frightened!'

'I feel pretty frightened myself,' said George, settling down. 'I should have jumped out of my skin if I'd seen that light tonight.'

The boys stole back to their room. Soon they were in bed and asleep. The wind still howled round the house, but they didn't hear it. They were tired out with their long walk over the hills.

Next day was so busy that it was quite difficult to find time to remember the night's happenings! They were reminded of it by one thing, though!

Mrs Penruthlan was seeing to their breakfast, and making bright conversation as usual. She was never at a loss for words, and chattered all day long either to the children or to the dogs.

'Did you sleep well with that howling gale blowing all night long?' she asked. 'I slept like a top. So did Mr Penruthlan! He told me he never moved all night, he was that tired!'

The children kicked each other under the table, but said nothing. They knew quite a lot more about her husband's nights than she did!

After that they had very little time to think of anything but picking fruit, podding peas, rushing here and there, carrying things for the Barnies, helping them to put up benches, barrels, boxes and chairs for the audience to sit on, and even mending tears in some of the stage clothes! Anne had offered to sew on a button, and at once found herself overwhelmed with requests to mend this, that and the other!

It was an extremely busy day. Yan appeared as usual and was greeted uproariously by Timmy, of course. All the dogs loved him, but Timmy was quite silly with him. Mrs Penruthlan sent Yan on endless errands, which he ran quickly and willingly.

'He may be a bit simple, but he's quick enough when he thinks there's some food he's going to share!' she said. So it was 'Fetch this, Yan!', 'Do that, Yan!' all day long.

The Barnies worked hard, too. They had a quick rehearsal in which every single thing went wrong; the Guv'nor raved and raged and stamped, making Anne wonder why they didn't all run away and stay away!

First there was to be a kind of concert party. Then there was to be a play, most heart-rending and melodramatic, with villains and heroes and a heroine who was very harshly treated. But everything came right for her in the end, Anne was relieved to find!

508

Clopper the horse was to have no definite performance of his own. He just wandered on and off the stage to get laughs and to please everyone, or to fill awkward gaps. There was no doubt he would do this to perfection!

Julian and Dick watched Mr Binks and Sid doing a small rehearsal on their own in a corner of the farmyard. How well those back legs and front legs worked together! How that horse danced, trotted, galloped, marched, fell over, tied itself into knots, sat down, got up, went to sleep, and, in fact, did every comical thing that Sid and Mr Binks could think of. They really were very, very funny.

'Let me try the head on, Mr Binks,' begged Julian. 'Do let me. Just to feel what it's like.'

But it was no good. Sid wouldn't let him. Mr Binks had no say in the matter at all. 'Orders are orders,' said Sid, picking up the head as soon as Mr Binks took it off. 'I don't want to lose my job. The Guv'nor says if this horse's head is mislaid again, I'll be mislaid, too! So hands off Clopper!'

'Do you sleep with Clopper?' asked Dick, curiously. 'Having to take charge of a horse's head all the time must be a bore!'

'You get used to it,' said Sid. 'Yes, I sleep with old Clopper. Him and me have our heads on the pillow together. He sleeps sound, does old Clopper!'

'He's the best part of the show,' grinned Julian. 'You'll bring the barn down with Clopper tonight!'

'We always do,' said Mr Binks. 'He's the most important member of the Barnies, and he gets paid the worst. Shame.'

509

'Yes, back legs and front legs are badly paid,' said Sid. 'They only count as one player, see, so we get half pay. Still, we like the life, so there you are!'

They went off together, Sid carrying the horse's head as usual under his arm. He really was a funny little man, cheery and silly and bright.

Julian suddenly remembered something at dinner-time. 'Mrs Penruthlan,' he said, 'I suppose that awful wind didn't cause any wrecks last night, did it?'

The farmer's wife looked surprised. 'No, Julian. Why should it? Ships keep right out to sea round these coasts now. The lighthouse warns them, you know. The only way any ship could come in now would be to nose into one of the coves at full tide, and then she'd have to be very careful of rocks. The fishermen know the rocks as well as they know the backs of their hands, and they come into the coves at times. But no other craft come now.'

Everyone heaved a sigh of relief. The flashing light hadn't caused a wreck last night, then. That was a mercy! They went on with their meal. Mr Penruthlan was there, eating away as usual, and saying nothing at all. His jaws worked vigorously up and down, and it was impossible to think he had no teeth to chew with. Julian glanced at his hands, covered with black hairs. Yes, he had seen those hands last night, no doubt about that! Not wielding a knife and fork, but sliding into pockets.

The evening came at last. Everything was ready. A big table was placed in the kitchen, made of strong trestles and boards. Mrs Penruthlan gave the two girls a most enormous white cloth to lay over it. It was bigger than any cloth they had ever seen!

'It's the one I use at harvest-time,' said the farmer's wife, proudly. 'We have a wonderful harvest supper then, on that same table, but we put it out in the big barn because there's not enough room here in the kitchen for all the farm workers. And we clear the table away afterwards and have a dance.'

'What fun!' said Anne. 'I do think people are lucky to live on a farm. There's always something going on!'

'Town folk wouldn't say that!' said Mrs Penruthlan. 'They think the country is a dead-and-alive place, but, my word, there's more life about a farm than anywhere else in the world. Farm life's the *real* thing, I always say!'

'It is,' agreed Anne, and George nodded, too. They had now spread out the snowy-white cloth and it looked lovely.

'That cloth's the real thing, too,' said Mrs Penruthlan. 'It belonged to my great-great-great-grandmother, and it's nearly two hundred years old! As white as ever and not a darn in it! It's seen more harvest suppers than any cloth, and that's the truth!'

The table was laid with plates and knives and forks, cruets and glasses. All the Barnies had been invited, and there were the children, too, of course. One or two of the villagers were staying as well, to help. What a feast they would all have!

The larder was so crammed with food that it was difficult to get into it. Meat pies, fruit pies, hams, a great round tongue, pickles, sauces, jam tarts, stewed and fresh fruit, jellies, a great trifle, jugs of cream – there was no end to the things Mrs Penruthlan had got ready. She laughed when she saw the children peeping there and marvelling.

'You won't get any high tea today,' she told them. 'You'll get nothing from dinner till supper, so that you can get up a good appetite and really eat well!'

Nobody minded missing high tea with that wonderful supper to come. The excitement grew as the time came near for the show. 'Here come the first villagers!' cried Julian, who was at the barn door to help to sell the tickets. 'Hurrah! It will soon begin! Walk up, everyone! Finest show in the world. Come along in your hundreds! Come along!'

CHAPTER ELEVEN

The Barnies – and Clopper

WHEN THE big barn was full of villagers, and a few more
boxes had been fetched for some of the extra children, the
noise was tremendous. Everyone was laughing and talking,
some of the children were clapping for the show to begin,
and the excited farm dogs were yapping and barking at the
top of their voices!

Timmy was excited, too. He welcomed everyone with a
bark and a vigorous wag. Yan was with him, and George
was sure that he was pretending that Timmy was his dog!
Yan looked cleaner than usual. Mrs Penruthlan had actually
given him a bath!

'You don't come to the show and you don't come to the
supper unless you bath yourself,' she threatened. But he
wouldn't. He said he was frightened of the bath.

'I'll be drowned in there,' he said, backing away from
it hurriedly. It was already half full of water for him!

'Frightened are you!' said Mrs Penruthlan grimly, lifting
him up and plunging him into the water, clothes and all.
'Well, you'll be more frightened now! Take your clothes
off in the water and I'll wash them in the bath when you're
clean. Oh, the dirty little so and so that you are!'

Yan screamed the place down as Mrs Penruthlan

513

scrubbed him and soaped him and flannelled him. He felt very much at her mercy, and decided not to annoy her in any way while he was in that dreadful bath!

She washed his ragged pants and shirt, too, and set them to dry. She wrapped him in an old shawl, and told him to wait till his things dried and then put them on.

'One of these days I'll make you some decent clothes,' she said. 'Little rapscallion that you are! What a mite of a body you've got. I'll need to feed you up a bit!'

Yan brightened up considerably. Feeding up was the kind of treatment he really liked!

Now he was down in the barn, welcoming everyone with Timmy and feeling quite important. He yelled with delight when he saw his old great-grandfather coming along!

'Grandad! You said you were coming, but I didn't believe you. Come on in. I'll find you a chair.'

'And what's come over you, the way you look tonight?' said the old man, puzzled. 'What've you done to yourself?'

'I've had a bath,' said Yan, sounding proud. 'Yes. I took a bath, Grandad. As you ought to.'

Grandad aimed a cuff at him, and then nodded to various people he knew. He had his big old shepherd's crook with him, and he held on to it even when he sat down on a chair.

'Well, Grandad, it must be twenty years since we saw you down here,' said a big, red-faced villager. 'What've you been doing with yourself all these years?'

THE BARNIES – AND CLOPPER

'Minding my business and minding my sheep,' said Grandad, in his slow, Cornish voice. 'Yes, and it might be twenty years before you see me again, Joe Tremayne. And if you want to know something I'll tell you this. It isn't the show I've come for, it's the supper.'

Everyone roared with laughter, and Grandad looked as pleased as Punch. Yan looked at him proudly. His old grandad was as good as anyone, any day!

'Sh! Sh! Show's going to begin!' said somebody, when they saw the curtain twitching. At once the talking and shuffling stopped, and all eyes turned to the stage. A faded, rather torn blue curtain was drawn across.

There came a chord from a fiddle behind the scenes, and then a lively tune sounded out. The curtain was drawn back slowly, halting on its rings here and there, and the audience gave a long sigh of delight. They had seen the Barnies many times but they never tired of them.

All the Barnies were on the stage, and the fiddler fiddled away as they struck up a rousing song with a chorus that all the villagers joined in most heartily. Old Grandad beat time, banging his crook on the floor.

Everything was applauded heartily. Then someone called out loudly: 'Where's old Clopper? Where is he?'

And old Clopper the horse came shyly on, looking out of the sides of his eyes at the audience, and being so very bashful that old Grandad almost fell off his chair with laughing.

The fiddle struck up again and Clopper marched in time

515

to it. It grew quicker, and he ran. It grew quicker still and he galloped, and fell right off the stage.

'Hoo-hoo-hoo-hoo!' roared someone. 'HOO-HOO-HOO-HOO!' It was such an enormous guffaw that everyone turned round. It came from Mr Penruthlan, who was writhing and wriggling in his seat as if he was in great pain. But he was only laughing at Clopper.

Clopper heard the giant of a laugh and put a hoof behind one ear to listen to it. Grandad promptly fell off his seat with joy. Clopper caught his back legs in his front legs and fell over too. There was such a pandemonium of screams and guffaws and yells from the delighted audience that it was surprising the roof didn't fall in.

'Off now,' said a firm voice at the side of the stage, Julian looked to see who it was, as Clopper obediently turned to shuffle off, waving one back leg to the admiring villagers. The voice came from the Guv'nor who was standing where he could watch the whole show in detail. His face was still unsmiling, even after Clopper's antics!

The show was a great success, although it could not have been simpler. The jokes were old, the play acted was even older, the singing was a bit flat, and the dancing not as good as the third form of a girls' school, but it was so merry and smiling and idiotic and good-natured that it went with a terrific swing from start to finish.

As for Clopper, it was his evening! Every time his head so much as looked in on the stage, the audience rocked with joy. They would, in fact, have been delighted to have had one actor only, all the evening, and that actor, Clopper, of course. Julian and Dick watched him, fascinated. How they both longed to try on those back and front legs, and put on the head, and do a little 'cloppering' themselves!

'Sid and Binks are awfully good, aren't they?' said Dick. 'Gosh, I wish we could get hold of legs and a head and do that act at the Christmas school concert, Ju! We'd bring the house down. Let's ask Sid if we can have a shot some time.'

'He won't lend us the head,' said Julian. 'Still, we could do without that, and just try the legs. I bet we could think of some funny things to do, Dick!'

Everybody was sad when the curtain went across the stage, and the show was over. The fiddle struck up 'God Save the Queen', and everyone rose loyally to stand and sing every word lustily.

'Three cheers for the Barnies!' yelled a child, and the hip-hurrahing rose to the rafters. Grandad waved his crook too vigorously and hit a very large farmer on the back of his neck.

'Now, old Grandad!' said the farmer, rubbing his neck, 'are you trying to pick a fight with me? No, no, I'd be afraid to take you on. You'd get me by my hind leg with that crook like you do your sheep, and down I'd go!'

Grandad was delighted. He hadn't had such an evening for forty years! Maybe fifty. And now for that supper. That was what he had really come for. He'd show some of these sixty-year-old youngsters how to eat!

The villagers went home, talking and laughing. Two or three of the women stayed on to help. The Barnies didn't bother to change out of their acting clothes, but came into the kitchen as they were, grease-paint running down their cheeks in the heat. The barn had got very hot with so many people packed in close together.

The children were simply delighted with everything. They had laughed so much at Clopper that they felt quite weak. The play had amused them too, with its sighings and groanings and threats and tears and stridings around. Now they were more than ready for their supper!

The Barnies crowded round the loaded table, cracking jokes, complimenting Mrs Penruthlan, smacking everyone on the back, and generally behaving like a lot of school children out for a treat. Julian looked round at them all. What a jolly lot! He looked for the Guv'nor, surely for once he too would be smiling and cheerful.

But he wasn't there. Julian looked and looked again. No, he certainly wasn't there.

'Where's the Guv'nor?' he asked Sid, who was sitting next to him.

'The Guv'nor? Oh, he's sitting in solitary state in the barn,' said Sid, attacking an enormous slice of meat-pie laced with hard-boiled eggs. 'He never feeds with us, not even after a show. Keeps himself to himself, he does! He'll be having a whacking great tray of food all on his own. Suits me all right! I never did get on with the Guv'nor.'

'Where's Clopper – the horse's head, I mean?' asked

518

Julian. He couldn't see it beside Sid anywhere. 'Is it under the table?'

'No. The Guv'nor's got it tonight. Said he wasn't going to have it rolled about under the table, or have jelly or gravy dropped all over it,' said Sid, taking six large pickled onions. 'My, Mrs Penruthlan is a wonder! Why don't I marry someone like her, instead of getting thinner and thinner inside Clopper's back legs?'

Julian laughed. He wondered who was going to take the Guv'nor's tray into the barn. He noticed that Mrs Penruthlan was getting one ready, and he went over to her.

'Is that for the Guv'nor?' he asked. 'Shall I take it for you?'

'Oh, thank you, Julian,' said the busy farmer's wife, gratefully. 'Here it is, and ask Dick to carry in a bottle and a glass for him, will you? There's no more room on the tray.'

So Julian and Dick together went out to the barn with the food and drink. The wind still blew strongly and rain was beginning to fall again.

'There's no one here,' said Julian, looking round. He set down the tray, puzzled. Then he saw a note pinned on the curtain. He went to read it.

'Back in an hour,' he read. 'Gone for a walk. The Guv'nor.'

'Oh well, we'll leave the tray then,' said Julian. He and Dick were just turning to go when they caught sight of

something, the back and front legs of Clopper the horse!
They stopped, each with the same thought in his mind.

'Everyone at supper! The Guv'nor gone for an hour.
Nobody would know if we tried on the legs!'

They looked at one another, and read each other's mind.
'Let's have a go at being Clopper!'

'Come on, quick,' said Julian. 'You be the back legs
and I'll be the front ones. Quick!'

They got into them hurriedly, and Julian managed to do
up most of the zip. But it wasn't right without the head.
Had the Guv'nor taken it with him? Surely not? It would
be quite safe in the barn.

'There it is, on that chair under the shawl,' said Dick, and they galloped over to get it. Julian picked it up. It was rather heavier than he had imagined. He looked inside it to see how far his head went in it, wondering how to work the eyes and mouth.

He put his hand inside, and scrabbled about. A lid fell open in the side of the neck, and out came some cigarettes, scattering over the floor. 'Blow!' said Julian. 'I didn't know Mr Binks kept his cigarettes in Clopper. Pick them up, Dick, and I'll put them back. Thanks.'

He put the cigarettes back in the little space, and shut the lid on them. Then he put the head carefully over his own. It felt extremely strange.

'There are eye-holes in the neck,' he said to Dick. 'That's how Mr Binks knew where he was going. I kept wondering why he didn't bump into things more than he did! Now – I'm ready. The head seems to be on firmly. I'll count – one-two, one-two – and we'll walk in time. Don't let's start any funny tricks till we're used to Clopper. Does my voice sound funny inside the neck?'

'*Most* peculiar,' said Dick, who was now bending over so that his back made the horse's back, and his arms were round Julian's waist. 'I say, what's that?'

'Someone's coming, it's the Guv'nor coming back!' said Julian in alarm. 'Quick, gallop out of the door before we're caught.'

And so, to the Guv'nor's enormous surprise, Clopper galloped very clumsily out of the barn door just as he was

coming in, almost knocking him over. At first he didn't realise it was Clopper, then he let out a loud roar and gave chase.

'I can't *see*,' panted poor Julian. 'Where am I going? Oh thank goodness, it's an empty stable! Quick, let's un-zip ourselves, and you'll have to take this head off for me, I can't manage it myself.'

But alas and alack! The zip got stuck and wouldn't come undone. The boys tugged and pulled but it wasn't a bit of good. It looked as if they had got to be Clopper for the rest of the evening!

CHAPTER TWELVE

A trip to the tower

'BLOW THIS zip!' said Julian, desperately. 'It's got *absolutely* stuck! It's so difficult for us to undo it from the inside of the beastly horse. Oh, this head. I *must* get it off.'

He pushed at the head but somehow or other it had got wedged on him, and Julian felt that short of pulling his own head off he would certainly never get Clopper's off!

The horse sat down, exhausted, looking a very peculiar shape. Julian leaned the head against the wall of the stable and panted. 'I'm so *hot*,' he complained. 'Dick, for goodness' sake think of something. We'll have to get help. But I daren't go back to the barn because of the Guv'nor, and we really can't appear in the kitchen like this. Everyone would have a fit, and Sid and Mr Binks would be furious with us.'

'I think we were asses to try this,' said Dick, pulling viciously at the zip again. 'Ugh! What use are zips, I'd like to know. I feel most uncomfortable. Can't you get in some other position, Ju? I seem to be standing on my head or something.'

'Let's go and scout round the kitchen,' said Julian trying to get up. Dick tried to get up too, but they both fell down

524

on top of one another. They tried again and this time stood up rather shakily.

'It's not as easy as it looks, is it, to be a two-man horse,' said Julian. 'I wish I could get these eye-holes in the right place. I'm absolutely blind!'

However, he managed to adjust them at last, and the two boys made their way cautiously and clumsily out of the stable. They went carefully over the farmyard, Julian counting one-two, one-two, under his breath so that they walked in time with one another.

They came to the kitchen door and debated whether to try and catch someone's attention without going in. There was a fairly large window near by, open because of the warmth of the kitchen. Julian decided to take a look through to see if George or Anne were anywhere near. If so, he could call them outside.

But he reckoned without the clumsiness of the big head! It knocked against the window-frame, and everyone looked up. There were shrieks at once.

'A horse! Farmer Penruthlan, one of your horses is loose!' cried a villager who was helping with the supper. 'He looked in at the window!'

The farmer went out at once. Julian and Dick backed hurriedly away and trotted in very good style over the farmyard. Where now? The farmer saw their moving figure in the darkness and went after them.

Trot-trot-trot went the horse desperately then gallop-gallop-gallop! But that finished them, because the back

525

and front legs didn't gallop together, got entangled and down went the horse! The farmer ran up in alarm, thinking that his horse had fallen.

'Take your knee out of my mouth,' mumbled an angry voice, and the farmer stopped suddenly, astounded to hear a human voice coming from the horse. Then he realised what was happening – it was the stage horse with two people in it! Who? It sounded like Julian and Dick. He gave the horse a gentle kick.

'Don't,' said Dick's voice. 'For goodness' sake whoever it is, un-zip us! We're suffocating!'

The farmer let out a terrific guffaw, bent down and felt for the zip. One good pull and the horse's canvas skin came in half as the zip was undone.

The boys clambered out thankfully. 'Oh – er – thanks awfully, Mr Penruthlan,' said Julian, rather embarrassed. 'We – er – we were just having a canter round.'

Mr Penruthlan gave another hearty roar and went off towards the kitchen to finish his meal. Dick and Julian felt very thankful. They carried the legs and head of the horse cautiously towards the barn. They peeped in at a window. The Guv'nor was there, striding up and down, looking extremely angry.

Julian waited till he was at the far end of the barn, and then hurriedly pushed the legs and head in the door, as quietly as he could. When the Guv'nor turned round to stride angrily back the first thing he saw was the bundle that was Clopper! He raced over to it at once, and looked out of the door.

But Julian and Dick had gone. They could own up the next day when things were not quite so exciting! They slid quietly into the kitchen, feeling hot and untidy, hoping that nobody would notice them.

George and Anne saw them at once. George came over. 'What have you been doing? You've been ages and ages. Do you want any more to eat before everything is finished up?'

'Tell you everything afterwards,' said Julian. 'Yes, we do want something to eat. I've hardly had a thing yet. I'm starving!'

Mr Penruthlan was back in his place eating again. He pointed with his knife at the boys sliding into their seats. 'Ock-ock-oo,' he said, beginning to laugh, and added a few more equally puzzling words.

'Oh, they've been to help you catch the horse that peeped in at the window, have they?' said Mrs Penruthlan, nodding. 'Which horse was it?'

'Clopper!' said the farmer, quite clearly, and gave a loud guffaw again. Nobody understood what he meant, so nothing more was said. George and Anne guessed, though, and grinned at the two boys.

It was a wonderful evening altogether, and everyone was sorry that it had to come to an end. The village women and the two girls stacked the dirty dishes and plates and the boys carried them to the sink to be washed. The

Barnies gave a hand where they could, and the big kitchen was full of chatter and laughter. It was very pleasant indeed.

But at last the kitchen was empty again, and the big lamp turned out. The village women went home, the Barnies departed. Old Grandad took Yan's hand and went back to his sheep, saying dolefully that he'd 'et a mort too much and wouldn't be able to sleep a wink, so he wouldn't.'

'Never mind. It was worth it, Grandad,' said Mrs Penruthlan, and shut and locked the kitchen door. She looked round, tired but happy. There was nothing she liked better than to spend hours upon hours preparing delicious dishes for people and then see them eaten in no time at all! The children thought she was truly wonderful.

They were soon all in bed and asleep. The Penruthlans were asleep, too. Only the kitchen cat was awake, watching for mice in the kitchen. She didn't like a crowd. She liked the kitchen to herself!

Next day was fair and warm, though a stiff breeze still blew. Mrs Penruthlan spoke to the four children at breakfast-time.

'I'll be busy today cleaning up the mess. How would you like to take a picnic lunch of some of the remains of the supper and stay out all day? It's a nice day, and you'll enjoy it.'

Nothing could be better! Julian had already planned to make his way to the old tower once used by the Wreckers, and explore it. Now they would have all day to do it in!

'Oh, yes, Mrs Penruthlan, we'd love to do that,' he said. 'We'll get the picnic ready. You've plenty to do!'

But no, Mrs Penruthlan wouldn't let anyone deal with food but herself. She proceeded to pack up enough food for twelve people, or so Julian thought when he saw her preparations!

They set off together happily, with Timmy at their heels. The four farm dogs accompanied them for some way, tearing on in front and then tearing back trying to make Timmy as mad as they were. But Timmy was sedate, walking along as if to say, 'I'm taking these children for a walk, I've not time to play with you. You're only farm dogs!'

'Do we want Yan with us if he turns up?' asked George. 'Do we particularly want him to know what we are doing today?'

Julian considered. 'No, I don't think we *do* want him with us. We may find out something we don't want him to know, or to spread around.'

'Right,' said George. 'Well, just you send him off, then, if he comes. I'm fed up with him. Thank goodness he's a bit cleaner than he was!'

Yan did appear, of course. He came up silently on his bare feet. Nobody would have known he was trotting behind if it hadn't been for Timmy. Timmy quite happily left George's heels and went to say how-do-you-do to Yan, jumping up at him in delight.

George turned round to see where Timmy was, and saw
Yan. 'Julian, there's Yan!' she said.

'Hallo, Yan,' said Julian. 'Buzz off today. We're going
somewhere alone.'

'I'm coming too,' said Yan, strutting along behind. He
still looked fairly clean.

'No, you don't come too,' said Julian. 'You buzz off.
See? Off you go. We don't want you today.'

Yan's face took on a sullen look. He turned to Anne.
'Can't I come too?' he said, pleadingly.

Anne shook her head. 'No, not today,' she said. 'Another
time. Take this sweet, Yan, and go away.'

Yan took the sweet and turned away, his face sulky. He disappeared over the field and was soon lost to sight.

The four children and Timmy went on together, glad of their warm pullovers when the wind blew strongly. Julian gave a sudden groan.

'I shall be jolly glad when we've had our lunch,' he said. 'This bag of food is so heavy it's cutting into my shoulders.'

'Well, let's wait till we get to the tower and we can put the bags down,' said Dick. 'We'll do a little exploring before we have our lunch. I should think Mrs Penruthlan meant us to stay out to dinner, tea and supper, the amount she's packed for us!'

They hoped they were going in the right direction. They had looked at a map, and found various lanes which they thought would eventually lead to the tower, and had worked out which was the best direction to take.

Julian had his compass and was going by that, leading them down lanes, across fields, along little paths, and sometimes along no paths at all! He felt sure, however, that they were going right. They were making for the coast, anyway.

'Look, there are two hills side by side, or cliffs, are they?' said Anne, pointing. 'I believe they are the hills between which we saw that tower.'

'Yes, you're right,' said Dick. 'We're nearly there. I wonder how people got there when the tower and house were lived in. There appears to be no proper road at all.'

They walked on, over a rough field. They soon found themselves in a very narrow, overgrown lane, deep-set between hedges that almost met overhead.

'A green tunnel,' said Anne, pleased. 'Look out for those enormous nettles, Ju.'

At the end of the lane an overgrown path swung sharply right, and there, not far from them, was the tower! They stood and stared at it. This was where the light had flashed a hundred years ago to bring ships to their doom, and where the light had flashed only the other night.

'The tower's falling into ruins,' said Dick. 'Large pieces have dropped out of it. And I should think the house is in ruins, too, though we can't see enough of it at the moment, just a bit of the roof. Come on. This is going to be fun!'

The tower didn't look the frightening thing it had seemed on the stormy night when the boys saw the flashing light. It just looked a poor old ruin. They made their way to it through high thistles, nettles and willow-herb.

'Doesn't *look* as if anyone has been here for years,' said Julian, rather puzzled. 'I rather wish we'd brought a scythe to cut down these enormous weeds! We can hardly get through them. I'm stung all over with nettles, too.'

They came to the house at last, and a poor, tumbledown ruin it was! The doors had fallen in, the windows were out of shape, and had no glass, the roof was full of holes. An enormous climbing rose rambled everywhere, throwing masses of old-fashioned white roses over walls and roof to hide the ugliness of the ruin.

532

A TRIP TO THE TOWER

Only the tower seemed still strong, except at the top, where parts of the wall had crumbled away and fallen. Julian forced his way through the broken door way into the house. Weeds grew in the floor.

'There's a stone stairway going up the tower!' he called. 'And I say, look here! What's this on each stair?'

'Oil,' said George. 'Someone's been carrying oil up in a can, or a lamp, and has spilt it. Julian, we'd better be careful. That somebody may be here still!'

CHAPTER THIRTEEN

In the Wreckers' tower

DICK AND Anne came hurriedly up to the old stone stairway when they heard what Julian and George had said. Oil! That could only mean one thing, a lamp in the tower.

They all stood and looked at the big splashes of oil on each step.

'Come on up,' said Julian at last. 'I'll go first. Be careful how you go because the tower's in a very crumbly state.'

The tower was built at one end of the old house, and its walls were thicker than the house walls. The only entry to it was by a doorway inside the house. In the tower was a stone stairway that went very steeply up in a spiral.

'This must once have been the door of the tower,' said Dick, kicking at a great thick slab of wood that lay mouldering away beside the stone doorway. 'The tower doesn't seem to hold anything but this stone stairway, just a look-out, I suppose.'

'Or a place for signalling to ships to entice them on the rocks,' said George. 'Oh, Timmy, don't push past like that; you nearly made me fall, these stone steps are so steep.'

As Dick said, the tower seemed to hold nothing but a stairway spiralling up steeply. Julian came to the top first and gave a gasp. The view over the sea was astonishing. He could see for miles over the dark cornflower-blue waters. Near the coast the churning of the waves into white breakers and spray showed the hidden rocks that waited for unwary ships.

George came up beside him and stared in wonder, too. What a marvellous sight, blue sky, blue sea, waves pounding over the rocks, and white gulls soaring on the stiff breeze.

Then Dick came up, and Julian gave him a warning. 'Be careful. Don't lean on the walls at all, they're crumbling badly.'

Julian put out his hand and touched the top of the tower wall near him. It crumbled and bits fell away below.

Big pieces had fallen away here and there, leaving great gaps in the wall round the top of the tower. When Anne came up also, Julian took her arm, afraid that with such a crowd up there someone might stumble against a crumbling wall and fall from the tower.

George had hold of Timmy's collar and made him stand quite still. 'Don't you go putting your great paws up on the wall,' she warned him. 'You'll find yourself down in the nettles below in no time if you do!'

'You can quite well see what a wonderful place this is for flashing a light at night over the sea,' said Dick. 'It could be seen for miles. In the old days, when sailing ships got caught in the storms that rage round this coast at times,

536

they would be thankful to see a guiding light.'

'But what a light!' said Julian. 'A light that guided them straight on to those great rocks! Let me see now. Are those the rocks near those coves we went to the other day?'

'Yes, I think so,' said Dick. 'But there are rocks and rocks, and coves and coves round here. It's difficult to tell if they are the same ones we saw.'

'The ships that sailed towards the light must have been wrecked on the rocks down there,' said Julian, pointing. 'How did the wreckers get there? There must have been a path from here somewhere.'

'The Wreckers' Way, do you think?' said Dick.

Julian considered. 'Well, I don't know. I imagine that the Wreckers' Way must have been a way leading to the sea from inland somewhere, certainly a way that was convenient for the villagers to use. No. I'll tell you what *I* think happened!'

'What?' said everyone.

'I think, on a stormy night long ago, the people who lived here in this house went up into the tower and flashed their false light to any ship that was sailing out on the waters. Then, in great excitement, they watched it sailing nearer and nearer, perhaps shown up by the lightning, perhaps by the moon.'

Everyone imagined such a ship, and George shivered. Poor wretched ship!

'When the ship reached the rocks and crashed on them, the signallers in the tower gave a different signal, a signal

537

to a watcher up there on the hills,' said Julian, pointing behind him. 'A watcher who was standing on the only spot from which the flash could be seen! Maybe the light gleamed steadily to entice a ship in, but was flashed in code to the watcher on the hills, and the flashing said, 'Ship on rocks. Tell the others, and come to the feast!'

'How simply horrible!' said Anne. 'I can't believe it!'

'It *is* difficult to think anyone could be so heartless,' said Julian. 'But I think that's what happened. And then, I think, the people who lived in this house went down from here to the near-by coves and waited for their friends to come along the other way, the Wreckers' Way, wherever that is.'

'It must be a secret way,' said Dick. 'It must have been a way known only to those villagers who *were* Wreckers. After all, wrecking was against the law, and so this whole business of showing lights and wrecking ships must have been kept a dead secret. We heard what old Grandad said, that every Wrecker who knew the way had to vow he would tell no one else.'

'Old Grandad's father probably lived in this very house, and climbed the stone stairway on a wild night, and lit the lamp that shone out over the stormy sea,' said Julian.

'That's why Yan said he was frightened of this tower,' said George. 'He thinks his grandad's dad still lights it! Well, we know better. Somebody else lights it, somebody who can't be up to any good either!'

'And, don't let's forget, somebody who may still be about somewhere!' said Julian, lowering his voice suddenly.

'Gosh! yes,' said Dick, looking round the little tower as if he expected to see a stranger there, listening. 'I wonder where he keeps his lamp. It's not here.'

'The oil splashes are on almost every one of the stone steps,' said Anne. 'I noticed as I came up. I bet it's a big lamp. It has to give a light far out to sea!'

'Look, it must have been stood on this bit of the wall,' said Dick. 'There are some oily patches here.'

They all looked at the oily patches. Dick bent down and smelt them. 'Yes, paraffin oil,' he said.

George was looking at the wall on the other side of the tower. She called to the other three.

'And here's a patch on *this* side!' she said. 'I know what happened! Once a ship had been caught by the light and was on its way in, the men with the lamp put it on the *other* side of the tower to signal to the watcher on the hills, to tell him the ship was caught!'

'Yes. That's it,' said Anne. 'But who could it be? I'm sure nobody lives *here*, the place is an absolute ruin, open to the wind and the rain. It must be somebody who knows the way here, sees to the light, and does the signalling.'

There was a pause. Dick looked at Julian. The same thought came into their minds. *They* had seen somebody wandering out in the stormy night, twice!

'Could it be Mr Penruthlan, do you suppose?' said Dick. 'We couldn't *imagine* why he was out here in the storm the first night we came out to watch for the light.'

'No, he's not the man with the light, *he's the watcher on the hills!*' said Julian. 'That's it! That's why he goes out on wild nights, to see if there's a signal from the tower, flashing to say that a ship is coming in!'

There was an even longer pause. Nobody liked that idea at all.

'We know he tells lies, we know he goes through people's pockets, because we saw him,' went on Julian after a few moments. 'He fits in well. He's the man who goes and stands in that special spot on the hills and watches for a light!'

'What does he do after that?' said Anne. 'Didn't we

hear that there were no wrecks here now, because of the lighthouse higher up the coast? What's the point of it all, if there isn't a wreck?'

'Smuggling,' said Julian shortly. 'That's the point. Probably by motor-boat. They choose a wild night of storm and wind, when they will be neither seen nor heard, wait out at sea for the signalling light to show them all's clear, and then come into one of these coves.'

'Yes, and I bet the Wreckers' secret way is used by someone who steals down to the cove and takes the smuggled goods!' said Dick, excited. 'Three or four people, perhaps, if the goods are heavy. Gosh! I'm sure we're right.'

'And it's the watcher on the hill who tells his friends, and down they go to the coves together. It's most ingenious,' Julian said. 'Nobody sees the light on the tower except the boat waiting, and nobody sees the signal inland except the one watcher on the hills. Absolutely fool-proof.'

'We are lucky to stumble on it,' said Dick. 'But what puzzles me is this. I'm pretty certain that the man who lights the lamp didn't come the way *we* came – we'd have seen trodden-down weeds or something. We should certainly have found some sort of a path his feet had made.'

'Yes. And there wasn't anything, not even a broken thistle,' said Anne. 'There must be some other way into this old house.'

'Of course there is! We've already said there must be a

way for the man who lights the lamp to get down to the coves from here!' said George. 'Well, that's the way he gets here, of course. He comes up the passage from the cove. How stupid we are!'

This idea excited them all. Where was the passage? Nobody could imagine! It certainly wasn't in the tower, there was no room for anything in that small tower except for the spiral staircase leading to the top.

'Let's go down,' said Anne, and began to descend the steps. A slight noise below made her stop. 'Go on,' said George, who was just behind her. Anne turned a scared face to her.

'I heard a noise down there,' she whispered.

George turned to Julian immediately. 'Anne thinks there's somebody down there,' she said, in a low voice.

'Come back, Anne,' ordered Julian at once. Anne climbed back, still looking scared.

'Would it be the man who does the lamp?' she whispered. 'Do be careful, Julian. He can't be a nice man!'

'Nice! He must be a beast!' said George, scornfully. 'Are you going down, Ju? Look out, then.'

Julian peered down the stone steps. There was really nothing for it but to go down and see who was there. They couldn't possibly stay up in the tower all day long, hoping that whoever it was would go away!

'What sort of noise did you hear?' Julian asked Anne.

'Well, a sort of scuffling noise,' said Anne. 'It might have been a rat, of course, or a rabbit. It was just a noise,

543

that's all. Something's down there, or somebody!'

'Let's sit down for a moment or two and wait,' said Dick. 'We'll listen hard and see if we can hear anyone.'

So they sat down cautiously, George with her hand on Timmy's collar. They waited and they listened. They heard the wind blowing round the old tower. They heard the distant gulls calling, 'ee-oo, ee-oo, ee-oo'. They heard the thistles rustling their prickles together down below.

But they heard nothing from the kitchen at the foot of the tower. Julian looked at Anne. 'No sound to be heard now,' he said. 'It must have been a rabbit!'

'Perhaps it was,' said Anne, feeling rather foolish. 'What shall we do then? Go down?'

'Yes. I'll go first though, with Timmy,' said Julian.

'If anyone is lying in wait he'll be annoyed to see our Timmy. And Timmy will be even more annoyed to see him!'

Just as Julian was getting up, a noise was quite distinctly heard from below. It was, as Anne had described, a kind of scuffle, then silence.

'Well, here goes!' said Julian, and began to descend the steps. The others watched breathlessly. Timmy went with Julian, trying to press past him. He hadn't seemed worried about the noise at all! So perhaps it *was* only a rat or rabbit!

Julian went down slowly. Who was he going to find – an enemy, or a friend? Careful now, Julian, there may be somebody lying in wait!

CHAPTER FOURTEEN

The secret passage

JULIAN PAUSED on the last step of the spiral staircase and listened. Not a sound came from the nearby room. 'Who's there?' said Julian, sharply. 'I know you're there! I heard you!'

Still not a sound! The kitchen, overgrown with weeds and dark with ivy and the white rambling rose, seemed to be listening to him, but there was no answer!

Julian stepped right into the room and looked round. Nothing was there – nobody was there! The place was absolutely empty and quiet. Julian went through a doorway into another room. That was empty, too. The old house only had four rooms altogether, two of them very tiny, and every one of them was empty. Timmy didn't seem disturbed at all, either, nor did he bark as he certainly would have done if there had been any intruder there.

'Well, Timmy, it's a false alarm,' said Julian, relieved. 'Must have been a rabbit, or even a bit of wall crumbling and falling. What are you sniffing at there?'

Timmy was sniffing with interest at a corner near the doorway. He stood and looked at Julian as if he would like to tell him something. Julian went over to see what it was.

There was nothing there except for some rather flattened

545

weeds, growing through the floor. Julian couldn't think why Timmy should be interested. However, Timmy soon wandered away and went all round the place, wondering why they had come to such a peculiar house.

'Dick! Bring the girls down!' shouted Julian up the stone stairway. 'There doesn't seem to be anyone here, after all. It must have been some small animal that Anne heard.'

The others clattered down in relief. 'I'm sorry I gave you all a shock,' said Anne. 'But it did sound like somebody down there! However, I'm sure Timmy would have barked if so! He didn't seem at all disturbed.'

'No. I think we can safely say that it was a false alarm,' said Dick. 'What do we do next? Have our lunch? Or hunt about to see if we can find the entrance to the passage that leads from here down to the coves?'

Julian looked at his watch. 'It's not really time for lunch yet, unless you're all frightfully hungry,' he said.

'Well, I'm *beginning* to feel jolly hungry,' said Dick. 'But, on the other hand, I feel I can't wait to find that passage! Where on earth is the entrance?'

'I've been in all four rooms,' said Julian. 'None of them seems to have anything but weeds in them, no old door leading out of the walls, no trapdoor. It's a puzzle.'

'Well, we'll all have a jolly good hunt,' said George. 'This is the sort of thing I like. Timmy, you hunt, too!'

They began to explore the four rooms of the old house. As weeds grew more or less all over the floor they felt that there could be no trapdoor. If there had been, and the man

546

with the lamp used it, the weeds would surely have shown signs of it. But they grew quite undisturbed.

'Listen,' said Julian at last. 'I've got an idea. We'll make Timmy find the entrance.'

'How?' said George at once.

'Well, we'll make him smell the oil drips on the steps, and follow with his nose any others that have dripped in the weeds,' said Julian. 'I don't suppose the lamp dripped only on the steps. It must have dripped all the way from the passage entrance, wherever it is, to the top of the tower. Couldn't Timmy sniff them out? They would lead us to the entrance we're trying to find!'

'All right. But I'm beginning to believe there *is* no entrance,' said George, getting hold of Timmy's collar. 'We've looked over every single inch of this house. Come on, Tim, you've got to perform a miracle!'

Timmy's nose was firmly placed over the oil-drip on the bottom stair. 'Sniff it, Timmy, and follow,' said George.

Timmy knew perfectly well what she meant. George had trained him well! He sniffed hard at the oil and then started up the stone steps for the next oil patch. But George pulled him back.

'No, Tim. Not that way. This way. There must be other oil drips on the floor of the house.'

Timmy amiably turned the other way. He found an oil drip at once, on a patch of weeds growing on the floor. He sniffed it and went on to another and another.

'Good old Timmy,' said George, delighted. 'Isn't he

clever, Ju? He's following where the man walked when he carried that lamp! Go on, Timmy, where's the next drip?'

It was an easy strong-smelling trail for Timmy to follow! He followed it, sniffing, out of one room into another, smaller one. Then into a third, bigger one, which must have been the main room, for it had a very big fire-place, his nose to the ground. In fact, he went right into the hearth, and there came to a stop. He looked round at George and barked.

'He says the trail ends here,' said George, in excitement. 'So the entrance to the secret passage must be in this big fire-place!'

THE SECRET PASSAGE

The others crowded to the hearth. Julian produced his torch and shone it up the chimney. It was an enormous one, though part of the top of it had now fallen away. 'Nothing there,' said Julian. 'But – hallo – what's this?'

He now shone his torch to the side of the big fireplace and saw a small, dark cavity there, barely big enough for a man to get into. 'Look!' he said, excited, 'I believe we've found it. See that small hole? Well, I bet if we crawl through that we'll find it's the way to the secret passage! Good old Timmy!'

'We shall get absolutely *filthy*,' said Anne.

'You *would* say that!' said George, scornfully. 'Who cares? This could be very important, couldn't it, Ju?'

'Rather!' said Julian. 'If we're on to what we think we are, and that's Smuggling with a big S, it *is* important. Well, what about it? Lunch first, or exploring that hole?'

'Exploring, of course,' said Dick. 'What about letting old Tim go first? I'll give him a leg-up.'

Timmy was hoisted up to the black hole, and disappeared into it with delight. Rabbits? Rats? What were the children after? This was a fine game!

'Now I'll go,' said Julian, and clambered up. 'It's a bit difficult to squeeze into. Dick, you help Anne and George up next, and then you come.'

He disappeared, and one by one the others also hoisted themselves to the hole and crawled in, too.

The hole was merely an entrance to a narrow standing-place at the side of the chimney. Julian got down from the hole, and stood still for a moment, wondering if this was just an old hiding-place, and not an entrance to anywhere, after all. But then, just to the right of his feet, he saw another hole that dropped sharply down.

He flashed his torch down, and saw iron hand-grips at one side. He called back and told the others. Then he descended into the hole, at first using the grips for his feet and then for his hands as well.

The hole went down as straight as a well. It came to a sudden end, and Julian found himself standing on solid ground. He turned round, flashing his torch.

There was the passage in front of him! It must be the one that led down to the coves, the one that the man with the lamp must have used long ago, when he went to gloat over the groaning ships on the rocks.

Julian could hear the others coming down the shaft. He suddenly thought of Timmy. Where was he? He must have fallen headlong down the hole and found himself suddenly at the bottom. Poor Tim! Julian hoped he hadn't hurt himself, but as he hadn't yelped, perhaps he had fallen like a cat, on his feet!

He called up to the others. 'I've found the passage. It starts at the bottom of the shaft. I'll go along it a little way and wait for you all to come. Then we can keep together in a line.'

Soon everyone was safely down the shaft. George began to worry about Timmy. 'He *must* have hurt himself, Ju! Falling all that way; oh, dear, where is he?'

'We'll soon come across him, I expect,' said Julian. 'Now, keep close together, everybody. The path goes downwards pretty steeply, as you might expect.'

It certainly did. In places the four children almost slithered along. Then Julian discovered iron staples fixed here and there in the steepest places, and after that they held on to them in the most slippery spots.

'These iron staples would be jolly useful to anyone coming *up*,' said Julian. 'It would be almost impossible to climb up this passage without something to help the climber to pull himself up. Ah, here's a more level stretch.'

The level part soon became much wider. And then, quite suddenly, it became a cave! The four came out into it in surprise. It was rather low-roofed, and the walls were made of black rock that glistened in the light of the torch.

'I wish I could find Timmy,' said George, uneasily. 'I can't even hear him anywhere!'

'We'll go on till we come to the cove,' said Julian. 'This must lead us right down to the shore, probably to the very cove where the ships were wrecked. Look, there's a kind of rocky arch leading out of this cave.'

They went through the archway and into yet another passage that wound between jutting rocks, which made it rather difficult to get through at times. Then suddenly the passage divided into two. One fork went meandering off towards the seaward side, the other into the cliff.

'Better take the seaward side,' said Julian. They were just going to take the right-hand passage when George

551

stopped and clutched at Julian. 'Listen!' she said. 'I can hear Timmy!'

They all stopped and listened. George had the sharpest ears of the lot, and she could hear him barking. So could the others after a few moments. Bark-bark-bark! Bark-bark-bark! Yes, it was Timmy all right!

'Timmy!' yelled George, making the others jump almost out of their skins. 'TIMMY!'

'He can't hear you all this way away,' said Dick. 'Gosh, you made me jump. Come on, we'll have to take the cliff passage. Timmy's barking comes from that direction, not this.'

'Yes, I agree,' said Julian. 'We'll go and collect him, and then come back and take the other passage. I'm sure it leads down to the sea.'

They made their way along the left-hand passage. It was not difficult, because it was much wider than the one they had already come down. Timmy's barking became louder and louder as they went down. George whistled piercingly, hoping that Timmy would come rushing up. But he didn't.

'It's funny that he doesn't come,' said George, worried. 'I think he must be hurt. TIMMY!'

The passage wound round a corner, and then once more divided into two. To the children's surprise they saw a rough door set into the rocky wall of the passage on the left-hand side. A door! How very extraordinary!

'Look, a door!' said Dick, amazed. 'And a jolly stout one, too.'

552

'Timmy's behind it!' said George. 'He must have gone through it and it shut behind him. Timmy! We're here! We're coming!'

She pushed at the door, but it didn't open. She saw that it was lightly latched, and lifted the old iron latch. The door opened easily and all four went through into a curious cave beyond. It was more like a low-roofed room!

Timmy flung himself at them as soon as they came through the door. He wasn't hurt. He was so pleased to see them that he barked the place down! 'Woof! WOOOOOF!'

'Oh, Timmy, how did you get here?' said George, hugging him. 'Did the door click behind you? My word, what a strange place this is! It's a storeroom – look at all the boxes and crates and things!'

They looked round the strange cave, and at that moment there was a soft click. Then something slid smoothly into place. Julian leapt to the door and tried to open it.

'It's locked! Somebody's locked it, and bolted it! I heard them. Let us out, let us *out*!'

CHAPTER FIFTEEN

Locked in the cave

DICK, GEORGE and Anne looked at one another in dismay. Someone must have been lying in wait for them, someone must have captured Timmy and shut him up. And now they were captured, too!

Timmy began to bark when Julian shouted. He ran to the door. Julian was hammering on it and even kicking it.

A voice came from the other side of the door, a drawling voice, sounding rather amused.

'You came at an awkward time, that's all, and you must remain where you are till tomorrow.'

'Who are you?' said Julian fiercely. 'How dare you lock us in like this!'

'I believe you have food and drink with you,' said the voice. 'I noticed the packs on your backs, which I presume contain food. That is lucky for you! Now be sensible. You must pay the penalty for being inquisitive!'

'You let us out!' shouted Julian, enraged at the cool voice with its impertinent tone. He kicked the door again out of temper, though he knew that it wasn't the slightest use!

There was no reply. Whoever it was outside the cave door had gone. Julian gave the door one last furious kick and looked round at the others.

'That man must have been watching us from somewhere. Probably followed us all the way to the old house, and saw the packs on our backs then. It must have been him that you heard down in the house when we were in the tower, Anne.'

Timmy barked again. He was still at the door. George called him. 'Tim! It's no use! The door's locked. Oh dear, why did we let you go into that hole first? If you hadn't run on ahead and somehow got yourself caught, you'd have been able to protect us when those men lay in wait!'

'Well, what do we do now?' said Anne, trying to sound brave.

'What *can* we do?' said George. 'Nothing at all! Here we are, locked and bolted in a cave inside the cliff, with nobody near except the fellow who locked us in. If anybody's got any ideas I'd like to hear them!'

'You do sound cross!' said Anne. 'I suppose there isn't anything to do but wait till we're let out. I only hope that man remembers we're here. Nobody else knows where we are.'

'Horrid thought!' said Dick. 'Still, I've no doubt that Mrs Penruthlan would raise the alarm, and a search-party would set out to find us.'

'What a hope they'd have!' said George. 'Even if they did trace us to the old tower, they wouldn't know the secret entrance to the passage!'

'Well, let's look on the cheerful side,' said Julian,

undoing the pack from his back. 'Let's have some food.'

Everybody cheered up at once. 'I feel quite hungry,' said Anne in surprise. 'It must be past our dinner-time now. Well, anyway, eating will be something to do!'

They had a very good meal and felt thankful that Mrs Penruthlan had packed up so much food. If they were not going to be let out till the next day they would need plenty to eat!

They examined the boxes and crates. Some were very old. All were empty. There was a big seaman's chest there, too, with 'Abram Trelawny' painted on it. They lifted the lid. That was empty too, save for one old brass button.

'Abram Trelawny,' said Dick, looking at the name. 'He must have been a sailor on one of the ships that the Wreckers enticed to the rocks. This chest must have been rolled up on the beach by the waves and brought up here. I dare say this cave was the place where the man who owned that old house took his share of the booty and hid it.'

'Yes, I think you're right,' said Julian. 'That is why it has a door that can be locked. The Wreckers probably stored quite a lot of valuable things here from different wrecks, and didn't want any other Wrecker to creep up from the cave and take them. What a hateful lot they must have been! Well, there doesn't seem anything of real interest here.'

LOCKED IN THE CAVE

It was very, very boring in the cave. The children used only one torch because they were afraid that if they used the others they had brought they might exhaust all the batteries, and then have to be in the dark.

Julian examined the cave from top to bottom to see if there was any possible way of escape. But there wasn't. That was quite clear. The cave walls were made of solid rocks, and there wasn't a hole anywhere through which to escape, big or small!

'That man said we'd come at an awkward time,' said Julian, throwing himself down on the ground. 'Why? Are they expecting some smuggled goods tonight? They've signalled out to sea twice already this week, as *we* know. Hasn't the boat they expected come along yet? If so, they must be expecting it tonight, and so we've come at an awkward time!'

'If only we weren't locked in this beastly cave!' said George. 'We might have spied on them and seen what they were up to, and might even have been able to stop them somehow, or get word to the police.'

'Well, we can't now,' said Dick gloomily. 'Timmy, you were an ass to get caught; you really were.'

Timmy put his tail down and looked as gloomy as Dick. He didn't like being in this low-roofed cave. Why didn't they open the door and go out? He went to the door and whined, scraping at it with his feet.

'No good, Tim. It won't open,' said Anne. 'I think he's thirsty, George.'

There was nothing for Timmy to drink except homemade lemonade, and he didn't seem to like that very much.

'Don't waste it on him if he doesn't like it,' said Julian, hastily. 'We may be jolly glad of it ourselves tomorrow.'

Dick glanced at his watch. 'Only half past two!' he groaned. 'Hours and hours to wait. Let's have a game of some sort, noughts and crosses would be better than nothing.'

They played noughts and crosses till they were sick of them. They played word-games and guessing games. They had a light tea at five o'clock and began to wonder what Mrs Penruthlan would think when they didn't turn up that evening.

'If Mr Penruthlan is mixed up in this affair, and it's pretty certain that he is,' said Julian, 'he'll not be best pleased to be told to fetch the police to look for *us*! It's just the one night he won't want the police about!'

'I think you're wrong,' said George. 'I think he'd be delighted to have the police looking for lost children, and not poking their noses into *his* affairs tonight!'

'I hadn't thought of that,' said Julian. How slowly the time went by. They yawned, talked, fell silent, argued and played with Timmy. Julian's torch flickered out and they took Dick's instead.

'Good thing we brought more than one torch!' said Anne.

Half past nine came and they all began to feel sleepy.

'I vote we try to go to sleep,' said Dick, yawning hugely.

'There's a sandy spot over there, softer to lie on than this rock. What about trying to sleep?'

They all thought it was a good idea and went to the sandy spot. It certainly was better than the hard rock. They wriggled about in the sand and made dents for their bodies to lie in.

'It's still hard,' complained George. 'Oh, Timmy darling, *don't* snuffle all round my face. Lie down beside me and Anne and go to sleep, too!'

Timmy lay down on George's legs. He put his nose on his paws and heaved a huge sigh.

'I hope Timmy's not going to do *that* all night,' said Anne. 'What a draught!'

Although they thought they couldn't possibly go to sleep, they did. Timmy did, too, though he kept one ear open and one eye ready to open. He was on guard! No one could open that door or even come near it without Timmy hearing!

At about eleven o'clock Timmy opened one eye and cocked both ears. He listened, not taking his head off George's legs. He opened the other eye.

Then he sat up and listened harder. George woke up when he moved and stretched out a hand to Timmy. 'Tim, lie down,' she whispered. But Timmy didn't. He gave a small whine.

George sat up, fully awake. Why was Timmy whining? Was there something going on outside the door, men passing perhaps, on their way to the cove? Had the light

559

been flashing out to sea and had it brought in the boat the men were waiting for?

She put her hand on Timmy's collar. 'What is it?' she whispered, expecting Timmy to growl when he next heard something. But he didn't growl. He whined again.

Then he shook off George's hand and went to the door. George switched on her torch, puzzled. Timmy scraped at the door and whined again. But he still didn't growl.

LOCKED IN THE CAVE

'Ju! I believe someone is at the door!' called George, suddenly, in a low voice. 'I believe Timmy can hear a search-party or something. Wake up!'

Everyone awoke suddenly. George repeated her words again. 'Timmy's not growling. That means it's not our enemies he hears,' she added. 'He'd growl like anything at the man who locked us in.'

'Be quiet for a moment and listen,' said Julian. 'Let's see if we can hear anything ourselves. We haven't got Timmy's sharp ears, but we might be able to hear *some*thing.'

They sat absolutely still, listening. Then Julian nudged Dick. He had heard something. 'Quiet!' he breathed. They listened again, hardly breathing.

They heard a little scrabbling noise at the door. Then it stopped. George expected Timmy to break out into a fusillade of barks at once, but he didn't. He stood there with his head on one side and his ears cocked. He gave an excited little whine and suddenly scraped at the door again.

Somebody whispered outside the door, and Timmy whined and ran to George and then back to the door again. Everyone was puzzled.

Julian got up and went to the door himself, his feet making no sound. Yes, there was most certainly somebody outside, two people, perhaps, whispering to one another.

'Who's there?' said Julian suddenly. 'I can hear you outside. Who is it?'

There was dead silence for a moment, and then a small familiar voice answered softly:

'It's me. Yan.'

'Yan! Gosh! Is it really you?'

'Yes.'

There was an amazed silence in the cave. Yan! Yan at this time of night outside the door of the very cave they were locked in! Were they dreaming?

Timmy went mad when he heard Yan speaking to Julian. He flung himself at the door, barking and yelping. Julian puts his hand on his collar. 'Be quiet, idiot! You'll spoil everything! Be *quiet*!'

Timmy stopped. Julian spoke to Yan again. 'Yan, have you got a light?'

'No, no light. It is dark here,' said Yan. 'Can I come to you?'

'Yes, of course. Listen, Yan. Do you know how to unlock and unbolt a door?' asked Julian, wondering whether the half-wild boy knew even such simple things.

'Yes,' said Yan. 'Are you locked in?'

'Yes,' said Julian. 'But the key may be in the lock. Feel and see. Feel for the bolts, too. Slide them back and turn the key if there is one.'

The four in the cave held their breath as they heard Yan's hands wandering over the stout door in the dark, tapping here and there to find the bolts and the lock.

Then they heard the bolts being slid smoothly back. How they hoped their captor had left the key in the lock!

'Here is a key,' said Yan's voice suddenly. 'But it is so stiff. My hand isn't strong enough to turn it.'

562

'Try both hands at once,' said Julian urgently.

They heard Yan trying, panting with his efforts. But the key would not turn.

'Blow!' said Dick. 'So near and yet so far!'

Anne pushed Dick out of the way, an idea suddenly flooding into her mind. 'Yan! Listen to me, Yan. Take the key out of the lock and push it under the bottom of the door. Do you hear me?'

'Yes, I heard,' said Yan, and they heard him tugging at the key. There was a sharp noise as it came suddenly out of the lock. Then, lo and behold! it appeared under the bottom of the door, slid through carefully by Yan!

Julian snatched it up and put it into the lock on his side. He turned the key, and unlocked the door. What a wonderful bit of luck!

CHAPTER SIXTEEN

Wreckers' Way

JULIAN FLUNG open the door. Timmy leapt past him and yelped with delight to find Yan standing outside. He fawned on the boy and licked him, and Yan laughed.

'Let's get out of here, quick!' said Dick. 'That man may be along at any moment, you can't tell.'

'Right. Explanations later,' said Julian. He hustled everyone out, took the key from the inside lock and shut the door. He inserted the key into the outside lock and turned it. He shot the bolts, took out the key and put it into his pocket. He grinned at Dick.

'Now if that man comes along to see how we are he won't even know we're gone! He won't be able to get in to see if we're there or not.'

'Where shall we go now?' asked Anne, feeling as if she was in a peculiar kind of dream.

Julian stood and considered. 'It would be madness to go back up the passage and into the old house,' he said. 'If there's any signalling going on, and there's pretty certain to be, we shall be caught again. We'd be sure to make a noise scrambling out of that hole in the fireplace.'

'Well, let's take that other passage we saw, the right-hand hand one,' said George. 'Look, there it is.' She shone her torch on it. 'Where does it lead to, Yan?'

'To the beach,' said Yan. 'I went down it when I was looking for you all, but you weren't there, so I came back and found that door. There is nobody on the beach.'

'Well, let's go down there, then,' said Dick. 'Once we feel we're out of danger's way we can plan what's best to do.'

They went along the other passage, their torch showing them the way. It was a steep tunnel, and they found it rather difficult going. Anne managed to give Yan a squeeze.

'You were clever to find us!' she said, and Yan gave her a smile which she couldn't see because of the dark.

They heard the sound of waves at last and came out into the open air. It was a windy night but stars were shining in the sky, and gave quite a fair light after the darkness of the passage.

'Where are we exactly?' said Dick, looking round. Then he saw they were on the same beach as they had been a few days before, but a good way farther along.

'Can we get back to the farm from here?' said Julian, stopping to consider exactly where they were. 'Gosh! I think we'd better hurry. The tide's coming in! We'll be cut off if we don't look out!'

A wave ran up the sand almost to their feet. Julian took a quick look at the cliff behind them. It was very steep.

They certainly couldn't climb it in the darkness! Would there be time to look for a cave to sit in till the tide went out again?

Another wave ran up, and Julian's feet felt suddenly wet. 'Blow!' he said. 'This is getting serious. The next big one will sweep us off our feet. I wish the moon was out. These stars give such a faint light.'

'Yan, is there a cave we can go to, a cave open to the air, not inside the cliff?' said George, anxiously.

'I'll take you back by the Wreckers' Way,' said Yan, surprisingly. 'Come with me.'

'Of course, you said you knew the Wreckers' Way,' said Julian, remembering. 'If it comes out near here, we're in luck's way! Lead on, Yan. You're a marvel! But do hurry, our feet got wet again just then, and at any moment a giant of a wave may come!'

Yan took the lead. He led them into cove after cove, and then came to a larger one than usual. He took them to the back of the cove, and led them a little way up a cliff path.

He came to a great rock. He squeezed behind it and the others followed one by one. Nobody could ever have guessed that there was a way into the cliff behind that rock.

'Now we are in the Wreckers' Way,' said Yan proudly, and led them on again. But suddenly he stopped and the others all bumped into one another. Timmy gave a short, warning bark, and George put her hand on his collar.

'Somebody's coming!' whispered Yan, and pushed them back. Sure enough, they could hear voices in the distance. They turned and hurried back. They didn't want to walk into any more trouble!

Yan got to the front and led them back to the big rock. He was trembling. They all squeezed out behind it, and Yan went along the cliff face to a tiny cave, really only a big ledge with an overhanging roof. 'Sssssssss!' he said warningly, sounding like a snake!

They sat down and waited. Two men came out from behind the rock, one a big man, and one a small one. Nobody could see them clearly, but Julian hissed into Dick's ear: 'I'm sure that's Mr Penruthlan! See how enormous he is!'

Dick nodded. It was no surprise to him to think that the giant farmer should be mixed up in this. The five children held their breath and watched.

Yan nudged Dick and pointed out to sea. 'Boat coming!' he whispered.

Dick could see and hear nothing. But in a few moments he did hear something, the whirr of a fast motor-boat! What sharp ears Yan must have! The others heard the noise, too, through the crashing of the waves on the rocks.

'No light,' whispered Yan, as the noise of the boat grew louder.

'He'll be on the rocks!' said Dick. But before the boat got to the rocks, the engine stopped. The children could just make out the boat now, swaying up and down beyond

568

the barrier of rocks. Evidently it was not going to try and come any farther in.

Now the watchers could hear voices again. The two men who had come down Wreckers' Way were standing below the big rock that hid the entrance, talking. One leapt down to a rock farther down, and disappeared. The other man was left standing alone.

'It was the big man who leapt down,' whispered Julian. 'Where's he gone? Ah, there he is! You can just see him moving behind that rock down there. What's he got?'

'A boat!' whispered Yan. 'He has a boat down there, pulled up high out of reach of the big waves. There is a pool there. He is going to row out to the other boat.'

The children strained their eyes to watch. The sky was quite clear, but the only light they had was from the stars, and it was difficult to see anything more than moving shadows or outlines.

Then there came the sound of oars in rowlocks, and a moving black shadow of a rowing-boat and man could be seen faintly, going over the waves.

'Does he know the way through that mass of rocks?' wondered Dick. 'He must know this coast well to risk rowing out through the rocks at high tide in the dead of night!'

'Why is he doing it?'

'He's getting smuggled goods from the motor-boat,' said Julian. 'Goodness knows what! There, I've lost him in the darkness.'

So had everyone. They could no longer hear the oars either, for the crashing of the waves on the rocks drowned every other sound.

Beyond the rocks lay the motor-boat, but only Yan's sharp eyes could see it even faintly in the starlight. Once, in a sudden silence of the waves, there came the exchange of voices over the water.

'He's reached the motor-boat,' said Dick. 'He'll be back in a minute.'

'Look! The second man is going down to the cove now, going to help the first one in, I expect,' said Julian. 'What about us escaping through the Wreckers' Way while we've got the chance?'

'Good idea,' said George, scrambling up. 'Come on, Timmy! Home!'

They went to the great rock and squeezed behind it once more into the entrance of the Wreckers' Way. Then, Yan once more leading, they went up the secret passage, flicking on the torch very thankfully.

'Where does the Wreckers' Way come out?' asked Anne.

'In a shed at Tremannon Farm,' said Yan, to the astonishment of everyone.

'Goodness, so it's very nice and handy for Mr Penruthlan!' said George. 'I wonder how many times he has been up on the hills at night, and has been warned by the tower light to go down Wreckers' Way to the cove and collect smuggled goods from some boat or other! A very

570

good scheme, it seems to me, and impossible for anyone to find out.'

'Except us!' said Dick in a pleased voice. 'We got on to it pretty well. There's not much we don't know about Mr Penruthlan now!'

They went on and on. The passage was fairly straight and had probably been the bed of an underground stream at some time. The way was quite smooth to the feet.

'We've walked about a mile, I should think!' groaned Dick, at last. 'How far now, Yan? Shall we soon be back?'

'Yes,' said Yan.

Anne suddenly remembered that nobody knew how it was that Yan had found them that night. She turned to him.

'Yan, how did you find us tonight? It seemed like a miracle when we woke up to find you outside that locked door!'

'It was easy,' said Yan. 'You said to me: "Go away. Do not come with us today." So I went back a little way. But I followed you. I followed you to the old house, though I was frightened.'

'I guess you were frightened!' said Dick with a grin. 'Well, go on.'

'I hid,' said Yan. 'You went up into the tower a long time. I came out into the room below, and . . .'

'It was *you* we heard scuffling there, then!' said Anne. 'We wondered who it was!'

'Yes,' said Yan. 'I sat down on some weeds in a corner,

and waited till you came down, and then I hid again: but I watched you through a hole from outside. I saw you go through the fire-place. One minute you were there. The next you were gone. I was frightened.'

'So it was you who flattened down that patch of weeds that Timmy sniffed at?' said Dick. 'Well, what did you do next?'

'I was going to come too,' said Yan. 'But the hole was so dark and black. I stood in the fire-place for a long time, hoping you would come back.'

'Then what happened?' said Dick.

'Then I heard voices,' said Yan. 'I thought it was you all coming back. But it wasn't. It was men. So I ran away and hid in the nettles.'

'What a place to choose!' said George.

'Then I was hungry,' said Yan, 'and I went back to Grandad's hut for food. He cuffed me for leaving him, and he made me work for him all day. He was angry with me.'

'My word! So you've been on the hills all day, knowing we were down in that passage!' said Julian. 'Didn't you say anything to anyone?'

'I went down to Tremannon Farm to see if you were back when it grew dark,' said Yan. 'But you weren't there. Only the Barnies were there, giving another show. I didn't see Mr or Mrs Penruthlan. I knew then that you must still be down in that dark hole. I was afraid the men had hurt you.'

'So you came all the way again in the dark!' said Julian, astonished. 'Well, you've got pluck, I must say!'

572

'I was very frightened,' said Yan. 'My legs shook at the knees like my old Grandad's. I climbed in at the hole, and at last I found you.'

'With no torch to light the way!' said Dick, and clapped the small boy on the back. 'You're a real friend, Yan! Timmy knew you all right when you came to the locked door. He didn't even bark! He knew it was you.'

'I wanted to save Timmy too,' said Yan. 'Timmy is my friend.'

George said nothing to that. She was thinking rather unwillingly that Yan was a remarkably brave young man, and that she had been silly and unkind to resent Timmy's

573

liking for him. What a good thing he *had* liked Timmy!

Yan suddenly stopped. 'We are there,' he said. 'We are at Tremannon Farm. Look above your heads.'

Julian flashed his torch upwards, and stared. An open trapdoor was just above them.

'The trapdoor is open!' he said. 'Someone came down here tonight!'

'And we know who!' said Dick, grimly. 'Mr Penruthlan and his friend! Where does that trapdoor lead to, Yan?'

'Into a corner of the machine shed,' said Yan. 'When the trapdoor is shut, it is covered with sacks of corn or onions. They have been moved to open the way down.'

They all climbed out. Julian flashed the torch round the shed. Yes, there were the machines and the tools. Well, who would have thought that the sacks he had seen in here the other day were hiding the trapdoor that led to the Wreckers' Way!

CHAPTER SEVEENTEEN

Long after midnight!

A RAT suddenly shot out from a corner of the shed, and tore across to the open trapdoor. Timmy gave a bark and leapt after it. He just stopped himself from taking a header through the trapdoor by sliding along on all four feet and coming to a stop at the entrance.

He stood up and looked down the hole, his head cocked to one side.

'Look, he's listening,' said Anne. 'Is there someone coming, those men, perhaps, with the smuggled goods?'

'No, he's only listening for the rat,' said Julian.

'I tell you what we'll do! We'll shut the trapdoor and pile sacks and boxes and everything on top of it! Then when the men come up, they'll find themselves trapped. They won't be able to get out. If we can get the police in time, they'll be able to catch them easily.'

'Good idea!' said Dick. 'Super! How mad those two men will be when they come to the trapdoor and find it shut! They can't get out the other way because the tide's up.'

'I'd like to see Mr Penruthlan's face when he sees the trapdoor shut, and feels a whole lot of things piled on top of it!' said Julian. 'He'll make a few more of his peculiar noises!'

'Ooh – ah – ock,' said Dick, solemnly. 'Come on, help me with the trapdoor, Ju, it's heavy.'

They shut the big trapdoor and then began to drag sacks, boxes and even some kind of heavy farm machine on top of the trapdoor. Now certainly nobody could open it from underneath.

They were hot and very dirty by the time they had finished. They were also beginning to feel very tired. 'Phew!' said Dick. 'I'm glad that's done. Now we'd better go to the farmhouse and show ourselves to Mrs Penruthlan.'

'Oh dear, do we tell her about her husband, and how he's mixed up in this horrid business?' said Anne. 'I do so like her. I expect she's very worried about us, too.'

'Yes. It's going to be a bit difficult,' said Julian, soberly. 'Better let me do most of the talking. Come on, we'll go. Don't make too much row or we'll set the dogs barking. I'm surprised they haven't yelled their heads off already!'

It *was* rather surprising. Usually the farm dogs barked the place down if there was any unusual noise in the night. The five children and Timmy left the machine shed and made their way towards the farmhouse. George pulled at Julian's arm.

'Look,' she said, in a low voice. 'See those lights up in the hills? What are they?'

Julian looked. He could see moving lights here and there up on the hills. He was puzzled. Then he made a guess. 'I bet Mrs Penruthlan has sent out searchers for us,' he said, 'and they've got lanterns. They're hunting for us on the hills. Gosh, I hope all the Barnies aren't out after us too.'

They came to the farmyard, moving very quietly. The big barn, used by the Barnies for their show, was in darkness. Julian pictured it full of benches, left from that night's show. The memory of Mr Penruthlan turning out the pockets of the clothes left and hunting through the drawers in the chest used by the Barnies, came into his mind.

A sharp whisper made them stop very suddenly. George put her hand on Timmy's collar to stop him growling or barking. Who was this now?

None of the little company answered or moved. The whisper came again.

'Here! I'm here!'

Still nobody moved. They were all puzzled. Who was waiting there in the shadows, and for whom was he waiting? The whisper came again, a little louder.

'Here! Over here!'

And then, as if too impatient to wait any longer, the whisperer moved out into the yard. Julian couldn't see who it was in the dark, and he quickly flashed his torch on the man.

It was the Guv'nor, grim-faced as ever! He flinched as the light fell on his face, took a few steps back and disappeared round a corner. Timmy growled.

'Well! How many *more* people wander about at night here?' said Dick. 'That was the Guv'nor. What was *he* doing?'

'I give it up,' said Julian. 'I'm getting too tired to think straight. I shouldn't be in the least surprised to see Clopper the horse peering round a corner at us, and saying "Peep-bo, chaps!"'

Everyone chuckled. It was just the kind of thing Clopper *would* do if he were really alive!

They came to the farmhouse. It was full of light, upstairs and downstairs. The curtains were not drawn across the kitchen window and the children looked in as they passed. Mrs Penruthlan was sitting there, her hands clasped, looking extremely worried.

They opened the kitchen door and trooped in. Yan too. Mrs Penruthlan leapt up at once and ran to them. She hugged Anne, she tried to hug George, she said all kinds of things at top speed, and to the children's dismay they saw that she was crying.

'Oh, where *have* you been?' she said, tears pouring down her face. 'The men are out looking for you, and all the dogs, and the Barnies too. They've been looking for ages! And Mr Penruthlan's not home, either. I don't know where *he* is, he's gone too! Oh, what a terrible evening. But thank goodness you're safe!'

Julian saw that she was terribly upset. He took her arm gently and led her to a chair. 'Don't worry,' he said. 'We're all safe. We're sorry you've been upset.'

'But where have you *been*?' wept Mrs Penruthlan. 'I pictured you drowned, or lost on the hills, or fallen into quarries. And where is Mr Penruthlan? He went out at seven and there's been not a sign of him since!'

The children felt uncomfortable. They thought they knew where Mr Penruthlan was, getting smuggled goods from the motor-boat, and carrying them back with his friend, up the Wreckers' Way!

'Now just you tell me what you've been doing,' said Mrs Penruthlan, drying her eyes, and sounding unexpectedly determined. 'Upsetting everybody like this!'

'Well,' said Julian, 'it's a long story, but I'll try to make it short. Strange things have been happening, Mrs Penruthlan.'

He plunged into the whole story, the old tower, Grandad's tale of the flashing light, their journey to explore the tower, the secret passage to the Wreckers' cove, their imprisonment and escape, and then Julian stopped.

How was he to tell poor Mrs Penruthlan that one of the smugglers was her husband? He glanced at the others desperately. Anne began to cry, and George felt very much like it, too. It was Yan who suddenly spoke and broke the news.

'We saw Mr Penruthlan in the cove,' he said, glad of a chance to put in a word. 'We saw him!'

Mrs Penruthlan stared at Yan, and then at the embarrassed, anxious faces of the other children.

'You saw him in the cove?' she said. 'You didn't! What was he doing there?'

'We think, we think he must be one of the smugglers,' said Julian, awkwardly. 'We think we saw him get into a

boat and row to the motor-boat beyond the rocks. If so, he
– well – he may get into trouble, Mrs Penr—'

He didn't finish, because, to his enormous surprise, Mrs
Penruthlan jumped up from her chair in a rage.

'You wicked boy!' panted Mrs Penruthlan, sounding
suddenly out of breath. 'You bad, wicked boy, saying
things like that about Mr Penruthlan, who's the straightest,
honestest, most God-fearing man who ever lived! Him a
smuggler! Him in with those wicked men! I'll box your
ears till you eat your words and serve you right!'

Julian was amazed at the change in the cheerful little
farmer's wife. Her face was red, her eyes were blazing,

and somehow she seemed to be taller. He had never seen anyone so angry in his life! Yan went promptly under the table.

Timmy growled. He liked Mrs Penruthlan, but he felt he really couldn't allow her to set about his friends. She faced Julian, trembling with anger.

'Now you apologise!' she said. 'Or I'll give you such a drubbing as you've never had in your life before. And you just wait and see what Mr Penruthlan will say when he comes back and hears the things you've said about him!'

Julian was much too big and strong for the farmer's wife to 'give him a drubbing' but he felt certain she would try, if he didn't apologise! What a tiger she was!

He put his hand on her arm. 'Don't get so upset,' he said. 'I'm very sorry to have made you so angry.'

Mrs Penruthlan shook his hand off her arm. 'Angry! I should just think I *am* angry!' she said. 'To think anyone should say those things about Mr Penruthlan. That wasn't him down in Wreckers' Cove. I know it wasn't. I only wish I knew *where* he was! I'm that worried!'

'He's down Wreckers' Way,' announced Yan from his safe vantage-point under the table. 'We put the trapdoor down over him.'

'Down Wreckers' Way!' cried Mrs Penruthlan and to the children's great relief she sank down into a chair again. She turned to Julian, questioningly.

He nodded. 'Yes. We came up that way from the beach

– Yan knew it. It comes up in a corner of the machine shed, through a trapdoor. We – er – we shut the trapdoor and piled sacks and things on it. I'm afraid, well, I'm rather afraid Mr Penruthlan can't get out!'

Mrs Penruthlan's eyes almost dropped out of her head. She opened and shut her mouth several times, rather like a goldfish gasping for breath. All the children felt most uncomfortable and extremely sorry for her.

'I don't believe it,' she said at last. 'It's a bad dream. It's not real. Mr Penruthlan will come walking in here at any moment, at any moment, I tell you! He's not down in the Wreckers' Way. He's NOT a bad man. He'll come walking in, you just see!'

There was silence after this, and in the silence a sound could be heard. The sound of big boots walking over the farmyard. Clomp-clomp-clomp-clomp!

'I'm frightened!' squealed Yan, suddenly, and made everyone jump. The footsteps came round the kitchen wall, and up to the kitchen door.

'I know who that is!' said Mrs Penruthlan, jumping up. 'I know who that is.'

The door opened and somebody walked in. Mr Penruthlan!

His wife ran to him and flung her arms round him. 'You've come walking in! I said you would. Praise be that you've come!'

Mr Penruthlan looked tired, and the children, quite dumb with amazement at seeing him, saw that he was wet

583

through. He looked round at them in great surprise.

'What are these children up for?' he said, and they all gaped in surprise. Why, he was talking properly! His words were quite clear, except that he lisped over his S's.

'Oh, Mr Penruthlan, the tales these bad children have told about you!' cried his wife. 'They said you were a smuggler. They said they'd seen you in Wreckers' Cove going out to a motor-boat to get smuggled goods, they said you were trapped in Wreckers' Way, they'd put the trapdoor down, and . . .'

Mr Penruthlan pushed his wife away from him and swung round on the astounded children. They were most alarmed. How had he escaped from Wreckers' Way? Surely even his great strength could not lift up all the things they had piled on top of the trapdoor? How fierce this giant of a man looked, with his mane of black hair, his shaggy eyebrows drawn over his deep-set eyes, and his dense black beard!

'What's all this?' he demanded, and they gaped again at his speech. They were so used to his peculiar noises that it seemed amazing he could speak properly after all.

'Well,' began Julian, awkwardly, 'we – er – we've been exploring that tower – and – er – finding out a bit about the smugglers, and we *really* thought we recognised you in Wreckers' Cove, and we thought we'd trapped you, and your friend, by shutting the trapdoor and—'

'This is important,' said Mr Penruthlan, and his voice

sounded urgent. 'Forget all this about thinking I'm a smuggler. You've got things wrong. I'm working with the police. It was someone else down in the cove, not me. I've been on the coast, it's true, watching out, and getting drenched, as you can see, all to no purpose. What do you know? What's this about the trapdoor? Did you really close it, and trap those men?'

All this was so completely astonishing that for a moment nobody could say a word. Then Julian leapt up.

'Yes, sir! We did put the trapdoor down, and if you want to catch those fellows, send for the police, and we'll do it! We've only got to wait beside the trapdoor till the smugglers come!'

'Right,' said Mr Penruthlan. 'Come along. Hurry!'

CHAPTER EIGHTEEN

Dick gets an idea!

IN THE greatest surprise and excitement the five children rushed to the kitchen door to follow Mr Penruthlan. Yan had scrambled out from beneath the table, determined not to miss anything. But at the door the farmer turned round.

'Not the girls,' he said. 'Nor you, Yan.'

'I'll keep the girls here with me,' said Mrs Penruthlan, who had forgotten her dismay and anger completely in this new excitement. 'Yan, come here.'

But Yan had slipped out with the others. Nothing in the world would keep him from missing this new excitement! Timmy had gone too, of course, as excited as the rest.

'What goings-on in the early hours of the morning!' said Mrs Penruthlan, sitting down suddenly again. 'To think that Mr Penruthlan never told me he was working to find those smugglers! We knew it was going on, around this coast, and to think he was keeping a watch, and never told me!'

Julian and Dick had quite forgotten that they felt tired. They hurried over the farmyard with Mr Penruthlan, Yan a little way behind, and Timmy leaping round like a mad thing. They came to the machine shed and went in.

'We piled . . .' began Julian, and then suddenly stopped. Mr Penruthlan's powerful torch was shining on the corner where the trapdoor was fixed.

It was open! Unbelievably open! The sacks and boxes that the children had dragged over it were now scattered to one side.

'Look at that!' said Julian, amazed. 'Who's opened it? The smugglers have got out, with their smuggled goods, and they've gone. We're beaten!'

Mr Penruthlan made a very angry noise, and flung the trapdoor shut with a resounding bang. He was about to say something more when there came the sound of voices not far off. It was the Barnies returning from their search for the children.

They saw the light in the shed and peered in. When they saw Julian and Dick they cried out in delight. 'Where were you? We've searched everywhere for you!'

Julian and Dick were so disappointed at finding their high hopes dashed that they could hardly respond to the Barnies' delighted greetings. They felt suddenly very tired again, and Mr Penruthlan seemed all at once in a very bad temper. He answered the Barnies gruffly, said that everything was all right now, and any talking could be done tomorrow. As for him, he was going to bed!

The Barnies dispersed at once, still talking. Mr Penruthlan silently led the way back to the farmhouse with Julian and Dick trailing behind. Yan had gone like a shadow. As he was not at the farmhouse when they walked wearily into the kitchen, Julian guessed that he had scampered back up the hills to old Grandad.

'Five past three in the morning,' said Mr Penruthlan, looking at the clock. 'I'll sleep down here for an hour or two, then I'll be up to milk the cows. Send these children to bed. I'm too weary to talk. Good night.'

And with that he put his hand to his mouth and quite solemnly took out his false teeth, putting them into a glass of water on the mantelpiece.

'Oooh – ock,' he said to his wife, and stripped off his wet coat. Mrs Penruthlan hustled Julian and the rest upstairs. They were almost dropping with exhaustion now. The girls managed to undress, but the two boys flopped on their beds and were asleep in half a second. They didn't stir when the cocks crowed, or when the cow lowed, or even when the wagons of the Barnies came trundling out into the yard to be packed with their things. They were going off to play in another village barn that night.

Julian awoke at last. It took him a few moments to realise why he was still fully dressed. He lay and thought for a while, and a feeling of dejection came over him when he remembered how all the excitement of the day before had ended in complete failure.

If only they knew who had opened that trapdoor! WHO could it be?

And then something clicked in his mind, and he knew. Of course! Why hadn't he thought of it before? Why hadn't he remembered to tell Mr Penruthlan about the

Guv'nor standing in the shadows, and his whispered message: 'Here! I'm here!'

He must have been waiting for the smugglers to come to him, of course, he probably used local fishermen to row through the rocks to the motor-boat that had slunk over to the Cornish coast, and those fishermen used the Wreckers' Way so that no one knew what they were doing.

The Barnies often came to play at Tremannon Barn, nothing could be easier for the Guv'nor to arrange for the smuggling to take place then, for the Wreckers' Way actually had an entrance in the shed near the big barn! If a stormy night came, all the better! No one would be about. He could go up on the hills and wait for the signal from the tower which would tell him that at last the boat was coming.

Yes, and he would arrange with the signaller too, to flash out the news that he, the Guv'nor, was at Tremannon again, and waiting! Who was the signaller? Probably another of the fishermen, descendants of the old Wreckers, and glad of a bit of excitement.

Everything fell into place, all the odd bits and pieces of happenings fitted together like a jigsaw puzzle. Julian saw the clear picture.

Who would ever have thought of the owner of the Barnies being involved in smuggling? Smugglers were clever, but the Guv'nor was cleverer than most!

Julian heard the noise outside, and got up to see what it was. When he saw the Barnies piling their furniture on the wagons, he rushed downstairs, yelling to wake Dick as he went. He must tell Mr Penruthlan about the Guv'nor! He must get him arrested! He had probably got the smuggled goods somewhere in one of the boxes on the wagons. What an easy way of getting it away unseen! The Guv'nor was cunning, there was no doubt about that.

With Dick at his heels, puzzled and surprised, Julian went to find Mr Penruthlan. There he was, watching the Barnies getting ready to go, looking very dour and grim. Julian ran up to him.

'I've remembered something, something important! Can I speak to you?'

They went into a near-by field, and there Julian poured out all he had surmised about the Guv'nor.

'He was waiting in the dark last night for the smugglers,' said Julian. 'I'm sure he was. He must have heard us and thought we were the men. And it must have been he who opened the trapdoor. When they didn't come, he must have gone to the trapdoor and found it shut, with things piled on it. And he opened it, and waited there till the men came and handed him the goods. And now he's got them hidden somewhere in those wagons!'

'Why didn't you tell me this last night?' said Mr Penruthlan. 'We may be too late now! I'll have to get the police here to search those wagons, but if I try to stop the Barnies going now, the Guv'nor will suspect something and go off at once!'

Julian was relieved to see that Mr Penruthlan had his

teeth in again and could speak properly! The farmer pulled at his black beard and frowned. 'I've searched many times through the Barnies' properties to find the smuggled goods,' he said. 'Each time they've been here I've gone through everything in the dead of night.'

'Do you know what it is they're smuggling?' asked Julian. The farmer nodded.

'Yes. Dangerous drugs. Drugs that are sold at enormously high prices in the black market. The parcel wouldn't need to be very big. I've suspected one or other of the Barnies of being the receivers before this, and I've searched and searched. No good.'

'If it's a small parcel it could be hidden easily,' said Dick, thoughtfully. 'But it's a dangerous thing to hide. The Guv'nor wouldn't have it on him, would he?'

'Oh no, he would be afraid of being searched,' said Mr Penruthlan. 'Well, I reckon I must let them go this time, and I must warn the police. If they like to search the wagons on the road, they're welcome. I can't get the police here in time to stop the wagons going off. We've got no telephone at the farm.'

Mr Binks came up at that moment, carrying Clopper's front and back legs. He grinned at the boys. 'You led us a fine dance last night!' he said. 'What happened?'

'Yes,' said Sid, coming up with Clopper's ridiculous head under his arm as usual. 'Clopper was right worried about you!'

'Gosh, you didn't carry old Clopper's head all over the

hills last night, did you?' said Dick, astonished.

'No. I left it with the Guv'nor,' said Sid. 'He took charge of his precious Clopper while I went gallivanting over the hills and far away, looking for a pack of tiresome kids!'

Dick stared at the horse's head, with its comical rolling eyes. He stared at it very hard indeed. And then he did a most peculiar thing!

He snatched the head away from the surprised Sid, and tore across the farmyard with it! Julian looked after him in amazement.

Sid gave an angry yell. 'Now then! What do you think you're doing? Bring that horse back at once!'

But Dick didn't. He tore round a corner and disappeared. Sid went after him, and so did somebody else!

The Guv'nor raced across the yard at top speed, looking furious! He shouted, he yelled, he shook his fist. But when he and Sid got to the corner, Dick had disappeared!

'What's got into him?' said Mr Penruthlan, amazed. 'What does he want to rush off with Clopper's head for? The boy must be mad.'

Julian suddenly saw light. He knew why Dick had snatched Clopper's head. He knew!

'Mr Penruthlan, why does the Guv'nor always have someone in charge of Clopper's head?' he said. 'Maybe he hides something precious there, something he doesn't want anyone to find! Quick, let's go and see!'

CHAPTER NINETEEN

Mostly about Clopper

AT THAT moment Dick appeared again, round another corner, still holding Clopper's head, with Sid and the Guv'nor hard on his heels. He hadn't been able to stop for a moment, or even to hide anywhere. He panted up to Mr Penruthlan, and thrust the head at him.

'Take it. I bet it's got the goods in it!'

Then Sid and the Guv'nor raced up too, both in a furious rage. The Guv'nor tried to snatch Clopper away from the big farmer. But he was a small man and Mr Penruthlan was well over six feet. He calmly held the horse's head out of reach with his strong right hand, and fended off the Guv'nor with the other.

Everyone ran up at once. The Barnies surrounded the little group in excitement, and one or two farm men came up too. Mrs Penruthlan and the girls, who were now up, heard the excitement and came running out as well. Hens scattered away, clucking, and the four dogs and Timmy barked madly.

The Guv'nor was beside himself with fury. He began to hit the farmer, but was immediately pulled away by Mr Binks.

Then one of the farm men shouldered his way through

the excited crowd, and put his great hand on to the Guv'nor's shoulder. He held him in a grip of iron.

'Don't let him go,' said the farmer. He lowered Clopper's head and looked round at the puzzled Barnies.

'Fetch that barrel,' he said to Julian, and the boy got it at once, placing it in front of the farmer. The Guv'nor watched, his face going white.

'You leave that horse alone,' he said. 'It's my property. What do you think you're doing?'

'You say this horse is your property?' said the farmer. 'Is it entirely your property, inside as well as outside?'

The Guv'nor said nothing. He looked very worried indeed. Mr Penruthlan turned the head upside down, and looked into the neck. He put his hand in and scrabbled about. He found the little lid and opened it. Out fell about a dozen cigarettes.

'They're mine,' said Mr Binks. 'I keep them there. Anything wrong with that, sir? It's a little place the Guv'nor had made for me.'

'Nothing wrong with that, Mr Binks,' said the farmer, and put his hand in again. He pulled at the lid, and ran his finger round the hole where Mr Binks kept his cigarettes. The Guv'nor watched, breathing quickly.

'I can feel something, Guv'nor,' said Mr Penruthlan, watching the man's face. 'I can feel a false bottom to this clever little space. How do I get it open, Guv'nor? Will you tell me, or do I smash Clopper up to find it?'

'Don't smash him!' said Sid and Mr Binks together.

They turned to the Guv'nor, puzzled. 'What's up?' said Sid. 'We never knew there was a secret about Clopper.'

'There isn't,' said the Guv'nor, stubbornly.

'Ah, I've found the trick!' said Mr Penruthlan, suddenly. 'Now I've got it!' He worked his fingers about in the space that he had suddenly hit on, behind the place where Mr Binks had his cigarettes. He pulled out a package done up in white paper, a small package, but worth many hundreds of pounds!

'What's this, Guv'nor?' he asked the white-faced man. 'Is it one of the many packets of drugs you've handled

round this coast? Was it because of this secret of yours that you told Sid never to let Clopper out of his sight? Shall I open this packet, Guv'nor, and see what's inside?'

A murmur arose from the Barnies, a murmur of horror. Sid turned fiercely on the Guv'nor. 'You made me guard your horrible drugs, not Clopper! To think I've been helping you all this time, helping a man who's only fit for prison! I'll never work with Clopper again! Never!'

Almost in tears poor Sid pushed his way through the amazed Barnies and went off by himself. After a few moments Mr Binks followed him.

Mr Penruthlan put the white package into his pocket. 'Lock the Guv'nor up in the small barn,' he ordered. 'And you, Dan, get on your bike and get the police. As for you, Barnies, I don't know rightly what to say. You've lost your Guv'nor, but it's good riddance, I'll tell you that.'

The Barnies stared after the Guv'nor as he was dragged away by two farm men, over to the small barn.

'We never liked him,' said one. 'But he had money to tide us over bad times. Money from smuggling in those wicked drugs! He used us Barnies as a screen for his goings-on. It's good riddance, you're right.'

'We'll manage,' said another Barnie. 'We'll get along. Hey, Sid, come back. Cheer up!'

Sid and Mr Binks came back, looking rather solemn. 'We're not going to use Clopper any more,' said Sid. 'He'll bring us bad luck. We'll get a donkey instead and work up another act. Mr Binks says he couldn't wear

Clopper again, and I feel the same.'

'Right,' said the farmer, picking up Clopper's head. 'Get the back and front legs. I'll take charge of old Clopper. I've always been fond of him, and he won't bring any bad luck to *me*!'

There was nothing more to be done. The Barnies said rather a forlorn goodbye. Sid and Mr Binks shook hands solemnly with each of the children. Sid gave Clopper one last pat and turned away.

'We'll go off now,' said Mr Binks. 'Thanks for everything, Mr Penruthlan. So long!'

'See you again when next you're by here,' said Mr Penruthlan. 'You can have my barn any time, Sid.'

The Guv'nor was safely locked up, waiting for the police. Mr Penruthlan picked Clopper up, legs and all, and looked down at the five children, for Yan was now with them.

He smiled at them all, looking suddenly quite a different man. 'Well, that's all finished up!' he said. 'Dick, I thought you'd gone mad when you went off with old Clopper's head!'

'It was certainly a bit of a brainwave,' said Dick, modestly. 'It came over me all of a sudden. Only just in time, too, the Barnies were nearly on their way again!'

They went over to the farmhouse. Mrs Penruthlan had already run across. The girls guessed why, and they were right!

'I'm getting a meal for you!' she cried, as they came in.

'Poor children, not a mite to eat have you had today. No breakfast, nothing. Come away in and help me. You can turn out the whole larder if you like!'

They very nearly did! Ham and tongue and pies went on the table. Anne picked crisp lettuces from the garden and washed them. Julian piled tomatoes in a dish. George cooked a dozen hard-boiled eggs at the stove. A fruit tart and a jam tart appeared as if by magic and two great jugs of creamy milk were set at each end of the table.

Yan hovered around, getting into everybody's way, his eyes nearly falling out of his head at the sight of the food. Mrs Penruthlan laughed.

'Get away from under my feet, you dirty little ruffian! Do you want to eat with us?'

'Yes,' said Yan, his eyes sparkling. 'Yes!'

'Then go upstairs and wash those dirty hands!' said the farmer's wife. And, marvel of marvels, Yan went off upstairs as good as gold, and came down with hands that really were almost clean!

They all sat down. Julian solemnly put a chair beside him, and arranged Clopper in such a way that it looked as if he were sitting down too! Anne giggled.

'Oh, Clopper! You look quite real. Mr Penruthlan, what are you going to do with him?'

'I'm going to give him away,' said the farmer, munching as hard with his teeth as he did without them. 'To friends of mine.'

'Lucky friends!' said Dick, helping himself to a hard-boiled egg and salad. 'Do they know how to work the back and front legs, sir?'

'Oh yes,' said the farmer. 'They know fine. They'll do well with Clopper. There's only one thing they don't know. Haw – haw-haw!'

The children looked at him in surprise. Why the sudden guffaw?

Mr Penruthlan choked, and his wife banged him on the back. 'Careful now, Mr Penruthlan,' she said. 'Mr Clopper's looking at you!'

The farmer guffawed again. Then he looked round at the listening children. 'I was telling you,' he said, 'there's only one thing these friends of mine don't know.'

'What's that?' asked George.

'Well, they don't know how to undo the zip!' said the farmer, and roared again till the tears came into his eyes. 'They don't know how to – how to – haw-haw-haw-haw – undo the ZIP!'

'Mr Penruthlan now, behave yourself!' said his amused wife. 'Why don't you say straight out that you're giving Clopper to Julian and Dick, instead of spluttering away like that?'

'Gosh, are you really?' said Dick, thrilled. 'Thanks most awfully!'

'Well, you got me what I wanted, so it's only right and fair I should give you what *you* wanted,' said the farmer, taking another plate of ham. 'You'll do well with Clopper, you and your brother. You can give us a show one day before you leave for home. Haw-haw – Clopper's a funny one, see him looking at us now!'

'He winked!' said George, in an astonished voice, and Timmy came out from under the table to stare at Clopper with the others. 'I saw him wink!'

Well, it wouldn't be surprising if he did wink. He's really had a most exciting time!

Bonus Blyton

Behind the Scenes with the Nation's Favourite Storyteller

THE LIFE AND TIMES OF

Enid Blyton

1897 On 11 August, Enid Mary Blyton is born at 354 Lordship Lane, East Dulwich, London. The family moves to a semi-detached villa at 95 Chaffinch Road, Beckenham, Kent.

1899 Enid's brother Hanly is born on 11 May.

1902 Another move to 35 Clock House Road, Beckenham. Enid's brother Carey is born.

1907 Enid starts at St Christopher's School for Girls, Beckenham. The family moves again, just a couple of doors down, to 31 Clock House Road, Beckenham.

1911 Enid enters Arthur Mee's children's poetry competition and is thrilled to have her verses published. Plus, Arthur Mee asks to see more of her work!

1912 The Blyton family moves to 14 Elm Road, Beckenham.

1916 Enid decides to become a teacher and goes to Ipswich High School to train. She starts work at Bickley Park School in 1919.

> **Did you know?** A comedy spoof of *The Famous Five*, called *Five Go Mad in Dorset*, was aired on Channel 4's first night of broadcasting, 2 November 1982. It's famous for featuring Dawn French and Jennifer Saunders and for the phrases 'lashings of ginger beer'. It's fun, but has nothing to do with Enid's novels. They produced a second film the following year, *Five Go Mad on Mescalin*.

1917 In March *Nash's Magazine* publish her poems.

1920 Moves to Southernhay, Surbiton, to work as a nursery governess.

| 1922 | Enid's first book *Child Whispers* is published. Enid also contributes to *Teachers' World*. |

| 1923 | Meets Major Hugh Pollock, an editor at her publishers. Earns more than £300 from her writing – the price of a small suburban house. |

| 1924 | Enid writes a book for Hugh, they fall in love and marry on 28 August. They move to Chelsea, London. |

| 1925 | Annual earnings reach £1,095.10s.2d – equivalent to an executive's salary! |

| 1926 | Enid and Hugh move to Elfin Cottage, a house in Shortlands Road, Beckenham. She purchases 'Bobs' a black and white smooth-haired fox terrier.

Sunny Stories for Little Folks, edited and written by Enid Blyton, is published. |

| 1927 | Purchases her first typewriter and forces herself to learn how to use it and also learns to drive. |

| 1929 | Family moves to Old Thatch in Bourne End, Buckinghamshire. |

| 1931 | Enid's first daughter, Gillian Mary, is born on 15 July. |

> **Did you know?** Enid used several made-up names throughout her career, including Mary Pollock, but her readers worked out it was really Enid Blyton.

| 1933 | Enid is a bestseller! *Letters from Bobs*, 'written' by her dog Bobs, sells 10,000 copies in its first week! |

1935 On 27 October, Enid gives birth to Imogen Mary, her second child.

1937 *The Adventures of the Wishing Chair* is published. Like many of Enid's stories, it first appeared in *Sunny Stories*.

1938 Enid, Hugh and daughters move to 'Green Hedges' in Buckinghamshire. Her first full-length novel for children, *The Secret Island*, is published, and so is *The Enchanted Wood*.

1940 *The Naughtiest Girl in the School* is published.

1940 Eight Blyton books are released, including *The Adventurous Four*, and *The Twins at St Clare's*. A year later, 22 books are published.

Eileen Soper

1942 *Five On a Treasure Island*, the first book about the Famous Five, is published, illustrated by Eileen Soper.

Enid's marriage to Hugh ends in divorce, and the following October, she marries Kenneth Darrell Waters.

1943 Despite paper shortages caused by the Second World War, 23 of Enid's books appear, including *The Mystery of the Burnt Cottage*, the first of the Mystery Stories.

1944 Twenty-four Blyton books are published, including *The Island of Adventure*.

1946 *First Term at Malory Towers* is published.

1949 Another busy Blyton year, with 32 books out, including the first of the *Barney Mysteries*. Noddy appears in the *Sunday Graphic*, and in November *Noddy Goes to Toyland* is published. The first of *The Secret Seven* series is published.

1950 Enid forms her own company, Darrell Waters Limited, which controls the copyrights for all her work.

1952   Enid has 44 titles published, and forms the Famous Five Club.

The Story of My Life, Enid's autobiography for children, is released.

1953   Enid stops writing for *Sunny Stories* to concentrate on *Enid Blyton's Magazine*. The pantomime *Noddy in Toyland*, is performed. It took Enid only two weeks to write! *The Famous Five* play is produced for the Prince's Theatre, London.

1956   Enid's makes her first appearance in *TV Comic* with Noddy and Bom. She buys Manor Farm at Stourton Caundle.

1957   The film of *Five On a Treasure Island* is serialised. Sadly, Enid's health begins to decline.

1962   Armada Books launch a paperback list featuring Blyton titles – so even more children have access to her books.

1963   The last book for each of *The Famous Five* and *The Secret Seven* series are published.

> **Did you know?** Enid interviewed A.A. Milne for an article in *Teachers' World* in 1926. He presented her with an advance copy of his latest book, *Winnie the Pooh*.

1964   A film of *Five Have a Mystery to Solve* is released.

1965   The last full-length Blyton books are published – *The Man Who Stopped to Help* and *The Boy Who Came Back*.

1967   On 15 September, Enid writes in her diary: 'My darling Kenneth died. I loved him so much. I feel lost and unhappy.'

1968   Enid dies peacefully in her sleep in a nursing home in Hampstead, London on 28 November.

Get to Know ...

Anne

Anne is the ten-year-old sister of Julian and Dick. She likes wearing dresses and playing with dolls but she shares enough qualities with her cousin George that they become good friends as the series develops. Just like George, Anne puts other people first and prides herself on her honesty. She likes horse riding and is captain of games at her school. It has to be said, though, that Anne isn't a fan of adventures – although she's good at organising her siblings and cousin, and sorting out meals and other arrangements wherever she happens to be. People think she is passive, but she won't always let others get the better of her – Julian once described her as changing from a mouse into a tiger.

Anne says ...

> You ought to be glad I like messing about with the food and getting it ready for you.

Other people say ...

> Anne has been at work - you know how she loves to put everything in its place. We don't need to worry about anything when she's about. Good old Anne!

Five Facts

The Famous Five make an appearance in *The Secret Seven* when Colin brings his set of *Famous Five* books to the cave in *The Secret Seven Win Through*.

Enid planned to stop *The Famous Five* after six books but her fans demanded more! **'The children would not allow it and Enid Blyton is glad,'** said the blurb of book seven ...

... and then, in *Five Go to Mystery Moor*, Enid wrote, 'when I finished the twelfth, in came thousands of letters again. "But you can't stop at twelve. Please go on for ever!" So here is the thirteenth for you.'

When *Five On a Treasure Island* was produced as an eight-episode **television serial** in 1957, Enid auditioned the children who played Julian, George, Dick and Anne.

The famous **Red Arrows** nicknamed a special flying formation 'Enid' (there were five planes, of course).

Cover to Cover

Anyone who has been a fan of *Doctor Who* in the past 50 years will have their 'own' Doctor – the one they grew up with. Many of the *Famous Five*'s readers will have collected the series with a particular cover style. So, which covers show *your* Famous Five? Why not ask your teachers, parents and grandparents?

1942

1967

1970

1974

1978

1983

1985

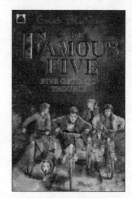

1991

1994

2000

2001

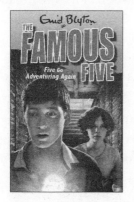

2010

2012

Writing the Famous Five Books

Enid Blyton taught herself to type in 1926. She typed faster than most typists, even though she used just two fingers. She said she could easily write 10-12,000 words a day and the reason she did not write more was because her arms became tired.

This helps to explain why it took Enid Blyton only four to five days to write a *Famous Five* book of approximately 40,000 words in length. When she started the first in the series, *Five On a Treasure Island*, she knew only what type of book she had to write and its length. She put her typewriter on her knees, closed her eyes and waited for the story to come into her imagination.

After a few minutes she saw four children – and soon knew their names and relationships. She was pleased when Timmy appeared because she knew her readers liked animals in their stories.

Gradually the setting grew in her imagination. Kirrin Cottage, the sea and a rowing boat, and an island with a castle on the top. She heard the children talking and playing in her head and saw George scowling at the others.

The ideas kept surging up from her imagination and she found it hard to keep up on her typewriter. She said it was like watching a film inside her head and she did not know what was going to happen until she started to write what she saw.

She kept to a daily timetable while writing a book, starting at ten o'clock and stopping for lunch at one o'clock. She would start again about a quarter to two and would finish writing for the day at about half past four. She didn't really like noise and interruptions but when I came home from school I would run in to say 'hello' and grab the pages she had written that day. I read them in my bedroom and at tea-time I would beg her to tell me what happened next, but she never would and I would have to wait until the next day.

She had far more to do in a day than just writing. She read over what she had written that day and corrected any proofs of other books that her publishers had sent her. She would check artists' pictures carefully, then carefully pack the pictures up again – and there was no Sellotape in those days, only sealing wax. Then she would have to answer all her letters – at least 50 every day; some business letters and some from children. She answered them all and never used a secretary.

She was the busiest person I have ever known, yet she still had time to read, to talk, to arrange her flowers, to play golf or tennis, or to garden. However, when she was writing a long book she had little time for anything else but she did not mind because, for her, writing was not work – it was pleasure.

This article was written by Gillian Baverstock, Enid Blyton's elder daughter. Gillian was born in 1931 and died in 2007.

If the crime fits ...

Can you remember which villain is responsible for which crime in *The Famous Five* stories?
Match the perpetrator (1-8) with the crime (A-H) ...

1. Mr Andrews *(Five Go Off to Camp)*
2. Mr Barling *(Five Go to Smuggler's Top)*
3. Gringo *(Five Have Plenty of Fun)*
4. Will Janes *(Five Go to Billycock Hill)*
5. Ebenezer and Jacob Loomer *(Five Go to Demon's Rock)*
6. Maggie Martin *(Five On a Hike Together)*
7. Mr Rowland *(Five Go Adventuring Again)*
8. Llewellyn Thomas *(Five Get Into a Fix)*

A. Kidnapping
B. Stealing jewels
C. Faking his own death
D. Stealing a scientific formula
E. Trading stolen goods
F. Smuggling
G. Stealing fighter aircraft
H. Trapping the Five in the lighthouse

Answers: 1. E; 2. F; 3. A; 4. G; 5. H; 6. B; 7. D; 8. C

More classic stories from the world of

Enid Blyton

The Famous Five Colour Short Stories

Enid Blyton also wrote eight short stories about the
Famous Five. Here they are, in their original texts,
with brand-new illustrations. They're a perfect
introduction to the gang, and an exciting new way to
enjoy classic Blyton stories.

Don't miss the first thrilling Secret Stories adventure!

The Secret Island

When Peggy, Mike, Nora and Jack find a secret to unravel, their adventures soon begin.

The Arnold children long to run away from their unkind aunt and uncle. But when they escape to a mysterious, deserted island with their friend Jack, they have no idea that an incredible adventure is just beginning …